# Love's Dangerous Undercurrents

## Part 1

Love's Dangerous Undercurrents is a work of fiction. All the characters, organizations, and incidents portrayed in this novel are either product of the author's imagination or used fictitiously. Any resemblance to actual persons, living or dead, business establishments, events, or locals is purely coincidental.

ISBN: 9781542489034

# By: Trish Collins

~ ~ ~ ~ ~ ~ ~ ~ ~

## Lucky Series

Lucky Day - Book 1

Lucky Charm - Book 2

Lucky Break - Book 3

Lucky Rescue - Book 4

Lucky Shot - Book 5

Lucky Honeymoon - Book 6

Lucky Me - Book 7

Lucky Number - Book 8

Lucky Guy - Book 9

Lucky Couple - Book 10

Lucky Bet - Book 11

Lucky O'Shea's - Book 12

## Daphne's Story

Daphne's Escape - TBA

Daphne's Oasis - TBA

Daphne's Revenge - TBA

## Jacobs Series

Riptides of Love

Book 1 - Parts 1 & 2

Love's Dangerous Undercurrents

Book 2 - Parts 1 & 2

Breaking Waves of Love

Book 3 - Parts 1 & 2

Love's Storm Surge

Book 4 - Parts 1 & 2

Impact Zone of Love

Book 5 - Parts 1 & 2

Love's Sunset - TBA

# Love's Dangerous Undercurrents

Part 1

Book 2 - Series

A Jacobs Novel

~~~~~~~

## Trish Collins

# PROLOGUE

Katherine Jackson, one of the most sought-after agents in New York City, lay in her bed the morning of one of her best author's book signing. The one that was going to hopefully change Liz McGreary's life. At least, Kat hoped it was going to work out for her. She didn't really believe in true love herself, but who knew, maybe Liz and Ben could be different. Liz had gone to California to research her new book and fell head over heels for a surf shop owner. This alone simply amazed Kat because Liz always used her daughter, Paige, as an excuse not to get involved with men. Even though Liz's daughter was eighteen and now going to start college.

Liz had been alone a long time after her first husband died. For her to allow Ben Jacobs into her life, there had to be something there. Then when Liz found out she was pregnant, after leaving California and Ben behind, Kat knew they belonged together. Ben had called frantic with worry about Liz. Kat knew it was the right thing to do to set them up at the book signing. So, Ben could show up and make Liz see they belonged together.

Kat never involved herself in anyone's personal life before, and she hoped she was doing the right thing. She hadn't really cared enough about anyone, before Liz, to get involved. This could backfire on her and become a PR nightmare. If Liz refused his proposal and Ben went ballistic, not that she thought that was going to happen, but she could admit, she felt anxious, not being able to control the outcome. Kat thought about how much Liz deserved to be happy, she practically raised Paige by herself. She was one of the most honest and loving people Kat knew. As her agent and best friend, she knew how hard Liz had it. She was the only person Kat could depend on, not that she would ever admit that to anyone.

Kat arrived at Liz's hotel, with coffee in hand, her heart pounding, and a small bead of sweat formed on the back of her neck. Kat stood at the door dressed in dark gray slacks and a white blouse with her short blonde hair spiked up. She liked that she was tall, and her hair just made her feel even taller, and the spikes gave an edgy look. She knocked and waited for Liz to answer the door. As she stood there, a small fear was building, because Liz had not answered her cell phone, and with Paige staying at her dorm, Liz might have had a break down or at least a bad night.

"It's me, Liz. I tried calling but you didn't answer your phone." Kat said, as she heard Liz start to move around inside. The door opened and sure enough, Liz looked horrible. Dark circles under her eyes showed she did not sleep well. Her cheeks still looked sunk in from losing weight because of her pregnancy, she had been sick, and right on cue, she turned and ran for the bathroom.

Kat stepped inside and took in the bedding on the couch and the TV was still on. "I guess asking how you feel today is really a no brainer and I'm just guessing here, but you didn't sleep well either." It did not take Liz long before she returned.

"Where's my coffee?" Liz reached for the cup.

Kat handed it to her. "You can drink it now, after that, I thought it made you sick." Liz tried to smile, but Kat could see it wasn't a real smile, but one that she hoped would make it so.

"The smell of it did, but I'm good now. I need this coffee. What time is it?"

"It's eleven o'clock, and you're supposed to be at the bookstore at noon. So, when I couldn't get a hold of you, I got a little worried," Kat watched Liz move around the room.

"Sorry, I must have turned off my alarm. I didn't get much sleep last night."

"I can see that, you look like crap. Go shower and I'll do your makeup, maybe we can get you ready in less than an hour." Kat wanted Liz to look amazing, so suggesting doing Liz's hair and makeup was not only to get her there on time, but also, when Ben saw her, Kat wanted Liz to look her best.

"Oh thanks, you're too kind," Liz said as she took her coffee and went into the bathroom. Kat was thinking she should have called Ben, so she would know what he was going to do. Thinking, Kat paced the small room, she knew this was going to work for Liz, in the rational part of her brain, however, in the cynical part, that never believed there was a man out there that could or would put the needs of someone before his own. Kat worried that Liz was in for a major let down. If that happened, she'd be there to support her. Then she would hunt Ben down and hurt him bad.

Liz emerged from the bathroom and Kat sat her down and went to work on her hair and makeup. "Is Paige coming to the book signing?" Kat asked as she worked the final pins into Liz's hair.

"Paige said she was going to try to make it, at least for a little while," Liz stood to get dressed.

"Paige needs to be there today," Kat said in a harsh tone.

Kat's manner drew Liz's attention. "Kat, she just got here and I'm sure she wants to familiarize herself with the campus." Paige was going to Boston University and had just arrived the night before.

Kat didn't give a shit what Paige had going on, because she needed to be there for her mother. Liz would need her if things didn't turn out well and if by some amazing feet, it did work out, she needed to be there so she could meet Ben. "She can do that later, it's important that she be there for you. I think she can give her mother one afternoon, the mother who has given her everything."

"Kat, what is going on, you've never insisted Paige be there before. So why today?"

Kat had to be careful, or she was going to tip Liz off. Liz was a very intelligent woman and didn't allow too much to get by her. "I just think with everything going on, you need her support. With her being at school, and you having a baby, I think you need her there and you would never ask her, that's all."

"Alright, but there's something going on here, Kat, I know you," Liz was dressed and was ready to go.

"There's nothing going on, I just think she should support her mother, she's an adult now, and she should know that it's a two-way street," Liz watched Kat as she grabbed her purse.

"Okay, let's go, and if you think she needs to be there, then call her and tell her."

"I think I'll just do that," Kat followed her out the door.

Kat was going to make sure that Paige showed up, once they made their way into the bookstore, she would call her. She wanted this day to be over, all this tension was starting to make her shoulders hurt. Kat parked the car around the back of the store, so Liz could go in without fans stopping her. Kat had no idea how many people were standing out front in line already, and she had no way of knowing if Ben stood in that line. This all just upped the tension and anticipation. Once she had Liz sitting at the table the store provided for her, Kat started to scan the crowd.

Kat needed to talk to the store manager and make that call to Paige before Liz started signing books, so she could be by her side just in case she needed anything.

Kat had everything she could in order, Paige was coming, and she hoped like hell Ben was in the line somewhere. She couldn't believe she was buying into all this when she, herself, disbelieved real love existed. Well, she knew it didn't exist for her and never would. There wasn't a man out there that would work hard enough to make it pass the walls she built up around herself. Kat knew she had her reasons for those walls, and her oh-tough attitude, was for her protection. Sitting next to Liz as she watched fans walk up to the table for Liz's autograph. Kat scanned the line again, but the way they formed the line, it was hard to see past the bookshelves. The line weaved up and down the shelves so she could only see the few people before they moved to the table.

Pulled from her thoughts Kat heard Liz say. "I need something to eat because my stomach is not cooperating with me. Could you get me some more coffee, too?" Kat nodded and got up to go across the street to the coffee shop. She met Paige as she got to the double doors. An employee from the bookstore didn't want to allow Paige in, so Kat made it known it would not go over well if they didn't allow the author's daughter in. The man guarding the door nodded and pushed the door just a bit wider to allow Paige access into the store as Kat walked out, she told Paige she was going to get her mother some food and something to drink. Once Kat made her way out of the building, she scanned the line again, but still didn't see Ben. She crossed the street and went inside the coffee shop.

There was a small line, so Kat looked impatiently over the menu, when the hair on the back of her neck rose. She trusted her instincts, but she didn't want to turn around to see what made her react. She heard his voice and closed her eyes. *"Oh hell,"* she said under her breath.

"Well, if it isn't Little Miss Sunshine, in the flesh." She didn't turn around maybe he'd go away. Her left eye started to twitch, *what the hell was he doing here? I'm going to kill Ben when I see him for bringing his asshole brother.*

"I know you heard me, Kat," he said louder. She still didn't turn, and the line moved up one space and she hoped she could order and get the hell out of there. She knew he was watching her. She just tried to breathe. Suddenly, he was right behind her, speaking in her ear.

"I know what you did," his whispering breath made her shiver. She didn't know why he had this effect on her.

"Oh yeah, and what did I do now?" She stepped forward so he wasn't so close, and he moved up too.

"You set this whole thing up for Ben, you know they belong together. I didn't know you were such a romantic." She needed air, so she took a big, ragged breath. He was so close to her back, she felt his heat and she needed him to step back.

"If you know what's good for you, you'll step back and that's the only warning I'm going to give you." He did take a small step back, but not enough for her. She would hate to make a scene, but she would if he forced her. This man just knew how to push her buttons.

"You always threaten with violence when I make you uncomfortable. Have you noticed that?" She stepped up and he did too. She had already suckered punched him once before, when she went to California to check on Liz.

"You just seem to piss me off, and as far as setting this up, it was what was best for Liz. If you say anything about this conversation, or refer to it in the future, I'll hurt you," she had to swallow hard.

"So, you keep saying, and for the record, I think they belong together, too." She felt him move in closer again. She needed to find out what Ben was going to do.

"Do you know what Ben's going to do?" She asked over her shoulder and knew he was right there behind her.

"No, but he's wearing that stupid shirt with her book cover on it, so I'm sure he's going to make an ass out of himself." Kat thought what Ben was doing was sweet and just the fact that he didn't care what anyone thought of him, made Kat melt just a little. She felt Jeff move even closer, so she moved up to order. Once Kat placed her order with the salesclerk and paid, she turned, and Jeff was right there.

They were face to face to one another, and she said, "Step back, you're in my space." She tried to sidestep him, and he went the same way, so she stepped in the opposite direction, and he did, too. It looked like they were dancing in the aisle. She tried to step back, but hit the counter, he had her trapped, and that's when the sucker punch hit. "I said step back," and once he bent over, she escaped to the other end of the counter, where the pickup line was. She refused to look his way as she picked up her order.

She could see him out of the corner of her eye, as she tried to get out before he could get close again. However, he stepped right in front of her, very close to her face. "One day when you go to do that, I'm going to be ready for it. Then I'm going to pin you down, and we'll see what happens next." He moved even closer, so he could whisper into her ear, "And we both know there's going to be a next time." She couldn't stop her reaction to him, as she felt her nipples harden, and knew she needed to stay far away from him. She was thankful when he stepped back and she just walked out the door.

Kat repeatedly took deep breaths as she walked back across the street to the bookstore. She hadn't been prepared to see him. When she had gone to California, she met Jeff, and she didn't like him at first sight. He was the kind of guy who thought he could simply smile pretty and get a girl out of her panties. Even if he had a great smile, and gorgeous brown eyes that had these gold flakes in them, she would not ever fall for someone like him. He was a type of man she loved to chew up, spit out, and hand him his balls. Kat made men question their own self-worth. She had a gift for it. She didn't consider herself a man hater, but when the men came on with so much confidence, she would make sure when they walked away they no longer were so self-assured. She hated the controlling ones the most. Kat liked to string them along until she could get them to beg her, and then she'd dump them. She was the one with control and she would not ever give that up to anyone ever again.

Back inside the safety of the bookstore, she looked for Ben again. She spotted him as he just came around the last set of bookshelves. She almost didn't recognize him, because he now had a full beard covering the bottom half of his face. She couldn't help herself when she gave him a dirty look and then mouthed, "I'm going to kill you." She held up the drinks and food from the coffee shop. Kat walked to the table where Liz sat at and gave her the items Liz requested. This was it, in the next five minutes, Ben would be at the table, and hopefully Liz's life would change. She found herself looking at Ben and then back to Liz. She waited as the anticipation was killing her, she couldn't wait for what was about to happen next.

Liz said to a group of woman that came up to the table. "Hi ladies, how are you today?" Kat watched as the women parted and Ben stood there. She held her breath as Ben came around the table and got down on one knee. Kat felt her emotions all caught up in Ben's proposal. How his sweet words, humble expression, and how he laid his heart out for all to see. She had no doubt he loved Liz, and she knew Liz loved him, too. It was a once in a lifetime occurrence. Liz had agreed to marry Ben, and Kat went into agent mode, she started to tell everyone what to do. Kat heard Liz protest and tell Ben she was at a book signing.

Kat said over the cheers, "Not anymore, everyone who is still in line, Ms. McGreary is done for today. Please leave your name, and address, you will receive your signed copy in the mail." There was the group that had helped Ben, and he wanted their information. As Kat took down names that's when she felt *him* watching her. She looked up and sure enough, there *he* was standing against the wall. Jeff smiled when she looked his way. *Oh, hell he's going to be a problem. She would need to put an end to this.* Once she finished doing her job, she walked over to where he stood to make sure he knew she wasn't going to put up with any of his shit.

Within the next month, Ben and Liz made plans for their wedding, once he found out Liz was pregnant, he wanted to marry as soon as possible. Kat was happy it worked out for them, Liz would move to California to be with Ben. Kat would help with the wedding plans from New York, and she would be the go between Liz and Paige, who was in Boston at school. Liz did not want anything big, so all they had to do was pick out the dresses, flowers, and shoes. Liz planned to have the ceremony on the beach, and the reception was going to be at Linda's house, Ben's mother.

Once Liz had the wedding planned, all that there was left to do was to fly out to California, she knew she would be near Ben's brother. This did not make her happy, because she knew he would use this short opportunity to try to drive her crazy. She needed to turn the tide on him and get under his skin.

Kat and Paige left the East Coast after Paige's last class the Friday before the wedding. They would have just the weekend, and then both had to get back. All the girls were staying at Linda's house, and the men stayed at their own places. Ben was not happy with those arrangements, but Kat was happy with them, because she didn't have to see Jeff. Linda had planned a small bridal shower for Liz on Friday night after the rehearsal. Kat wasn't into the shower so much because it just wasn't her thing. However, Liz was enjoying herself, meeting all Linda's friends and opening gifts from people she didn't know. Kat just sat in the background watching Liz open towels with Paige's help and she thought about how much Liz deserved to have this happiness.

The men went to a bar for Ben's bachelor party, which he didn't want. Therefore, Kat had a sinking feeling they would show up any minute, and crash the shower, which she hoped Jeff wouldn't be with Ben when they did. An hour later, the front door flew opened, and sure enough, the men came in. Kat couldn't help but watch him walk in and his eyes scanned the room until they landed on her. Linda made a big stink about the men crashing the shower, but it was almost over anyway. Ben went straight to Liz and kissed her, and it was time for her to make herself scarce, so she slipped out of the room and went to the restroom. What Kat didn't know, was that Jeff followed her. When she emerged from the bathroom, he was waiting in the hall for her. At first, it looked like he was just waiting to use the restroom. She tried to step around him, careful not to touch him, but he moved so they would not be able to pass each other.

She muttered under her breath that it hadn't been long enough. "What did you say?" He smiled at her.

"Nothing, excuse me," she tried to get by him again, but he wouldn't budge. "Is this how it's going to be, because we both know I can get you the hell out of my way?" She stepped closer to him, and he didn't move back, as she thought he would.

"What fun would that be if you didn't try to sucker punch me. If I recall the last time you did that, I told you what would happen." He watched her wet her lips as her tongue darted out and she smiled.

"I just might change it up and knee you in the balls, or I could always just crush your windpipe, not that, that would be good for the wedding tomorrow, with you being the best man." Her entire body was tingling as it betrayed her. Sparring with him turned her on, she liked to fight, whether it was physical or mental and right now, it could be both.

She didn't expect him to step even closer, it made her step back as her back hit the wall behind her. In a second, she went from having a little fun, into panic mode, and she reacted by stomping on his foot with her heel. She didn't anticipate him leaning forward into her. He grabbed a hold of her and pulled her into him pinning her arms at her side. They were face to face, with her body pressed against his, and everything inside of her wanted to kiss him.

"Well, well, I guess you did mix it up, but for some reason, I don't think this is how you saw it working out for you."

"What the hell is going on here?" Liz's voice rang from the end of the hallway and Jeff released her and stepped back.

"Just the same old shit, but this time, I think I got the upper hand," he said with a huge smile.

As Kat went to walk away, she turned to him and said, "Abruti," she was calling him a fool in French. She didn't know why, but it made her feel better.

"You two had better be on your best behavior tomorrow, you might want to stay out of each other's way," Liz passed them to use the restroom.

"Wait up, Kat," she heard Jeff say as she made her escape. Kat didn't stop. She went through the living room where the shower was wrapping up and then straight up the stairs to her room. It had been a long day, she worked that morning, along with the flight, and she was exhausted. It was the only way she could explain why she had enjoyed the sparing match with Jeff. Thank God, he didn't follow her up to her room. Now all she needed to do, was keep her distance from him tomorrow, and then she would be heading home again, far away from him.

Liz had planned a noon ceremony. Linda had arranged for a hair stylist to come to her house to do every one's hair and makeup. Kat spiked hers as usual. The morning was very busy with preparations, and she had no time to think. Liz had selected beautiful lavender strapless dresses, with a fitted bodice, and a flowing skirt, for both her and Paige. They were very similar to Liz's dress, but hers had lace overlay, over her bodice that tied around her neck, and it was a beautiful eggshell color. Once everyone was ready, they all loaded into the limo to head to the beach, where the men had made a walkway and a flat platform for everyone to stand on, for the wedding ceremony. White cloth draped over the platform with lavender rose petals scattered around, with a lovely archway for Ben and Liz to stand under, it was very beautiful, simple, but elegant, and it suited Liz perfectly.

Liz didn't want anything big and extravagant, but Ben insisted he wanted it to be special for her. He convinced Liz to buy a wedding dress, and he wanted her to have the limo to take her to the wedding. Ben got his brother and Owen, his teenaged employee that was part of the family, even though not related, to build the stage on the beach. It was the small things he did for her, that melted Kat's heart. At first, she didn't like Ben and gave him a hard time. Of course, Kat gave everyone attitude, but she wanted to know if Ben truly cared for Liz. When Kat had come to California, Ben stood up to her and didn't let her attitude deter him in pursuing Liz. That gained Ben a lot of respect from Kat and considering she did not put much worth in men, that was a huge step.

Liz hadn't said much all morning. Kat wasn't sure if it was just nerves, or she wasn't feeling well. "Liz, you okay, you're quiet. You're not thinking about changing your mind about marrying Ben, are you?" Paige sat next to Liz as Kat, and Linda sat across from them.

"No, I'm not changing my mind. I was just thinking how happy I am. I love Ben. He is such a wonderful man. I keep thinking how much my life has changed and how much more it's going to change," Liz pulled Paige just a bit closer. "Do you like Ben, Paige, I know you didn't really get time to get to know him?" Liz looked uncomfortable as she asked, with Ben's mother watching.

"I like Ben, Mom, I think he's great, and he definitely loves you and that's all that matters to me. I'm sure in time, I'll get to know him better, when I come back for school breaks. But while I'm at school, it gives you and Ben time to get used to the fact that you're married and having a baby," Paige smiled at her mom.

Linda didn't comment on the conversation between Liz and her daughter, but she wanted Paige to know she was always welcomed. "I happen to know Ben is very fond of and impressed with you, Paige. When they came back from Boston, he told me all about you. I hope that when you do come home, we can spend some time together. I'm not sure if your Mother told you, but I take in stray family members." Linda had taken in Owen, and now Liz, as her added family members. She absolutely adored Liz and not just because she was giving her the grandkids she always wanted. Liz must be fond of her too because she asked Linda to walk her down the aisle. Linda was giving Liz the support she never got from her own mother. At this moment, Linda couldn't be happier. "Now, if I could only get Jeff to settle down and maybe date just one girl, I could have some hope for him."

"Well good luck with that," the words were out of Kat's mouth before she realized everyone was watching her. "What?" She asked.

"I just think it's funny every time the two of you get together you're fighting, pushing each other's buttons, or like last night in the hallway, you were..." Liz didn't get to finish because Kat cut her off.

"Stop right there, Liz McGreary, I know it's your wedding day and all, and Jeff's mother is in the car, but don't go getting any ideas that there is anything or ever will be anything going on between us." Kat turned to look at Linda when she said, "I'm sorry, Linda, you are a very nice person, and I like your other son, but Jeff just irritates the hell out of me. I would kill him with my bare hands." Everyone in the car was smiling at her. "Don't you guys look at me like that?"

"Okay Kat, if you say so." Liz said that as they pulled up to the beach and the limo driver opened the door for them all to get out. Liz took a deep breath and got out. She could see Ben, Jeff, and Owen standing on the platform. Ben's sister, Dannie, was there, too, she had gone to the beach early to set everything up, it was just family, so there were no chairs. Paige took Liz's hand and started her walking toward Ben. Dannie put on the music and Paige was the first to walk down the walkway.

Kat stood waiting for Paige to make her way down the aisle, she couldn't help but look Jeff's way, and sure enough, he was staring right at her. She took several shallow breaths as she started down the walkway. It was a beautiful day, and she took in the scene of the makeshift wedding chapel. With the flowers, and the heart shaped archway, it was very romantic looking, Kat had to admit. This wedding suited her best friend to a tee. Liz never liked a big fuss, and she didn't think you needed to spend a lot of money to have nice things.

Unlike her, she spent money, because she had it, and never paid must attention to how much things cost. She worked hard for her money and spent it hard, too. She made her way down and turned to see Liz's arm wrapped through Linda's arm. It was nice to know Liz was going to have a great support system of family here in California.

Liz was stunning in her dress, as the skirt blew in the breeze. It was very whimsical and the look on Liz's face showed her happiness. Kat took her eyes off Liz and glanced over to Ben. His expression was very serious, but his eyes said everything. How he loved and treasured Liz. Kat could feel just the smallest of jealousy and envious creeping in because she asked herself, how it would feel to have love so true, to have someone love you with everything they had to give. Kat watched as Linda stepped back, and Ben took Liz's hand, and it didn't surprise her one bit when Ben kissed Liz. She couldn't help it when that made her smile.

The ceremony didn't last long, both Liz and Ben said their own wedding vows, and before she knew it, they were husband and wife. She had to admit, it was very sweet. The photographer took so many pictures, ones of just Ben and Liz, and then of the complete bridal party. He even took some silly ones. He had Ben in the middle between Kat and Paige, where Paige was kissing his cheek and Kat looked like she was going to slug him. Then he took one with Liz, Jeff, and Owen. Both Owen and Jeff held Liz across their arms as Liz rested her head on her arm. The picture of just her and Jeff, as the maid of honor and best man, was the one that she wasn't happy about. They arranged them so Jeff looked like he was whispering in her ear, and she was supposed to have a shocked expression on her face. She knew he would take advantage of this opportunity. She'd tried her best not to allow anything he said to make her react in anyway. She would plaster a shocked look on her face and give nothing else away. After all, this was for her best friend, and she would let Liz know later she owed her big time.

As much as she tried to prepare herself for this picture, when Jeff leaned in and whispered with just the faintest breath, "Kat, I want to fuck you so hard," she couldn't help the shiver that ran down her body, and the photographer got his picture. She needed to get away from him. Kat went to help Dannie put everything in her van and thank goodness, Jeff was still needed for pictures, which kept him busy. Between Owen, Paige, and Dannie, the beach looked as if the wedding never happened. They were all going back to Linda's house for the reception. Ben and Liz took the limo, so that left her to drive back to the house with Jeff and Linda, Paige went with Owen, and Dannie drove her van full of the wedding supplies.

They were the first ones back, Kat had a feeling Liz and Ben would be awhile and she had no idea where Paige and Owen were, but she helped Linda get the food set up. All Kat knew, was Jeff was nowhere around, and that suited her just fine. Once she finished, she wanted to get out of this dress, it was long, and every time she went up and down the back steps, she had to make sure she didn't step on it. As Kat worked side by side with Linda, it was a comfortable feeling until Linda started taking about Jeff.

"So, that was such a cute picture of you and Jeff, it looked as if he really did say something to make you blush." Kat looked up at Linda to see if she was sincere, or if she was trying to feel Kat out. In Kat's line of work, she was a good judge of character. "I'd love to have a copy of all the pictures, Liz made a beautiful bride." Kat could hear Linda's voice starting to break up. "I've always wanted a big family, and God blessed me with three wonderful children, but I was losing hope that one day, they would find love and give me the grandkids, I've always wanted. I was very surprised to find out Liz was pregnant, and I'm happy to get Paige."

"You do seem to have a lot of love to go around. I'm glad Liz is going to have you because her own mother wasn't there for her. Liz is the kind of person who deserves to have people that love her." Kat didn't look at Linda as she just kept putting the meat on the platter.

"What about you Kat, do you have a big family? Because I always have room for one more, I know you have been a great friend to Liz, and you're always welcome here any time." Kat could hear the little voice inside of her that told her not to trust. Linda was now Liz's family, not hers no matter what Linda said. Kat laughed to hide her insecurities, because her family loved her, but she pushed them away.

"Well, my family is a mess, but I'm sure you don't want to get into all that. This is a celebration and not the time or the place." Kat took the tray outside, this conversation was getting just a bit too heavy, and a subject she wasn't going to discuss. Kat noticed that Paige and Owen were back. They were talking about surfing. Kat overheard Owen offering to give Paige lessons when she came back into town. She thought that didn't take long, and the way they were smiling at each other, she'd be surprised, if somewhere down the road, they didn't get together. Kat wondered how Liz would feel about that. "Hey, I want to learn to surf, too, do I get lessons, too?"

Linda said from behind her, "Are you kidding, they'll give lessons to anyone. I'm sure when you come back and have a little more time, someone would be glad to give you lessons."

Jeff asked, "Who needs lessons?" Kat turned around so fast to see him standing close to her. Where in the hell did he come from? She noticed he changed out of his suit into a pair of dark jeans and a button-down shirt. She needed to change, too, but that's when Ben and Liz showed up.

"Oh, Kat, could you go inside and get the champagne out of the fridge, I forgot to grab it." Kat turned and Jeff was right there, damn this man liked to be right up her ass. She side stepped him and went inside, happy to get away from him. All she had to do was get through this day, and then she was going home. She thought once she changed and went back outside she would try to stay in the group of people, so there would be no way he could try to pull anything.

Kat was deep in thought, and didn't realize Jeff followed her inside. It's so unlike her, she was always aware of her surroundings and the people around her. Once again, he was right there when she turned around after getting the champagne out of the refrigerator. "What is it with you? Are you getting that much enjoyment out of aggravating the shit out of me? Because I must tell you, I'm trying hard here not to make a scene. But, you keep pushing your luck. I will not be responsible for my actions." She stepped closer to him and narrowed her eyes as she said, "Or is that what you want?"

Jeff strode even closer and once again, she took a stride back and hit the fridge. They did this same song and dance repeatedly. However, this time she was not going to freak out, she'd keep her cool. In a spilt-second decision, she reached out, pulled him in, and kissed him with everything she had. The kiss was supposed to make him want her, but she felt it, too. As their tongues intertwined with each other's, her body went on high alert. He pulled her in close and she could feel how he reacted to her, too.

Jeff made a sound and pushed her back until she had nowhere to go. He pressed his body against her and his hands moved to her ass. Somehow, she forgot where she was, that she was supposed to be avoiding him. She found herself lifting her leg to get closer to him, but the dress restricted her from lifting it too far. Jeff slid his hand up her leg to lift her dress. At that moment, it hit her, what the hell was she doing? She pushed hard on his chest and pretended that this whole display hadn't affected her at all and walked away.

# ~ 1 ~

Kat Jackson was sitting at her desk, looking out her corner office window on the thirtieth floor of the building she worked in. The view of New York City was stunning as she thought about how things in her life had changed in the last couple of months. Liz, her best friend, actually, her only real friend, fell in love and got married. Liz was now in California with her new husband, who owned a surf shop out there. They were waiting for their twins to be born.

Kat was feeling strange, feeling as if she had all these loose ends and even loneliness. This was something so foreign to her because she never allowed anyone to get close, so they couldn't disappoint her. Right now, her life did not feel full or as rewarding as it once had. She was successful as one of the top literary agents in New York. She made a lot of money, and she had the best of everything, but now, with the one person she let in living so far away, none of that seemed to matter. Even though they talked almost every day, Liz was on bed rest, but it was not the same.

In some ways, Kat had always felt she had a considerable advantage over her friend. Liz's inexperience with men and sex made her look to Kat to help her through her books' sex scenes. Liz was one of her best writers, and before meeting Ben, she needed just that little support, and now Liz did not need her for any of it. Kat's intercom buzzed, pulling her from her thoughts.

"Ms. Jackson, there's a call for you on line one, a gentleman named Ben Jacobs."

"Thanks, Vikki. How much time do I have before my next appointment?"

"You have twenty minutes," the voice said from the little box on her desk.

"Thank you," Kat picked up the receiver and hit the button, "Ben, what can I do for you?"

"Kat, I need your help," she could hear the desperation in Ben's voice as she leaned back in her chair.

"Well, of course, you do, I do you one favor, and now you want something else." She had set up the book signing where Ben had proposed to Liz.

"This is big, Kat, and I know it's asking a lot, but Liz..."

"Liz, what? Is she okay, the babies?" Immediately Kat was concerned.

"You know she's on bed rest, and it's driving her crazy. Actually, she is driving me crazy. I've done everything I can to make her happy. I can't be with her twenty-four-seven, so I hired someone to help, and she keeps running them off."

"So, what do you want from me? I can call her and give her a pep talk," Kat knew Liz was a little crazy, but what could she do from New York.

"I need you to come to California," the line went silent.

Before Ben could get the rest of his words out, Kat had to stop him. "NO!"

"Kat, Liz needs you," he pleaded with her.

"NO," she repeated.

"Why not? You're the only person I know Liz can't run off, please, Kat. I'll beg if I have to. Is that what you want?"

"As much as I would enjoy that, Ben, I have a job and a life in New York. I love Liz, and you know that, but I can't just pick up and move to California. Liz is not my only client, you know." There was no way she wanted to go back after what had happened at the wedding.

"Please, Kat, I promise to keep Jeff far, far away from you. I'll even hold him down so you can beat the crap out of him if he bugs you. She needs you, just until the babies are born, then I promise, I'll never ask anything of you again."

The thought of beating the crap out of Ben's brother Jeff was a plus, but that would mean she'd have to see him again. The only way she could guarantee that nothing could ever happen between them was to stay in New York. She thought how Jeff had cornered her at the wedding reception, then the kiss that sent a shiver down her spine. She couldn't allow him to get that close again.

"Kat, you there, come on, this is for your best friend. I have to get some help here. You know I'm desperate if I'm calling you." She knew he must be extremely in despair.

"I still have meetings that I have to be here for Ben. I can't just give up everything to go running off to play nursemaid." Kat knew that sounded bad, but she did have other obligations.

"I'll pay for you to fly back and forth. I just need some relief, and when you need to go back, you go. I'll take what I can get." Kat knew if she kept talking to him, she would cave.

"I'll think about it. I have an appointment waiting," Kat had to get off the phone before she did something stupid and foolish.

"Okay, but I'll pay for whatever you need. Just come, please."

"Bye, Ben," Kat hung the phone up. She needed a minute to get her thoughts together before she turned back into the tough as nails agent.

The thought of that kiss crept in, and Kat squashed it. She wasn't going there, well likely she would. The sound of her assistant reminding her that her appointment was waiting put her back in work mode.

Kat went through the rest of her day, kicking publisher's assess and getting her client the best deals possible. The call from Ben was on her mind all day. She needed to call Liz, and then she would assess if she genuinely needed to go. If she went, she would need to keep tight control of herself and not allow anyone under her skin. Because there was one person that could crack her hard-core resolve, and he was the big reason why she didn't just pack her bags.

It seemed that Jeff could get her so pissed off and arouse her all at the same time. Kat wasn't used to feeling like this, oh, she could have a guy get her hot and turned on, but she knew it didn't mean anything. It was just sex, and when she was done, she'd turn back into the cold-hearted bitch. The guy got the picture real fast when she was finished with him. She always had control, and that's just how she liked it. No one would ever control her fate again.

That dark night so many years ago, when she trusted a boy, and he betrayed her in the worst way. She made herself a promise that night, if she survived, she would never allow anyone to take advantage of her again. This was her motivation every time she went into the gym to build and strengthen her body. She took self-defense classes and knew how to shoot the gun that she carried on her at all times. The fact that she knew she could take care of herself was the only thing that made her feel safe.

Kat knew she could do most of her business from California. She didn't need to be in New York to talk on the phone, and many people did meetings via conference call. Therefore, she could help Liz and still do her job. Nevertheless, it was Jeff holding her back. He was going to be a problem in the biggest way. If only she could just use him, then kick him to the curb and out of her life, but she knew that wouldn't happen. So, the only way was not to allow him in the first place. She had to find out if Liz truly needed her, so she pulled out her cell phone and dialed Liz's number.

On the second ring, Liz picked up, "Hello Kat, and no fat jokes, they're getting old."

Just the sound of Liz's voice made Kat laugh. "I just can't help myself. You're a big easy target, one, you're on the other side of the country, and two, I can."

Kat could hear the annoyance in Liz's voice. "I thought you were my friend. You know, I could find a new agent." That statement made Kat laugh harder.

Kat missed sparring with Liz like this, "You could, but you know that wouldn't be in your best interest. I make you a lot of money."

Liz's voice was full of satisfaction, "I think you have that backward. I write books, and you make a lot of money off of me by getting me a great contract."

"Okay, okay, no fat jokes, happy? How are you doing? I hear you're going crazy with this bed rest."

"Oh, and where did you hear that? Don't tell me Ben called you, didn't he?"

"I hear you keep running off everyone he gets to help you. Is that true, Liz, are you?"

"The people Ben hired were nosy. I didn't like them helping me dress. Someone I don't even know wants to undress me, help me into the shower, and they didn't even buy me dinner." Liz laughed at her own joke.

"Nosey, how?" Kat asked.

"Once they found out I'm a writer, they wanted to know all about what I was writing and what was going to happen next. I think one even tried to snoop through my computer. So yeah, I ran them off, wouldn't you?"

"Liz, Ben asked me to come and help you. Of course, I've already seen you naked, so I don't have to buy you dinner first. I know what you're writing, so I don't need to snoop. I'll come if you really need me, but if you don't think you need…" Kat trailed off.

"Oh, my God, that would be great, Kat. When can you come? It will make being stuck in this bed so much better if I have you here all the time." Liz sounded so happy that Kat didn't have the heart to tell her. She didn't really want to come.

"Wait. Don't get all crazy. I can't be with you all the time. I will have to fly back and forth when I have to be here, and I'm going to need a few days to get this all set up." Kat knew this was a big mistake, but she just couldn't say no to Liz. It seemed she had a soft spot for a woman in need. It was the first thing that had made Kat work so hard for Liz when she walked into her office all those years ago. She had told her about how her first husband had died, and she needed to make money to support her daughter. Kat did everything she could for Liz, and they became best friends.

Kat buzzed her assistant, "Vikki, I need you in here, please."

"Yes, Ms. Jackson."

Kat looked over her calendar and tried to move around her schedule when Vikki walked in. Vikki sat quietly and waited for Kat to give her orders. However, Kat didn't say a word. She just kept looking over month after month on her calendar.

"Ms. Jackson, is there something wrong with your schedule?"

"Yes, there is. I need to go out to California, and I will be gone for four to six months. I'm going to need you to hold down the homestead. That will mean I'll be doing all my meetings through conference calls. I'll need you to set that up and let me know if that's not possible. I will be racking up the frequent flyer miles."

"Is everything alright with Liz...? Ms. McGreary, I mean Mrs. Jacobs?"

"Yes, she's on bed rest for the remainder of her pregnancy and going crazy, from what I'm told. I need to help her stay on track with her book if we want to make the deadline. She only has a few months until the rough draft needs to be turned in." Kat got up from her desk and started putting files in her briefcase. "I might need you to fly back and forth at some point. Will that be a problem?"

"I'm going to get to go to California, not a problem. Will I get to meet Liz's...? I mean Ms., I mean Mrs. Jacobs's husband. It was so romantic the way he proposed to her at the book signing. Almost like one of her books."

"Vikki, relax. I know you call Liz by her first name. I'm sure she wouldn't have it any other way. I'm not sure about meeting Ben. You might regret that. That family has a way of sucking everyone into their fold, and before you know it, you're on a surfboard in the Pacific Ocean. You might want to rethink going."

Vikki's eyes got huge when she said, "Surfing, oh my, I don't think I could do that. I have no coordination." She went back to looking through her phone at Kat's appointments.

"Hey, they got Liz out there, and if I didn't see it with my own eyes, I wouldn't have believed it. She was great, but of course, Ben was her teacher, so I'm sure he gave her extra "private" instruction, if you know what I mean." Kat cleared her throat, "Well, anyway, I'm going to need to leave as soon as possible, so if you could work that out for me, I'd appreciate it."

Vikki got up and said, "Yes, Ms. Jackson, I'll get right on it."

Kat watched Vikki walk out, and she thought, what am I doing. *This is going to be a big mistake. I'll need to find a good gym out there because I will have a lot of sexual frustration to work off.* Her mind wandered to the man that she knew would cause all that sexual frustration. He was the kind of man who had a great smile as he charmed you out of your panties. Then once he got what he wanted, he was gone and moved on to the next woman. Not that she was much different. However, she never led the guy to believe there was going to be more. She made sure they knew upfront she didn't do relationships. This was the difference between them.

She could never allow a man like Jeff to see her weaknesses. Letting any man really know the person she hid inside was something she couldn't ever do. Trust was something Kat didn't do easily. If she could only get her fill of Jeff, then she'd be able to get him out of her system. Nevertheless, she knew the minute the thought went through her mind, it could never be. He would be the one to make her house of cards crumble, and she couldn't risk that. She worked too hard to make herself tough and strong to allow any man to make her weak again.

Kat went back to gathering up what she would need to bring with her. She would do what she had to do to help Liz. She would not allow him to take up any more of her time or energy. A buzz from the intercom let her know Vikki had made the necessary arrangements. Kat walked over to her desk, hit the button, and heard Vikki's voice.

"Ms. Jackson, I set everything up. You have three meetings you can't do by video chat. I put them in your calendar with an asterisk. Is there anything else I can do for you before I leave for the day?"

"Yes, Vikki, I'd like it if you could make my travel arrangements and remind me to give you a raise. I don't need any other agent trying to steal you away from me while I'm gone."

"That's not going to happen, but I won't say no to a raise. I'll get right on your flight. When do you want to leave, and will you need a hotel?"

"I want to travel sometime tomorrow, and you don't need to make arrangements for a hotel. I will do that when I get there. Thanks, Vikki."

"Yes, Ms. Jackson."

"I do appreciate just how efficient you are, I know I expect a lot, and you never disappoint."

"I try my best, Ms. Jackson, and I'll get right on the travel plans."

Vikki had been working for Kat for years now. She had lasted longer than any other assistant had. Kat knew the value of someone that could work with her and get the job done. Vikki didn't take compliments very well, but she did do a great job. Kat made a note in her planner to double Vikki's holiday bonus, and she'd give it to her early.

Kat went to her closet to get out her extra shoes and her favorite black boots. The ones with heels that made her stand over six feet. The ones she hoped would make her tower over *him,* so she could look down on him. That thought put a big smile on her face. *Oh yeah, how will he like that?* She wore the boots when she had male clients come into her office. It was one way she felt more superior and in control. They were part of the mask and shield she wore, so no one would ever see that girl. The one that was weak and helpless. Kat knew she wasn't that girl anymore, and she would never allow herself to be again. That was the old girl they called Katherine, not the new and improved Kat. Her parents never liked her nickname, but Kat had to reinvent herself. Therefore, she changed what everyone called her to how she wore her hair, short and spiky. She pushed those thoughts out of her mind. She had too much to get done before she left.

Kat hoped like hell Ben would not have Jeff picking her up from the airport. She would hate to have to kill him before the babies arrived. Kat was pleased when she saw Owen waiting at the gate. Kat knew her luck would run out soon enough, but she was hoping for the long term.

"Hey, Owen, how's things going with school?" Kat knew Owen had started community college at the same time Paige, Liz's daughter. Ben was paying for him to go, so she had a feeling he was working hard. She knew he didn't want to let Ben down.

He smiled and said, "It's school, but I like it. Let me take your bag. Do you have any more we need to get from the baggage area?" Kat liked Owen. He was a sweet kid, with his blonde hair that was too long and blue eyes. If she were eighteen again, he would definitely be on her radar. Not that she made the best choices when she was younger. He took her bag, they walked to the baggage claim, and Owen's eyes lit up when he saw how many bags she had. "All these bags yours? Holy crap! You moving here or something?" Kat just laughed and shook her head.

"Oh God, I hope not, I'm here just to help Liz, and then I'm going home. I wasn't sure what I was going to need, so I brought several things." Owen grabbed a cart, and she helped him load her luggage onto it. "I hear Liz is having a hard time of it lately," Kat said as they walked to Owen's car. His vehicle was an older model Chevy. She hoped all her stuff would fit in the small car. "Do you think everything is going to fit?" However, Owen had it all loaded up in no time, and she thought they were on their way to Liz and Ben's apartment over the surf shop. Kat watched out the windshield as Owen drove. "So, is Liz as bad as Ben said because I can't believe she has changed that much being pregnant?"

"Well, you know, I like Liz a whole lot, but I have to say, I try to stay out of all that. From what I've seen, Liz's mood swings have Ben going out of his mind. One minute, Liz is laughing, and in the next, she's crying. She's getting big, of course. She is having twins, after all. Liz thinks Ben doesn't find her attractive anymore. Ben's done everything he can think of to let her know that he loves and adores her. I think that's why he called you, so you could control her like you do everyone else." Owen glanced over at her, and she had to laugh. This kid just pegged her for the control freak that she was.

"I'm not all that good with being compassionate and sympathetic, but I know Liz, and she knows me. She won't get away with pulling all that shit, and as far as Ben not finding her attractive, I will straighten her out. I don't know any other man that loves anyone the way Ben loves her." It was true she had seen it over and over because he always put her needs before his own, so she knew he hadn't changed just because Liz was pregnant. If anything, she would bet her life that he loved her more, if that was even possible. Kat didn't know how that felt, to have that kind of love, that all-consuming feeling, of wanting no one else and knowing they only wanted you. "We're going straight to the apartment, right? I'm going to need to find a hotel and rent a car." Kat was thinking aloud about all the things she needed to do.

"No, I was instructed to take you to Linda's house. Once she knew you were coming, she wouldn't allow you to stay in a hotel. She has that big house and all those rooms, so if that's not what you want, you'll need to take it up with her. Just if you're going to do something different, I want to be there when you tell Linda." Kat had no idea why he wanted to be there, and then he said, "Linda likes to get her way, and you seem to have no problem saying what you think, so the way I figure it, it's going to be one hell of a fight." This kid just cracked her up. The image that ran through her head was of her and Linda duking it out.

"Sorry to disappoint you, Owen, but I'm fine with staying at Linda's. When we stayed there for the wedding, Linda was a very gracious host, and I don't think I'll be there very often anyway. I'll be with Liz during the day, and I work out in the evenings. Hey, do you happen to know of any good gyms close, between Linda's and Liz's place?" She would definitely need to get in some hard workouts. The thought of seeing Jeff came to mind, and Kat had to get him out of her head. She needed to focus on what she came here for and not obsess over him. They pulled up into Linda's driveway, and she was sitting on her big porch. She came out to the car to greet them.

"Well, there you are. Did you have a nice flight? I set up the room you had last time if that's okay?" Owen started to get the luggage out of the car. "Owen, can you handle getting Kat's bags?" He nodded, so Linda put her arm through Kat's and walked her inside. Kat wasn't sure what to make of Linda. She just didn't notice or paid no mind to the fact that Kat pulled away just a little. Linda kept talking, "Now, I have two vehicles, so you won't have to rent one, and you should have everything you need, but if you don't, just ask, and you're welcome to anything. If you want anything special to eat, just put it here on this pad on the fridge." Linda was talking so much Kat's head was spinning. "I know Ben appreciates you coming to help with Liz. We've all tried to help out, but Liz has not been herself lately." What had Liz turned into, because that was the second or third time someone had said that about her? Once Owen had her bags in the house, hauling them up to her room, it was time to get away from Linda and see for herself what was going on with Liz.

"Owen, can I follow you back to the shop, so I'll know how to get there, and I don't get lost. I think I'm going to need to see Liz. Just to make sure she hasn't grown two heads or horns." Both Owen and Linda laughed. She drove Linda's Town Car to the shop and followed Owen into the back parking lot. Kat knew they lived on the third floor over the store. She had never been inside their apartment, but she knew Ben and Liz would likely want to buy a house when the babies were born. Going up and down three flights of stairs with two babies in tow wasn't going to be easy. Kat walked up all the flights of stairs and knocked on the door. It opened immediately, with Ben standing there. He grabbed her and pulled her into a hug, and she thought he must have lost his mind. "What the hell are you doing?" He stepped back.

Before she could say any more to Ben about the hug, she heard Liz. "Is that Kat? Tell her to get her ass in here." *Oh, no, she didn't just say that* Kat walked past Ben, and he pointed to their bedroom. She walked down the hall and into the room where Liz was lying in bed, and she turned and shut the door.

~ ~ ~ ~ ~ ~

Jeff Jacobs was pacing around in the surf shop he owned with his siblings. Usually, he was selling surfboards or ordering for the store, but nothing was going on today. The store was empty, except for him. Owen had left to pick up Kat from the airport, Ben was upstairs with Liz, and his mother was at her house, waiting on Kat to arrive. Therefore, he was holding down the fort. Dannie, his sister, was supposed to come in and do some of the office work that Ben usually did.

With Liz being pregnant with twins and on bed rest, Ben's plate was full. Jeff couldn't help thinking of how it was making his mother very happy. Liz was going to give her grandkids, and his sister was now staying in California. His mother would now move onto him. She liked to be involved in her kids' lives. He wouldn't necessarily call it meddling, but she pushed in a subtle way. They all knew Linda loved her family deeply. The way she always looked at the family, bigger was better, and now that Ben had fulfilled his obligation to the bigger part, he knew he would be next on her list.

All his adult life, he never felt anything special about a woman. He dated all the time with different women, and he had his share of sex. However, no one ever made him feel beyond lust. No one had ever felt as if his soul mate or that he would give up everything for them. Jeff watched his brother go from having only his work to being ready to move to New Jersey to be with Liz. The change in Ben was like watching him do a total three-sixty. He saw how crushed Ben was when Liz left, everything he was willing to go through to get her back. When he went to Boston with Ben for Liz's book signing, and Ben wore that t-shirt with Liz's book cover, he knew Ben had it bad for Liz. How did his brother know Liz was the only one for him? He had no idea. Jeff never thought that Ben would find someone in a million years, much less get married before he did. Ben never really dated, but when he saw Liz, something just clicked, and that was it.

Jeff only knew of one person that could turn him upside down, and he didn't like her much. Was he attracted to her? Yes, she was sexier than hell. She was so rough and tough, not the kind of woman he dated. This woman had walls so high around her, he didn't think anyone could climb over them. If they could just have great sex, the kind that knew it could be and walk away. He'd be right on that. However, she was his sister-in-law's agent, so there was no walking away. Not that he thought she'd go for it because she hated him as much as he did her.

From the time he laid eyes on her over the summer when she was here to visit Liz, he couldn't seem to control his reaction to her. That first night when Ben asked him to double date to keep Kat busy to spend time with Liz. He knew something was going on between them. She pranced around the place as if she owned it, and her confidence was attractive initially. Still, somehow, she made him feel like they were competing as they danced. She had said she didn't want him to touch her, but then he had the feeling she was trying to get him to have contact with her. It seemed the more she protested, the more he liked it. He could feel her get uneasy, but then she would turn it around to make him crazy. He liked to get in her space, and she turned violent and sucker-punch him. It was what they did.

Jeff closed his eyes as he remembered the one kiss they shared. It was the hottest kiss he had ever had, but then she walked away as if she didn't feel anything at all. Jeff was glad when she went back to New York. He didn't want to be thinking about Kat, but now she was back to help Liz through her pregnancy. He knew she would avoid him, which was ok because he didn't really want to see her either. It didn't matter. But, when he was with her or watching her, he felt more alive than he ever had. He would not beg a woman to spend time with him. Women came to him, not the other way around. He would just go on with his life as if she wasn't there.

He would date whomever he wanted, just he had before he met her. However, in the last couple of months, he hadn't really dated that much. Not since Ben had pointed out that some of the women he dated might have stronger feelings for him than he had for them. Once his eyes opened, there was no way of going back into obliviousness. He couldn't lead them on when he didn't care for them in the same way. Jeff told himself he would put all his effort into working at the shop. Ben had given him more responsibility, and with Ben gone most of the time, he needed to do his share. Was he just making excuses for not wanting to date anyone? No matter how hard he tried, Kat would work her way back into his mind.

The thought of making a deal with her for a sex-only relationship crossed his mind. Would she ever go for something like that? He didn't know, but he wouldn't find out unless he asked. Jeff smiled, now just sex with her. That's what he wanted. How would he go about asking, and would she refuse him, just so she could throw it in his face? If she did reject him, he would have to live with the knowledge that he was wrong about her, or maybe she didn't want him. He had been telling himself that the kiss they shared had affected her, too. No matter how hard she tried to hide it. However, if he started this, would it backfire on him? His mind was flipping back and forth over getting involved with Kat. Should he or should he not?

Jeff never put this much thought into dating or sex with a woman before. If he had wanted to date someone, he asked. But then again, he just seems to attract women, and there was minimal effort on his part. However, with Kat, it's so much more complicated, with her being Liz's agent. Then there was Kat herself, he didn't really understand. He had never met anyone like her. Her personality was big and hardcore, not his type at all. He liked his women soft and gentle with some curves. Even Kat's body was hard. She was thin but muscular, a body he would love to get his hands on, but for the life of him, he couldn't understand why.

As he thought of that day on the beach when Liz showed Kat how she could surf, Kat stood watching in that teeny-tiny bikini. He remembered his reaction to her because it had pissed him off. On the one hand, he had to get a closer look, and on the other, he knew it wasn't in his best interest, yet the closer he got to her, his body went straight to arousal. He watched her smile, and the sheer joy of her watching Liz showed by her excitement. He knew he should have stayed in the water, but he couldn't help himself, and that's when he lashed out at her. Kat talked to Liz about how great she did and how she would love to learn, but it was too bad she was going home. The words were out of his mouth before he even thought about it.

He remembered saying to her, "Is it too bad? Because I think it's perfect timing," as she turned around to face him. He scrutinized the tic in her left eye and knew he was affecting her. Yet, somehow, that made him feel better about being mad at his own reaction to her. Liz stepped between them, and it was probably a good thing because he knew now most likely she'd sucker punch him or worse. At the time, he thought, once she went home, things would return to normal. However, it happened again when he went to Boston with Ben for Liz's book signing. All those feelings of anticipation of seeing her again. When Kat had set Ben up to be with Liz, he saw genuine emotions from her that day also. She always tried to hide her feelings, he didn't know why, but the minute she knew anyone could see them, she pulled that pissed-off tough act.

"What are you doing, sleeping standing up?" Jeff opened his eyes to see Ben standing in front of him. He must have been so deep in thought he didn't hear him.

"I was just thinking, trying to decide whether or not I want to change this display." He lied through his teeth, but in no way did he want his brother to know he was thinking of Kat. "What are you doing down here, and who's with Liz?" He knew the answer before Ben opened his mouth.

"I never thought in a million years I'd say this, but I was so happy to open the door and see Kat standing there. I even hugged her." Jeff experienced a crazy feeling that came over him because the image of his brother's arms around Kat did something to him. In his rational mind, he knew Ben loved Liz more than life and had only felt relief to get some help. As much as Jeff tried to put the feelings of jealousy aside, he couldn't help how he felt.

"What's wrong with you? Your face just got a look as if you're pissed off. I know I haven't pulled my weight around here lately. But now that Kat is here, I'll be able to get my mind back on work," Ben watched Jeff shake his head.

"I know, you have been stretched thin, and it has nothing to do with any of that. I just hate you had to call her." Jeff didn't have to clarify who the "her" was that he was talking about, and the look in Ben's eyes said it all. "Now, don't look at me like that. I just hate having her here."

"Right, I know how you two don't get along, and I'd totally appreciate it if you stayed away from her," Ben said as he hid his smirk behind his hand, and that pissed Jeff off more.

"Right, like I want any part of that. I have no problem with that request." He needed to walk away before his brother noticed anything else, and he turned as he heard Ben say, "I needed her here, Jeff, she's the only one I know Liz can't run off, and Liz trusts her." He didn't turn around. He just said, "I know, and for you and Liz, I'm glad she's here." He didn't want to admit it, but somewhere deep down, he was happy about it too. "Where is she staying? You know, just so I don't run into her."

"Kat's staying at mom's house for now." Jeff didn't say any more, and Ben watched him walk away. *Oh, hell, this was going to get interesting.* He knew his brother, and there was definitely something there where Kat was concerned. Whether or not Jeff knew it himself, but he was in for the ride of his life. Ben didn't envy Jeff. Kat was a hand full compared to Liz. Ben thought he'd take his relationship and the hard times that came with it, ten times over, rather than what Jeff was getting himself involved in.

Ben walked to his office, where he would try to get some work done for the first time in a long time. His sister Dannie had been helping, and she had been using his office. He pushed her work aside and turned on his computer. On the screen was the picture of his and Liz's wedding. He was so happy, even with everything going on. He had Liz, and they were having twins. Ben opened his e-mail, and there were two hundred, and he went to work. They would need more space soon with Dannie staying and with Jeff doing the ordering for the store now. Both of them would need an office of their own. He wasn't sure how he felt about sharing his computer and space with them.

# ~ 2 ~

Kat walked into Liz's room and gave her the look, the one that said, "*Just who the hell did she think she was talking to?*" "I will give you two seconds to rephrase your last question and comment to your husband." She crossed her arms over her chest and stood there tapping her foot waiting.

"Kat, I'm so glad you're here, come sit on the bed and tell me what's going on with you." The look on Liz's face showed she was truly glad to see her, but Kat didn't budge until Liz did as she asked. "What, why are you looking at me like that," Kat just stood her ground and stayed by the door not showing any movement. "Okay I'm sorry, is that what you want?"

"I told you what I wanted," she paused "Did I not make myself clear?" Kat still stared at Liz, not giving anything away.

"Kat, Ben is gone, he took off the second you shut that door, because he can't wait to get away from me, and that's when he's not trying to pawn me off on someone else. That's why he called you," Kat could tell Liz was sure in a funk.

"No, that's not why he called, he called me, one, because he loves you and wants the best for you," Liz made a pfft sound as if she didn't believe her. "Two," she went on, "He knows I'm not going to put up with any of your shit, like the crap that is coming out of your mouth," she mimicked Liz's words "Is that Kat, tell her to get her ass in here?"

"What are you going to do to me Kat?" Liz asked sarcastically, "Beat up a pregnant woman," and Liz saw Kat smile the most wickedly smile. Kat watched Liz draw back.

"Do you really want to take the chance to find out Liz, what I can do to you," Kat now stepped closer to the bed.

"Umm, no not really, it's just, I'm stuck in this bed, and nobody wants to stay with me. I'm fat and my husband doesn't want me anymore." Kat knew Liz was going crazy, but she hadn't realized it was this bad.

"Look, I see where you're coming from. I'd go bat-shit if I was trapped in that bed, too. However, from what I hear, you are not acting like yourself. Your hormones must be through the roof. I know you can't control that, but that still doesn't give you the right to talk and act out. Now you know, I'm not the compassionate and care giving type, and I'm not going to cut you any slack." Kat examined Liz's reaction to her words, she hated to be so hard on her, but she could see Liz needed to have some boundaries, because she was spinning out of control. That right there, was Liz's problem. She didn't have control, not over what she did, or the outcome with the babies.

"Okay, first let's start with talking about Ben," Kat went and sat on the bed next to Liz. "Have you talked to him about how you feel? Because, I sincerely doubt he has fallen out of love with you," Kat handed Liz a tissue, because the tears streamed down her face.

"He won't touch me. We came back from the honeymoon at the lake. I went to the doctors and that was the end. Now, I feel fat and unwanted," Liz wiped away the tears.

"Men are stupid when it comes to this, most likely Ben's afraid he's going to do something to hurt the babies or you. You know he's so big, it just might hit the babies and stunt their growth." That made Liz laugh, the way Kat knew it would.

They talked through all of Liz's concerns and now Kat was going to have to have a conversation with Ben, one that she wasn't looking forward to. It had surprised Kat, that Liz and Ben hadn't talked about all this. But then again, they hadn't been together all that long to really know each other. This was not Kat's area of expertise. However, to keep everyone sane and get through this pregnancy, she was going to have to get right in the middle of Ben and Liz's relationship. Kat got Liz to rest, and she headed downstairs to talk with Ben.

Kat found the back stairs that lead to the shop, took a deep breath, and proceeded through the door. Now she knew she could run into Jeff, but she needed to speak to Ben without Liz overhearing them. She couldn't help it when her eyes darted around the store scanning for him. She didn't want him to sneak up on her, because if she saw him first, then she could prepare herself. However, she didn't see him, so she released the breath she held and went to Ben's office and knocked on the door.

"Come in," she heard him say.

Kat entered and the first thing she noticed was the mess on his desk and he was deep in thought. She could tell Ben must be under a lot of pressure. The last time she was in his office, was when she had come to check on Liz and his office was neat and organized. He looked up and was surprised to see her.

"Kat, who's with Liz?" He started to get up and Kat sat in the seat across from him.

"Relax, Liz is sleeping, I need to talk to you," she wasn't sure how to proceed. How was she going to get into Ben and Liz's sex life? She noticed him relax just a bit as he sat back in his chair. "Okay, I'm going to say, I'm here under direst," she watched his brow on one side lift.

"Just don't tell me you're leaving, anything else I can handle." Kat wasn't so sure, once she opened this box there was no closing it.

"I had a long talk with Liz. I have to say she is a mess."

"Tell me something I don't know."

Well, here go's nothing, "She doesn't think you're attracted to her anymore, because you won't touch her." Just by his expression she knew that wasn't true, but it didn't matter because Liz thought it true. "I can see you haven't changed how you feel about her, but it's all about how she feels about herself." Kat waited for Ben to absorb what she said and added, "I don't want to get into your sex life, Ben, believe me, I don't, but Liz feels she has no control over her life. She can't get out of bed. She has no control over what happens with the babies, and she can't get you to respond to her sexually."

Kat saw the anguish in Ben's expression as he ran his hand over his face and though his hair. "Kat, I just don't know what to do. I love Liz, more now, than I ever thought possible, but I'm scared, I don't want to hurt her or the babies. I've been going crazy trying to make her happy, and nothing seems to work. I feel I'll never make her happy. I tell her every day, I love her and that she's beautiful, but she doesn't seem to take it in. It's as if she thinks, I'm just saying the words because I have to."

"What does the doctor say about sex?" Here's where it was going to get interesting, because there was going to be a fine line, she was going to have to walk.

Ben took a deep breath and looked at his folded hands on his desk, "He didn't say we couldn't, but said to be easy and if she feels any pain to stop. I just can't risk hurting Liz or worse the babies."

"That's what I thought, but have you expressed how you feel to Liz? I'm sure you're aware there's other ways to have sex besides intercourse. If you're afraid of going too far, you can wear a cock ring that won't allow you to go." She stopped herself, because this was her best friend's husband she was talking to, and she changed the subject. "You can't tell her she's beautiful, either, because you have to make her feel it. What did you do before, you know before the babies? How did you make her feel comfortable with you? And she's going to have to get out of that apartment, too."

Ben looked up, and she could tell he was thinking about what she said about the sex. Now he was staring at her with confusion. "Liz is on bed rest, how am I going to get her out of the apartment?" Kat could see in Ben's eyes, he was so stressed, he didn't understand.

"You don't plan on staying there after the babies are born, do you? I think if you bought a house, Liz wouldn't feel so trapped," she could see he was overwhelmed. The poor man has been running ragged, and she could see circles under his eyes and a deep crease in between his brow. "Ben, if Liz was setting up a nursery, picking out clothes for the babies, it would keep her mind off being on bed rest. You see where I'm going with this. She needs to feel in control of something. She can order things online and we can set up something for her so she can be in the room when everything arrives. Liz can pick out paint, you get my point, she needs control. Liz needs some control over something."

"I've thought about a house, but I didn't want to buy one without Liz, because what if she didn't like it?" He had a good point, because Liz would not be able to go from house to house to look for one.

"I have an idea, the house Liz rented, she liked it right, and you have a history there. Why not try to buy that house? She can get outside, see the ocean, and watch you surf. And…" she paused, "You could surprise her with it." Kat watched the biggest smile come across Ben's face and he got up and came around the desk. She got this uneasy feeling when he pulled her to her feet, "Don't you dare hug me again," she said, but he didn't listen. He wrapped his arms around her and hugged her tight and then he did something she knew he was off his rocker, because he kissed her on the cheek. "I swear to God. I will cut you off at the knees if you do that again."

Jeff stood outside Ben's office, as he was about to go in, he heard voices, the door was ajar, pushing it open so he could see inside. What he saw made his blood boil. His brother had Kat in another hug, and he kissed her, "What the hell is going on in here? Your wife is upstairs and you're down here kissing her best friend." Both Ben and Kat turned to see Jeff in the doorway.

Ben paid no mind to his brother's obsession, when he kissed Kat again and she punched him. He stepped back and said, "Yes, I kissed her because she is a genius." Now both Kat and Jeff were looking at him as if he'd lost his mind. Ben went back to his desk, picked up his phone, and dialed a number, "Yes, my name is Ben Jacobs, and I want to know who owns the house at 11039 Ocean Way." Jeff turned his attention to her with the look of "What the fu—," she stepped out into the hall and Jeff followed, as she knew he would.

"What the hell is going on?" She could see he was mad, not that she understood why, because she should be the one angry.

"I just had to talk to Ben about Liz," Kat watched how Jeff's face turned red, and anger marred his face.

He cut her off, "It didn't look like talking was going on. What would have happened if I didn't walk in right then?" She smiled, because at that moment she saw jealousy, it was the only explanation for why he was acting this way.

"You might have wanted to wait five seconds to see me beat the shit out of your brother. But now, what I want to know, why is it any of your concern?" She saw when he realized what he was doing and covered his anger. Kat turned and started to walk away, but over her shoulder, she said, "Kat one, Jeff zero."

Jeff just groaned aloud at the thought that there might not be a way to win this game against her. He walked back into Ben's office. He thought how she wasn't here for two seconds, and she was already affecting him. Jeff watched his brother as he spoke to someone on the phone. Ben looked to be very excited over something. "Yes Sir, I will, thank you." Ben hung up.

"What the hell is going on, I come in here, and you're hugging and kissing Kat?" Ben told him what Kat has suggested about buying the house and how that would make Liz happy. Jeff could see Kat's point, but kissing her, he didn't want to see his brother's arms or lips any were near her again. "Yeah, but you kissed her," he said it as if he dared to kiss a frog or lick a pile of shit. Ben just laughed, and somehow that just made him madder.

Kat went up to the apartment with a huge smile, with her work finished, Ben would buy the house, Liz would be happy, and to top it all off Jeff was jealous of his own brother. This was easier than she thought, and maybe she would be on a plane back home in no time. Was that what she really wanted? *Yes, I need to go home.* Kat checked on Liz and then grabbed her laptop and her phone and went into the living room to get some work done. As she tried to pull up contracts and look over the list of new potential clients, he kept slipping back into her head and she said aloud, "Get the hell out of my head."

"Kat, who are you talking to," she heard Liz from the other room, *shit now she woke Liz up.*

"Just talking to myself," she got up and went into the bedroom, "You need anything?"

"I'm hungry and bored, what are you doing out there?" Liz looked to Kat from under the covers.

"I was trying to get some work done," she looked around the room and found no TV, "You don't even have a TV to watch in here? You can't even watch movies."

"You know, I'm not really a TV watcher," Kat heard her say as she walked out the door to get her cell phone.

When Kat came back in she said, "Well, that's about to change." She started looking something up on her phone and dialed a number,

"Yes, this is what I wanted," Liz just watched Kat go to work. "Hi, I want to know if I buy a TV and DVD player and a bunch of movies, if I can have the Geek Squad to come and set it up. Yes, just a minute," she turned to Liz and asked, "What's the address here?" Then she said into the phone, "Yes, I need it all delivered, and I'll pay extra if you can have that here for me today. Yes, it's the third-floor apartment." She gave them the address of the apartment and how many movies to send over, told them to pick out a variety of new releases, and then hung up.

"Oh, my God, did you just do what I think you did? I can watch movies on my computer, I didn't need a TV."

A few hours later, the TV was installed and all the movies stacked next to it. It was starting to get late, so Kat made her next call to the deli down the street, and she ordered sandwiches. Kat made a nice comfortable pallet on the floor in front of the TV, who knew she was so domesticated.

"What are you up to Kat?" She heard Liz ask, but didn't answer, but asked a question of her own question, "What time do you expect Ben to come back?"

"He should be here any minute, why?" Kat heard the knock and went to get the food and once she came back, she went to the bed to get Liz.

"Let's go," she pulled the covers back and that's when she got her first real look at just how big Liz had gotten. *Holy crap, no wonder Ben was afraid to touch her. She looked like she could pop at any moment.* Liz was such a small woman to begin with, only standing about five foot. Now she looked as round as she was tall. When Liz started to protest, Kat said, "You've been in this bed all day, out you go." Kat slid Liz's feet to the side of the bed and helped her up. They took five steps to the pallet on the floor and Kat asked, "You have to use the restroom first? Because I have a feeling once I get you down, it's not going to be easy to get you up again." Liz just made a sound of disgust. The trip to the bathroom and back to the blankets tired Liz right out.

The minute she got her settled Ben walked through the doorway. "What's all this?" He looked around the room.

"I ordered sandwiches for dinner, and you can pick a movie to watch, but I'd start with a chick flick if I were you. The rest is up to you, gotta go," she walked out of the room when Ben went to kiss Liz, and she shut the door behind her. Kat gathered up her work stuff and went to her borrowed vehicle. Well, she had made it through the first day and her encounter with Jeff wasn't entirely bad. She did enjoy the expression on his face when he walked into Ben's office. She pulled out her phone. She needed to find a gym to workout, especially if she was going to be seeing him every day.

Kat was looking through her phone when someone knocked on her window. She jumped and let out a grasp. Jeff stood there laughing at her. She pushed the button for the window. "What the hell do you want?"

"Jeff one, Kat one," he said as he walked away. Kat could feel her eye twitching, she needed that workout more now, than she did before. Once she caught her breath, she put the key in and revved the engine to life, maybe she could run him over.

Jeff walked away with just the smallest of satisfaction catching her off guard, after she had caught him acting all crazy this afternoon. Just something snapped in him when he saw Ben's arms around her, kissing her. He knew it was silly to think anything was going on between his brother and Kat. Ben loved his wife Liz, the way he hoped to feel someday about a woman. However, the spiky blonde did things to him that he couldn't explain. She always made it a competition between them, and if not for anything else, he was a competitor. He never liked second place, second was just the first loser. He would get her to come to him if it was the last thing he did. The instant the thought went through his head, he knew she'd never come to him.

Never giving into him, but that didn't stop him from thinking how sweet that would be if she did, when she did.

He walked up to his apartment and then watched her from his window until he no longer could see her taillights. How has he allowed this to get so far, she had him chasing after her? Thinking of her too much, Jeff walked away from the window. He needed something else to think about, Jeff thought what could he do, he could call one of the girls he knew would just jump at the chance to go out tonight. That didn't really entice him, so he went back down to the store. Ben had talked to him about clearing out one of the storerooms in the back to make offices for him and Dannie. Some hard work should do the trick.

His cell phone beeped, he had a text, and he pulled it from his pocket. It was Cindy, she wanted to know what he was doing, he texted back, "working." Her next text said, "You're always working, what's with that," with a sad face after it. He smiled, but didn't answer, because he didn't know what to say to her. He said aloud to himself, "Sorry baby, a crazy blonde has gotten under my skin, and I can't seem to get her out." Jeff knew she wouldn't appreciate his response, so he just put his phone away and went back to working on the storeroom.

Boxes that had never been broken down were the easy part, but all the old shelves and display cases they were the pain in the ass. Jeff didn't know what to do with them, so he pulled his phone back out again and called his brother to find out what he wanted to do with all the crap.

"This had better be really important, because I'm busy," he heard the raggedness in Ben's voice.

"Sorry to interrupt, but I'm in the storeroom looking at all this old shelving, not sure what do with it.

"What the hell are you doing in there?" Jeff could tell Ben was going to come down to see what he was doing.

"Don't come down. I just didn't want to throw stuff out that we might need." He knew Ben would come anyway. He shouldn't have bothered his brother.

"Look, give me a little bit and I'll be down." He heard him cover the phone and talk to Liz, and then he was back. "I'll be right down." Jeff tried to stop him, but the line went dead. Oh great, now he disturbed his night with Liz. He didn't really want the company because he was trying to work off thoughts of Kat.

Within ten minutes, not only was Ben there, but Owen, too. They worked together and in no time had the space for two offices cleared. Ben had made plans for the next couple of days for them to get some wood and put up walls. It would be nice to have his own space, even if it was in the back of the store, and he knew Dannie had talked to Ben about revamping their website. Graphic design was what she did, so if she had to stay and work for the shop, she wanted to do what she knew best. She wanted them to start selling merchandise over the internet. If things took off, they would need more space anyway. They could be looking for a warehouse soon for all the extra stock and more employees.

Once they finished, all Jeff wanted was a shower and then go to bed. He knew the next couple of days were going to be fun, between working and making offices. It would be just what he needed to keep thoughts of her out of his mind. He smiled at the thought of her shocked look when he scared her today. If he was going to have to put up with her invading his world, then he might as well have some fun with it. Once he had time to think about it, he knew that she would drive him crazy in return.

~ ~ ~ ~ ~ ~

Kat pulled into Linda's driveway, the entire way home, her thoughts of how Jeff could sneak up on her. Normally she could sense someone's presence, and took pride in that she could detect danger and react. Somehow, Jeff could slip in under her radar and not only scare the shit out of her, but he managed to get too close. As Kat knew all too well, that was not going to do, because she needed to be aware of her surroundings, always. If at any point, Jeff caught her off guard, she knew, she could physically hurt him, but what she didn't want him to see was the fear. When those overwhelming feelings of fear came over her of an attack, she went into survival mode.

Grabbing her belongings from the car, Kat went inside. Linda was sitting in her living room watching a show on TV and Kat realized, she herself didn't watch that much TV. After hours at work, she'd go to the gym and then home and look over contracts and work a few more hours before going to bed and starting all over the next morning.

"Hey Kat, how's Liz?" Kat pulled from her thoughts by Linda's question.

Kat walked into the room and sat, letting out a breath "Well, I can see what everyone was talking about," she curled her legs under her. "Liz is as big as a house and trapped in that apartment with no control over anything. I can see why she's going crazy, but I hope the few suggestions I made to Ben, will help."

Linda smiled, "What kind of suggestions? I know Ben could use all the help he can get. I've tried to help, but he's feeling so helpless. Short of Liz having the babies, I didn't see any reprieve." Linda hit the volume button, so they could talk.

"I suggested, Ben buy the house that Liz rented. I know she loved it there, and Ben could surprise her with it. Liz could get out of that apartment, even get outside, and maybe watch the guys surf." The expression on Linda's face said, she approved. "I think if Liz could set up the nursery, you know, pick out paint and order stuff on the internet, she'd feel a little more in control. And that's what I think Liz's real problem is, no control, and this is coming from the ultimate control freak."

"How did Ben take your suggestion? I bet he went nuts over it, but I love the idea. I'm surprised, I didn't think of it, because I could see

Liz much happier in her own house setting up the nursery. I know pregnant woman have that nesting instinct." Linda shook her head as if the idea pleased her.

"I don't know anything about pregnant woman, but I know Liz. Linda, I'm sure you were worrying about the babies and not thinking of Liz, wait that didn't come out right. I didn't mean..." Kat trailed off when Linda held up her hand.

"Don't worry, I know what you meant. I think a fresh set of eyes could see what the rest of us could not. So, what is Ben going to do about the house?" Linda watched Kat and thought how smart of a woman she was, and even though Kat played the part of tough and hard, she knew Kat had a much softer and caring side to her as well. "Did you eat any dinner?"

At that moment, her stomach growled loudly, and she realized she hadn't eaten anything all day. "I haven't eaten anything. I guess I got caught up with Liz today and forgot to eat." Linda stood and walked into the kitchen as Kat followed. "Oh, Ben is researching who owns the house and considering buying it." She watched Linda get a plate out of the cabinet and dish some leftovers on to it. "You know you don't have to serve me, I know I'm your guest, but I'm going to be here for a while, and it would make me feel better if you didn't go out of your way for me. I should be compensating you for my stay, not having you wait on me." Linda turned and gave Kat a look of discuss. Kat knew what was coming next.

"Listen here missy," Linda pointed her finger at Kat, "Don't even attempt to give me money and as far as serving you, I'm not here most nights. I eat early and have social engagements. Tonight, I waited for you and didn't go to play bridge. So, as you can see, I won't be here to wait on you hand and foot, but you are still my guest and will act as such." Linda put her chin in the air and Kat noted that she was set in her ways. Linda wouldn't change how she did things.

"Okay, I apologize if I insulted you by offering money. I'm just not used to people doing things for me. I wouldn't want to disturb your social calendar. I appreciate you allowing me to stay here." Kat knew she had to pick her battles with Linda, and on this one, she wouldn't win. This was Linda's home, and her rules, not that Kat followed rules set by others well. Linda seemed to accept her apology and went on as if they didn't just have words.

"I hope Ben can buy the house. I think it would be perfect for them. They'll have to watch the kids when they get a little older around the water. That's why I never owned a house on the beach," Linda took the food out of the microwave and placed the plate in front of Kat, almost daring her to say something. Kat maybe rough and tough, but Linda had the experience of being a mother and knowing how to get her children to behave. Kat might not know it yet, but Linda was about to pull her into her family and love her as she did her own kids. She liked Kat's spunk and determination, but she could read Kat like a book. There was a story behind Kat's facade and Linda would find out what her deal was but wouldn't force Kat to tell her. She'd gain her trust, which Linda knew wouldn't be easy, but she was confident in her talents.

Kat got an uneasy feeling as she ate. Linda scrutinized her, she might be another person she needed to avoid, as her list was getting longer by the minute. First Jeff, now Linda, Kat thought she might need to get her own place, besides it wouldn't hurt to have a place to stay when she came to visit Liz. A house was something Kat never owned, she had her penthouse apartment in the city, but would she like having a house of her own? She had plenty of money, why hadn't she ever thought to buy a house before now. Because she liked the hustle and bustle of the city, and if she wanted a house, she'd have to move out of the city. Oh, she could have a brownstone or a townhouse but a real house on land, she'd have to maintain, as in mow the lawn. The image of herself out mowing grass in spiked heels made her laugh to herself. Linda pulled her from her thought when she spoke.

"Do you have an apartment in the city? New York is such a magical place. I've been a couple of times over the years. I took the boys and Danielle to see the Empire State Building and the Statue of Liberty, but they were very young."

"Yeah, the city does have its attractions. It also has its ugly side, too." Kat knew all too well about the ugly side of the city and people in general. Something she needed to remember even now, that she wasn't in the city. Every place has its unpleasant side, but somehow being in California, made it appear the undesirable were better hidden. You didn't see people sleeping in doorways or on park benches, although she knew there must be homeless people here, too. It was more you'd have someone trying to steal your money by swindling you on a land deal or stealing your identity. Not that didn't happen back home, but the crime in the city was almost everywhere. It must be the open space and the clean streets that gave her false sense of security.

"Every place has a violent side," Linda watched as Kat reacted to her words.

"Yes, I'm sure it does. That is why I've made every effort to be able to defend myself. I have a gun with a concealed weapon permit and I'm very comfortable using it if I must. Being a single woman in New York City can be dangerous, if your clueless and naïve. By the way, I need to find a gym while I'm here. I have to keep in shape, and it won't take long to get rusty."

Linda was reading in between the lines, Kat's words, and her body language. Something told her that Kat had been that naïve person at one point, and that was why she put on that arrogant bold manner, the don't even attempt to give her a hard time attitude. Now that Linda could see through Kat's smoke screen, she knew how she would win Kat over.

"Linda," Kat noticed Linda watching her too closely and that was something she couldn't have. "Do you know of a gym, one that might have a boxing ring, I like to kick box." Kat got up from the table to clear her dishes. "Do you like the dishes to be rinsed and put into the dishwasher?" Yep, she'd needed to stay clear of Linda. She was too perceptive, and the way she was observing her every move, that was one reason, she put her back to Linda to keep her from seeing too much.

"I don't use the dishwasher unless I have the family over. It's just me, so I usually just hand wash my dishes. The dish detergent is in the pump on the sink, and you can just put the clean dishes in the rack. I'll put them away, because I happen to be very particular about how my dishes get put away and where my stuff is." Kat nodded her head as she washed her plate and sliver wear. Linda could feel Kat avoiding looking at her, and she was about to prove another one of her suspicions. "I'm not sure about the gym, but you could ask Jeffery, he would know all those kinds of places." Linda heard Kat make a noise in the back of her throat of disgust and she could tell she was rolling her eyes. It made Linda smile, because the way Kat always professed her dislike of her second born. She wondered if there was a love hate attraction going on. Tomorrow she'd feel Jeffery out and see how he felt about Kat. Just maybe she could do a little subtle match making.

"I'll find one on my own, thanks anyway. I'm just used to working off stress and kicking some butt at the gym, it helps so I don't hurt stupid and irritating people. It's my way of anger management." Kat finished the dishes, turned to face Linda, and could see that Ben's mother was about to try to pull her into her family. Linda, Ben, and his family were Liz's new family now, not hers. She didn't have much of a relationship with her own parents, and that's how she liked it.

"I'm heading to bed, it's been a long day, and I'm tired, thanks for dinner." Kat walked by Linda and started up the stairs, where she could escape from Linda's watchful eyes.

"Kat, I'll leave a key for the house on the counter for you." Linda stood at the bottom of the stairs, and for the first time, she appreciated Kat's cute little figure. *Oh yeah, Jeffery won't know what hit him.*

Once Kat was in the safety of her temporary living quarters, she changed into a tank top and a pair of shorts. She would have to work out in her room for tonight, because there was no way she'd be able to sleep, not with someone, the one person that kept seeping into her subconscious, and aggravating the hell out of her. She knew if she went to bed now, she'd only be thinking how he could get under her thick skin, and over her high barriers to reach her, like no other.

Kat started with a warmup, just to get her blood flowing. She did some low impact jumping jacks. She didn't want Linda to hear her and come to investigate, so she needed to be quiet. Then she went to her bag that she would take to the gym and pulled out her weighted gloves. As she went through her routine of punches and kicks, once fully warmed up, she could feel some release of pent up frustrations of the day. Kat went into her uppercut punches, jabs, and her combo series. This wasn't going to make everything in her mind go silent, but it would help. Next, she did her sit ups, and pushups with her hands on the floor and feet on the chair to make them harder. There wasn't much more she could do in her room, but at least, she broke a sweat. Tomorrow, she'd need to find a real gym, one she could work off her demons.

Kat went to shower, and to try to get some sleep.

# ~ 3 ~

Jeff was up early the next morning, and he had gone surfing with Owen, now he watched wood being unloaded from the delivery truck for the new offices. He couldn't wait to get started on the space that would be his. It was funny how he was feeling because he never wanted to be stuck working at the shop, and now he was looking forward to getting more involved. He went from never wanting to be there, to always being at the shop, and he was happy about it. When Ben pushed him to take on more responsibility, he didn't feel overjoyed about it at first. As Ben pulled back at the shop, Jeff had to step up, and it gave him a sense of pride. He belonged here. He felt it, as he never did before.

His father had opened the surf shop before he was born, as a kid, he remembered hating working all summer when the other kids played. He swore when he grew up, he'd never work here, but when his father died, everything changed. Ben's plans to go off to college changed. He had to stay to work, and everyone had to pull more than their weight. Jeff was in high school at the time, but he knew he wouldn't be going off to college, either. It was Ben who pulled the shop into the age of computers and scanning the merchandise. He set up the system the store used now to reorder merchandise, by keeping track of what they sold. It was time for Jeff to make his mark on the shop. If this deal he had in the works for selling Shafford Surf Boards went through, it could be big for the shop.

"What's going on?" Kat's voice caught Jeff by surprise. He turned to see her standing next to him.

"We're making offices in the back for Dannie and me." He must have been so deep in thought, because he hadn't even heard her car pull into the lot.

"Oh, so will there be a bunch of construction workers around, with their shirts off?" She asked, and then added, "Maybe I could get Liz down here, and we could watch." Jeff made a noise and Kat laughed.

"Oh yeah, the workers will most likely have their shirts off and if you can get Liz down here, she will probably enjoy the show, because we are the construction workers." Now he was laughing, "And we'll even have tool belts." He said, the last part as if he knew, she'd like to see that.

"I'll find a way to get Liz down here. Just so, I can watch you hit your thumb with the hammer." That made Jeff step slightly closer to her.

"Don't you worry Kat, I know how to pound nails in and if you want to watch, all the better." Oh yeah, he hoped she'd come and watch.

Kat side stepped him and went up the stairs to Liz's apartment. He watched her every move, and noticed she was wearing clothes that looked as if she'd be going into her office. Kat wore a navy-blue suit jacket with a skirt and killer heels. He hadn't realized when he was talking to her that they were the same height. Now, he could see her legs as she went up the stairs. He was admiring her shapely calf muscles, and damn, she had nice legs. He didn't realize the dude unloading the wood was standing next to him admiring Kat too, until he spoke.

"Hot damn, who is that? I wouldn't mind getting me a piece of that." Jeff just turned as he felt the anger build inside.

"I bet you would, but she eats men alive." Jeff wanted to say more, but he didn't want this dude to take Kat on, as a challenge. "I'd know, so take my advice, and steer clear of her. Besides, she lives in New York." Jeff signed the paperwork the man handed him.

"That's a damn shame, because she could eat me alive if she wanted to." The man turned and walked away.

As Kat walked up the stairs to Liz's apartment, she thought how she was going to get Liz down all these flight of stairs. What did they do when she had to go to the doctors? They had to have a way, she thought as she knocked. Ben opened the door with a big smile on his face, as if he had a good night. Not that Kat wanted to know why he was smiling that way.

"Good morning, Kat," he stepped back to let her in, and thank God, he didn't hug her, as he did the day before.

"Hi Ben, how do you get Liz to the doctors when she has to go?" Kat could see the question puzzled him. "How do you get Liz down the steps?" She rephrased her question because she wanted to get Liz out of the apartment today.

"Ah, we have a wheelchair, and it takes all of us to carry her down, why?"

"I want to get her out of this apartment today, and you guys are building offices today downstairs. I thought she'd like to watch." She could still see confusion in Ben eyes, so she went on. "I'm sure you'll be taking your shirt off," she paused hoping he'd get it, but nope, so she went on. "You know, so she can watch you with no shirt, working." Finally, he got what she was saying.

"Oh, I see where you're going with this. Okay, let's see if Liz wants to go downstairs."

Of course, Liz wanted out of that apartment. So, Ben loaded her into the wheelchair, and it did take all of them to carry her down the stairs. Kat noticed Jeff was smiling the entire time, as they strained to go down three flights of stairs. Once they had her down the stairs, Ben set up one of the best lounge chairs they sold in the store, so Liz could see everything they were doing.

"Kat, I'm so glad you suggested this. I have to say, I was going crazy looking at the same four walls." Liz was smiling as the men started to bring wood inside to start building walls. At first, it was just Ben and Jeff, Owen would join them when he got out of class later. Kat went to get herself a lounge chair and some lemonade for Liz. Every so often, Ben would look over at Liz, and she smiled back. Kat thought how she managed to get right in the middle of her friend's relationship. How she needed to keep suggesting things that put them together, as if they had lost their way. She had a little chuckle over it because she was the one that didn't believe in true love, and here she was, caught up in their romance. Kat pulled out her computer so she could try to get some work done. She didn't want Jeff to think she was here for him. This was for Liz, even if that tool belt hung low on Jeff's waste was a turn on. Kat had to ignore him, as her phone rang, she took it outside to answer, because it was too noisy with them working.

"Yes Vikki, I received the contract, but I don't like the wording. I want to amend some of the provisions, how many books Mr. Wilkins has to write before we can renegotiate his contract and the percentage that he'll make per book." Kat listened to her assistant as she turned to walk in the opposite direction and saw Jeff watching her. He walked toward her, then stopped, and grabbed more wood off the pile. Once more looking her way and then went back inside. Kat let out a breath, as she realized, Vikki was still talking to her, and she had no idea what she had said. "Sorry Vikki, I didn't hear what you said, we must have a bad connection."

Once the conversion was over, Kat took a couple of minutes to get herself together. She didn't know why she felt just a bit disappointed over Jeff not trying to get into her space. It was crazy that she felt this way because she should be happy he just looked at her and walked away. It was as if when she prepared herself for him, he didn't engage her, but when he could sneak up on her, he took full advantage. That was just it. She couldn't allow him to get the best of her, so what could she do to make him react to her. "Oh, yes, I know what I could do."

Kat walked back into the building and went to her seat, but before sitting, she removed her jacket. The white kami she wore under her jacket was very thin, and she was aware what could be seen, or what it appeared someone could see. To make sure Jeff noticed, she asked, "Ben do you know of a good gym close by, one that has a boxing ring?" Both Ben and Jeff turned their attention on her, as she knew they would.

"Um, well let me think." Ben wasn't sure he wanted to tell Kat, the only place that had a boxing ring, was the all men's boxing club, on the bad side of town. He knew Kat wasn't going to appreciate the fact that she couldn't just walk in and be welcomed because of her gender.

"There's O'Leary's Boxing Club on Board Street, but that's a men's only club," Jeff answered for Ben. "There's also some martial arts places, that might do kickboxing, not sure if they have a ring or not. Why, do you need to beat someone to release all that pent-up frustration you have." Ben stepped away from Jeff and went to sit next to Liz to watch the show.

Kat could feel her eye starting to twitch, and she had to regain her composure. She stepped up to Jeff, right in his face. "Why, are you volunteering to be that someone, because I would definitely enjoy kicking your ass?" The evil smile that spread across her face was proof, of just how much she would enjoy hurting him. The thought of him hitting the mat played in her mind for the briefest moment before Jeff spoke again.

"You think you could take me? I have what?" His heated sexual pursuit over her body, with that thin white top and her heels, made him laugh. "I have to have at least fifty, maybe sixty pounds on you, and I don't physically hurt women, not even ones that irritate the hell out of me." Jeff was aware his brother and sister-in-law were watching the confrontation. He tried to hide the sexual desire to wrestle Kat down and do what he'd been fantasizing about doing to her. He didn't understand why, but this sparring was making him extremely aroused. Jeff knew if he was feeling the sexual electricity between him and Kat, so was everyone else in the room. He couldn't control it, there was something that drew him to her. He had no clue what that was, except for the sexual pull, because he didn't like anything about her. The women he was attracted to were soft spoken and easy going, not rough and aggressive, and yet here he was, engaging her.

"Oh, I have taken on men way bigger than you and left them begging for mercy." Now it was her turn to step back and let her eyes sweep over every inch of his body, as if she was assessing all his strengths and weaknesses. Jeff took the bottom edge of his t-shirt and pulled it over his head. Kat watched him, and she kicked off her heels. Then he removed his tool belt, his eyes never leaving hers.

What she did next surprised the hell out of him because she unbuttoned her skirt and slowly pulled the zipper down. Jeff heard Liz tell Ben to do something, because this was going to get out of hand, but Ben didn't move, and neither did he. When her skirt hit the ground, she had tight black workout shorts on and that skimpy top. Holy shit, she was a vision that made him hard as concrete. She started bouncing back and forth on the balls of her feet in a fighting stance as if she was going to fight him right there.

"Ok, that's enough," Ben said as he stepped between them. He pointed his finger in Jeff's direction and said, "Jeff, go see if Dannie needs help in the shop. Kat put your clothes back on, there isn't going to be any fighting here today. You both really need to find a place to work this out, physically or just get down and get it over with, because you are going to be by each other."

Jeff just grabbed his shirt and walked away, because one his hard on was impossible to hide, and two, he was so close to dragging her up the stairs to fuck the hell out of her. He had to shake that thought out of his head, because he knew she'd never just give into his desires.

If he were going to admit it to himself, just how much he wanted her, he'd have to admit this wasn't going to be easy and soft. Was that what attracted him to her, because he knew he'd have to really work for a woman, for the first time in his life.

Kat turned to face Ben, shaking her head, because she didn't know why she let Jeff get to her. "Why did you stop it before I could show him what the floor tastes like? You do know, I could drop him like a fly, right?" She took her skirt, glided it back into place, and slipped her feet into her heels. "I thought you'd appreciate watching me hurt your brother."

"I have no doubt you'd hurt him, that's why I had to stop it. I need him to help with putting up these walls. Otherwise, I'd be doing it by myself. Kat, I don't know what's really going on between you two, and I don't think I want to know, but I need you here, and I can't keep Jeff away from you. From what I see, there is enough sexual tension, and electrical current, to light the entire state, and I don't want to get in the middle of that. For the rest of us who must be around you two, I wish you'd have mercy on us, and have a hard roll in the hay, knock some boots and get it over. Please." Ben sat next to Liz again and kissed his wife.

"Unfortunately, it's not that easy Ben, because believe me, if it was, the deed would already be done. Your brother just brings out everything in me that says fight. I truly don't know what it is, but I can't just allow him to take any part of me." Kat knew she already said too much and needed to get out of there. "Hey, with Liz down here, I'm going to take off for a bit, you know find a gym. I'll be back in a little while." She gathered up her computer, briefcase, turned and walked out the door.

"Holy crap, when they finally realize they can't just beat the shit out of each other to get it out of their system, it just might be the hottest sex ever, I hope when it happens, Kat shares it with me, so I can put in my next book." Liz fanned her heated face as Ben strained to lay next to her, because she took up the entire chair. He pulled the chair Kat had left closer and snuggled in close as he could to her.

"Not hotter that our first time, because nothing was better than getting inside of you." Ben ran his hand over her huge belly and kissed her forehead. "You know, I remember every second, the way I wanted to take you slow. Your frantic need," he said into her ear and felt her shiver as his hand moved up to cup Liz's amazing large breasts. She was well endowed before her pregnancy, now even with her belly big with their twins, her body still did it for him. How could she ever think he didn't find her even more appealing? "You were so tight, and there was nothing between us, just skin to skin." He heard her laugh, and to him, it was one of the sweetest sounds.

"And most likely, that is why I look like this now," she ran her hands over her huge stomach.

"And if you remember, I told you, if I was so lucky to have my wife carry my child, a few stretch marks would be worth it. Just so you know, nothing in the world could ever change how I feel about you, or how my body reacts to yours." He took her hand to drag it over his jean-covered erection to prove his point. "I love you, Liz Jacobs, and absolutely love the sound of that, too. I hope you never feel like I don't want you, physically, or emotionally, because Liz, I need you more than my next breath." His lips covered hers, if they were anywhere else, he'd be doing a whole lot more. He heard his name breathlessly from her, his body craved her. "Liz, I need you, but I can't get you up the stairs."

"There's always your office," he heard Liz whisper. Ben moved so fast to get Liz in the wheelchair and went through the shop, if anyone was in his office, he was going to kick'em out.

Jeff was glad to be able to walk away first, he knew it was childish, but somehow it made him feel if he won. He was aware this was far from being over with Kat. Most likely, she'd end up hurting him physically, because he couldn't hit her or restrain in any way, and she'd get hurt. If he could only figure out a way that it didn't turn into a competition every time they came anywhere near each other. Jeff turned just in time to see Ben wheeling Liz down the hall to his office, and he knew where that was going to lead. Maybe he'd go and knock on the door in five minutes, but the thought that Ben was with Liz, made him wonder where Kat went. After work, he'd ride by some of the gyms and see if he could find his mom's car. Then he'd know where she'd be working out. It was very stalk-ish of him, and he'd be appalled if he could help it. Kat made him crazy, and drove him to desperate measures, something he never ever had done before for a woman.

Kat pulled out of the lot behind the shop, before she pulled into a gas station to look up gyms on her phone. She didn't want Jeff sneaking up on her again and giving him the satisfaction of startling her. The tension in her back and neck was giving her a headache. Maybe she'd get a massage while she was at it. Ben had Liz and she needed to relieve the sexual frustration, along with her normal restlessness she always felt. Being in California, had in some way, relaxed her and in other ways, made her feelings of control non-existent. That was a state she didn't like being in. Control was important to her because it meant she could prepare for whatever came her way.

She could feel the lack of sleep, and the fact that she hadn't worked her body to sheer exhaustion last night, allowing her demons to start creeping in. Kat knew, because she could feel those old feelings of hating herself, or the person she used to be. The person that didn't have control over what someone did to her because she was weak.

She only allowed the feeling to consume her for a few minutes, to make sure she never forgot what she endured. Once, she grieved for her lost innocence, and the fact that she stayed quite all these years, to allow this man to maintain his freedom. There was nothing to be done now, too many years had passed. What she could do, is never forget, even when everything in her, never wanted to remember.

Kat took a deep cleansing breath and let it out, as if to purify her soul. She needed the control, to balance out the demons. The only way she found, was to work her body, so her mind could deal with the fear of not being a victim. When Kat worked out, it was to make her body stronger and allow her to mind the freedom of knowing she could handle herself. If her body couldn't handle a situation, she always had the security of knowing her gun wasn't far.

"Okay, enough of that, now a gym," she looked down at her phone to see the listing of all the gyms within ten miles. She knew she'd have to do the legwork and go to each one. A gym to her had to be a place she felt comfortable. It had to have all she needed to get the best workout. Back in N.Y., she had several different places she worked out in, because each offered something she liked, and she was prepared to do the same here. It amazed her how uncomfortable she felt to have to find new places that she took for granted at home.

People knew her, like the trainers and the gym rats, that she would spar with, verbally or physically if they were brave enough. Along with the guys that attempted to come onto her, and she set straight. She'd have to start all over, not that she had a problem telling guys, or anyone else, what was on her mind. However, at her places, they already knew her and that she wasn't going to go out with any of them. Most of them knew when to leave her the hell alone altogether.

Well, she'd start with the one closest to the shop, because most likely, she'd be leaving from there. She set her GPS, so she didn't get lost. Driving in California felt weird, because even though she had a car, she never drove it. In the city, you walked or took a cab because parking was almost impossible.

The first place was a yoga studio. When Kat walked inside, she got a good feeling from it. She went to the small counter, where a young girl was talking on the phone, so Kat waited and glanced around. When the conversation ended, she asked if Kat needed any help. Kat explained she was here on business for a few months and was interested in short-term membership. The young woman showed her the studios where classes took place and went over class schedule. Kat paid for six months, took the schedule, and headed for the next place on her list. She went through the list quietly. She knew the moment she stepped inside if she'd get what she needed. By the time, she finished with her list, she had memberships for not only yoga, but also a big-name gym, and a small martial arts academy. Each having something she needed, the yoga for her piece of mind and flexibility, the big gym to do her strength training, she even signed up for some sessions with a trainer, and last, the martial arts to keep her body prepared to fight. Tomorrow she'd check out the boxing club, even if it were for men only. She'd prove she could handle herself. Kat had been gone for hours and needed to get back to Liz.

Studs for the walls were close to being up and the office space were coming along, when Jeff spotted Kat stroll in. He had been able to concentrate with her gone, even if their earlier confrontation replayed in his mind. It was her bare feet, tight little shorts, and the nothing there top, that gave him thoughts of stripping her naked. The short break when he went into the store to help and Ben had taken Liz to his office, was what he needed to regroup. Jeff knew Kat would be back, but at least he wasn't sporting the boner, as he was earlier.

Although they had been working for hours, Jeff didn't take off his shirt as Ben had, but suddenly, he felt over heated. Liz was in her chair watching Ben's every move, and Kat moved to sit next to her. As they started talking, Jeff couldn't help trying to overhear their conversation. He knew she went looking for a place to work out. It would save him from stalking her if he knew her routine, but Ben saved him the trouble of asking if she found what she was looking for.

"Actually, I found three places. There's a nice little yoga studio not far from here, and the big gym on Main Street. Oh yeah, and a martial arts place that has a great layout. The instructor seems to be very knowledgeable in his art."

Jeff's heart was pounding in his chest at the thought of Kat working with some instructor, him putting his hands on her. *Oh man, what is wrong with me, she's free to do whatever the hell she wants to. I need to get a grip, but I do have a membership to the gym on Main and I took some Karate class when I was a kid. Maybe I might want to consider starting again, of course, not the same class she's taking.* Now the yoga, no way was he going that far, but to watch, *now I could get into that.* Jeff thought, didn't he date a yoga instructor at one time. Most likely, but he had to think about what her name was, and if she was still in town. *Wait, could I use someone like that just to get close to Kat?* He knew the answer before the thought was complete, especially since his brother had pointed out how his dating habits affected the women he dated.

Pulled from his thoughts, Jeff listened as Ben asked Kat about the boxing club. Because the thought of her working with a male instructor at the martial arts studio hit him hard, the thought of her in an all-male gym truly pissed him off. When he heard, her tell Ben, she hadn't considered the boxing club yet, an amazing amount of relief washed over him.

He was trying his best to just keep working and not act as if he cared about anything she said, but he knew by his reaction to her doing, what he guessed was her normal routine. He had feelings for her, deeper than just wanting a sexual romp in her bed, because a fierce possessiveness to keep her for himself and protect her, came over him. The thought made him laugh, because Kat didn't desire or need anyone to protect her or control her.

"What's so funny over there?" It took Jeff a minute to comprehend that Kat was talking to him. He had been so lost in his own thoughts, he hadn't realized he had laughed aloud.

"What?" Luckily, he was saved when Dannie walked into the back to check on how the offices where coming.

"Wow, looks great so far. I want the office closest to the back door. I have a feeling once Ben lets me revamp the website, I'll be going in and out." Dannie walked into the open space that would be her office and turned around as if deciding where she was going to put all her furniture. "So, can I go down to the computer store and pick out my desk and everything?"

"Don't get ahead of yourself, we still have a lot to finish before, any furniture gets moved in. Just because you see walls, doesn't mean it's ready yet. We still have to figure out electric, and maybe a bathroom you and Jeff can share back here." Dannie just gave her older brother a dirty look and Ben laughed. "You can go and look at furniture and pick out a computer, but I don't want anything delivered just yet. I want to go over the computer you pick out to make sure it has everything you'll need."

"Ben, I'm not stupid, you know. I know what I'll need to run the website and inventory once we launch the web-store. I worked at a major graphic design company and managed several big accounts all at the same time. So, I think I can handle this." Dannie knew her brothers still looked at her as being the baby of the family, but she was no longer a child, and now it was a good time to prove it. "And, just so you know, I'm not getting some big clunker like you have. I want a laptop, that I can take to where I'll need it. But, still can be added to the main system, so I can access records for the store, and you'll be able to do the same for any warehouse inventory."

Dannie knew by the look on Ben's face, she impressed him, but she wasn't finished with what she planned to do for the store. As Ben, had told her, she had to wait until they launched the new line of surfboards that Jeff was handling. It involved buying into a franchise, so the store was putting out a great amount of money. He didn't want to start anything new before they saw how the new line of surfboards worked out. That didn't stop her from planning and organizing what she'd need. When Ben gave her the freedom, she'd be ready.

"Wow, this is really looking like offices, do I get one, too?" Everyone turned to see Owen walking in and both Jeff and Dannie said in unison, "You have to wait your turn." Everyone started laughing.

"Hey, now that Owens here, can I go pick out my stuff for my office," Dannie asked.

"I want to go, too," Liz had been so quiet it was almost as if everyone had forgotten she was sitting there.

Jeff wanted to take a break from the manual labor, to get away from the feelings he was realizing were growing inside of him. "I'll go work in the store, and Owen can work with you Ben, until the girls get back. I have ordering to do anyway, if we're not too busy," he took his shirt and headed for the store once again. This time, he knew no matter how hard Kat fought him, he'd have to convince her he could be the man she needed, because he never had such strong feelings for anyone before. If he didn't at least attempt to see where this all would lead him, he'd always wonder what if.

# ~ 4 ~

Kat and Dannie packed Liz into the back of Dannie's van and drove to look at furniture for the new offices. Kat felt a small calm come over her as she released a breath and tension that had been building inside of her all day. She knew she could go to the gym tonight and get rid of some of the uneasy feelings that Jeff instilled in her. Kat thought how it was going to be impossible to stay clear of him and his effect on her. She knew she couldn't allow Jeff to get any closer to her and yet she couldn't stand by and pretend he didn't exist.

"So, Kat, what was all that about this morning with Jeff? Tell me you weren't going to truly, fight him? I mean, I know you could probably hurt him, but why?" Liz asked from the back seat, she was sitting behind the driver's seat. Kat could see Liz from the front passenger seat and turned to give Liz a dirty look.

"What happened this morning?" Dannie was now asking, *oh great now Jeff's sister was going to know there was something going on between her and Jeff.*

"Liz…" Kat's tone was of warning.

"Crap, I miss all the good stuff. Kat, if you are going to beat the crap out of my brother, I want to be there to watch." Dannie glanced in Kat's direction and then back to the road.

"Honestly, I need to go work out at the gym. I can get a little hostile, and I'll take it out on the person, I dislike the most." There, now that should set the record straight. Kat didn't want anyone else aware of the growing tension between her and Jeff. It was bad enough that Liz and Ben knew.

Liz laughed from the back seat, "You, Kat, a little hostile, that's putting it mildly. I think the word you might be looking for is intensely hostile and when it comes to Jeff, he ramps up your engine to a new level of hostile."

"Oh, now my brother can be relentless, if he figures out how to annoy you. Both my brothers can be, although Ben grew out of it and Jeff never did." Dannie laughed and added, "Not that Jeff is a bad dude, he just had that middle child syndrome. He always needed attention, Ben was the oldest, so Jeff had to follow in his footsteps, and of course, I was the youngest and female."

Listening to Dannie talk about her brother gave Kat a small insight into why Jeff might do what he does. Kat wanted to know more, and the thought she could befriend Dannie to get that inside information, was intriguing.

Dannie went on, "Now, Ben was, and still is, our Daddy figure. He's the one we all go to when things go wrong. With Ben, he was always responsible for everything after our father's death. Jeff never truly had to take on any responsibility, and he preferred it that way, to let everyone else handle things." As Kat listened, she glanced to see Liz smiling at her, and Kat knew, Liz realized what she was doing. Thank God, they pulled into the computer/furniture store and the conversation ended.

~ ~ ~ ~ ~ ~

Jeff kept busy for the rest of the afternoon, he knew the girls had returned but hadn't seen Kat anywhere. He looked up as Dannie entered Ben's office and watched as she stopped short when she spotted him. She started to turn to leave then stopped again, as if she couldn't make up her mind.

"Did you need something?" he asked her.

"Yeah, I was going to do some work, but as I can see, you're already in here. I can use Mom's office. It's going to be so nice to have my own space when the offices are finished, because sharing Ben's office, is getting old fast." Dannie sat down in the chair on the other side of the desk and looked at Jeff.

"What? I know that look." He could tell his sister was going to give him a hard time about something.

"I just want to know what's going on with you and Liz's friend. In the car, Liz asked Kat if she was going to really fight you. And... I find myself wondering, first, why she'd want to kick your ass, and second, why she hung on every word I said about you." She was watching him very closely, most likely to see his reaction. He tried to keep his expression neutral.

"Kat and I have a hate-hate thing going on. She didn't like me from the moment she laid eyes on me. At the time, she didn't like Ben either, but now it's just me she can't stand." He smiled as he said, "I just annoy her, and I have to say I quite enjoy doing so."

"So, you're not attracted to her in the least bit then, or maybe it's that you are, and she won't give you the time of day? Not like your other lady friends."

Jeff just snorted as he shook his head, "Look Dannie, I really have no idea what goes on in that woman's head. As far as me being attracted to her, I'm attracted to just about every woman out there, so you figure it out."

"Well, what's not to like, she definitely has the body." Dannie thought how she was more on the full figure side in body types, like her mother. Wearing a tight little bikini was not in her future.

"Her mouth for one, she's rude, and not a very nice person, to me anyway."

"Mmm, she was nice to me. Maybe it is you. Maybe you did something to her. Like agitate the shit out of her." She watched as a smile spread across Jeff's face, a big smile as if he enjoyed the idea of it. "You know what happens when you play with fire, right?" Dannie got up and walked out.

Oh, Jeff knew fire was what he was playing with when it came to Kat, and her tight little body. Most likely, he'd fry, before he knew, she put him in hot oil. Jeff leaned back in Ben's chair and thought about hot oil and spreading it all over her skin. His eyes closed as the image of his hands gliding over her body went through his mind. The sound of someone moaning aroused him even further as her skin was so soft. Jeff slipped into a fantasy. Kat was on a table with just a white sheet over the center of her body. Waiting for her massage, she was motionless, and Jeff appreciated her body from her head to toe. The shape of her ass as the sheet hugged it, he realized that's where he wanted to be. He stepped closer and when she moved, he placed some hot oil into his hands and started at her shoulders, with his palms flat against her skin, he worked her muscles and again he heard a moan. Yes, this is what he wanted, to move over her body and know she enjoyed his touch. As his hands progressed down her spine, he procured the sheet with his every stroke. He was so close to her gorgeous ass, very slowly his hands slid to her bottom.

"Napping again, aren't you sleeping at night?"

His brother's voice snapped Jeff out of his stupor and the vision of Kat's stunning body was gone. When he tried to sit up and almost tipped over the chair.

"Easy there, I didn't mean to startle you. I'm heading up stairs for the night. Owen is closing tonight, you got any plans tonight, a big date maybe?" Jeff didn't want to talk to his brother now, because he wanted to get back to his fantasy.

"No, I have no big plans. I was thinking I might go work out, but I have a little more to do here first," he said as casual as he could manage. His fantasy left its mark on his crotch, and he didn't want to get up with Ben still there.

"Jeff, tell me you're not going there, to the gym to annoy Kat, because I have to say you two are getting out of control. After what happened today, you two need to work this out, what almost happened." Ben corrected himself as he leaned against the door jam and folded his arms over his chest.

"That's not the plan, to annoy her. But, when she's around, she does things to me, I can't explain. On one hand, I'm so attracted to her, and on the other hand, I can't stand her. I'm confused. I don't know what I'm feeling." Jeff ran his fingers through his hair.

Ben stepped inside his office and shut the door behind him. Jeff knew where this was going. Now, should be honest with his brother, or should he deny everything? His brother sat across from him and let out a big breath as if he needed to consider what he was about to say.

"Jeff, I want to know where you see this thing going with Kat. Because from what I've seen, up until this morning, the two of you have enough pent up sexual tension that it just might kill the both of you."

"To be totally honest Ben, I don't know. I'm not sure. I'm strong enough to handle Kat. She is in my head all the time, I find myself looking for her. When we have those confrontations, I have never been so aroused and so fucking hard in my life. I want to drag her kicking and fighting somewhere and do her. A part of me wants to try to bring down her walls and find what she is hiding. And then, there's the part that she is not easy, I have to work for her." Jeff shook his head because he wasn't sure if he was making any sense.

"She challenges you, and she drives you crazy." Ben leaned into the desk, "She does things to you, changes you, and makes you think."

"Yes," Jeff's voice was soft but distressed even tortured.

"You my brother, have a tough road ahead of you. I don't envy you. My best advice for you, is to talk to Liz, she knows Kat better than anyone does. Don't worry about her telling Kat, because if you ask her not to share your conversation, she'll keep it to herself. Liz prides herself on being trustworthy, and she just might enjoy having one up on Kat."

"I'll think about it. I'm not sure I'm there just yet." Jeff watched Ben get up and start for the door.

"You surfing in the morning?" Jeff asked to Ben's back.

"No, can't leave Liz until Kat gets here. You goin'?"

"Yeah, I think Owen doesn't have class until late tomorrow. If Kat gets to your place early enough, come join us. You haven't been in a while." Jeff noted that Ben hadn't gone surfing in months and he missed not seeing him out on the water.

"I know I have more important things to do." Now Ben turned to look back at him.

"I'm not saying your plate hasn't been full, but you need some time to be free. And you know how an hour of surfing can make everything better."

"I know, I might show up, you never know." Ben walked off and now Jeff was thinking about talking to his sister-in-law about Kat. He knew Ben was right. Liz could give him some insight into the spiky blonde that has wormed her way into his life.

~ ~ ~ ~ ~ ~

Kat walked through the doors of the gym, and she could feel that familiar pull, as the young woman behind the desk smiled at her. She scanned her membership card and moved to the locker room. The need to work her body was over whelming, she must dispel the demons that would haunt her, if she let them.

Quickly Kat changed and went to the first small room that didn't have a class going on. She started her warmup. With the music playing in her ears, she could lose herself. Soon, her body began to sweat, and her muscles tighten as she watched herself in the floor to ceiling mirror. She distinguished how her body moved, and each move had to be perfect, perfection was the only standard she'd accept. With every defense passage she made, she didn't have to think, because she'd done them so many times before. Kat subconsciously went through her kicks, and punches. Once her physique was wet with sweat, she moved to the main gym.

Kat noticed how the men watched her, not that she cared if they left her alone. Today, she was working her upper body. As she moved to each machine, Kat scanned her surroundings. She hoped the vibe she was sending out would keep anyone from approaching her. In the corner of her eye, she spotted him.

"Shit," *why was he here*? Damnit, she was here to get him out of her system, and to expel her demons, but mostly to work off the sexual tension he caused in her body. Now what was she going to do? She decided that if he stayed away, and on the other side of the gym, she would just finish and leave. Did she truly want him to leave her alone? Yes, because that was what was in her best interest. She went through her routine but couldn't help how her eyes shifted to where he was. Kat tried her best not to allow Jeff to see that, she was watching him.

"Okay, I can't take it. I need to go upstairs and run on the treadmill, and this way, I can look down on him. He can't sneak up on me then," Kat whispered to herself. She moved to the staircases that took her to the second-floor balcony that overlooked the floor below. As she set the speed and the incline, she watched him. The band underneath her feet started to move and she began a slow jog.

He moved to the Smith machine and loaded the barbell with weights. She had a practically clear view of him, as she pretended to watch the TV suspended from the ceiling. Jeff effortlessly picked up a bench and moved it beneath the bar. *Oh Yeah, he's working his chest,* her eyes roamed over him as he lay on his back with his legs straddling the bench. Kat ramped up the speed on her treadmill, without taking her eyes off him. She noticed how much weight he was lifting and exactly how many reps he did, before standing and glancing in her direction. Quickly, she diverted her attention and studied something on the other side of the gym. He smiled and went to start his next set.

"Shit, he knows I'm watching him, how pathetic," again she increased the speed.

Jeff knew exactly where Kat was, from the minute he walked through the door, he searched for her. He stared from a safe distance through the glass doorway in amazement. Alone, in her own little world, her moves sharp and calculated, and yet, very fluent, and passionate. Shocked by Kat's flexibility, as she did sidekicks over her head and spinning kicks, he couldn't take his eyes off her.

Finishing his last set, he moved to the side of the machine where he could see her, but she couldn't see him clearly. Adding more weights, he continued with his work out. His thoughts moved to his fantasy from earlier, as he mindlessly lifted the weight over his chest. He felt the pain before he realized he hadn't counted his reps. He locked the weight into place and stood, looking to the treadmills. To his surprise, she was gone. Surveying the gym for her, his mind spiraled with what to do. Should he go after her, or just let her go, he knew what he wanted? The split-second decision made, he was going after her. He was chasing her, he hated the thought, but he couldn't stop himself.

Kat had made it to the car she was using, just as she heard Jeff calling her name. She closed her eyes, and thought that maybe, she could pretend she hadn't heard him. Unlocking the door, she threw her bag into the car and stood in the safety of the space between the car and the opened door. Jeff now stood on the other side of the door, giving her the space she needed.

"Hold up a minute," Jeff sounded winded.

"What can I do for you?" She asked, and when Jeff's brow lifted, Kat added, "What do you want?"

"I just thought we needed to talk after what happened this morning, and before things get out of control. I was thinking," he trailed off.

"Boy, we are in trouble," she said under her breath. He smiled at her and stepped around the opened door, eliminating the barrier she was using as protection from him. Kat leaned against the car and crossed her arms over her chest.

"We need to try to be civil, you're going to be here for a while, and we are going to have to see each other. I think we should go out and spend some time together."

"Like a date," her voice raised. "No!"

"Not a date, just two people getting something to eat, and working to find some common ground. You know, I'm not really a bad dude."

"Pifft," Kat made a sound as she rolled her eyes.

"What, I'm not. You don't know anything about me. You've decided you didn't like me from the second you set eyes on me. I don't judge someone by their looks," he shifted closer. She tried to step back, only to realize she had nowhere to go.

"I happen to be very good at judging people, it's part of my job. I also know your type, how you operate. I don't like men that use women. You give them that great smile of yours, giving them false hope, and take what you want, leaving a huge path of devastation behind you." Kat's entire demeanor changed, she was no longer was calm. A streak of aggressiveness hummed through her body, and she stepped forward.

"Um, hold up. I don't leave a path of any kind of devastation. Yes, I date, but I don't go out to hurt anyone." Jeff held up his hands in his defense and stepped back. "Kat," as he spoke her name he could see something more was going on, so he asked, "Are we really talking about me or someone else?"

That statement snapped Kat out of her stupor, and she put her shield back in place. "Look," she exhaled. "I don't think it's a good idea for us to spend any more time together than absolutely necessary. It's bad enough we don't have a choice, can't we just agree to dislike each other and leave it at that." Kat knew spending any more time with Jeff was a bad idea for her wellbeing. She couldn't believe she allowed her emotions to get the best of her in front of him. She thought hopefully he hadn't noticed how her reaction was over the top. Although she knew, he had noticed something wasn't right.

"One dinner Kat, I think we should at least try. You might find you like me because I'm not all bad." He gave her that hundred-watt smile, trying to soften her up.

Unfortunately for Jeff, Kat long ago had fallen for a great smile and trusted the words of someone, and she wasn't going there again. Not that she couldn't handle herself, because she knew she was very capable and had the ability to take care of any situation. However, this was Jeff, not the one who hurt her, who attacked her. The only way Jeff could hurt her, was if she allowed him to.

Jeff could see Kat had an internal battle going on and he didn't want her to say no. "Kat, listen, no pressure, it's just dinner and some conversation, get to know each other. I'd like to know more about you, what you do for fun and maybe share what I like to do." He watched her shake her head and thought for sure she was going tell him not happening.

"Okay, against my better judgment, one dinner," she heard herself say and had no inkling why she just agreed to have dinner with him.

"When's good for you?" Jeff could feel the blood rushing through his body. He would have one night to change her mind about him. Would he see a different side of her? This was going to be it, he knew, he'd find out if he could be with her. This one night would hold so much promise and possibility he almost couldn't wait.

"I can't do it until Ben is off at night, so he can be with Liz. Or I'm sure I could get your mother to sit with Liz." Kat was deep in thought, why she was doing this, when Jeff interrupted her.

"No, I don't want my mother to know anything about us going out. If you hadn't noticed, she will make so much more out of us spending any time together. I'm not kidding. She will have us married with kids." He saw the surprise on Kat's face at the thought and for the first time he realized her hair, it lay flat not spiked up as he usually saw it. From working out, it had fallen around her face, it gave her a softer look, not so tough. Wondering how it would feel to tighten his fists in it, he immediately felt his body reacting to the vision and needed to end this conversation before he did something stupid like kissed her.

"Let me know when, and for both of our sake, don't tell anyone in my family. Not even Liz, okay? I don't need the shit from them." He stepped back away from her to put distance between them. She nodded her response and stepped into the car. "Good night, Kat." He watched her get into his mother's car and couldn't help feeling his life was about to change, he just didn't know if it was for the better.

Kat drove to Linda's house on autopilot, wondering what just happened. Why was she doing this, in her conscious mind, she knew this was a terrible idea. She knew under no circumstances could he change her mind about him, it was the only way to protect herself. How was she going to keep her distance if essentially, she liked him? Tonight, he cut right through her defenses, any other time she would have cut the guy down. However, with Jeff being Ben's brother, she had to be cautious, she had to see him again. The ways she would normally handle a man didn't apply. Kat thought she'd attempt to put the evening off if she could, until she could come up with a plan.

Pulling into Linda's driveway, Kat wasn't looking forward to having one of her little talks tonight. Where Linda looked too deep into her life and watched her too closely. The woman made Kat feel uneasy, as if she knew everything Kat hid from the world, all her secrets.

To Kat's surprise, the house was empty, relief flooded her body. She needed a shower and had work to do before her attempts for sleep. The work out made her body hum with adrenalin, and the endorphins in her body made her feel so good. She was addicted to the feelings, they were the only way she could relax her mind, keep the old memories from resurfacing and haunting her in her sleep.

"Okay, I'm not going there. Old news," she said to herself as she stepped into the shower.

~ ~ ~ ~ ~ ~

Completely stoked after his conversation with Kat, he went back into the gym. He hadn't finished his work out and needed to work his body if he planned to get any sleep tonight. Deep in thought, he hadn't appreciated the pretty young thing that saddled up next to him. He knew then he had changed, because he didn't even give her another thought as he grabbed his shirt and moved to the other side of the gym. There was just that one person that had him turning inside out for her, even chasing her down in the parking lot, so he could have his chance. He hoped like hell that she didn't tell anyone about them going out. If he could just get through the night without anyone knowing, it would be great. Because he had a feeling, after their night together, everyone would catch on very quickly, especially if they ended up in bed.

"No, don't go there, bro," he said under his breath. The thought of her sweaty body and her hair flat, still did things to him. "You're one sick dude." Then every time he saw her went through his mind and he couldn't remember a time he didn't think she was sexier then hell. She might have pissed him off, but that had so much more to do with how she made him feel. The fact that she didn't fall at his feet, didn't help either, and yet he found that fact intriguing and fascinating.

Watching her tonight in her tight shorts and a sports bra had him intrigued. The sheer confidence she displayed was exciting. He tried to think of any other woman he knew that had that kind of self-assurances. One that didn't care what others thought of them, most of the woman he dated needed reassurance, told they were pretty or sexy. Somehow, he didn't think Kat needed any one's approval, much less reassurance. Another thing about her he found sexy and so different from any other woman. Her movements displayed control over her body and mind.

He knew there was so much more to her that he didn't know, like when she made the statement about him leaving a path of devastation. What was up with that? She seemed to go to a strange place, then recovered, as if she passed through time. Had someone hurt her, that thought unleashed enormous anger in him. The rage that surged through him, if he ever found out someone had harmed her, he'd do some serious damage to the dude's face.

The next few days passed as Kat did her best to avoid Jeff. Every time she walked to and from her car, she knew he might be lurking, waiting to ambush her. She tried to convince herself that he had changed his mind about going out. Wondering how long he would allow her to put off their dinner. She called it a dinner because she refused to call it a date. Dreading the thought of spending an entire evening with Jeff, being alone near each other, had Kat shuddering. She figured if she were more obnoxious, the evening would end sooner. At least that was the plan.

~ ~ ~ ~ ~ ~

Jeff was aware it had been three days since his conversation with Kat, and he knew Ben had off two out of the three. So, Kat was avoiding him, she didn't need to take care of Liz. He would let her have the illusion of getting out of their date a little longer, but he wasn't going to let it go on for too long. Besides the fact of it was driving him crazy, and made him feel anxious, he knew it was Kat's strategy. The evening wasn't going to be easy, he assumed. No, Kat never made anything easy. She had a way of making everything hard, including his junk. She showed up each night in his dreams. So much so, that he didn't want to wake up. He needed to know one way or the other if the feelings he was having for her would lead to something more. If it wasn't anything, he wanted in a relationship or if he couldn't get past her hard shell, he needed to know now. Jeff walked through the store, heading for the stairs and leaned his head into Ben's office.

"Ben, I'm heading up stairs for a minute, I'll be right back. Can you cover the floor for me? You know we really need to hire someone else, right, with Owen in school and all."

"Yeah, I know. I'm gonna' start looking soon, I thought with Dannie here, we would be covered, but it doesn't ever seem to be enough." Ben shook his head as if the fact that he had to hire someone was another thing on his long list of things to do.

"I won't be long, oh yeah, I finished ordering. You know, if you need me to do more, I can." Jeff could see Ben was beyond his coping mechanism because Ben's usually controlled, and reasonable personality was showing cracks.

Ben tilted his head, "Who are you?"

"Funny, you know, never mind, forget I offered then."

"No, no, I can't forget it. It's just words I never envisioned coming out of your mouth."

"I know, believe me. I never thought I'd say it and mean it."

After his conversation with Ben, Jeff thought of how he'd try to do more. As he moved to the third-floor apartment, his mind rehearsed what he was going to say. Preparing for anything Kat could say was the key, he thought she would try to back out. He wouldn't let that happen, if he had to, he'd pull Liz into it, because he was sure she would be on his side. He knocked on the door and held his breath.

# ~ 5 ~

When no one answered the door, Jeff took the key that Ben kept in the flowerpot and unlocked the door. He listened for voices and knew Liz had to be in the bedroom, because she was on bed rest. He moved quietly through the living room and down the hallway. With the door to the bedroom closed, he knew Liz could be sleeping. As he moved closer to the closed door, wham, he was pinned against the wall with his arm-twisted behind his back. Kat was behind him with her soft voice in his ear.

"How the hell did you get in here? The door was locked. I could've hurt you." He exhaled with his face plastered to the wall in front of him. She pulled the smallest bit to get him to speak.

"I knocked, no one answered, then used the key Ben has in the flower-pot on the landing outside. I needed to talk to you. Do you mind letting go of my arm? Although, I'm enjoying your body pressed up to mine." She released him immediately as he anticipated she would.

"Liz is resting, so be quiet. If you don't want her to overhear you," her voice still soft as she moved to the living room. Kat stepped around the sofa to allow the space she needed. "Why are you here?" Kat thought she was safe from him if she stayed inside and was careful when she went to her car. She hadn't expected him to let himself in the apartment and scare the crap out of her.

"I thought you were going to let me know about going out. You wouldn't be avoiding me, now would you, Kat?" He moved toward where she stood and noticed how her body grew tight and uneasy. Her breathing excelled and she stepped away from him.

"I've been busy," she moved to the kitchen to stop his pursuit.

"Okay, you know I'm not going to let this go, right? Ben is off tonight, and that means you're free, I will pick you up at my Mom's around seven. Mom should be out with her book club tonight, so she won't get the heads up about us going out for dinner." He could see she wasn't happy with him telling her what to do. "Look, you could have set the time and date if you wanted to and since you didn't, I'm doing it."

"FINE, SEVEN," she said through clenched teeth.

He smiled and stepped into her space as he said, "It's going to be fun, you'll see."

"Now, go way," Kat moved to the door as she dismissed him.

That was fine, he didn't really care, he got what he came for and just for good measure, he made sure he touched her as he moved through the doorway. He had a feeling she was going to come out fighting. He decided no matter how she acted, he would be nice and civil to her. If anything, it would drive her crazy. He just couldn't allow her to get to him and pull him into a confrontation. Calm was the key, and control over his behavior.

Kat walked around in circles through the small apartment, mumbling to herself. Mad at herself for permitting Jeff to bully her into going out tonight. How stupid could she be? If only she hurt him as she heard him moving through the apartment. He wouldn't want to go out with her if she had broken his nose. That thought made her smile because there was always time. No, she couldn't just hit him unprovoked, but she could have when he let himself in. The key, she moved to the door and found it in the flowerpot just as he had said.

Putting the key in her pocket, she went back inside. Now at least he can't get in anymore, at least she hoped he couldn't, pulled from her thoughts when Kat heard Liz calling for her, "Kat, I need to use the bathroom."

She moved to the bedroom to help Liz and Kat wondered if she should confide in Liz about Jeff. She knew Liz would keep it to herself if she asked her to. However, once she told Liz what was going on in her head, she no longer could deny what was happening with in her.

"Who were you talking to?" Liz asked, and Kat was totally baffled by the way she did that, how could she hear anything and yet she knew.

"Jeff stopped by to give me a fax that came in for me," she lied.

"Oh, I didn't know if you were on the phone, I just heard voices." Kat wondered if Liz was getting super hearing, stuck in the bedroom most of the time, as if she didn't want to miss anything. She wanted to kick herself for telling Liz that Jeff was there, because now she might tell Ben, and then it would get back to him. Well, they were going out tonight, so if Ben found out, it would be after their date, no dinner.

~ ~ ~ ~ ~ ~

Jeff kept busy, and the afternoon passed quickly, but every time he had a minute to think, it was of her. How would the night go, would he kiss her? Most likely, at least a good night kiss. The thought of the one and only kiss they shared still sent his blood roaring through his body. He had no idea how that was possible, he kissed so many women and had never experienced anything like it. He wanted to climb over that first wall that surrounded her if she would allow him to see even a glimpse of who she truly is. She must have her reasons for the protection, maybe she was hurt by someone. That was the only logical explanation he could come up with, and it made him feel for her. Was it a lover, or maybe a family member? Seven couldn't come fast enough for him. He couldn't remember feeling so obsessed with anyone else, like how he was with Kat.

His Little Miss Sunshine, that made him smile, because the thought of the first time he called her that came to mind. Little did he know then, that she would sweep in and consume him.

~ ~ ~ ~ ~ ~

Kat slipped out the second Ben walked through the door. She had so much to do before Jeff came to pick her up. She questioned whether she had time to do a quick work out and decided against it. Once in the driveway of Linda's house, Kat's nerves sent impulses through her body. She had to sit and catch her breath, a reaction she hated. The anxiety and inner turmoil that so often accompanied her when she had thoughts of being alone with a man. She tried her best to control her apprehension because she recognized she was safe. Sometimes, Kat had to repeat her reassurance to herself repeatedly, until that terrified girl was gone, and the confident woman emerged. Kat took several deep breaths and got out of the car, only to find the house was not empty. Linda was working in the kitchen, and so Kat went to say hello, against her better judgment. Something she seemed to be doing a lot lately.

"Hi Linda, how's things going?" Kat walked to the fridge and took out a bottle of water.

"Oh, hi Kat, it feels like I haven't seen you in days," Linda laughed.

If Kat had her say, it wasn't long enough. Not that Linda was a bad person, she wasn't, but she had powers, motherly powers. As if she knew when her children told her a lie, or did something they shouldn't have done. Just because she wasn't one of Linda's children, didn't matter to her. Linda had enough love to spread around to everyone she saw fit. Owen, the young kid that worked in the shop, she felt he was hers, and she made sure everyone knew it. Kat didn't want to end up one of hers. She had her own family to fight to keep away.

"How is Liz doing? I heard she went to the store with you and Dannie. I bet she liked that, you know, getting out." Linda turned to face Kat, "I think you're doing a great thing for Liz and Ben. Taking care of Liz, it takes an enormous amount of pressure off Ben."

Kat wasn't sure how to take Linda sometimes, so she under played her compliment. "I'm just looking after my investment. If Liz doesn't write, or can't fulfill her contract, I lose money, besides the fact that it doesn't go over well with my boss."

"Now come on Kat, we both know you're here for more than just an investment or money," Linda wasn't going to let Kat slide.

Now studying Linda, Kat decided she would be straightforward with Linda. "Yes, Liz is my friend, and I care about her. Linda, can I ask you something," Kat would put all her cards on the table.

"Anything."

"What exactly are you up too? I can see you scrutinizing me, and at times, I see your wheels turning. In my line of work, I need good instincts, to be able to read people. Therefore, I know you have a plan. I'm going to tell you right here, do not include me in any of it. I maybe overstepping here, but I don't need a mother, or a family, because I have both. I'm not like Liz, who needed both. I don't want or need it." Kat saw the surprise in Linda's eyes, but then determination set in.

"Fair enough Kat, not many have the balls to call me out. I have plans for all my children, but what I want for them isn't anything that every mother wants for their child. I want them happy. I want to see them fall in love and have families of their own."

"What I want to know, is where you see me in this plan, because I am not imagining your attempts to pull me in. I have no plans to move, I like New York, so whatever you're thinking, count me out." Kat could see this wasn't going to deter Linda.

"I'll tell you exactly what I see happening. I think you are perfect for my son, and I'll tell you why. You will keep him in line and kick his ass when he needs it. As much as you try to make people dislike you by being aggressive and rough around the edges, it's what just might attract people to you. Not that I don't see right past all that, you are caring, and I think you love cautiously but deeply." Kat didn't like where this conversation was going and needed to put the kibosh on Linda's plans.

"Hold up, Linda I can't stand to be in the same room with your son, much less anything more. I am NOT THE ONE FOR JEFF. Let me make that perfectly clear. I'm working on tolerating him, for Liz's sake and again, I live in N.Y."

"I'm aware how the two of you are together, anyone who is in the same room can feel the sexual tension between the two of you. You can protest and fight me on this if you want Kat, but I'll tell you right now, it's not going to change the outcome."

Kat shook her head. This could not be happening. She didn't want to be in love with anyone, and especially not him. She could see Linda wasn't going to let this go. She needed to go home and get away from these people, sooner rather than later.

~ ~ ~ ~ ~ ~

Jeff showered, shaved, and now was on his way to pick up Kat. He had high hopes for the night, but it could go either way. The scenario he was hoping for would be that Kat walked away not hating him more than she did now. That would be a start anyway, and he could work from there. Dragged from his thoughts as he pulled into his mother's driveway, he noticed her car was gone. "Thank God for small favors," he said as he got out and walked to the door. Pulling out his key, he unlocked the door and went right in.

Kat heard movement in the house and knew Linda had left for her book club over an hour ago, she moved to open the door to her room, cautiously she moved to the stairs. Slowly, not to make a sound, she moved down each step. He stood in the living room, and she let out the breath she held. "Do you not have any boundaries? First, you let yourself into your brother's place, and now here you are, standing in your mother's living room, when I know I locked the door." As Kat stood against the wall still on the stairs, she gave him a once over. He was wearing jeans and a white golf shirt, not that she hadn't seen him in regular street clothes before, but somehow this didn't fit her image of him. His board shorts and a tank top, along with his laid-back personality were more fitting.

"Yeah, I have a key, not that my mom locks the doors most of the time. I didn't mean to scare you," he moved closer to where she stood. "You ready to go?"

"I just need to grab my bag. You know, I could have shot you, right?" Kat turned and went to get her purse.

Jeff shouted, "You won't need it."

"I at least need my phone," she yelled back down at him. Once back in her room, she took several deep breaths and repeated to herself that, she could do this.

Jeff held the door for her, and as she walked by him caught his scent. Pissing her off, she didn't need to be taken in by him. It was best for her to remember that. The faster she walked away from these crazy people the better.

As they walked to his truck, he watched as she slipped her phone into her back pocket. He loved how her jeans hugged her ass, and if by any miracle, he might get his hands on it. Once at his truck she turned and gave him a look as he stood next to her.

"You don't have to do that," she said.

"Do what?" He was very close to her.

"Open doors for me, I'm a big girl."

"You are no girl," his eyes quickly moved over her body before making it back to her face. "You are a lady, and my mother would have my head if I didn't have manners." He opened the door and waited as she climbed in. Of course, watching her ass had nothing to do with manners. He closed the door and rounded the front getting in the drives seat.

"Why couldn't I have just met you at the restaurant?" She looked out the window, as if she had no cares, but he knew better.

"One, because we are supposed to be spending time to get to know each other, and two, you don't know where you're going, and three, you can't just walk out," he liked the sound she made, and smiled on the inside.

"You know that won't stop me. I'll call a cab if I have to." She didn't like to feel trapped, and she wouldn't allow him to make her feel that way.

"I know, let's just try to have a good time tonight, okay." They became quiet and Jeff enjoyed the closeness his truck cab insured. He could see her profile as she looked out the window. He noticed her hair spiked as usual, and how her nose dipped, but it was how she smelled. He couldn't figure out what it was, but whatever it was, he knew he liked it. He glanced down at her legs as she crossed them, he could see she had on open toe shoes with red polished toes peeking out. The thought of when he'd ever noticed what kind of shoes his date wore before.

"I had a talk with your mother today," she said casually.

"Oh shit, that doesn't sound good. You didn't tell her about tonight?" All she needed was just a hint that he might be interested in Kat, and she would be up his shit in a heartbeat. Although he knew it was coming, with his brother married, now it was his turn as far as his mother saw it.

"I didn't have to, not that I told her. She is a relentless woman, she has this crazy idea that we're meant to be. As in a couple, you have any notion how she might have gotten this in her head?"

"Not from me, if that's what you're asking. I try my best to keep my mother out of my business, but that's easier said than done."

"Well, I would appreciate it if you would straighten her out. I tried, but she didn't seem to want to listen."

Jeff laughed hard at Kat's righteousness. As if, he could deter his mother, but he would have liked to be a fly on the wall for that conversation. "I bet that didn't go well, you are probably the only person to give my mother a run for her money in the strong will department."

"It's not funny, Jeff. I don't need your mother conspiring, undermining, me while I'm here. I tried to tell her, I'm going home the second Liz doesn't need me anymore. I'm not moving here, I like New York."

"Calm down, no one is asking you to move here," *not yet anyway*. Wow, where the hell did that come from? They hadn't even made it through a dinner together, must less her moving here.

"You need to take care of this, that's all I'm saying."

"Okay, I'll talk to her, not that I think it's going to do any good."

Jeff parked the truck out front a brick building nestled with other small businesses. With the words, Mamma Mia's Pizzeria painted on the large plate glass window, Kat knew they had arrived. She remembered her strategy for the evening, act rude and obnoxious. Under no circumstance would she fall for him, or any of his charming ways. That was when he opened the door for her, and the shield went into place.

She moved around him, ensuring they didn't touch. When she tried to open the restaurant door Jeff was there, placing his hand over hers. Kat pulled away, not looking at him even if she could see he was smiling. Once inside, Kat looked around, there was a small counter with a display case below with desserts. Beyond the counter, was a dining room, booths lined the walls and tables took up the middle section. The place was small, but clean and quaint.

Jeff ushered her to a booth, and she sat on one side as he sat across from her. She thought that at least he didn't try to crowd her by sitting next to her. However, now she'd have to look at him the entire time they ate. This night couldn't pass fast enough for her. She tried to focus her attention on the menu because she didn't eat pizza. That wasn't in her healthy diet, because she worked too hard to keep in shape to eat crap. Kat could feel Jeff staring at her and she made the mistake of looking up at him.

"Why are you looking at me like that?" Kat could feel her forehead pinch. How did he make her feel uncomfortable in her own skin by just watching her?

"I know the menu inside and out, you're sitting in front of me, what else do you want me to look at?" Leave it to Jeff to come up with a smart-ass answer.

"Then, at least pretend to look at your menu," she said as she attempted to concentrate on her own.

Jeff picked up the menu, but didn't hide the fact the he was still staring at her. He studied her eyes and her long lashes, her eyes were the only thing he could see over the menu. He knew she had blue eyes because he's had a few occasions to gaze into them. The multi-blue pools were the prettiest he'd ever seen, and that said a lot, because blonde and blue eyes said California.

He broke the silence, "Do you know what you want?"

"As I said before, I don't eat pizza but guess a vegetarian pizza on thin crust will do." She said with an annoyance tone in her voice, letting him know she wasn't happy with his choice of food.

"Really, because I love a deep-dish pizza, with everything on it," he enjoyed her reaction to his choice.

"Ugh, how do you stay in such great shape eating all that crap?"

Laughing he answered, "I surf, work out when I can, and I guess good genes. Don't you ever eat something you shouldn't, ya know just because you like it."

"No."

Jeff stood and walked to the counter to order, she watched his every move. The way he strutted across the room, as if he knew she watched him, or maybe it was just how he moved. All smooth and confident, how she hated guys like that. Not wanting to be caught looking at him, she pulled out her phone and appeared to be checking her messages when he returned.

"Now none of that, no phones at the table," she heard him say, bossy much, she thought.

"I have to check my messages. I have clients I work for, you know," she put her phone on the table.

He surprised her when he said, "Kat, I want to know three things about you, that I don't already know."

Kat thought, did she want to play this game with him, "Only if you go first."

"Fair enough, I'll go first. I like to ride motorcycles. I own a Harley. I play the acoustic guitar and sing a little, not well. And..." he looked around as to make sure no one could overhear him, "I secretly like to knit," he said with a straight face. When she burst out laughing, he knew he had her. How beautiful was her smile, he wasn't sure he'd ever seen it before? When she caught her breath, he said, "You should do that more often."

"Oh, my God, you had me going there. Knitting, you Mister Macho," she shook her head.

After the waitress put a glass of water and lemon for her and a Coke for him on the table, Jeff said, "Your turn, Kat." He moved his brows up and down and she smirked at him.

"Okay, I passed the bar on my first try, I have a cat, and I studied in France," there he got his three things, not so painful.

"You have a cat, Kat. I find that ironic, where is it?"

Out of all the things she told him, he picks the cat to talk about, "My cat, Mr. Puss is at home." Now it was Jeff's turn to laugh. She just waited until he stopped, and asked, "What's so funny?"

"Only you could manage to emasculate even a male animal, by naming him Mr. Puss."

Kat smiled, "Why Jeff, do I emasculate you?"

"The way you strut around, might intimidate most men, as you already know, your effect on men, I'm sure. I don't find your confidence threatening. It's a turn on for me. Kat, you are so different from any woman I've ever met. I don't mind telling you that I'm very attracted to you." He watched her closely, how her breathing changed, because her reaction was going to be critical.

"Well, even IF I were attracted to you, we could not act on it. I'm all for just sex hook ups, but not with you." Kat sat back in the booth to put as much space between them.

Jeff's heart skipped a beat when Kat announced the all for sex hook ups but quickly doused. "Why not me? It might help relieve the sexual tension that's always between us. I know it would for me anyhow."

"Jeff, I'm going to be as honest as I can be without going in too much detail. I don't believe in love, so hook ups are the only thing I do. I have rules, I follow for sex, and they are agreed upon before any interaction takes place. I don't think you'd like my definition of sex, and I don't need you knowing my business. I don't openly share my private life with anyone." Kat stopped talking as the pizza arrived.

They ate in silence, as Kat knew the bomb she dropped on Jeff would take some time to sink in. She just hoped he wouldn't ask too many questions. It was the reason she couldn't be mixed up with him, and once he knew her hang-ups, she couldn't maintain her edge. Guys like Jeff, would take your weakness and exploit it. No man would have that much control or power over her ever again. There was no giving any part of her away. She kept her secrets tucked away.

"Kat, I understand why you might not want to get involved with me. We have ties, with me being Ben's brother and you're Liz's agent, but that doesn't mean we shouldn't see where this might take us." Jeff didn't want to let this go, he needed her to think about giving them a chance.

"That's just it, there is no us. There will not be an "us", because I can't have someone so close to me knowing my business."

"What kind of shit are you into Kat because you have me thinking all kinds of crazy and kinky stuff. I have a very vivid imagination."

"Don't," Kat stood and walked to the restroom. She needed time and space. This man could infuriate, stimulate, and downright push her buttons. She needed to go home to get as far away from him.

Jeff paid the check and was waited for Kat by the door. He wasn't ready to let go of them just yet, no matter what she said he knew there was something strong between them. He should have known she wouldn't just roll over and play nice. That just wasn't her style, he would have to do the legwork, that was all there was to it. When Kat walked out, he held up a box with a small bag on top.

"What's in the bag," she asked just as he knew she would.

"It's a surprise for later," he watched as her brow lifted in question. He held the door open for her and walked behind her to his truck. She just watched as he dug in his pocket for his keys. Once inside, the tension was there, humming between them. She broke the silence first.

"I hope you understand, how I need to keep my business and private life separated." Kat needed to end any notion Jeff had of them ever being together before it got into his head that she was a challenge.

"Not really Kat, but I respect your right to privacy. I would never betray your trust." Jeff glanced over at her as he drove back to his mother's house.

"Sorry if I don't open the flood gates wide for you and trust you. Don't take it personal. I learned a long time ago not to trust." She just looked out the window as she thought how she needed to shut up before she said something stupid.

"So, you've been hurt before, that's why you don't believe in love. After watching my brother with Liz, I know love is out there."

Kat's laugh sounded sad, "You can say I've been burned, and then some, but that's not something I talk about to anyone. Let's just say, I learn from my mistakes, and don't repeat them. Love is not out there for me, because I don't have what it takes and neither does any man out there. Can we drop it, please?" The truck grew quiet again until Kat spoke again, "So, tell me what's in the bag."

"I told you, and you'll have to wait until we get back to the house." He grabbed the bag from in between them and moved it to his lap, because he didn't think she'd try to take it from there. He was wrong, as she went for the bag, he moved it, and when her hand connected with his dick, he almost lost control of the vehicle. He grabbed her hand and held it still, "I don't think so, unless you're going for something else." She didn't pull free, as he expected, and his body reacted to her hand on him. "Kat, you're sending mixed signals here." He hated when she pulled away.

"Sorry, you're right." God, she needed to get away from him and was glad when they drove up to the house.

He parked and looked over at her, "Kat, I want to at least be friends. You may have your reasons for not liking me, but I don't think it's something we can't work on." He wanted so much more, but knew he had to start with something less threatening. He'd have to earn her trust, so if being her friend was what he needed to first, then it was step one.

They moved to the house, and Jeff went to the kitchen to get two forks. Kat followed him, as she sat at the breakfast bar, he stood at the end as he opened the bag and removed a smaller box. Kat watched him open the box and inside was a large slice of cheesecake. He slid it over to her and she just looked at the open box. This man was bad for her in so many ways.

"Ladies first," he leaned in as the look of total temptation crossed her face. He wasn't sure if it's the dessert or him, his body wanted it to be the latter. When her fork disappeared into her mouth and she moaned, his dick hardened. Kat's tongue licked her lips to get the small bit left on the side of her mouth. His mind reeling, he wanted to kiss her like their first kiss, hard and passion. For a few seconds, they just stared at each other.

She whispered, "Your turn." She watched as he picked up his fork and slid it slowly through the cheesecake. He put it to his mouth, but didn't open his lips, just touching it there and then offering it to her. She opened just enough so he had slip it in, oh damn this was hot.

"Hello," a load voice came from the front door, "Jeffrey, you here?"

Shit, it was his mother, why oh, why was this happening to him. Kat's sultry look immediately disappeared, and she moved to the sink. He stayed in place, because now he sported a huge boner, and the counter hid his bottom half.

"Oh, you two are together," she looked from Jeff to Kat and then at the dessert, taking in two forks. "Having some cheesecake?" Jeff could hear all the questions his mother wanted to ask but didn't. He needed to escape before she asked because he knew she would.

"I have to go, Kat walk me out," she gave him a dirty look, and he knew why. He was leaving her to deal with his mother's questions. She followed him to the door and stopped. "Outside, Kat," he held the door, so she moved though. She was mad and he got that.

She walked to the rail and turned on him crossing her arms under her breasts. His eyes went there as he could see her nipples harden.

"Up here, I'm up here Jeff. I guess you're going to leave me to clean up this mess. I swear to God. I am going to kill you." She really didn't need this crap, and tomorrow she would arrange to go home.

"Sorry," he stepped into her. "I didn't mean for her to come home and find us."

"Duh, she lives here. What am I going to tell her? I told you to take care of this."

He smiled, "Tell her to mind her own business, because that's what I'm going to tell her, butt out and mind her own business. Kat please, don't allow this to ruin the night, because I had a good time." He stood close looking at her. He needed to leave because he wanted to kiss her again. "Friends," he asked.

"That's all, friends," she said, but her body said so many other things.

He grasped her chin and pressed closer, as if he would kiss her, as he whispered, "Maybe." He knew she held her breath and stepped back.

The curtain moved in the window, and Kat noticed, "Ugh."

"She's watching us through the window, isn't she? Jeff asked.

# ~ 6 ~

Kat went in and Linda was still in the kitchen, she walked passed her as she grabbed the dessert and walked away. She heard Linda say, "Don't be like that Kat." Once in the safety of her room, she called the airline, and then she needed to tell Ben she'd be gone for a few days. She arranged for an evening flight, so she wouldn't leave Ben with no one to take care of Liz. Taking her carryon bag, she started to gather her toiletries, computer, and files. A small amount of relief came over her, knowing that tomorrow night, she would be home, to resume her life. Where no one looked too closely or pushed her into situations where she did stupid things. Like what happened with Jeff tonight, what was she thinking? Why was she engaging him? When she knew, it was not good for her?

Without a workout, she knew she was in for a rough night. Maybe she could go for a nice long run, work her legs. Once she finished packing, and changed clothes, with her music in her ears, she headed for the door. With any luck, she wouldn't see Linda. It was getting ridiculous, how this woman made her sneak around to avoid her motherly ways. Once outside, Kat walked to the end of Linda's driveway, as her mind replayed the evening, she started pounding the pavement.

~ ~ ~ ~ ~ ~

Alone in his apartment, Jeff didn't know what to do with himself. Nothing on TV interested him, he paced from one end to the other. He couldn't go surfing so late, but he needed to clear his mind. Jeff grabbed his helmet and headed down the stairs to get his bike. He uncovered his Harley, that he kept stored under the stairs. Having the wind blow against his face should help to ease his frustration. Kat left him feeling a need for her, to be with her. He backed his bike out and started it up, as he revved the engine, and pulled out onto the road. There weren't very many people out, so he could open her up.

Flying down the highway, he was still thinking about her and what she had told him about herself. The three things he asked her wasn't a surprise, except for the cat. The fact that she passed the bar exam did nothing for him because he knew she was smart, just as her telling him she studied in France. What she said about her past told him more, so he was right, someone hurt her. A horrible thought crossed his mind, had someone violated her, it would explain her obsession for physical fitness, and the body combat moves, she did in the gym. How could he find out what really happened to her? He could talk to Liz, but she was smart and would figure out why he wanted to know about Kat's past. He had internal battle in his head when movement up ahead caught his attention. Someone was out jogging this late of night. At least she dressed in reflective clothing.

"Wait, I know that shape," he slowed the bike to pull next to her. She ignored him and picked up her pace. He smiled at the fact that she couldn't outrun him. Then she made a split second turn down a small path. He drove to the other end of the path and turned off his bike to wait. Within a minute or two, she emerged from the trees and ran right by him. This time, he stayed put, because he knew she had to come back through. When she reappeared, he watched as she made her way to him. For once, he hadn't chased after her, it was a small consolation.

"Okay Jeff, this is getting a little ridiculous. I can't get you out of my head or get away from you. Why are you following me, didn't you get enough of me tonight?"

If she only knew how much more, he wanted of her, she'd run a lot faster. "I was taking my bike for a ride. I was not following you. I just happened to be passing by when I recognized it was you. What, were you going to do try to outrun me?"

He was laughing at her, the bastard, "No, I didn't know it was you. If I wanted company, I would have asked you to join me. Notice, I didn't ask?"

"Kat, what are doing running so late?" He asked, as he sat on his bike with both legs to one side.

"Running, why are you out?"

"I needed to think, and it was too late to surf. Kat, if I asked you a question would you answer honestly."

"I don't know, it would depend on the question," Kat didn't really want to get into a question and answer session with him but putting him off might make him push harder for an answer.

"Your statement about not believing in love got me thinking, when you said you got burned, it wasn't just a bad break up, was it?" He watched as everything changed in her. Her body became rigid, breathing accelerated, as she stepped away from him, and he didn't need to hear her answer.

"I have to go."

"Never mind, don't answer, but don't go." He could hear the desperation in his voice, but he didn't want her to leave.

Her shield back in place, she stepped into his space, because she'd make him understand, "Look Jeff, you need to stop thinking about me, that there might be more, I can't do it. I will never trust you, and there will always be a side of me nobody gets to see. I will never fall for someone, I won't allow it." She didn't realize a tear formed until it escaped, and she dashed it away.

"C'mere," he pulled her into his arms, even though she resisted at first. He whispered into her ear, "I'm sorry baby, I didn't mean to make you upset." He felt her sink into him, and he rested his chin on top of her head. "I'll always be honest with you, and anything you tell me, doesn't go any farther than us."

Her voice muffled, "I can't talk about that, you know more than anyone."

"You never told anyone what happened to you, Kat?" A surge of anger went through his entire body.

"No, I need to go," she pulled away from him and let her go.

"Kat, I know you think you can't trust me, and I get why, but please let me be your friend."

"Somehow, I don't think that's what you're out for, being my friend," looking in his eyes, she could see him deciding what he was going to say.

"Truth, yes, I want more. I'll put everything on the line here. I want you, because you do things to me Kat, things that I can't explain. When you verbally spar with me, I am so fucking hard it hurts. Is that enough truth for you or do you need more?" He took her hand and placed it over him, "See what you do to me? I want to kiss you, like we did at the wedding. I've thought about that one kiss so many times."

"Jeff, please stop. I can't give you what you want. I'm broken, and if you repeat that, I will kick your ass." The tough Kat was back.

"I haven't dated anyone since that kiss, and I'll take what I can get Kat. But, just know, I'm throwing my hat into the ring. I want a real date with you, Kat."

"No, that's not a good idea. I just told you."

"Okay."

"Wow, you given up that easy?" Kat wasn't sure if she were relieved or disappointed, he'd give up so easily.

"Nope, but you said no. I'm not about to force you. I'm like the magic eight ball, when it says no, you turned over again, until it gives you the answer you want." He smiled when she shook her head. On that note, it was getting late, and he didn't want her running back. He mounted the bike and nudged his head for her to get on. "It's getting late. I'll take you home, get on." He took the helmet off the handlebar to give to her.

Looking at his outstretched arm, skeptically she took the helmet and slung her leg over the bike. He waited until she fastened the helmet, and she slid her hands around his body. Her hands hugged him low, pressing her chest against his back, and once again, his body reacted. Jeff wanted to keep her on his bike, hugged up next to him. His mother's house was just a few miles away and they would be there all too soon. He tilted his head back, so she could hear him, "Want to go for a little ride?" When she nodded, he revved the gas and shifted through the gears. With no traffic, they moved freely down the road. As the bike went around the bends and curves, they leaned as one. Before he wanted, he pulled into his mother's driveway. He killed the engine and immediately felt the loss of her body when she climbed off.

"Wow, that was great. I've never been on a bike before." She couldn't remember the last time she did anything for fun. In the city, you couldn't just get on a motorcycle and freely go. You could barely drive a car safely, much less a bike like this one.

As he took the helmet from her, he pulled her in, "We can do it again, if you say yes to the date." One hand still holding the helmet, his other hand moved to around her thin waist. "Now, what about a good night kiss?"

"Jeff, do you really think that's a good idea, nothing can come of this," her voice going to a whisper.

"I can't think right now, but I know what I want Kat," he looked to her lips and right on cue she wet them. He leaned in waited a half a beat, when she didn't stop him, he moved very gently and touched his lips softly to hers. When she pressed in close, it was his undoing. The kiss moved quickly when he ran his tongue along the edges of her lips and a small sound escaped. His tongue was inside tangling with hers, he could feel her body reacting just as his own. He wanted so much more, but she pulled back.

"Please Kat, say yes," he rested his forehead against hers.

"I can't Jeff, good night," she backed up and then was gone.

Once again, he was walking away, wanting her more, and he didn't think that was possible. If something didn't give soon, he might have permanent damage, getting so hard with no release in sight, was not a problem he could ever remember having before.

Kat made it to her room, as she chastised herself the entire way. What was she thinking? She needed to stay far away from him. Just a minute ago, she was kissing him. He asked, and she just let him, and obviously, she was losing control. Her brain and common sense told her to put as much space between her and Jeff, but her body hadn't gotten the memo. She met guys like Jeff every day, and they did nothing but disgust her. His charming ways and that great smile that lit his face right up. He was a dime a dozen, so why was she reacting to him this way.

It scared her to have feelings of this magnitude and just the sheer fact that she came close to telling him her deepest secret. "He knows, not all of it, but he knows something happened to me. How could I be so stupid? I could never trust Jeff," *maybe?* "No." Because she knew no matter what he said, she'd never confide the truth.

Just talking and thinking about it, brought her to a place and time that was the darkest of her life. She would never allow him to have any power over her ever again. He already took so much from her as a teenager, and as an adult, she was strong and in control of her own destiny.

Kat showered and got ready for bed, she hated how this weighed on her. This was the reason she never got involved with anyone. If she couldn't trust them with the true Kat, how could she ever give her heart and soul to anybody? That brought her back to why there was not true love out there for her. Climbing into bed, she knew that tomorrow she would be home in her own bed. In her safe place, the thought made her chuckle. Was anyone safe in the city? In the city, no one cared about anyone else. No one looked too closely into why you were the way you were. They just took you at face value and she could put her best mask up.

She could smell the car seat leather and the nasty aftershave he wore. Her hands tied over her head with his belt biting into her wrists as she tried to free herself. His voice dark and aroused by her pain, "You are such a fucking slut, you tease me, and now I'm going to take what I want." He sat on her legs, so her body was plastered into the seat. He smiled when he pulled out a hunting knife and looked over the blade. She heard herself scream and begged him to stop. His smile widened, "Not until I get what I want, and no one can hear you, so keep begging, I like it." She felt the tears slide down her face as he ripped her blouse open and the cold knife slid under her bra, and he popped it. Kat yelled at the top of her lunges for him to stop.

"Kat, wake up, please dear, you're dreaming," Linda was sitting on the edge of Kat's bed.

Kat jumped back away from Linda, her breathing labored with sweat beading on her forehead. Linda tried to calm Kat, as she realized where she was, Kat knew what happened. It had been a long time since she had one of those dreams. All this talk with Jeff, dragged it back to the surface. Just a dream, and Kat relaxed, "I'm okay, Linda."

"Oh, Kat," Linda took Kat into her arms, and she tried to resist, but Linda wasn't going to have it. Kat gave in and let her hug her. "Do you want to talk about your dream?"

"No, that's the problem." Kat just wanted Linda to leave and pretend nothing happened.

"Kat, you were yelling for someone named William to stop." Linda could see this shook Kat, but she wasn't going talk about her dream.

Kat was thankful for the darkness in the room, because just the sound of his name made her cringe. "I'm fine, Linda, really. I need to get up early in the morning to get to Liz's, because I'm heading back to the city tomorrow night. I have meetings that I have to be there for." Kat had no idea why she was explaining herself to Linda, but she wanted her to get the hint and leave.

"Kat, I understand you might not want to talk about this, but just know, I'm always here for you if you ever do want to talk." Linda stood and turned pulling the door closed behind her.

Kat released the breath she held and threw her head back on the pillow and hit her head on the headboard. "Just great, I'm not getting any more sleep, and I'm going to have a headache." She rubbed her head as she slipped down in the bed. Thinking how this was all Jeff's fault, and his stupid, cute smile, sexy body, and his funny sense of humor. He was trying to break her down, soften her up, because she was a challenge to him. Now pissed at him, she knew it was better than falling for him. When she got home, she needed to find someone to have sex with, to get Jeff out of her head. Too bad, sex didn't help with her demons, only exercise kept the dreams away. What could she do now, it was five a.m., and there was no way she wanted to attempt to fall back to sleep. All she needed was to fall back into what woke her, but it would still be dark for another hour. Kat got up and dressed, grabbed her yoga mat, and headed for the beach.

~ ~ ~ ~ ~ ~

Jeff fell asleep thinking about her and woke with her on his mind. What could he do to convince her to go out on at least one date with him? A date, where he could hold her hand, kiss her, or better yet, pull her up close to him. He knew that before he ever thought he wanted more, that she had walls. Now he also knew why the walls were in place and why they were so high. Why she didn't like or trust men, that thought of someone hurting her, pissed him off again. The moment she allowed him to see she was vulnerable, his heart melted. Things started to make more sense to him now, the rude attitude, how she emasculates every male in her path. What dude would want a part of that? He did.

Getting up, Jeff knew Owen would be waiting for him at the beach, to surf. One of the best times to surf, was at sunrise, and it wasn't a bad way to start the day. Maybe he'd come up with a plan to talk Kat into that date. Putting on his wetsuit and grabbing an energy drink, he went out the back door where his board stood on his porch. Practically jumping down the stairs, Jeff felt better than he had about him and Kat, even if she hadn't agreed to anything yet.

Jeff met Owen on the path leading to the ocean, surprised to see him running late. "Dude, your late."

"What, no way, you're just early for a change." As they both made their way down the path, Jeff stopped short, and Owen almost smashed into the back of him. "Dude, what you doin'?" Once Owen got a look at what Jeff stopped for he said, "Oh shit, dude you ain't gonna fuck with her?"

"Not yet, but yeah, I am," Jeff said almost as he didn't realize he said it aloud. Both men stood at the top of the sand dunes watching Kat do yoga. Her purple mat spread over the hard sand close to the water, and once again, he was in awe as he watched her body move.

"Dude, you have it bad, I'm goin' surfing before she sees us and gets pissed. Something I want no part of, thank you very much, you do what you want." Owen moved around Jeff and headed for the water.

Jeff still watched, as she paid no mind to anyone around her. Slowly, he walked toward her as she balanced on one foot with the other one in her crotch, her hands pressed together in front of her as if she was praying. Kat moved fluently into the next pose, and Jeff almost swallowed his tongue. She moved the bent leg behind her, reaching back, and took hold of her foot, pulling it up over her head. She was in a complete standing spilt. "Holy shit," his body doing what it did every time she was close, but he was in his wetsuit and there was no hiding his body's reaction.

Once he was close to her, she said through greeted teeth, "Go away, Jeff."

Confused by her tone, he didn't understand, because she sounded mad, when he left her last night, she had let him kiss her. He thought that maybe that's why she was mad. "Kat, are you mad at me, did I do something you didn't like?"

"I said go away, far, far away. As a matter fact, go drown yourself, please." She could feel all the peace draining from her body. She needed this to get her through her day and the flight home.

"Kat, talk to me. Tell me why you're mad," he tried to step closer, wrong move.

She bent down, and snatched her mat, throwing sand everywhere. "Go fuck yourself, how's that?"

Not knowing what just happened, but knowing it was smarter to not go after her, he picked up his board and headed for the water. He knew she wasn't going to be easily convinced that he could be the man for her, to be the one to tame her. He smiled at the thought of taming her, as if anyone could control that wild Kat. Now he laughed because he cracked himself up. Paddling out to meet Owen, he had to figure out why she was mad.

Kat rolled her mat as she walked to Liz's house, placing it on the steps. Mumbling to herself as Ben opened the door for her. He stepped back, clearing room for her to enter. "I hate your brother and today I hate you, too, because I have to put up with him because of you."

"I won't ask what's he done now, lucky for you, you're going home. But don't be pissed off at me because I have to stay here." He leaned his head in the direction of the bedroom, "I hate to tell you, but she's not in a very good mood either. I gotta deal with Jeff every day. So, I think I win in the shitty day department." Ben started for the open door.

"Okay, I'll give you that, but I still hate you anyway," she walked down the hall to Liz's bedroom. Opening her door, Kat looked in on Liz, who was sitting up talking to herself.

"No, no, no, I don't like how this sounds, hitting the delete button," Liz looked up from her computer. "Kat, you're here early, or are you late?" She looked at her watch, "I've lost track of time. I've been trying to write, but nothing is coming out right."

"Do you need anything? I'm going to use your shower. I was doing yoga on the beach and need to clean up. I have sand stuck all over me and it's all because of Jeff. I hate that man." Kat didn't wait for Liz's response, she just turned and walked out.

"Well, okay then," Liz went back to her computer.

~ ~ ~ ~ ~ ~

After surfing, Jeff went into work to find his mother waiting for him in his almost finished office. The thought, maybe he could sneak out, without her knowing he saw her. "Don't even think about it Jeffery, get in here. I have to talk to you." How did she do that, she had her back to him? How did she even know he was there?

"Don't even think about what Mother, trying to avoid you, never, as if we could." The last part he said under his breath.

"It's Kat, Jeffery. I need to know what you know about what happened to her." That got Jeff's attention.

"What I might or might not know, I can't share. I've made a promise, but I'm sure you didn't promise anything yet, did you?" His mother shook her head. "Spill the beans, Linda, you know you want, too."

Linda's eyes squinted at her son, and she gave him the look. "Okay, sorry Mom, please tell me what you know, so I can help Kat."

"Last night she had a nightmare and was yelling for someone named William to stop hurting her. When I finally got her to wake up, she looked like a scared child, and reared away from me, as if I were going to hurt her. I tried to get her to talk about it, but she wouldn't have it."

"Losing your touch there, Mom, because I thought you could get a mute to tell you anything you wanted to know."

"This is not the time to joke, Jeffery, I didn't want to push her and make things worse. I think something very bad happened to her." The room became very serious, and the silence that stretched out, became uncomfortable.

"I told you, I can't share, but I do believe your right about something happening to her. I don't know what myself, so don't think about pumping for information, it isn't going to help." He couldn't help wondering if her dream was the reason she was mad at him this morning.

His mother broke through his thoughts when she spoke again, "Did you know she's flying home tonight, for at least a week, Ben said. She has to be in NY for meetings, isn't that when you have your first meeting with Shafford Surf Boards in the city?"

With everything going on, he had forgotten about the franchise, the surf shop was buying into, this was a big deal for the shop. Carrying this brand of surfboard was huge, because no other shop in California had this new and upcoming style of board. This company was massive on the east coast, and very exclusive to whom they allowed buying into their business. However, this was Jeff's baby, and he pushed for this with Ben. He wanted this to be his legacy for the shop.

Why did he not know Kat was leaving? She thought she could just run. Little did she know, he would see her sooner than she thought. He knew he needed to get help from his sister-in-law, and after that, there would be no hiding. Well, his mother already knew that's why she was in here. Jeff realized his mother wasn't truly looking for information as much as she wanted to give him. Maybe once they here without everyone looking on, they could make some headway.

# ~ 7 ~

Kat was so glad to be on her way home, far away from the prying eyes of those who looked a little too close into her life. As she sat in first class waiting for the plane to take off, her mind wondered back over the last few weeks. How had Jeff figured out what no one else had? She had kept her parents, family, and friends in the dark and it only took him a couple conversations with her to realize something had happened to her. Thank God, he didn't know the truth. He was just assuming, by her behavior. This is why, she could never allow Jeff in, because if he ever found out just how fucked up she was, he not only wouldn't want to have anything to do with her, but he would see her shame, and how weak she truly is.

Her attitude and tough persona has taken her far because most people didn't examine and scrutinize her every move. Jeff and Linda seem to be able to see right past her, "back off," vibe she sends out.

Then there was Jeff himself, sexy as hell, and he knew it. For the life of her, she couldn't understand why her own body reacts to him, any time he came near, her body went on full alert. She allowed him to get past all her defenses. Why would she agree to go out with him, even if it wasn't a date? Spending any amount of time with him, was not in her best interest, and she knew this, but there was something going on with her that she couldn't explain. All she knew, was this time away from him was time to think.

The plane pulled away from the gate, and Kat felt a small release. Her brain was in overdrive, she needed to sleep, but she didn't dare. After having the nightmare, the night before, she was afraid it might happen again. Once she was home, she could take a catch-up nap and if the dreams were back, then she would have to get back to her intense workouts. She was sure it didn't help that Jeff questioned her about what happened. She had kept the secret for so long, without anyone ever questioning her, and he seemed to know she was hiding something. It most likely was just her over sensitivity to Jeff, and the way he pushed her so far out of her comfort zone. Once the plane reached flying altitude, Kat pulled out her iPod, sat back in her seat, and closed her eyes.

~ ~ ~ ~ ~ ~

Two days, and Jeff was feeling the loss and excitement with the thought of seeing Kat again, in NY. He had time to go over all the things Kat had said, and her actions. Late at night it dawned on him, this wasn't a competition, between him and Kat as he once thought. It was Kat's way of protecting herself, coming on strong and hard. He now knew she was anything but and would have to proceed with caution. Jeff didn't truly know if he wanted to know all the details of what happened to her, or if she would even confide in him. It was obvious she didn't trust him, and he wasn't sure how he could change that fact.

The one thing he did know for sure, he needed to talk to his sister-in-law. That was going to be tricky because Liz would see right through him. Maybe he should just come clean with Liz right off the bat.

Jeff stood on the doorstep of his brother's apartment, took a deep breath, and knocked. Ben opened the door and didn't look so surprised to see him standing there.

"What do I owe the honor?" Ben said with a smile, as if he didn't know.

"I'm here to talk to your wife, and don't be a dick about it," Jeff walked passed his brother.

"If I recall, when I was trying to get Liz, you were a dick quite often. You know what they say about payback don'tcha?" Ben just walked behind Jeff to the bedroom where Liz was resting. He stepped in front of Jeff, putting up his hand. "I'll tell her you're here." Ben went inside and shut the door. Jeff knew his brother was going to have a field day at his expense. He stood there and tried to take in calming breaths. The door opened and Ben stepped out in the hall.

"Sorry, she doesn't want to talk to you," Ben's huge grin told Jeff his brother was full of shit.

"I think, I'll hear it from her," he stepped around Ben and went in.

"Jeff, come and talk to me," Liz looked happy to see him.

"Hey Liz, how are you felling?" Jeff watched as his brother came in behind him and sat on the bed.

"Ben, I have a feeling Jeff would like to speak to me," she said as Ben snuggled in close to her.

"Oh, don't ruin my fun. I want to watch my brother squirm. He's had it easy all his life with women, and now he's going to have to work for it."

"Ben, out," Liz ordered.

"Oh, man," Ben got up and left the room, leaving the door open.

"Jeff, go close the door and then let's talk."

Jeff closed the door and pulled up a chair next to the bed. "I guess you know why I'm here. I'm not going to beat around the bush. I need to know some things about Kat."

"I'm not sure how much I can help you, because Kat is a very private person, and she'll only tell you or show you what she wants you to see and hear. I've known Kat for years, and I really don't know much about her."

"Okay, let's start with some stuff I know you know, like her address and phone number. I'm leaving for NY in a few days, for the franchise meeting with Shafford Board. I want to spend time with Kat on her home ground. I don't want her to know I'm coming Liz, so please don't tell her. Really, I don't want her to know we spoke at all. Can I trust you to keep this to yourself?"

"If you want my help, then I need to know what your intentions are toward Kat. I don't want to see either of you hurt, and I can't lose Kat."

"Liz, I don't know what my intentions are, but I do know I'm drawn to her like no other. I don't think it's just because she plays hard to get or pushes me away. Liz, I don't know if you know, Kat had something happen to her. I don't want to share anything she told me, which isn't much. It changed her life, and I'm giving you my word, I'm not messing with her." Jeff took a deep breath putting his head down and his arms on his knees. "I need to get her to trust me, and I'm not sure how to do that. I have a feeling, I remind her of the dude who might have attacked her. If that's what really happened to her, all I do know, is she hasn't told anyone."

"Oh, my God Jeff, do you realize how big this is? If something did happen to her, that was life altering and she told no one, but you. Don't you see, by her telling you anything at all, she, on some level, already trusts you? What do you have planned when you get to the city?"

Jeff went over his plan to surprise Kat at her office and go over the contracts from the meeting with Shafford Boards. Liz gave him all the information he needed to get in contact with her once he made it into the city. Jeff got up and kissed Liz on the cheek just as Ben returned to the room.

"What the hell are you doing," Ben didn't sound very happy.

"Oh, stop, Ben. He's just thanking me for helping him," Liz waved a hand at her husband.

As Jeff walked by Ben he said, "Now we're even." Ben just watched him walk out the door and he knew what Jeff was talking about, the time he walked in on him kissing Kat.

~ ~ ~ ~ ~ ~

"Jeff, now really isn't a good time for you to be going out of town. Kat's not here and… Wait, where do you have this meeting?" Ben asked and watched him closely.

"I know what you're going to say, but I made these arrangements way before Kat told you she had to go back to New York. In fact, this has been in the works for months, and you know it. I talked to you about selling Shafford Boards back when you first met Liz. I can't help it if their headquarters is in the city, and it's just a coincidence that Kat and I are going to be there at the same time." Jeff could see Ben knew this, even if he intended to look Kat up while he was there.

"Look, it's just a bad time, can you reschedule? With Owen at school and Kat gone, I need to stay with Liz, so that just leaves Mom and Dannie." Jeff could see Ben's stress, but they had waited months to get this appointment.

"Ben, we need to hire more employees, because you have a lot going on right now, and Owen is gone more then he's here. We need the help, and I waited a long time to get this meeting. I'm not sure they'll reschedule. They have so many other surf shops interested in carrying their line of boards. I'm sure they'll just say next and move on."

"I know this is your project and it's important to you, it's just timing, that's all," Ben blew out a ragged breath. "I'll start interviewing tomorrow for some floor people. It's going to feel weird to have new people working here, besides having to train someone, Owen trained himself."

"I know, but becoming a Shafford Board Franchise could be worth millions for the shop." Jeff was leaving in the morning for the big city. He would arrive in New York that evening, and then his appointment was the next morning. As much as he looked forward to the meeting with the major surfboard company, he felt a little nervous about this deal. This was going to be where he'd put his own stamp on Jacobs Surf Shop. Ben had run the shop for years and the shop was very successful now, but he wanted to leave his imprint on the shop. He also knew he had to be very careful, because if he screwed this up, it could cost the shop dearly. Not that Ben would allow him to have the final decision, so it wouldn't be entirely his fault if this went bad.

Once the meeting was over, he was going to find Kat, starting with where she worked. He wondered if she'd blow him off or would she play the game they've been playing. He now knew, he had to be careful, and yet, he had to have her, he wasn't proud of that fact. The games they've been playing were getting serious and they both knew it. She wanted him just as bad, although she seemed to have better control over her feelings. If he could get her to bring him to her apartment, where they could be alone, away from everyone watching them.

Because not only Liz and his mother, but Ben, too, have in some way, butted in, wanting to know what was going on between him and Kat. Only his sister has left him alone when it came to Kat, although she called him an idiot, which most likely he was where Kat was concerned. The way she made him feel, one minute she had him hard as nails, and the next he wanted to fix everything for her. Oh yeah, he looked forward to seeing Kat on her own home tuff. See where she worked, where she lived, and the thought of seeing Kat's apartment, where he could be alone with her excited him.

"Ok, so tell me again how long you're going to be gone," Ben had his head in his hands.

"I leave tomorrow and come back in two days, so I'll be gone a total of three days." Jeff watched his brother as he could see Ben was still thinking.

"You can't catch a flight back after the meeting finishes?"

"Ben, I told you weeks ago, about my plans, you didn't have a problem with them then. I don't want to hop right on a plane, because I want to be able to look over the contracts and if I have any questions or concerns, I can talk to them right away. Besides, it's only one more day and I think you'll live without me for three days."

"I know, I'm sorry. I'm just going crazy with Kat gone and trying to get any work done. This is going to be good for the store, I do know that, but with you gone, and Owen not here either, means I need to be out on the floor. I've been doing most of my work from upstairs, and now I'm going to have to get Mom or Dannie to stay with Liz, even though she has gotten better, she still has her days."

Ben gave Jeff all the financial paperwork for the shop that he needed to prove the shop was in good standings. Jeff still had a lot to do before he could just take off for the day. He went to his office to finish ordering, and he hadn't packed yet, either. Jeff sat back in his chair and thought how this would all go down, because he knew how he wanted it to turn out. With Kat, he never knew, the one thing that was for sure, is she wouldn't make it easy for him.

Jeff should have known his mother would be waiting for him the next morning. When she insisted on taking him to the airport, he also knew, she was going to interfere in her ever-loving way. His mother loved her children, with everything she had, even if at times it was overbearing. Linda would not let him go without putting in her two cents, her little insights into what she always seemed to be dead on. But Jeff had to draw the line at his mother giving him advice about his love life. He never needed her help before, and he didn't think he needed it now. Thank God, the airport wasn't far from their house and with security these days, he had to be there two hours early. His mother couldn't go on forever, or he'd miss his flight.

"Mom, you know I could have driven myself," Jeff sat in the passenger seat of his mother's car.

"Don't be ridiculous, Jeffery, no sense in paying for parking, when I can just as easily drive you." Linda pulled out onto the main street and didn't even give Jeff a second look.

"It wouldn't have anything to do with you wanting to butt in and give me your loving advice, would it? Because I should tell you, I've managed just fine until now without your help."

"You know what, Jeffery, your right, I haven't said anything about any of the other girl's you've dated. Only that I wished you'd settle down with just one. We both know, even if you're not ready to admit it to yourself, she is different from any other. Do you know how I know this? One, I'm your mother. I know you better than you think. Two, I have eyes. I could see that day we went to Liz's house for dinner how you reacted to Kat. You had a date with you, and yet, you still managed to keep an eye on Kat's every move. Every time the two of you are in the same room, it gets hotter than hell with the electricity that runs between the two." Linda fanned her face as if to make her point.

"And after the conversation about Kat's dream, I know she is not just one of the girls you hang out with, so don't bull shit me."

"Mom, what do you want me to tell you, yes she is different. I don't know why I'm drawn to her." Jeff sighed, as if this entire situation stressed him out.

"What's your plan once you're in New York?"

Jeff went over how he planned to get in contact with Kat under the pretense of going over the contracts for the dealership. He told his mother how he had spoken to Liz, so he knew how to connect with her. Linda smiled at the mention of Liz's name, or it might have been because she was hatching a plan and now she would include Liz. He needed them both to just butt out and let him find his way, because he didn't need any more to worry about. Getting Kat to trust and open to him was going to be enough for him. He couldn't think about what his mother and Liz might be up to.

His mother cut into his thoughts, "Jeffery, you remember when you were a kid, and we had those stray cats at the shop? How you worked so hard to get the momma cat to trust you and take food from you?" His mother's random statement had his mind wondering, what she was talking about.

"What," Jeff looked at her.

"How patient and determined you were, and once the mamma cat figured you weren't going to hurt her, she let you hold her kittens. Kat will know you're not going hurt her, but that's going to take patience and that same amount of determination. We both know something happened to her to make her skittish. I'm sure, as I am your mother, it was something horrible."

He should have known his mother would know exactly how to tell him what he had to do. He never gave his mother the credit she deserved, raising three kids, for the most part, by herself. She kept the surf shop open after her husband died, with two teenage boys, and a daughter still in middle school. Yeah, Ben stepped up and helped, but his mother was a tough lady. They pulled into the drop off and turned to his mom.

"Thanks, Mom, for the talk and everything else you do," he hugged her and got out.

~ ~ ~ ~ ~ ~

Kicking the hell out of the punching bag, that was in front of Kat felt so good, her body hurt from her over working every muscle. The last few days being home, was what she needed, to get back to her normal routine. She hadn't had another dream, except for the one she had on the plane. At least no one in first class acted as if she was crazy, she didn't think she yelled out. The dream just shook her awake, as she damned herself for falling asleep. Going back to the gym at night, working her body and mind into exhaustion, along with meditation and yoga, did the trick. She was sure it didn't hurt, that she was also far away from the one man who could make her come unglued.

Kat had contemplated telling Ben she couldn't return to California. She tried to think how she could get out of going back, although she knew Liz needed her. It wasn't going to be much longer before the babies would be born, and soon it would be winter break for Paige. Liz's daughter could help, maybe when Paige came to California she could come home again. It was the time in between that worried Kat, because if she allowed Jeff to get any closer, he would find out just how messed up she was. That was something she worked too hard to cover up and change about herself. She didn't want him to bring it all back. That's why a relationship with him was out of the question, along with the fact that he was Liz's brother-in-law.

Now seeing Jeff's face on the bag in front of her, she punched it harder. That smirk of a smile, he had, as if he knew her. The way he could get by her defenses. The way his eyes had that gold flake in them, made them sometimes twinkle when he looked at her. Punch, *man-whore*. Two more punches, *ass-hole*, kick, *sexy- shit. Why did he have to be so damn sexy?* She bounced from foot to foot in her fighting stance, catching her breath. The thought of riding on his bike, her body pressed close to his, and the wind blowing by. How freeing it felt, yet, it was one of the most dangerous things she's done. Having him so damn close, and the smell of him, did things to her that could bring her house of cards tumbling down.

She put her hands on her knees as she bent over. She could feel the twinkling of stars dancing in front of her eyes. Between breathing hard and over working out, she knew she might faint. She had to get her breathing under control or hit the floor. She closed her eyes, the image of Jeff's arms around her as she pressed her face into his chest. His comfort, her breathing slowed, and her eyes popped open, "No don't do that." Some guy a few feet away looked over at her with her outburst, as he pulled out his ear buds.

"What, I wasn't doing anything." The guy now stepped closer.

"I wasn't talking to you, so go back to your workout." She was being rude to make him stop his forward motion, and he stopped, putting his hands in the air as if he understood and turned to go back to what he was doing.

Now she was not only furious with Jeff, but also extremely pissed at herself. She had to come up with a strategy to get him to back off. Normally being rude and obnoxious sent a man in the opposite direction. She didn't really have to do much more than that. No man tried to bypass her armor. They just figured she was a bitch. Of course, that was how she portrayed herself, and how she liked it.

This thing with Jeff was different, first, she didn't intimidate him, and he seemed to like it when she was a bitch to him. Jeff took her bad arrogance as verbal sparring, and said it made him hard. What the hell was wrong with him? She couldn't be nice to him, because he would take that as she wanted to be with him. If she was nasty to him, he became aroused. She already told him, she didn't do relationships, so she couldn't tell him she met someone. He wouldn't believe she bats for the other team, but she had to show him, she wasn't his type. He had her backed into a corner, and that was a place she didn't like to be.

~ ~ ~ ~ ~ ~

The flight was long, but it gave Jeff time to think about his mother's advice. He had it playing in his head like a movie, how he wanted tomorrow to go. First thing he needed to do, was get his bags and then call down a taxi to ride by Kat's office building. Then, check into his hotel, the one he hoped he'd be spending only one-night. He wanted to see her, it had been days, and he could admit he missed her.

Jeff had to remember, he was here for business. This was very important for the shop. He had to be on his game tomorrow at the meeting with Shafford Surf Boards. Once he went to the hotel, he had to go over all the paperwork Ben gave him. Jeff might not have gone to college, but he was no idiot. Just because he never showed initiative in the shop before, didn't mean he couldn't be an asset. It just wasn't where he wanted to be, before now. Working in the surf shop was a given, and something he used to hate, up until recently.

When Ben met Liz, he took time off, left him in charge, and gave him more responsibility. It changed something in him, because it wasn't just going to work selling surfboards anymore, once Ben trusted him to order merchandise for the entire store and make the decisions on new merchandise. That's how he ended up here in NY, meeting with one of the top of the line surfboard companies. He had pitched his idea to Ben, and he agreed with Jeff, that it would be a good thing for the shop.

Now, he was watching the luggage go around the turnabout, waiting for his bag. This airport was busy, everyone from the flight stood shoulder-to-shoulder waiting. All he knew, was he wanted to catch a glimpse of Kat, and again he felt as if he was stalking her. He only had one bag that he checked in, because he wasn't going to be in the city long. Long enough, he hoped, to get into Kat's good graces, and if things went well, her bed. His mother's advice came to mind about patience and getting Kat to trust him. That was going to mean going slow, and for the long haul, but his body didn't want to go slow.

He had met Kat months ago, and they had been doing this dancing around each other. It felt to him, like the longest amount of time he ever spent with someone without having sex. He knew that didn't say much about him, but something told him she was worth the wait, not that he hadn't dreamed and fantasized about that moment. When they finally be joined, just thinking about it now, aroused him.

"Shit," Jeff said as he watched his bag go by. He could try to catch up with it, but with the turntable so crowded, he didn't think anyone would let him in to grab his bag. He wasn't in California anymore, and New York was without a doubt, different. He guessed now was as good as any to start working on patience, but this time, he paid more attention to when his bag came around again.

It took another hour to clear the airport, and he thought she would be gone by the time he got to her office. Not sure if he should just go straight to the hotel, he hailed a cab. When the cabbie stopped and Jeff climbed in, he asked where to and he heard himself say Kat's office address in Manhattan. He knew he needed to see her, but he didn't want her to know he was in town just yet. Jeff sat back and watched the city go by as his thoughts went to how Kat was going to react to him being there. She thought she could get away from him, by running home. How perfect, he couldn't have arranged the timing any better. He smiled as the plan to go see Kat tomorrow after his meetings played through his mind. He'd make every effort to get her to take him back to her place. There, he would sweet talk and convince her he was the man, she not only needed, but also wanted. The cabbie pulled to the curb, "You're here. You need a receipt?"

"Yeah, that would be great," he swiped the business credit card through the card reader. The one Ben had given him, he never had a reason to use the card before now. He found that strange, but the cabbie passed the receipt through the small slot in the partition, Jeff took it and put the card and receipt in his wallet. As he climbed out, he thought of his mother's face when he handed her all the expense receipts. He was working on being more responsible and this trip was proof, because Ben would never allow him to handle such a big deal on his own if he didn't think he could. Not that Ben wouldn't be here himself, if he could leave Liz, but if he didn't think Jeff could get the job gone, he'd reschedule when he could go. The fact that Ben just handed over all the financial paperwork for the store and wished him luck, it made him proud, and nervous.

Standing on the sidewalk outside of Kat's office building made wanting to see her stir things in him. Although, he still couldn't understand why she was the one, the one to turn him inside out, made his body spark with electricity. All he did know, was there was no other he had ever wanted so badly, and now it wasn't just about sex. He wasn't going to fool himself, but yes, he still wanted that with her. After finding out something happened to her and it most likely was why she put on a big defense, he had to push to find out who she truly was, not that he didn't like the woman she showed the world, but he did think there was a softer side to her. He didn't want her finding him standing here, so he looked for a place to go, preferably somewhere inside.

Jeff pulled the collar of his jacket up, grabbed his suitcase, and slung his garment bag over his shoulder. He spotted a coffee shop across the street, it had gotten dark, and he knew it was going to be hard to see her if she was still here. He ordered coffee and sat next to a window in the shadows, so he could see the lights coming from the doorway across the street. He told himself how wrong this was, how obsessive and all consuming, she had become to him. Never feeling anything like this before, he wasn't sure what he was doing, but he knew he couldn't give up. He was going to see this to the end.

After a long day, Kat needed to get out of her office and to the gym. She went back to her stringent workout routine, and the dreams that had returned in California, went back to hell where they belonged. Now if she could only rid Jeff from her dreams, and get him out of her daytime thoughts, too, that would be great. The hard workouts didn't do anything about him, and her fear was that nothing would do, except for the one thing she couldn't give him. Kat grabbed her coat from her closet along with her gym bag, briefcase and headed for the door. Vikki, her assistant, had left hours ago, so Kat locked up behind her and headed for the elevators.

She hated the time change. It got so dark so early. Going to work in the dark, and leaving into the darkness with the cold, didn't do much for her mood. She could be on the beach, her thoughts told her. She told her reflection in the mirrored elevator doors, "Yeah, but he's there and I'd never get any peace." The thought of doing yoga on the beach was such a pleasant image. The sun on her skin, Kat closed her eyes just taking in the feeling. When she heard the chime to signal she arrived at the lobby, she let out the breath.

Walking passed the security guard, he looked up, "Evening, Miss Jackson," she dipped her head in greeting. She pulled her coat tighter around herself preparing for the cold blast to hit her once she walked through the doors. She hated the winter, well, it was in fact fall, but in New York City, it was still cold enough to snow in November.

Walking through the doors, she felt the cold air, but also the hairs on the back of her neck stood up. Immediately, she glanced around, surveying her surroundings. Not seeing anything out of the ordinary, but she didn't discard her instincts. Kat started moving in the direction of the gym, it was only a block away. Never giving into her fear, she watched everything. As she walked, she looked across the street and she could have sworn she saw Jeff in the window watching her. Kat laughed at herself, "What the hell is wrong with you, now you're seeing him everywhere," she said under her breath. She knew, with all reason, he was in California in the bright sunshine. He wouldn't be here, but something had her body on high alert.

He sat still as a statue, as he watched her, and he knew the minute she spotted him. Turning his head, so she couldn't see his face in hopes, she wouldn't truly recognize him. "Shit," he whispered because he didn't think she would see him. When he glanced back she was gone, should he follow her? No, that would be going too far, he needed to check into his hotel and get his head on what brought him here. He gathered up his stuff and headed back to the street.

# ~ 8 ~

The next morning, Jeff woke to his phone alarm going off. He couldn't believe he slept at all, with what he knew the day would hold. He rolled to turn it off and ran his hand though his shorter hair. He had gotten a haircut for this meeting because he wanted his appearance to be more of a businessman, not so much a surfer dude. His appointment was at nine-thirty, so he had time, but he wanted to be prepared. As he went over the paperwork once again, Jeff could feel the tension building in his shoulders. So much was riding on this for the shop, and he was the one who would have to prove, he could manage this part of the business. He knew everything there was to know about Shafford Surfboard, and yet, he couldn't shake feeling nervous. He had been surfing for as far back as he could remember, and he loved it, as did his father. Jeff decided as important as this was, he needed to just be him, and do as he always did, wing it.

~ ~ ~ ~ ~ ~

Kat knew she would have to return to California soon. No matter how she tried to put it off, it wouldn't last forever, she told herself. Once Liz had the babies, she could return to her life, safe, and free from him. Then, she would only have to see him once or twice a year when she went to see Liz. She knew if Jeff kept up his pursuit of her, she just might give in. She knew in the end, that wouldn't be good for her wellbeing. How had he managed to get by so many of her defenses, to get so close, where no other had? She had been giving him way too much of her time trying to figure out a way to get him to back off. Kat stepped away from her floor to ceiling window that overlooked downtown Manhattan. She still had a few more days before the inevitable and had work to do. Sitting behind her desk, she called for Vikki. It was going to be a long day. For the next few hours, Kat went over contracts with her assistant and meetings with clients.

~ ~ ~ ~ ~ ~

Jeff arrived, and now had his visitors pass, walking to a hallway with six elevators, with a crowd. He entered and noticed his floor was lit. He stood toward the back and watched the light above the door flash as it passed each floor. It stopped as people got out and more got on, Jeff moved closer to the door. When the doors opened on his floor, he squeezed past a group of women and saw an appreciative look from them. He just smiled and nodded, as he exited, walking to the double doors.

The receptionist smiled at him as she said, "Welcome to Shafford, May I help you?" She was cute enough, Jeff thought, but he felt nothing. No little zing, or any interest at all.

"Hello, my name is Jeffery Jacobs, here to see Mister Jameson." Jeff watched as she looked to her computer screen, and when she glanced back to him, she smiled again.

"Please have a seat Mister Jacobs, Mister Jameson's assistant should be with you shortly," she gestured toward a comfortable looking seating area.

When Jeff observed the room, it wasn't as impressive or grand as he would have thought. There were several couches in deep reds, and black positioned in small quaint arrangement. Not what he would have expected, but what did he know about a corporate headquarters. Sitting on the closest couch, he placed his briefcase on the floor. As he assessed the waiting area more, he notices on the far wall, a large mural of a vintage surfer. He didn't know what he expected, maybe a big glass sculpture with a fountain in the middle of the room.

At this point, all he wanted to do was get this over with, his nerves hammered though his body. So much rode on this deal, and he knew what this would mean for the shop. Trying to slow his heart and relax, he took a deep breath and closed his eyes. He knew, he was as prepared for this meeting as he could be, the thought of once it was over, he would see Kat, made him smile. He realized as much as he wanted this all to go well, he wanted to see her just as bad. He heard his name, grabbing his briefcase he stood and followed an attractive young woman to a boardroom.

"Please have a seat. Can I get you anything to drink?" She stepped back as he walked into the room.

"No, thank you, I'm good," again he sat in the closest seat near the door.

"Mister Jameson will be with momentarily," she turned and walked out.

This was it.

Hours later, Jeff walked out of the building and took his first deep breath of relief. The meeting went well, and he thought he understood everything Mister Jameson had explained, how the partnership worked. His main concern, was just how many Shafford boards the shop would have to sell, and the space the store would have to dedicate to their products. He pulled out his phone and dialed his brother's number. As it rang, he had to move back inside the building to hear and to get out of the cold.

"Jeff, how did it go?" He knew his brother would be waiting to hear from him. Jeff smiled at the concern he heard in Ben's voice.

"It went well. I just have a few concerns about the sheer number of boards we must move. When I get back, I'll have to move the entire store around to accommodate the Shafford line, because they're not just surfboards. I knew they had other products. I just didn't think since we are such a small shop they would want us to carry their full line. The way they put it, we're the first shop in California to be a Shafford dealer, so they want us to be full service. I explained again that we aren't that big, he insured me they checked us out, and get this, they agreed to give us money to expand."

"Holy shit, you're kidding me." Jeff could hear some commotion in the background and realized his mother was there too. Ben spoke to someone else a second, then came back and said, "Jeff, I'm putting you on speaker before Mom has a heart attack."

Jeff went over everything he had just told Ben and went on to tell them everything. Of course, his mother didn't wait a minute to ask if he had seen Kat yet.

"Mom, I haven't had the chance to see her, but I want her to look over all the paperwork I have to sign. I'm sure since she is a lawyer, she'll know if there's a problem with the contracts. So, I'm heading over there as soon as I get off the phone with you."

"Good, now do not screw this up." His mother always had the utmost confidence in him.

"Wait, I didn't know Kat was a lawyer," Ben said. "I knew she worked out some of the best contracts for her clients, now it all makes sense."

"I have to go," Jeff needed to move, so he could get to the part of this trip he dreamt about. He walked through the doors again to hail a cab. Once he was on his way, the anxieties of seeing her came to the surface. Thinking and wondering what exactly he wanted from her. He knew he wanted her under him in the worst way, but did he want more. The need to be with her ran deep, something he never felt before. That had to mean something, just what, he didn't know. He wasn't even sure she would see him, or she just blow him off. For all he knew, she could be out of the office, or with a client. He wouldn't know until he showed up.

Kat's assistant buzzed her, as she worked on a new writer's book deal. The last thing she expected when she picked up the phone was to hear Vikki's voice breathless, as if she ran a marathon. She was whispering and Kat almost couldn't hear her.

"Kat, you have the most amazing looking guy here to see you. He is so hot, oh my God, and he just smiled at me. I think, I just died and went to heaven." Vikki was swooning about someone in her outer office.

"Vikki…" when she didn't answer, Kat said her name again, "Vikki, who is in my outer office." Goosebumps spread across Kat's body, and she held her breath waiting for the answer.

"Oh, sorry, Kat, it's just he's watching me, and I can't think." She still spoke in a low voice, "Jeffery Jacobs to see you, you have to see this guy Kat, I mean Ms. Jackson." Vikki seemed to gain her wits about her and attempted to gain her professionalism.

Now it was Kat's turn to be speechless, her mind raced. What was he doing here? She could send him on his way or see what he wanted.

"Ms. Jackson," the question-hanging, while she waited for her directions on what to do with the hunk sitting looking at her.

"Give me two minutes and send him in," Kat laid her head on her hands and took several deep breaths. She needed more than the two minutes that she told her assistant but had to pull herself together quickly. She crossed her legs under her glass desk and tried to relax. When she heard the knock and Vikki opening the door, what she saw was something she never expected in a million years. Jeff walked into her office dressed in a suit, navy blue with thin white pinstripe. He smiled and Kat felt her heart stop.

"Hello Sunshine, miss me?" He said, before Vikki could leave the room, and the look she shot Kat was of shock. Jeff walked in as if he owned the place, confident and so sure of himself. She watched as he came around her desk and leaned in to kiss her on the cheek.

"Wow speechless, never would have thought possible. You of all people, always have something to say." She knew he was goading her, but she wouldn't allow him to provoke her.

Wanting to ask what the hell he was doing in NY, and why he was standing in her office, instead she asked, "What brings you here?"

Jeff walked around her office. It was all glass and chrome, very modern. He couldn't help his reaction when he noticed her legs crossed under her glass desk. Her long-toned legs as she rocked her crossed foot slightly. He drew his eyes away to look at her face, liking how she watched him. He moved to a glass bookshelf on one wall picking up a small crystal animal, but what caught his eye were the music boxes she displayed. When he went to pick one up, she was there to stop him, obviously annoyed by his presence.

"What are you doing here, in my office, Jeff?" She asked with no more patience.

"I'm here on business," he smiled when she laughed. Knowing she didn't believe, him he added, "I had a meeting with Shafford Surfboard this morning in Manhattan, and I need your help. That's why I'm here." He could have sworn he saw disappointment cross her face, but then it was gone.

"My help, you say, please do tell," she said as she stepped away from him, putting distance between them. "Have a seat," she sat behind her desk as Jeff took one of the seats across from her.

Jeff knew what she was doing, giving herself space. He would take care of business first, and then he'd get down to business. He reached for his briefcase and took out the documents from earlier as he said, "I don't know if you were aware that we planned to become a licensed Shafford dealer. I pretty much understand everything, but Liz suggested, I have you look over the contracts, just to make sure the surf shop is covered. It means a lot of money for the shop, going out for the initial buy in, but we're hoping it will expand the business. We'll be the first shop on the west coast to carry this line of board, along with their other products."

Kat took the stack of papers and placed a small set of glasses on her face as she looked over the first page. Occupied with the paperwork, gave Jeff a chance to study her. He didn't know she wore glasses, but somehow it was sexy. She must have sensed his attention and looked up, he just tried to look as if he was waiting for her to finish. When she went back to reading, he studied her some more, her blonde hair spiked up as usual. Dressed in a pale blue business suit, he allowed his eyes to sweep over her chest down to where her jacket closed. Which brought his eyes back to her glass desk, and how he could see her skirt ride high on her thighs?

"Stop it," her voice startled him. "I can feel you looking at me, so stop it." She didn't even look up at him.

"I'm just enjoying the view, and let me tell you, I like this glass desk, it's got me wondering how strong it is."

"Strong enough, but you won't find out, so forget it." She kept reading, and he noticed how low his chair sat compared to her desk. He wondered if that was by design, to make her sit taller. Did it make her feel, as if she had advantage over her clients? He stood and began to walk around her office again, looking out the full view window over the city. It was getting dark out, the lights of the city lit the streets. Wondering if she could feel the pull he felt, everything in him wanted to pull her into his arms and kiss the hell out of her. He was going to do everything in his power to make tonight, the night he would know her better than any other would. Knowing she had things she never told anyone else, he wanted to be the one person to know her secrets. He thought would he be strong enough to handle her secrets. All he knew was, he wanted to be.

Kat was doing her best to concentrate on what she was reading, but she kept reading the same two lines. She could see him in her peripheral vision as he walked around and once he stopped directly behind her, she could feel the hair on her neck rise. She tried to take a cleansing breath, clear her mind of him, because this was important to the surf shop. This was not her area of expertise. She wasn't a corporate attorney as her father. She thought about mentioning to Jeff about making an appointment, but instead, she heard herself ask, "Can I take this home and go over it better, when I have more time?"

Jeff smiled, because if he had his way, she wouldn't have any time tonight to go over paperwork. "Sure, it's getting late. Have dinner with me, Kat." He went to her now and pulled her from her chair into his arms. Just as Jeff leaned in to kiss away her refusal, her phone buzzed.

Kat was so glad for the interruption, stepping back she pushed the speaker button. "Yes, Vikki."

"I'm sorry to disturb your meeting with mister hottie, but your parent's driver just called, and they are waiting for you out front in their limo."

"Thank you, Vikki, and just so you know, you're on speaker." Kat heard the gasp and the click as Vikki disconnected. Knowing how much he was going to like what he overheard, Kat turned to him and said, "It seems you have my assistant all hot and bothered. Maybe she'll like to have dinner with you because I have other plans." Thankful for the intrusion, but she hated it was with her parents.

It was never good when they came into the city from Long Island. They always tried to get her to spend time with them, and she truly loved them, but in some ways, she blamed them for not knowing what happened to her, well her mother anyway. Not that they knew the truth, but they never seem to care when she changed, they never wanted to know why. Just a phase, they said. It's being a teenager. Back then, she went from the naïve girl next door, with her long blonde hair and very little make-up, to changing everything about herself. Her mother was more involved in her social calendar, what charity ball that was coming up, what to wear, then in what was going on with her. Her Dad was a workaholic, and with that, he didn't know half of what went on at home.

"Kat, you still with me," he asked. He could see she went somewhere but recovered quickly. "I wanted to take you, not anyone else, but I understand your parents are waiting for you. I'll walk you out. You know, we appreciate you doing this for us." They walked out together, and Kat stopped to speak to Vikki, whose face was red as she nodded her head. Jeff pretended he didn't notice, he continued to step out of the small office. He waited for Kat to speak to her assistant. His thoughts going to his plans for the evening, how those plans won't be happening. Maybe if he walked her out and introduced himself to her parents, he could convince them they had plans for the evening.

The ride down was quiet, because the elevator was full, so Jeff used this to move in close to Kat. He could smell her unique scent and couldn't help taking it in. She stepped slightly to the right and away from him. He smiled and moved with her. As they hit the lobby and everyone exited, he placed his hand on her lower back. She didn't say anything just looked at him. Once they walked through the door, she turned to ask for the hotel he was staying. At that moment, the driver opened the door to the limo parked right in front of the building. A very well dressed man stepped out and called to Kat, but he called her Katherine. She looked in his direction and went into his open arms.

"Daddy," Jeff just stood waiting for the embrace to end. He wanted to meet Kat's mom and dad.

"Your Mother and I are in town to see a show. We wanted to have dinner with you. We know your busy, but we never get to see you, so we won't take no for an answer." Once her father noticed him standing there he asked, "Who is your friend, where is your manners, introduce us please, Katherine."

"I'm sorry, Daddy, this is…"

Kat didn't get a chance to finish, because Jeff put out his hand and said, "Jeffery Jacobs, Kat's boyfriend, nice to finally meet you Sir." The look on Kat's face was of total shock and then her eye started twitching.

"Well son, nice to meet you, too, boyfriend," he repeated. Her father looked at Kat as she tried to recover. Jeff knew he'd pay for this later, but he couldn't pass up this opportunity to get to know this part of her. Placing his hand on her back, he pulled her in as he kissed her cheek. "I'm Roger Jackson, and Katherine's mother, and I would love for you to join us for dinner." Roger's smile told Jeff he was happy to see his daughter with him, and somehow it did the same for him, too.

Through the opened door, a woman's voice came from inside, "Roger, darling, we need to get to dinner if we plan to get to the show in time."

"Yes, dear," he said as he gestured for them to get in.

As Kat climbed into the car, she couldn't believe how fast this situation had gotten out of hand. Jeff just introduced himself as her boyfriend and now her mother was going to add her take on the situation. This night just couldn't get any worse. At least she hoped it wouldn't. Jeff pushed in close next to her, as if they were in a compact car and not a limo. She was going to kill him once this night was over.

"Who is this, Katherine?" Her mother's eyes appraised him, appreciating what she saw. Gauging her mothers' reaction to Jeff, she knew her mother would run her mouth in front of him and she would have to do a lot of damage control.

"Mother, I'd like you to meet Jeff Jacobs," then through a clenched jaw she added, "My boyfriend. Jeff, this is my mother Frances Jackson." Her mother put out her hand to shake Jeff's hand, but he took hers in his and kissed her.

"Now, I see where Kat gets her beauty from." Kat wanted to gag, but her mother like every other woman melted.

That was all her mother had to hear, because from there, she asked question after question. Where they met, how long they have been dating, why she didn't know anything about him. Kat was surprised that she didn't want to know when the wedding date would be. Jeff answered all her questions as he poured on the charm and had her mother eating out of his hand in no time. That meant when she announced that they broke up, her mother would give her hell about losing a man like Jeff. Even her father had a few questions about what Jeff did for a living. She didn't know why, but that's when she started to boast about how he and his family owned a surf shop in California, and why he was here. She told them how they were buying into Shafford Surf Boards, and she was going over the contracts for them.

When the car stopped out front of the restaurant, the driver opened the door, and Roger got out first helping Frances. As Kat proceeded to exit, Jeff couldn't control his hands as they landed on her ass to help her. She just turned, giving him a death glare, and he laughed so loud, that her father said, "Now, none of that you two, wait until your Mother and I are long gone."

He heard Kat whisper how she was going to kill him, and hoped it was going to be in bed.

Dinner was good, Kat talked with her mother and Roger wanted to talk business. Jeff reached under the table to take Kat's hand, and again, she shot him daggers. He just smiled and leaned in to press a soft kiss to her lips, knowing she couldn't pull away. How just the simplest touch turned him on, he wanted the right to be able to touch her for real. He knew she was mad, but lots of great sex had come from anger. He'd show her, he could go with hot hard sex or soft and slow sex.

Roger mentioned to Kat that he heard William McDonnell was running for public office. Jeff felt Kat's entire body go stiff, and something shot across her face that looked a lot like fear. Jeff wasn't sure why this name would make Kat react this way. She recovered quickly, Jeff wasn't sure if he was reading her right. Once France announced they had to leave for their show, Roger insisted on paying the bill. As they walked outside, the limo driver opened the door. Jeff didn't expect to get back in, but when Kat got in, he followed. The theater wasn't far and once the car stopped Roger gave the drive instructions to drop them off at Kat's apartment and gave him her address.

"Dad that's not necessary, Jeff and I can take a taxi." She didn't want to spend any more time with him, much less alone in the back seat of her parent's limo. Her father wouldn't hear of it, he shook Jeff's hand and leaned in to say something for just Jeff to hear. When she heard, him say, "I will Sir. It was nice to meet you, too."

Her Father turned to give her a tight hug and said in her ear, "I like him." As her mother moved in next to pretend to kiss both cheeks, surprising she said nothing. Then her mother moved to hug Jeff, he hugged her briefly and released her.

Once the door shut and they pulled away from the curb, Jeff expected Kat to blast him. She moved to the other side of the seat and looked out the window. He'd wait her out, but one thing was for sure, he wasn't going to let her get away, not tonight.

Kat asked, "Do you want the driver to drop you off first?" She still wasn't looking at him, so he moved to her side of the car.

"No, I don't, Kat look at me. I know you're mad, so just let me have it."

All she said was, "Why?"

He knew she was asking why he told her parents he was her boyfriend. All he could say for himself was, "Because, it's what I want, for real, Kat. I want to have the right to touch you, when I want, to hold you."

"Jeff, I told you I can't do that. I can't give you a relationship. I'm fucked up and I can guarantee once you truly find out just how much, you won't want any part of me."

Jeff couldn't stand hearing the sadness in her voice. He eased her face to his, "Kat, there is nothing you could tell me about yourself that would change my mind. Nothing in your past will change how I feel." He took the opportunity when she closed her eyes to kiss her. The kiss started feather soft at first, but once their lips touched, she reacted by kissing him back. Her arms ran around his neck, her hands weaved through his hair, and it drove him mad. His tongue touched her lips, and she opened to him. He dreamed of kissing her again after their first hot kiss at his brother's wedding. His hands moved from around her neck to her back to pull her closer. Their tongues tangled, as each fought for control, but neither had any control. Jeff pressed her down onto the seat and that's when she freaked out. Shoving him back, once his brain caught up, he realized she wanted him off. He immediately pulled back, and that's when he saw fear in her eyes.

"I can't do this, I'm sorry." She moved as far as the seat would allow.

"Kat, it's me. I'm not going to hurt you. I would never do anything that you didn't want. Please trust me. I want you to be okay with us, even if that means we take things slow."

"What if, I don't want this? You going to walk away and leave this alone." Her voice filled with sorrow, and it broke his heart.

"No, Kat, I won't walk away. I'll be your friend and always be here for you." He took her hand in his.

"What do you see in me? Most guys run the other way, but you keep pushing closer. I don't understand you, Jeff." Kat didn't look so frightened anymore.

"I don't understand it either. I just know you drive me crazy."

Just then, the car came to a stop, and they were at her apartment. The moment of truth, would she allow him upstairs? He'd ask her and she said no, he would accept that, but he wasn't giving up.

"Kat, I want to go to your apartment with you. Are you going to be okay with that?"

She sat there for the longest time. He didn't think she was going to answer. Finally, she nodded, but said, "I need to know, before you go up with me, you'll follow my rules, because if you can't do that, then my answer will be no."

"Kat, I'll do whatever you need, always."

The driver opened the door, as if he knew they were ready to take this huge step. Kat stepped out as Jeff followed her up to the building, where she swiped a key card, and the outside door opened. Jeff couldn't believe the time had come, that Kat had agreed to have sex with him. Even if she had stipulations to protect herself, he'd do whatever she needed him to do. He thought back to when he first met Kat. The night at the nightclub with his brother, who set him up for a double date, so he could spend time with Liz. He was supposed to keep Kat busy. She came to check up on Liz, and to check out Ben, to make sure he wasn't after her money. That was a major fuck up, because in the end, Kat set Liz up for Ben to propose to her at her book signing.

He was taken back by Kat's badass attitude and the confidence that spewed from her. She was downright mean, and no other woman had ever treated him that way. Jeff, found it amusing to get under her skin. She declared right from the beginning, she didn't want him to touch her. The closer he got to her, without really touching her, the more she got irritated with him. They played this game, he got into her space or pissed her off, and she would react by getting physical with him. Now knowing she experienced something bad, and that was the only way she protected herself, Jeff felt bad for putting her though that. Would they be here if he didn't push her or refuse to give up? The truth was, there was something between them, and he wanted, no needed, to find out what the strong hold she had over him.

Kat said nothing until they were at her door. She couldn't believe she was going to do this with Jeff. She could think of so many reasons why this was a bad idea, but her body told her brain to shut up. Here is where she would have to go over her rules. Never having any trouble telling a man what she wanted, here with him, she felt very vulnerable. Would he change his mind once he knew, or walk away from her? Not caring what other men thought about her, rules made it easy. Jeff was different in every way because he knew something happened to her. He just stood there waiting for her. She took a deep breath and released it.

"You know, I have hang ups, I need to have complete control in bed. I don't need you to perform any sex acts on me. We will have sex with me on top, and you won't touch me in any way." As an afterthought, she added, "And, I don't do completely naked. Do you agree to my terms?" She couldn't look at him.

"Kat, I understand a few things about why you want these rules. I want you to understand, I want a lot more than just sex. I want to love you, whether that's as your lover or your friend. I will not hurt you. I'll agree to the rules this time, but when you can trust me, things will change. Understand?" He lifted her face to look in her eyes.

# ~ **9** ~

They moved into Kat's apartment, and her heart pounded as if it would leap from her chest. She never had this kind of reaction, yes, she'd get nervous, but knowing this was someone she couldn't just walk away from, and would forever know her hang-ups, scared her to death. Jeff didn't move to her or pressure her in any way. He stood waiting for her, she wasn't sure how to start this, because she never did this kind of thing in her home.

Taking Jeff's hand, she led him into her bedroom. Turning to him, she said, "I'm going into the bathroom to get ready, please remove what you need to, and lay flat on your back. When I come out, I need you to put your hands above your head and keep them there. There are condoms in the nightstand." With that, she walked away from him and closed the door to the bathroom.

Jeff wondered what he had gotten himself into, he wanted to be with her in any way he could. That he knew, but could he control his hands and not touch her? Whatever happened to her, had really screwed with her head. He didn't think the physical part of sex was the problem, but intimacy was another story. That had him wondering if she could ever give herself to anybody. Trust someone enough not to hurt her. Just the thought of some douche-bag doing horrible things to Kat, killed him. He heard her moving around in the bathroom, and knew she'd be out soon. Getting undressed, he placed his suit jacket over a chair and removed his shirt and tie, next taking his pants and boxers off. He got into position on the bed, thinking how essential it was to her to have all the control, he wondered if he could give her everything she needed.

When the door finally opened, he couldn't stop his eyes from roaming over her body. She still had on her bra and underwear. The white lace was sexy as hell, and that's what he needed to get his juices flowing. He was a little worried that with everything so calculated, he would have a hard time getting it up. No need to worry anymore with her standing at the end of the bed, he was instantly hard. He reached for the condom, sheathed his shaft, and placed his hands above his head as she asked.

Kat had given herself a serious talking to in the bathroom. Convincing her reflection, she could do this, saying how this was just Jeff, and not some stranger. He had agreed to her rules, but once she opened that door, would he keep to his promises? She hadn't been looking for someone to love her, as he said. Not thinking she needed anyone, and believing love didn't truly exist, even after seeing it with her own eyes, watching Liz and Ben fall in love. Now expecting twins, they couldn't be happier. Liz is sweet, loveable, and a caring person, and she deserves to be loved and happy. Not the same for her, she was mean, callous, and thrived on conflict kind of person. Who, or why, would anyone want a part of that? This question had plagued her mind. Putting up her brave warrior shield, she left the safety of her bathroom.

Watching Jeff closely, reaching for the nightstand, make her heart pulsate though out her body. She took in how his body moved, the muscles in his shoulders, his flat abs. When Jeff rolled the condom over himself, his eyes never leaving hers, the strangest feeling overtook her body. A calming sensation she never felt before sex. She'd always had to fight her demons, using every breathing technique she ever learned to get past her fear. Kat realized that was it, she wasn't fearful, because she knew Jeff wouldn't physically hurt her. Emotionally was an entirely different story, because there, he could hurt more than her body. She was having a hard time disconnecting physical and emotional, all because she felt safe.

"Kat," he said her name to get her to move. She was just standing at the end of the bed regarding him. He didn't want to make any moves toward her.

"Sorry it has to be like this," she said, not knowing why she felt the need to apologize. She never made apologies for her actions before. Somehow, this was different, she never had a connection to the men she had sex with before.

"Don't be, this is just the beginning for us Kat, and if this is what you need than that's what I'll do. To be honest, it's going to kill me not to be able to touch you." The smile that statement put on Kat's face eased the mood and she climbed onto the bed.

"You've thought about touching me?" she moved up his body as if a wild cat stalking her prey.

"You're kidding, right? I haven't thought about much more than touching every inch of you. Kiss me Sunshine." Keeping his hands above his head, he wanted her mouth on his. Now straddling him, she rested one hand on each side of his head. She bent close to his face, their lips only inches away.

"I like to know, I've tortured you," touching her tongue to the corner of his mouth. His eyes closed, seeing him giving into her, the power within her amplified. His lips parted as she teased her tongue over his. She could feel his chest rising, as her breasts pressed close to his body. As if he needed air, Kat knew the feeling because she couldn't get enough air into her lungs.

Jeff's hands balled into fists to keep from touching her. God, he wanted to flip her and run his hand everywhere over her body. Having her hips pressed over his cock and her tits rubbing his chest had him so hard. He wanted to be inside her, but didn't want this to be over, because he was afraid she would pull away afterwards. His thoughts started to jumble when their tongues twisted as he fought for any kind of control. Kat broke the kiss as she pulled back to sit. Knowing all he could do was watch and allow her to decide what came next.

"Kat, you okay?" She looked bewildered, almost as if she didn't understand what was happening. "It's just me Kat, talk to me." When she still didn't say anything, he took one hand from its position and went to touch her. That's when she snapped out of her trance.

"No, don't touch me." She started to get off the bed.

Jeff couldn't help it when his hand reached out to stop her, "Kat, talk to me, its ok. If you can't do this, I'll understand. Just tell me what's going on in your head."

When she looked to where he held her, he released her. "Please."

"I… I just can't, this is a mistake," but she didn't move.

"Why Kat, why is it a mistake?" She looked away from him.

"It's different, and I'm not sure I can handle it, or give you what you want from me."

"Please, make me understand, you know I won't hurt you Kat. I have feelings for you that I can't shake." He took her wrist, rubbing his finger over her pulse.

"There lies the problem, when I have sex, that's all it is. This is different because it's not just sex for you. I don't think I can do it, open myself up to someone. I have things that I don't share with anyone, weakness, and fear. I put on a big front, only letting people see what I want them to see. If you know everything about me, you won't look at me the same way. You'll see me as weak and not the strong person, I've worked so hard to become, and I don't know if I can live with that."

"If you told me all your secrets, I wouldn't look at you any different than I do right now. I know you're strong, not just physically, but in every way. I think that was one of the things that attracted me to you, besides the fact that you're hot as hell." That made her smile, as he hoped it would. "Seriously Sunshine, from that first night at the night club, when you said you didn't want me to touch you, I've thought about nothing else. I'll wait until you're ready to tell me, I just want to understand and know how to help you. I want you to trust that I would never betray you. I want to be with you Kat."

He never expected her next move, but she crushed her lips to his. This time he put his arm around her to hold her to him. When she didn't object, his hands did what they wanted to do, roaming over her ass. Pressing her into him, immediately made his body respond and her moans egged him on. He had to remind himself not to roll her beneath him. Letting her lead was so much better that not being with her at all. Before he knew it, she had him ready to enter her. When she sank down his shaft, he thought he died and went to heaven. His dick hardened and when she sat forcing him deeper, he yelled.

"Fuck that feels so good. Ride me, Kat," he placed his hands lightly on her hips. She still had her panties on, and his fingers slipped under the garment. Kat arched back placing her hands on his thighs. He watched her as she rode him, her tits bounced and it made him want to reach up and slip the lace down so he could see her, feel her, but he knew if he made any move to touch any more of her, she'd freak. He could feel she was close, he moved his thumb to her clit. She hesitated ever so slightly but kept moving. His hips moved to meet hers, but he could see she was struggling.

"Come for me Sunshine, I need to feel those muscles clamp down on me." Just like that, she let go, the wave of her release squeezed him, and the sounds she made, sent him into heaven.

When he could breathe again, he realized Kat was lying on his chest. She didn't move, and he didn't know if she passed out or was just being still. He rubbed her back and asked, "You okay?"

"I just need a minute." Her face pressed into him.

Once again, he was at a loss of what to do, so he just held her. When the silence stretched out, his concerns grew. "Kat, what are you thinking."

She rolled off him and then stood righting her panties. He stood too because he needed to see her face. When she wouldn't look at him, he took her face in his hand and moved her so he could see her. Her eyes met his, and he could see something was wrong. The hard, tough Kat was gone. He needed to get her to open to him, because not knowing what to do was driving him crazy. Afraid to do the wrong thing, say something that sent her running.

"I'm going to take care of the condom, but when I get back, we are going to talk," with that, he stepped back and went into the bathroom.

Kat's mind wound tight, she didn't know how to handle what just happened. It wasn't often for her to have an orgasm during sex, and the one she just experienced, was such a hard release. Jeff just told her to let go and she did. It didn't hurt that she let him touch her when she never let any other. When she would normally get dressed, and then walk out, now that the sex was over, here she was at her own place and nowhere to go. She didn't want to offend Jeff by asking him to leave, but how did she deal with him. He wanted to talk, but what could she say, "I'm a freak and have no experience with this kind of situation." The door to the bathroom opened and Kat felt as if she couldn't breathe. She watched as Jeff put his boxers back on and then go to the light. Now darkness showered the room and knowing he couldn't see her, gave her comfort.

He took her hand in his and moved them back to the bed. Once he had her tucked under his arm he said, "I'm at a loss here Kat, on one hand, that was the best sex, but on the other, I'm so afraid I might do something wrong. I've never felt so insecure when it comes to any woman in my life. I always knew what my partner needed, but with you, I just don't know. I need you to guide me through this." When he heard her laugh, it caught him off guard. "What's so funny?"

"I was just thinking the same thing because I have no idea how to handle this situation. First, I've never had a man here at my house before, so when sex was over, I'd get dressed and leave. Second, I feel overwhelmed, this is going to be embarrassing, but I don't easily find release. Having hang-ups, makes it hard to be relaxed enough, but you say let go and it happens, like no other. If I tell you about what happened to me, I need you to promise you won't repeat it or hold it over me. You know I'd hunt you down and kill you." She held her breath waiting for his answer. Why was she going to tell him something she's never told anyone else, she didn't know?

"Kat, I don't want you to feel pressured into telling me, yes I want to know, so I can understand. Anything you say here, in this bed, is between us, and I wouldn't expect any less of you to come after me and make my death as painful as possible if I breached a word. I want to be your friend, lover, and the person you can trust." Jeff knew he needed to prepare himself for what Kat was going to tell him, because whatever it was, it had to be truly bad to mess her up the way it has.

"Before I tell you, I need one more promise."

"Anything."

"You can't try to fix this or somehow find the person responsible."

"Okay, but I'm going to find it hard not to do anything to make things better."

After a few minutes, she started her story, "I was in high school, a junior, and one of the most popular boys asked me out. We went out a few times and I had such a great time with him. I felt comfortable with him, so one night, he asked me if I wanted to go parking with him. He said we would only kiss, at the time, I very much wanted to do that. I was naïve and had no experience with boys."

"Once he drove to a remote place in the woods, he moved us into the back seat. Here's the hard part, we kissed, my first real kiss. He climbed on top of me, and I didn't stop him. When things started going too far, I tried to stop him. At first, he didn't seem angry, and I watched him remove his belt. He told me to put my hands above my head and so stupidly, I did as he asked. Before I knew it, he tied me to the armrest, and he pinned down my legs with his body. Telling him to stop just seemed to egg him on, but once he pulled out a knife, I started screaming."

"Ahh shit, this is going to be really bad. Son of a bitch, give me a minute." Jeff tried to pull himself together.

Kat waited, knowing how hard this was going to be, she needed the time, too. "He took the tip of the knife gliding it over my cheek, which made me stop thrashing. I pleaded with him, and I started crying, begging. He just laughed, said I was a tease, and he would have what he wanted. He unbuttoned my white blouse, running the knife under my bra, popping it open. I closed my eyes because I didn't want to see him looking at me. His hand squeezed my breast hard, and I cried out, he called me a fucking slut. I've never even been with a boy, much less be a slut. He then proceeded to pull up my skirt that I picked out just for this date. I thought it was so pretty, and he cut my fucking underwear off. I stopped screaming and fighting, I guess I just went somewhere deep in my mind. I told myself if I live through this, I'd never be a victim again. He began unzipping his pants, saying all kinds of stuff, to me but at that point, I wasn't listening to him anymore. Until he rammed into me, the pain was so bad, I couldn't keep it in. He said how he loved him some virgins because they were so tight. When I stopped fighting again, he took the knife trying to terrorize me. He ran the knife from my collarbone down my breast to my nipple. Even with the pain of the cut, I said nothing. I guess that made him madder because he ran the blade down my hip."

"He cut you, Kat, I'm trying to control my rage here, but why didn't you tell somebody?"

"His father had a lot of money, and he told me if I told anyone, nothing would happen to him, but everyone would know I was a slut and was asking for it. I believed him and I didn't want anyone to know. Unfortunately, he wasn't finished with me because he lost interest in fucking me. When he pulled out, I thought it was over, but he climbed up me and told me he was going to fuck my mouth. He put the knife to my neck and told me if I even thought about biting him, he'd slit my throat. I did as he said and when it was over, I wasn't that same naïve girl."

Jeff swallowed the bile that threatened to come up. Every muscle in his body was tight. He had questions, but wasn't sure if he should ask. She had told her story with absolutely no feeling as if it was someone else who went through this horrible ordeal. He needed to do something and at that moment, his thoughts of Kat's reaction when her father mentioned that dude tonight at dinner. Could he be the son of a bitch that raped Kat, because if he were, he would be breaking his promise?

"Kat, why didn't you tell your mother, she would have…" Kat cut him off.

"What would my mother have done, she didn't even notice something was wrong. I told her I was sick for two days after and when I changed, she blamed it on being a moody teenager. My mother was more involved in her volunteer work, charity balls, and tennis matches, than she was ever involved with her children. And don't think I was going to my Dad, although he would have killed the guy, I wasn't going to tell him what happened to me. He was at his office most of the time. It had been months before he realized I cut my hair. Which was down my back, and I cut it short. I didn't want anyone looking at me, I didn't want to look cute, and so I chopped it off. I patched up the cuts on my chest and hip, lucky they weren't that deep, and even if they were, I wasn't going to have anyone looking at them."

"You amaze me how strong you were, even back then. Kat, you must know, I don't think you're weak at all. You went through something I wouldn't wish on my worst enemy. Thank you for telling me, and I'm sorry."

"Don't be sorry or pity me."

"Kat, I don't pity you, but I do need to apologize to you for forcing myself into your space. I knew it affected you, I truly liked it when you would verbally spar or got physical with me. I thought of it as foreplay, and now knowing what I do, I can't help feeling like a real jerk."

"You are a jerk, but you woke up something in me. I've never felt desire for a man, much less a man that would want to deal with my problems. I put up my shields, my attitude kept men away. Until you, it turned you on when I was rude and put you down. I couldn't be nice to you because you'd think I was softening toward to you. I tried distancing myself from you, going back home, and then you show up here." She could feel his smile.

"So, what you're telling me is that I'm irresistible." He playfully rolled her, that's when she reacted swift and precise. He found himself on his stomach with his arm twisted behind his back.

"Jerk, just so you know, I can't have you on top of me. With your weight, I'd feel trapped." She whispered into his ear, and letting go of his wrist. "I don't want to hurt you, if I freak out, and I could.

"Kat, I want to ask you something, but I don't want to upset you." He rolled so now she was on top, but with the room dark, he couldn't see her reaction.

"Okay, ask but if I don't want to share, I'll take the fifth."

"Tonight, at dinner your father mentioned a man, William something or another." He felt her body react by tensing up. He knew before he asked, "That's the dude, isn't it?" Immediately, she was off the bed, and went into the bathroom, shutting the door. He heard the shower turn on. Obviously, she needed time, so as much as he wanted to go after her, he knew she wouldn't appreciate his intrusion.

Jeff thought about everything she said, because it was a lot to process. He couldn't even imagine what she went through, all alone. Not being able to tell anyone all these years, not even her parents, his mom came to mind, and how she would have reacted to someone hurting one of her children. Linda not noticing something was going on, not likely. Now he knew and had a name, someone her father knew. What could he do about it now, he gave her his word? What if he didn't technically come right out and tell her father, he wouldn't be breaking his promise to her, right? A plan hatched, he'd go see her father tomorrow before he had to return home.

Kat stood under the hot water, not moving. Repeating to herself "How did he know?" This man scared the crap out of her. He managed to unearth her deepest darkest secret in a matter of months. What was wrong with her, no one has ever been able to penetrate her self-protection? Jeff just steps into her life and her control is gone. He had to know by her response to his question that William was the one who raped her. She should have played it cool, but she never expected him to know his name. She needed time to think, but her mind wasn't cooperating, because it was just spinning round, and round. Sitting on the tile and rocking herself, she had to get rid of him. How, she had no idea, he saw too much. So, deep in thought she didn't hear the bathroom door open.

Jeff tried to give Kat her space, but she was in there too long. The hot water had steamed up the glass and he couldn't see her. When he opened the shower door, he still didn't see her, until he looked on the floor. Balled up on the floor with her head in her knees, he crouched down, putting his hand on her back.

"Kat," she didn't move. "Please look at me, I need to know you're alright."

Still not looking at him she asked, "How did you know who he was?"

Jeff turned off the water and sat next to her, "At dinner, when Roger said his name I felt your entire body go tight. I didn't know why, of course, but I've watched you Kat, for months, you could say I studied your body language. Trying to learn more about you, and what makes you who you are. All I needed to do was pay attention. You don't scare me. Well, you do, but not enough to run me off." Placing his finger under her chin to get her to look up at him he added, "I like who you are, the good, the bad, and even the ugly. Knowing what happened, doesn't change that. I desire you more now, and I want to be the man you need me to be."

Sitting there naked reminded her no one had seen her scars. Saving herself of ever having to explain what happened, but Jeff already knew. Could she allow him to see her, really see her? She'd come this far, she knew he wouldn't react badly.

"Jeff, I need to do something that I've never done," she stood but put her back to him. "No one has ever seen my scars, which is one of the reasons I keep on my underwear and bra. I need your help, because you already know, I need you to see them now."

Jeff turned her, but didn't look away from her eyes. "Kat, I want to see you, but I'm not going to gawk at your body. I want to love your body, taste your body, and most of all, I want to tease every inch of you. Understand I'm not here just to have fun and move on, what I'm looking for, is someone to share more. We'll work on the hang-ups, you'll see, okay? Just tell me if you don't like something and I'll stop or if you want to do something else. Whatever you want, I want. No pressure, just pleasure."

He kissed her, pulling her into his arms. Still in the shower and wet, feeling her pressed to him didn't make him move to dry off. Running his hands up her ribcage, just below her breasts he waited for her to stop him. When he felt her seek his touch, he moved higher, until she rested in his hands. Moving slowly his thumb brushed across her nipple, the moan she made sounded of pain. "What do you need Kat, tell me," tweaking her nipple.

"Kat, me touching you here, good, or bad," waiting for her answer he kept his touch soft.

"More, I need more," groaning as if she had her teeth clinched tight.

"Relax Kat, remember it's just me, we can stop anytime."

"Don't you dare stop. I've never had a man's touch like this. God, please." Kat couldn't understand the need that coursed through her body. Never wanting a man's touch as much as she wanted his, all the fear of being with him, dissipated. All she felt was deep need, overwhelming craving. She didn't feel threatened, no fear, just pleasure as Jeff touched her. His kisses moved to her neck, and she tilted to give him better access. She wasn't sure when they moved but was glad to have the support of the tile wall. Still being cautious, Jeff moved lower, caressing the top of her breasts. Knowing what would come next, she opened her eyes to watch his reaction, but his eyes closed. Watching his mouth close over her nipple was erotic, feeling the pleasure when he pulled it tight into his mouth, making her inner walls clinch. He moved to the other breast and Kat held her breath, because that was the one with the scar. Feeling over sensitive, her entire body tightened.

"Relax, Sunshine, breathe. Just loving your body and enjoying the hell out of it. You're beautiful, prefect, every fucking inch of you." Kat released the breath she held, as he moved down, over her flat stomach. His hands holding her hips, knowing he was touching the area of the other scar now covered with a butterfly tattoo. His words pull her away from her thoughts.

"Damn woman you have a six pack better than most men." His eyes were open now as his tongue mapped out each muscle. She sucked in and he chuckled. "Shit, your hips are like handles a man could hold tight to."

"Jeff, stop talking, I'm going crazy here thinking about what you're about to do." When his gaze met hers, she could see the twinkle of gold dancing in his brown eyes.

"You don't like talking during sex, got it," he went back to his mouth on her skin. "Oh, one more thing, and then I'll get down to business. You smell so damn good," running his nose down her center. "I have to know, have you ever…"

"No."

"Well, now that I know I have no competition, I'll use all my wicked skills." He pressed her legs open and noticed a little beautiful butterfly tattoo on her hip that went down into her smooth pelvic area.

"Cocky much?" she said with attitude.

"Oh, I'm plenty cocky, now shhh, because you don't like talking during sex."

She hated when he got the last word, but once his mouth touched her body, nothing mattered. He used his thumbs to spread her, his tongue swirled around the bundle of nerves and the sensation almost sent her over the edge. The awareness ran along her spinal cord and shot through her limbs. Every muscle in her body stiffened when he inserted a finger.

"You okay, Kat?" He didn't stop his pursuit but slowed.

"Fine," this time she could hear the need in her own voice.

"You ready for more?" More, oh God, she didn't think she could take much more. When she didn't answer, he stopped and looked to her.

"Don't stop."

This time he sucked her clit and added a second finger. She could feel the muscles in her neck as she clinched her teeth. He alternated between swirling and sucking, but it was when he opened his fingers and twisted them that sent her into an amazing orgasm.

Jeff was one happy son of a bitch. He couldn't help the pride he felt. Being the first to show her that kind of pleasure, was one of the best sexual experiences he ever had. Having Kat trust him enough to get this close, to love her body, and he did love loving her body. He stood, taking her mouth with his. Her hands tangled in his hair, holding him to her. His body was on fire, hot and hard. He didn't bring a condom with him, so he needed to stop before he went too far. Pulling away from her wasn't easy.

"Kat, I don't have any protection." He knew when it dawned on her what he was saying.

"I'm protected, and I haven't been with anyone since my last check up, so I'm clean, you?"

"I... You're protected, what the hell does that mean?" He placed his hands on the wall beside her head.

"I have an IUD because I don't take any medication that's not absolutely necessary. I don't need or want an unplanned pregnancy. In case you haven't noticed, I'm not the maternal type."

"That's bullshit and you know it, you may not want that now, but don't try to tell me you're not caring." He gentled, "I think you'd make a great mother, the momma bear."

"I think you're getting off the subject, we were talking about being clean, and you never answered."

"I'm clean. I haven't been with anyone since before Ben's wedding. I just had a physical for the increase in my life insurance policy. With the agreement with Shafford Boards, the shop is worth more." She pulled him into her and kissed him as her life depended on it. When her hands moved from around his neck to down his back, he hadn't realized just how much he wanted her touch. Unsure of his next move, he'd just let her lead. He still had his hands on the wall behind her. Knowing she had issues, he'd go with what ever made her comfortable. Having Kat with nothing between them would be a first for him. He was smart enough not to trust every girl that said she was on birth control. He trusted Kat completely, if anything, it would be him talking her into getting pregnant. He gave his head a slight shake because the thought was crazy. She didn't even want a relationship, much less marriage, and children with him.

"You with me Jeff?" her question in his ear pulled him out of his thoughts, when her hand closed over his shaft, he almost swallowed his tongue. Pushing into her hand, he moaned. God, having her hands on him as he had fantasized, but this was one hundred times better.

"I can't reciprocate the favor, at least not yet." When he realized what, she was saying, he kissed her, hard. Knowing that fucker who attacked her, forced his dick in her mouth killed him. He didn't care if she ever gave him a blowjob, because if it gave her horrible memories, then it could never be pleasure for him.

"I don't need that from you, Sunshine. What I need, is to be in you, feel you connected to me." Lifting her and pressing against the wall he said, "Wrap your legs around me." He could feel the strength in her legs as they clamped around him. She held her own weight, and that left his hands free to roam her body. Their bodies lined up and she slide down his dick, the feeling made him hiss. "Don't move, give me a second. I need to get control, because being inside of you with nothing, is going to make me lose it. Damn, that feels so fucking good." When she started to move, he took hold of her ass. He knew he wouldn't last long and wanted her to come with him.

"I'm not going to last, I need you to rub your clit, I want you to fly with me." She did just as he asked, and if that didn't make his control slip even further. It was when she started to clinch and squeeze his cock, and with her sounds, that sent his seed rushing. Bright lights flash in his closed eyes, and he found breathing impossible.

When they both came down from the high, Jeff released her legs. Taking her hand to draw her from the shower, he started to dry her off. She took the towel from him, and he let her. It was getting late, and he hoped she wasn't going to kick him out. He knew she had already done more with him than anyone else, but he didn't want to push his luck. Yet he wanted more, he wanted her sleeping next to him.

"Kat, I don't want to go back to my hotel, but if you don't want me to stay, I understand." She stood there just looking at him, most likely he was heading back to the hotel.

"I've never slept with anyone, so... I sometimes have dreams, although I haven't had one in a while."

"I know, you had one at my mother's house, she told me because she was worried about you. By now you should know not much gets by my mother." He saved Kat from having to say the words, "I'll just go..."

"No, I mean, not yet. Stay with me until I fall asleep. Please," it was so unlike Kat to ask for anything. He knew he most likely wouldn't sleep once she was in his arms, and going back to the hotel late would be hell tomorrow. He nodded his agreement because he wouldn't say no. For the longest time, she said nothing, and he thought she might be regretting allowing him to get close. What would he do if she pulled away now that he made it through her hard-outer shell? What was he thinking because he knew she'd try to pull away? So, what was he going to do when she did?

"Thank you," was all she said.

"For," he asked as he pulled her closer into him.

"You know, don't make me say it, okay."

"Good night, Sunshine."

"Why do you call me that?"

"I'll tell you some other time, now go to sleep."

# ~ 10 ~

Jeff held Kat until he heard her breathing slow, she made herself comfortable under his arm. When she snuggled up next to him, he felt all was right. Knowing this was just the beginning for them, he was in, and now he needed to get Kat to trust him enough to give him her heart. He had known for months she was going to be his end, and he had to prove to her she could count on him. Closing his eyes, a peace settled over him, this was where he belonged.

Kat lay in his arms thinking, *what am I doing? I don't sleep with men, and without a doubt, not Jeff. So why, why am I here? I told him things about me that no other person in the world knows. I've lived my life for me, the only one I could truly depend on. I lived with this secret for so many years and never felt the need to share with anyone. He brings things out in me, feelings, but I can't put any merit in what I'm feeling, because at some point, he will destroy those feeling. When that happens, I must be prepared. For now, Kat, have fun while it lasts, and when it's over, walk away with your heart intact and head held high. Never allow him to see he could hurt you, just as you never allowed William to see your pain. Yes, stay strong.* After telling herself everything she needed to hear, she relaxed.

When Jeff's mind became fully aware of where he was and whom he had in his arms, he didn't move. He opened his eyes to look at Kat, her body turned away from him, but she hadn't moved away. Her short blonde hair was relaxed, and he loved how amazing it smelled. Regarding her bare shoulder, made him want to run his finger over her skin. The skin he already knew was astonishingly soft. Now, she did move, and it gave him a prefect view of her back, he could see the muscle band across her shoulder blades. He never had been with another woman that worked out as Kat did. Last night, he didn't want to put too much emphasis on her body, because of what she had told him about her attack and the scars, he knew she was self-conscious. Never thinking he'd be attracted to a woman with bigger muscles than him. Not that Kat's physique was large for her frame, she displayed shear strength. Sexy didn't even come close to describing Kat. Last night when she wrapped her legs around his waist, God he loved that, the fact she could support her own weight. She worked hard, and it showed, he totally appreciated her. Glancing further down to where the swell of her ass gave way had him swallowing hard. He wanted to touch her, in the worst way.

A noise from the other room pulled any thoughts of Kat out of his mind. Getting up without disturbing the bed, he slipped on his boxers. Creeping through Kat's apartment felt strange, but not wanting to make a sound, he slid down the hall. The sound came from the kitchen area, singing. When he turned the corner, he saw a dark-haired woman cleaning the counters. He stood still, not wanting to scare her, because he could see she had ear buds in. Dancing around with her long braid swaying, singing out of tune had Jeff smiling. When she turned, and spotted him, she gasped throwing her arms to her chest. Jeff put up his arms, hands facing her.

Ripping her ear buds out she asked, "Who the hell are you? What are you doing in Ms. Jackson's apartment?" Breathing hard she stepped back, grabbing the broom, and pointing the handle at him.

"Hi, I'm Jeff, a friend of Kat." Jeff could see she wasn't sure if she believed him.

"A friend, as in you spent the night, kind of friend?" She sounded unconvinced, and the questionable look down his body, had reminded him he was standing there in his underwear.

"I guess, that would be true," he moved to the breakfast bar to block her view of him.

"Ms. Kat has never had an overnight guest, except Ms. Liz and her daughter, and she always tells me when they're coming. She never mentioned you staying."

"Sorry Miss…, but you have me at a disadvantage. I'm Liz's brother-in-law." That information seemed to ease her stance, she put the broom down.

"Do you want something to eat, not that I do Ms. Kat's cooking? I could whip up something. I guess you live out in California, too. She told me she'd be spending some time out there, how Ms. Liz needed her help." She looked down the hallway and turned back to him. "So, did you sleep in the guest room?"

"You don't think I'm sharing any information with someone I don't even know their name, do you?" Jeff sat in the seat in front of him, because maybe this person could shed a little light on Kat's life.

"Oh, sorry, I'm Shay. Ms. Kat's housekeeper, not that she really needs me. Don't tell her I said that." She pointed a spatula at him, and he made the gesture of zipping his lips closed. She nodded and went back to cracking eggs.

"Nice to meet you, Shay. I'm sure if Kat keeps you around, it's because she does need you."

"I clean things that never get dirty. She never cooks, and only uses one bathroom, and the living room never has anything out of place. She really doesn't spend that much time here."

"So, you said she doesn't have overnight guests, no men then, ah," and when she turned and smiled. He gave her one of his own, one of those hundred watts smiles.

"No, Ms. Kat doesn't bring her men home, ever."

"How long have you worked for her?"

A voice from behind them said, "Long enough to know she shouldn't be telling you anything. Of course, the way you have with women, I shouldn't be surprised. Thank you, Shay, I'll take care of our house guest." Taking over breakfast, Shay stepped away.

"Nice to meet you, Mr. Jeff, good luck," Shay, whispered the good luck part just for him and it made him smile, because she was on his side.

"You know, you weren't supposed to be here either. I asked you to stay until I fell asleep. Although, I'm sure Shay enjoyed the sight of you in your boxers," placing a plate in front of him, their eyes met.

Jeff stood and walked around to her. Kat had on a silk robe that didn't hide her body. Putting his arms around her and pulling her in close.

"I heard a noise, came to investigate. At least I put on my boxers, because who knows how I could have scared Shay if I didn't put them on."

"Eat and then you need to go." Here it goes because he knew she'd pull back.

"I have an appointment with your Dad this morning, so I have to get going." He kissed her and released her to shovel some eggs into his mouth. "Kat. just so you know, I'm not done here. Not by a long shot, but I won't push you or allow you to push me away."

"Allow me." She laughed and added, "I have news for you. I don't have anyone to answer to. I do as I please, just so you know. Don't think this changes anything because I don't do relationships. This is just sex, and nothing else."

"If you say so, but it's not that way for me." Shoveling more into his mouth, he turned to walk away. "By the way, I like the robe," he said over his shoulder.

Kat looked down at herself, noticing how her nipples had betrayed her. Hating how Jeff could make her body want him. They had had sex twice last night, and she wanted to chase after him for more. Usually having sex could last her for a long time, and she never did it twice in one night. For some reason, he made her want more sex. Not that she was very fond of sex, but she couldn't do without, it as Liz did for ten years. Feeling this need was new, and she wasn't sure if she liked it. Jeff had a way of making her feel comfortable with him.

Jeff dressed and needed to head to his hotel to shower and change. He had talked to her father at dinner about going over the contracts. Not that, that was on his mind, he needed to get her father's help to get the son of a bitch that raped Kat. Knowing of his promises, he'd have to tread very carefully. When he returned to the main part of the apartment, he knew Kat would be nowhere around, so he found a pad on the fridge. Writing a note to her, before leaving, he headed out.

After stopping at his hotel, he hopped in a cab, he was hoping he was doing the right thing getting Kat's father involved. If it were his daughter, he'd want to know, kill the dude, or at least kick the shit out of him. Once at the building, he decided he was doing the right thing, if he didn't betray Kat's trust. Ushered right into Roger's office, he walked in and amazed by how big it was. Roger was on the phone, looked up and held up one finger. Jeff sat in the chair and waited for him to finish, as he rehearsed what he wanted to say.

Once done Roger got up to come around the desk to shake Jeff's hand. "Good to see you, son."

"Me too, Mr. Jackson," Jeff stood, but wasn't sure how this was going to go down, or if her father would think the same once he said what he had to.

"Roger."

"Right, Roger, I know we talked about you looking over the contracts, but that's not why I'm here."

"Have a seat Jeffery, and this wouldn't be about my daughter, would it?" Roger showed Jeff to the far end of his office to sit more comfortably.

"Yes, it's about Kat," but before he could tell the man about what happened to his daughter Roger interrupted.

"Are you going to ask for her hand in marriage," he asked eagerly.

"Not this trip, I must confess, I'm not even Kat's boyfriend."

"But, you want to be?"

"Yes, I do, but I need to talk to you about a totally different situation and it's not pleasant. I'm walking a thin line here. I don't want to betray your daughter's trust. I made her a promise, so we need to play a game."

"A game, son, I'm not following you."

"I'm going to ask you some questions and lead you down a road, but you have to come to your own conclusions, so in the end, I didn't tell you anything. When did Kat change?"

Roger looked confused, but then thought about the question, "High school."

"Do you have any idea why?"

"Her mother said it was just a phase she was going through. Some things telling me it was not a phase."

"Who was she dating at the time?"

"Son, if you are trying to tell me something happened to my daughter, I think we would have known."

"Who," Jeff pressed.

"I don't know, just tell me what you came to tell me."

"I can't tell you, you need to figure it out. Yesterday, you mentioned someone."

"Jeffery, are you telling me William McDonnell did something to Katherine, because if you are, nod." Jeff moved his head slightly. "Son of a bitch," Rogers face turned red, he stood and started pacing. He went to his desk picking up his phone, "Judy, cancel the rest of my appointments for today." Once he hung up, he grabbed his suit jacket, "You comin,' Jeff?"

"Hell yes, but I promised Kat I wouldn't tell anyone or go after him." Getting on the elevator he said, "Roger, I can't tell you exactly what he did to her, but know he terrorized her. If I could, I'd kill him, and that would be too good for him."

"Son, I like you, and the fact you have my daughter's back. She never lets us take care of her, so I can rest a little easier knowing she has someone like you in her life."

"I want to be with your daughter, but as you know, she is very independent."

Roger laughed, "That's a nice way to put it, she's stubborn, and bull headed."

"This is how she protects herself, the attitude, how she carries herself. It's all to control things."

"When the time comes, and I hope it does, when you ask for her hand, I'll be a very content man. What did you say you did for a living again?"

"I own a surf shop with my family." Jeff was thinking Kat's dad the big corporate attorney, wouldn't be very impressed.

"Good, Katherine needs to have some fun in her life."

"Yes Sir, she deserves to have fun and more."

When they walked out of the building, Rogers's driver opened the door for them, and he gave him the address. It seemed Roger was aware of this William person. They drove in almost complete silence. Finally, Roger broke the quiet, "When did she tell you?"

"Well, she didn't tell me the complete story until last night, after dinner, but I had known something happened to her. I figured out who by the way she reacted to his name, but at the time, I didn't know the truth."

Roger looked a little disgusted, for not noticing anything was wrong. "Roger, she has hidden this from everyone, for a very long time. I guessed something bad happened, and she had a nightmare at my mother's house. So, give yourself a break if she wanted you to know, you would. Because Kat is who she is, the way she is, we only know what she wants us to know. The rest, she locks up tight."

"She told you."

Yes, Kat had told him what happened, with no emotion, no feeling whatsoever. Just the facts, nothing more, and nothing less, living with this burden had taken its toll on her. Not allowing William to have any power over her, not allowing what happened to control her life. It did come with a price, trust, hope, and ever-finding true love. No wonder she didn't believe in real love. Could he be the one to change that for her? He sure as hell hoped so. At this point, he was in deep, and after last night, there wasn't a doubt in his mind. Having her in his arms, he'd give everything to have that every day, but her love, to have her love.

They arrived, and Jeff could feel the surge of anger raging inside him. He needed to get a grip, because Kat would know if he did anything, like kill the dude. Roger put his hand on Jeff's knee and looked him in the eye. "Now, let me do the talking, William will attempt to play on your emotions, try to get you to hit him, and we're not going to fall for it. As much as I might want to rip him apart, my plan is to hit him where it'll hurt the most… financially."

They entered the offices of Chandler, Smith, and McDonnell Attorneys at Law. So, the scumbag was a lawyer, it figured. Jeff knew Roger Jackson was a man most in the corporate world didn't mess with. Just his presence, how he carried himself, spoke volumes. Walking up to the receptionist, Roger spoke quietly. She immediately left her desk and disappeared down a hallway.

Low and behold, two seconds later, Jeff got his first look at the man who hurt Kat. Bile rose in his throat, and his hands clinched at his side. He wasn't a very big man, yeah, he was dressed in an expansive suit, but that didn't stop him from looking like the fucking lunatic he was. The one who got off by hurting young girls, and Kat had been one of those, young and innocent. He took so much from her, and then went on with his life, never paying for what he did. How many more were out there suffering, because of him. Jeff could feel himself hyperventilating and needed to step back. Roger had been speaking to William, but Jeff couldn't hear a word they said to each other, because his emotions were getting the best of him.

"Son, you alright, pull it together," Roger said in a hushed tone and followed dickhead down the hall. Jeff took a deep breath and moved in behind Roger. Once the door closed behind them, Jeff just stood by the door and Roger went to the couch and sat.

"Mr. Jackson, what can I do for you, my secretary said this was very important." William sat across from Roger.

"Do you know who I am?" Jeff could see both men from where he stood, and the surprised look was priceless.

"Well, of course I know who you are. You're a legend in the corporate world."

"Do you have any idea why I might come to see you?" Roger's voice still sounded calm, Jeff wondered just how he was holding it together.

"I would hope you're here to contribute to my political campaign," and the son of a bitch smiled.

"I'm not only an attorney, but a father. I have a son and a daughter." This made Jeff stand taller, Roger was going for the kill. "I think you might know my daughter, perhaps you went to school with her. As a matter of fact, I think you dated a few times even." Jeff could see William wasn't fazed by Rogers statement.

"Really, what was her first name? Small world isn't it."

"My daughter is Katherine Jackson, she had long blonde hair." Roger sat still, not moving.

"No, I'm sorry, I don't remember her." Jeff felt his legs move and Roger held up his hand and Jeff stopped. It was the first-time William looked in Jeff's direction.

"Are you sure you want to play this game with me, William, because I don't play games I can't win."

"What do you want from me, money?" William didn't look so cool any more.

Roger laughed, "Son, I have more money than you could ever spend, and why would I want your money?"

"Then what, because the statute of limitation has long passed for anything I **might** have done as a juvenile. Legally, there isn't a damn thing you can do." Jeff felt his palms getting itchy, he opened and closed his hands.

"Did I say anything about the legal system, no, what I have planned for you has nothing to do with what's legal. First, there will be no campaign, rapist don't run for office. Second, you will leave this firm, tell them anything you want." Roger now sat back in his chair.

"I'm not going to give up everything for something that happened years ago, I was an angry kid whose father physically and emotionally abused him. I went for treatment, counseling, and anger management. I'm not the same person I was then. I have a wife and children to support."

"That all sounds nice William, but counseling and treatment should have been from prison. Knowing what I know about what you did, I'm positive there are more women out there. You know it's only going to take one publicly announcing what you did to them. Bad press will not only take you out of any political race, this will also make your partners drop you. As for your wife and children, I do feel bad for them, but look at it this way, if someone hurt your child what would you do to seek justice for them. The way I see it you had your freedom far too long and had the chance to meet your wife and have those children. Not paying for any of your crimes, I'm giving you the only chance to walk away from this, without me completely destroying you."

"This is black mail," William said.

"No son, I deal in facts, we both know all it's going to take is an accusation, and you're done." Roger got up from his seat because this meeting was finished. He'd make sure William would follow through, and along with his help, he'd ruin him. He'd set up a college fund for his children, because it wasn't their fault who they had as a father.

Jeff had held his tongue the entire time but had to say his peace. Stepping into William's face, Jeff said, "What you took from Kat has made her into a very strong woman. If she saw you on the street today, she would kick your ass, and I'd enjoy watching. I've seen with my own eyes the scars you left for her to bare. You are the biggest sort of coward, to force yourself on a girl and to take something they can never get back. I hope your wife knows what kind of a man she married. What they say about Karma, what goes around comes around, I hope it's true," with that, Jeff stepped back.

Once in the closed elevator, Roger asked, "It was bad?"

"Yes."

"I don't need to know the details, do I?" Both men stood facing the doors.

"No, Sir."

"I appreciate how you handled this." Confused, Jeff turned to look at Roger.

"Why, I just stood there. You're the one who did all the talking."

"Because son, I don't know the truth about what my daughter went through, you do, and you held it together. You came to me, knowing I'd help you. You're keeping her secrets, but you felt the need to defend her honor. Apparently, Katherine didn't feel as if she could confide in us at the time, and you have no idea how much of a regret that will be for me. I would have loved to see him pay for what he did, but at the time, I might not have wanted to put Katherine through anymore trauma, but this man should not be able to walk away, without paying for his crimes."

"I had to do something, and yet, I needed to respect Kat's right to her privacy, knowing how much trust it took for her to tell me what happened. So many things make sense now, not that knowing makes things easier for me. Dealing with my own anger, over what happened to her, isn't easy."

The doors opened as Roger turned to him, "I guess not, but not knowing doesn't help me either. I watched my beautiful daughter change before my eyes. She changed her appearance, her grades dropped, and she wanted us to refer to her by that hideous nickname. Even when she entered the corporate world, she used Kat. Her mother and I thought she was trying to get back at us for something."

Standing in the lobby Jeff had to be honest, "She changed for so many reasons, but you're right, Kat puts a lot of blame on your wife,

Roger. A mother should know what's going on in their child's life. If one of us kids came home, and everything changed, my mother would never allow it to go on. Still to this day, you can't keep a thing from her. All I'm saying is, Kat became someone she could see as strong, independent, and most of all, in control of her life." Jeff knew he might be overstepping his boundaries with Kat's trust, and Roger's acceptance to the blame.

"You seem to know my daughter quite well. Now I know why she always distances herself from her mother. I know Franny has her faults, but she loves her children. If she's guilty of anything, it was fear of pushing Katherine further away." Jeff nodded, but he knew if it were his mother, he'd never get away with pushing Linda away. She would be in his face in a heartbeat, because to, Linda there wasn't anything more important than her children.

The driver opened the door once again, but Jeff didn't move to get in. Roger glanced back, with a questionable look. Jeff wasn't sure why, but he felt the need for space. Kat's father moved back to him. Understanding, Roger put out his hand, and Jeff shook it.

"Thank you, son, you have no idea how much I respect you. It takes more to use words than a fist, even when using your fists would seem to be more satisfying. You are a man with integrity, and I admire that. Seeing you with my daughter last night, pleased both her mother and me. You might have misled us, but we could feel the electrical charge between Katherine and you. If you don't get discouraged, she will come around. I hope the next time you come to see me, it'll be under better circumstances."

"Yes Sir, until next time," Jeff knew there would be a next time because he wasn't giving up on Kat. Roger's smile spread wide as he nodded and walked away.

Jeff grabbed a cab once the limo pulled away from the curb and again gave Kat's office address. The ride gave him some time to think, but he needed to walk, so he pulled his coat tight to combat the cold, as he moved down the sidewalk. He wasn't used to this kind of weather, but the cold took on the emotion he felt. Not truly looking where he was going, just walking he noticed a beautiful shop with all kinds of expensive looking trinkets in the window. He thought maybe he'd buy something for Kat and send it anonymously. Show her the how it feels when someone is thinking of them. As Jeff walked inside the shop, he noticed all the little glass animals like she had in her office. They were all very pretty, but not really, what he was looking for. A salesclerk approached him, he didn't know if he could help him, because he had no idea what he had in mind.

"Hello, may I help you find something?" Right away, Jeff could see and hear how feminine he was. Not that it bothered him, but in the same sense, he wanted to make it clear he didn't bat for the other team.

"I'm looking to buy my lady friend something," Jeff motioned around the store. "She has all this kinda stuff in her office. So, I know she likes it, do you carry music boxes?"

"Oh yes, we carry a wide variety," moving down the aisle with a sway in his hips, that Jeff tried to ignore. The man stopped in front of a display, "As you can see," he gestured with his hand. "We also do custom music boxes, for a fee of course."

"Of course," Jeff repeated. "My friend has a few, so I'm not sure what to get her." Jeff looked over the ones on the shelf. He didn't see any of the ones he saw in her office. "If I only knew what she may want, or which ones she already has." Thinking aloud, Jeff knew he was in over his head with this music box thing.

"I might be able to help you there, if she purchased them from us, which we happen to be the best in the entire city," he giggled. "If I do say so myself," placing his hand over his heart.

"She might have bought them here, it's worth a shot," Jeff followed the clerk to the back.

The clerk smiled at him, "You're not from here, California, perhaps," his smile made Jeff a bit uncomfortable. When he didn't answer, the clerk went back to looking if Kat was in his system, "Your lady friend's name?" Jeff gave him Kat's name and waited.

"Oh yes, Ms. Jackson gets all her music boxes here. I can even do you one better, I know just the ones she wants," moving his fingers back and forth, then pointing to himself. "Oh yes, I'm the one who can most definitely get you what you're looking for."

Now it was Jeff's turn to give him a smile. One of those smiles that got him what he wanted. The man in fact swooned and fanned his face. Jeff didn't care, this man was going to be the answer to his prayers. Robert, the clerk, set everything up from what music to send first, and to having it delivered. Jeff didn't want Robert to pick out each one he'd send to her, so he gave him his email and Jeff would go through the list and pick the ones he wanted her to have. After paying, and Robert's little comment about Kat being a lucky woman, Jeff was on his way back to the hotel. He had one more night in the city and wanted to spend it with her.

# ~ 11 ~

Kat couldn't concentrate on what she was doing, her thoughts kept returning to Jeff, and just how good he made her body feel. Her mind was racing, she had to know if he was still in town. She picked up her cell and dialed Liz, because she'd know when Jeff would be returning to California. If she could have one more night with him, before things went back to the way they were, she wanted it.

"Hey, Kat," Liz sounded tired, and Kat wondered if she was getting enough sleep.

"Liz, are you sleeping enough? You sound tired."

"I am tired, all the time, no matter how much sleep I get. When are, you coming home? I miss you."

"Liz, I am home." She had been spending so much time there, it was starting to feel more like home than her own place. The weather was certainly better there, then here. She could be in a bikini on the beach right now.

"You know what I mean Kat. It's just that you've been gone so long. I keep asking Ben if you decided not to come back, and he didn't want to tell me."

"I wouldn't do that to you, Liz, you knew I had meetings that I had to be here for. It's not as if I left you all alone, and Paige should be coming home from school soon for Thanksgiving." Kat paused, then added, "And I needed a little space, not that it has done me any good. It seems you forgot to mention that Jeff was coming to the city. It would have been good to have the heads up, considering he just showed up in my office yesterday. He said you told him to come see me, to look over the contracts of course." Kat's tone was to let Liz know she wasn't happy with her.

"Okay, so the truth is, he came to me and asked for your information, intending to contact you. I told him to have you look over contracts for the shop. Kat don't be mad at me because I think Jeff's feelings for you are real. I want you to be as happy as I am." Liz sniffled a little, and Kat knew she was crying. "Damn hormones, I can't even write without sobbing."

"I'm not mad, just knowing he could show up, would have been nice."

"I didn't want to say anything, just in case he didn't come by." Kat knew Liz was playing matchmaker, along with Linda, both were pushing her and Jeff together.

"Listen, Liz," she said slowly as if it would help to stop her from pushing. "I... do... not... want... any... kind... of... relationship... with...Jeff, and if we should get together, it won't be because of love, I don't do love."

"If you get together, Kat you're so funny. I think you're the only one who doesn't see what's happening. What happened to, and I quote, "It's so electrifying when you first start a relationship and everything is fresh and new," unquote. When I was talking about meeting Ben, you were all into a relationship. What happened?"

"For you Liz, you're the relationship type. I'm the just sex type."

"Then, did you have sex with Jeff last night?" Liz didn't dance around the subject and Kat knew where this was going. What should she tell her about last night without giving too much away?

"I have to go, when is Jeff returning home?" She'd try to rush Liz into telling her if Jeff was still around for tonight.

"I'm not falling for that Kat, did you, or did you not, have sex with Jeff, because if you think after all I shared with you about Ben, that you're not going to tell me anything you're mistaken."

Liz waited and when Kat didn't answer, she jumped to her own conclusion. "Oh no, you did, and it sucked. Damn, I would have thought it would be so hot that you two would burn down your building."

"It didn't suck. Just the opposite, and now I have to go." As Kat hung up, she heard Liz say she knew it, but Kat didn't want to talk about it. After all that, she didn't even find out if Jeff was still in the city.

Liz hung up and turned to Linda who sat next to her on the bed. "It's started, as you heard, the deal is done. Not that she would share any details with me, but it didn't suck. I think being with Jeff is a big change for her, and it's going to take time."

"I don't want details, but I knew they would be perfect for each other. I just hope Jeff doesn't screw this up somehow. Of course, I've never seen him so taken back by a woman before, so I'm hopeful. I have a few tricks up my sleeve for when she gets back, to throw them together."

"I have a feeling it's not going to take much," both laughed.

Jeff had the entire day to mill around the city, but there was only one thing he wanted to do, so he stood in front of her office building. He wanted to get Kat alone, but he needed to do it with a little finesse. He wanted her to know this wasn't just about the sex. Although, the sex was great, and he knew it was only going to get better, once Kat trusted him. He thought of how he used his skills to make other women feel special, and yet, this was different. She was not the same as any other, and he wanted this more than he could imagine. It had always been just himself, having fun, no pressure, easy. This felt as if being himself wasn't going to be enough. She deserves more, more than he ever offered any other.

Kat had issues that ran deep, as anyone that had been raped. He wanted to show her that he could put her needs before his own. The fact that she never truly dated, is where he'd start. He needed to guide her though what a relationship means. Not wanting to wait any longer, he stepped into her office building.

Once he walked into her outer office, and Vikki looked up and saw him, she quickly glanced away. He knew she was embarrassed from the way she acted yesterday, and Jeff didn't want to add any discomfort. He just asked, "Is she busy?"

"Yes, Mr. Jacobs, she's on a conference call. You can have a seat, I'll tell her you're here."

"You can call me Jeff, and if you don't mind, I don't want you to tell her I'm here." He noticed she still wouldn't look at him.

"Oh, I like my job to much Mr. Jacobs, I have to announce you. I apologize for my behavior yesterday, it's just that we don't get many men in like you."

"Like me?" He questioned.

"We don't get many men in general, but the ones that come through here don't look like you." That made Jeff chuckle.

Again, he said, "Like me?"

"Well, tall, and tan, and hot, and you know, now you're just trying to embarrass me." He was having a little fun with her. "You wouldn't happen to have another brother, besides the one married to Liz."

"Nope, just a sister, sorry," he thought he heard her say something under her breath about men from California.

"Have you ever been to California? If not, you should come. We'll teach you to surf, and you'd get a tan." Just then, the door to Kat's office opened.

Jeff stood when Kat walked into the small room. She started talking to Vikki and stopped when she spotted him. He smiled and went to her, pulling her into his arms and kissed her. Not a little peck, no, he kissed her with everything he had. Kat responded, and then she pulled back when Vikki cleared her throat, saying something about needing to make copies. Vikki scurried out of the office, closing the door behind her. Seeing the surprise on Kat's face, made Jeff smile, he liked to keep her guessing.

Kat pulled away from him, giving him a dirty look, "What part about me keeping my personal life, private, don't you understand. I'm in my place of business, and that was very unprofessional. You ran off my assistant." Jeff just stood there smiling, then he moved closer, and she stepped back. Taking her hand, he led her into her office, closing the door behind them. He pinned her against the door, putting both his hands on the door over her head. Kat held her breath, she didn't feel threatened, just anticipation, looking in Jeff's eyes, seeing his intense brown stare. He moved one hand to her cheek moving his thumb over her bottom lip.

"God, you're beautiful," he kissed her.

"I'm not."

He moved his lips down over her neck, "You are, and your skin is so damn soft. You smell incredible, I could eat you up," his lips moved down the opening in her blouse.

Her voice hitched as she said his name, "Jeff."

"You have the sexiest legs I've ever seen," his hands went to the back of her thighs, dragging up her skirt. "Do you have any idea what you do to me?" Pulling Kat's leg up to his hip, he rested his hands on her tight bottom, "You fuckin' drive me crazy." He pressed his body against hers, showing just what she was doing to him.

"Jeff, Vikki is just beyond this door."

He chuckled as he picked her up, "Are you sure your desk is strong enough, because we're about to find out?" He walked with her in his arms, he placed her on the edge, and her phone buzzed. "Damn," he said and knew this was going to be bad timing.

Kat leaned back and pushed the button, "Yes, Vikki."

"Sorry to interrupt, but a package just arrived for you, from the Most Precious of Moments. I thought you'd want to know right away."

"Thank you, Vikki, I'm not waiting on a package from them. I'll be right out." Kat pushed Jeff to step back. "I need to get that," she straightened her skirt.

Jeff watched as she walked across the room and unlocked the door. He knew what was waiting for her, but it couldn't have come at a worse time. His body hummed for her, and he knew once she opens the music box, the connection they had would be broken. When she returned, he moved to the window behind her desk. Kat placed the box on the other side and opened it, pulling out a beautiful wrapped smaller box. He observed her reaction as she ripped away the paper. Her eyes became big as she looked in amazement, running her hand over the box. She opened it and her breath hitched when the music began to play. Standing there, just looking at the box in her hands, she didn't move. Then picking up the small card, she slid it from the envelope. She read, "This will be one of many. Beauty comes in many forms, but none more beautiful than yours." She immediately picked up her phone dialing it from memory.

"Hello, may I speak to Robert, please," Kat waited. "Robert, this is Kat Jackson, I received a music box today, and I need to know who sent it. The card wasn't signed, and I'd like to thank them."

Jeff watched closely to see if Robert told her who sent it, but she didn't even look his way. He heard her say, "What do you mean you don't know, nothing comes or goes without you knowing. What, they paid with cash, so you have no way to track who bought it. Just great, the card said something about one of many, if another music box is ordered to be sent to me, I want you to get the person's name Robert." Jeff didn't like the concern in her voice, but for now, he wanted to keep who sent it quiet. He looked down at the box she had placed on her desk it was the one Robert said she wanted. The next one was going to be one he wanted her to have.

Once she hung up, she went back to the box on her desk, picking it up and looking it over. "I wanted this music box, but I don't like that someone sent it to me. As if someone is in my head," her expression changed, and she turned to him. The look she gave him, as if she was scrutinized. "Wait, you wouldn't have anything to do with this, how would you know where I get my music boxes?" She stepped closer.

He didn't answer her question but asked one of his own. "Why would you think I had anything to do with this?"

"Because, you are the only man I know that has managed to see through me. You've accomplished what no one else has ever done. I've told you things about me, that I never planned to tell anyone. And, I must say, its freaks me out, how you could know me so well. Besides, you're the only one I know who could sweet talk Robert into not telling me. I bet he fell all over you, but how did you know?"

"You're giving me way too much credit here. As you said, how would I know where you get your music boxes? This is New York City, and there must be hundreds of places to get those things." He tried to pull her close to him again, but she held back.

"I need to know, as much as it freaks me out, I'd much rather know it was you. I don't like thinking someone is out there sending me things."

She was playing on his heart, but he couldn't lie to her, so he came clean. "I was walking and just happened on that store. I saw they had some of those glass animals in the window, so I went in. I wanted to get you something, but I didn't know what I was looking for until I talked to Robert." Now, he did pull her in close and she went. "Once I told him you had others, he said you most likely got them from them. He looked you up and told me you had one you wanted. I want to send you more, but ones I want you to have." He softly kissed her, "I want to show you," he kissed her again. "What you've been missing."

"What have I been missing?" He didn't answer her.

"I want to take you on a date tonight and then spend the rest of the night making love to you."

"Jeff, I don't do love, I can't give that to you," she started to pull back, but he held her.

"Let's just take it as it comes, I know you have stuff to work through. I'm safe Kat and you know I won't hurt you. Why not work through your sexuality with me, we can take it slow. I just want to be with you. Let me show you how good sex can be, not just what your body needs, but to truly learn to enjoy making love to someone. Please say yes." He pressed his palm to her face, running his thumb over her bottom lip.

"What do you want to do on this date?" She wet her lips and watched as his eyes followed her tongue. She had to change the subject, because she didn't want to discuss her sexuality, what her body wanted from him, but her head had to catch up. She had already trusted him with her deepest secret, could she trust him with more?

"Anything you want to do, just as long as we end up in your bed." He kissed her, "You owe me."

"Really, do tell, what I owe you." She looked at him from under her lashes, pulling away from him, and moved around her desk. As she moved she slid her hand along the glass desk, she knew exactly what he was talking about, "It wasn't my fault someone sent me a beautiful music box, if anyone owes anybody, it would be you whom owes me." The second he started to move her phone buzzed again.

"Yes, Vikki," Kat looked over at Jeff who was shaking his head. She smiled knowing just how he felt, but she was at work.

"Mister Lundqvist is on line two and he's not very happy."

"Thank you, Vikki, I'll calm him down." Kat picked up her phone, took a deep breath and then pushed line two. "Walter, what can I do for you?" She turned her back to Jeff and listened to her boss ream her out, about being gone. He said, "Why should they be paying for her office if she is never in it." "Walter, I told you, I had a family situation come up. I've kept up with everything here, and it's not as if I take off from work. I still have a very impressive client list, as you already know." She didn't want to do this now, with Jeff standing close enough to hear. "Walter, I'll have to call you back, I have a client waiting." Once she placed the receiver down, Jeff was at her side.

"Let me guess, your boss isn't happy with you being in California." He wrapped his arms around her.

"He can get over it, I work hard and make this company a bundle of money, and he knows it. He just doesn't like that I'm not here when someone calls for an appointment. I've passed some new clients to other agents, and when people expect to have me as their agent, and find out they have someone else, they become upset. Then it gets back to Walter, he calls to let me know that having happy clients, is very important in this business. Besides, Walter isn't used to me being gone, I never take time off."

"You ever think about going out on your own? I'm sure all your clients would follow you if you left."

"All of the client's sign a contract with the company, so they couldn't just leave. It would be as if I was starting over. I couldn't even be Liz's agent. If I were to leave I might want to do something different." She moved away from him and placed her music box on her shelf.

"What would you do," he asked thinking maybe she could do her different in California.

"I don't know, I've never thought about it before, but I'd do something with helping women." She wasn't sure about how she felt about changing careers this late in her life. Now that she thought about it, Kat knew she would help rape victims. She never turned to anyone after her own experience, feeling all alone, but now, after sharing her story with Jeff, it somehow freed her. Kat waved her hand as to dispel her thoughts, "It doesn't matter, because I'm not going anywhere."

"You could always get certified and teach self-defense classes, or even yoga, and I'm sure a bunch of other stuff. I know you work out hard," he moved around the desk. "Is it because you need to feel safe, to control any situation you might feel threatened?" Again, he drew her into him.

"I guess it has something to do with that, but mostly, it's to keep the nightmares at bay. When I work my body to sheer exhaustion, I can sleep. My mind and body can relax when I'm in my best physical shape. It's how I've always dealt with what happened to me." Kat had to lighten the mood because she didn't want to talk about this anymore. "I have a little more work to do before I can leave for the day, so you need to go. I'll call you when I'm done." She started to push him out the door.

"I'll just wait outside for you," he kissed her and began to move.

"Oh no, not in Vikki's office, she'll never get anything done." Jeff turned and gave Kat a huge smile.

Jeff had a few things he needed to take care of, like checking out of his hotel, and stopping in to talk to Robert about what he wanted to send Kat next. Once he did that, he was going to Kat's apartment, and with any luck, Shay would be there to let him in. He wanted to surprise Kat, something he knew no one had ever done for her before.

Kat watched Jeff walk out the door, and on one hand, she was so relieved and on the other, she missed him already. This was not good for her, and she needed to get a grip. He just always knew how to work past her walls. Could it be she wanted Jeff to be the one, to restore her faith in men? In her head, the warning bells rang loud and clear, but her body wanted this with him. She knew he wouldn't hurt her physically, but as far as anything else, she knew he could do more than she could handle.

Kat went to her desk, thinking she'd try to finish up so she could leave. Looking down through the glass, for the first time, realizing with clarity she had to release the last hold William had over her. She always insisted and told herself for so long he didn't have any power over her. He held one thing she never could manage to work through, to allow a man to make love to her, to feel that emotional connection to another person. Feeling strange, because she wanted that one last hold to be broken, but to get there, she had to take a chance with another man. Not sure how she'd feel when the time came, that was if she could follow through and allow Jeff to make love to her. He knew she could freak out, and he still wanted to help her work through her hang-ups. She would remind him again what could happen, because if she had a flash back, she might hurt him.

Kat pushed all those thoughts out of her mind for now because she had work to do, and a date to plan.

Jeff met Kat in front of her building, he noticed she changed into tight jeans, and she was wearing winter boots. She was very quiet and somehow it made him uncomfortable. He didn't know the quiet Kat, she always put everything right out there, in your face. He asked, "Everything okay?" When she didn't answer right away, he got concerned. "Kat, talk to me," he pulled her out of the stream of walkers. He never saw so many people walk without looking at anything in particular. Everyone in a hurry, no one paying any attention to anything, and yet, they knew what was around them.

"I'm fine, I've got something to talk to you about, and I am not sure how. I don't want this discussion to ruin the night because I want this time with you. As crazy as this sounds, after last night, all that I shared with you, I feel free. There's just one thing holding me back, and I'm scared. I've moved past what happened to me long ago, but with you, I realized I haven't totally gotten over things."

Jeff wrapped his arms around her, pulling her in close to him. He kissed her forehead and said, "It's okay Kat, I told you, we go at your pace. As long as you're not telling me things are over, anything else, I can handle."

"I'm not telling you I want it to end," she heard him release the breath he must have been holding. "What I'm saying, is I want to try to move past that last hurdle. I'm just not sure how my body will react, if I have a flash back…"

Jeff kissed away her words, because he understood, and he wasn't going to let that happen. He would remind her, every step of the way that he was touching her, he didn't want that asshole to be on her mind when they were together. He wanted to show her how great it felt to have someone love you, body, mind, and soul deep. Not that he ever felt like this about anyone else, he never felt such a strong pull, as he did for her.

When he pulled back he asked, "So what do you have in mind for our first date?" She just gave him a wicked smile.

"Oh, that would be a surprise. Let's go," she intertwined her gloved hand with his. Looking down, seeing her white glove against his tan hand, just proved how different they were. She knew he wasn't dressed warm enough to be outside for very long, but she still wanted to take him ice-skating in Rockefeller Center. They had just put up the huge Christmas tree, although not lit yet, it was still one of the great things to see in the city.

Kat pulled him to the curb and hailed a cab like the pro she was. Once the cabby stopped, she and Jeff hopped in, "45 Rockefeller Plaza, please," she told him. The man just nodded with his Met's baseball cap and pulled out into traffic. She knew Jeff most likely realized where they were going, but he didn't say anything. When she snuck a peak at him, he was smiling, and she couldn't help the feelings that flooded her system. He must have felt her looking at him because he turned and slid closer to her.

The cab stopped and she tried to pay, but Jeff wouldn't hear of it. This was a date, and he never in his life let a woman pay when they went out, and he wasn't going to start now. Once on the sidewalk, she again took his hand, and he liked it. Pulling him through the crowd, she stopped in front of the ticket booth. They got in the line marked for reserved skate sessions. Kat gave her name, ID, and the clerk punch a computer and tickets printed out. With tickets in hand, she again pulled him through a gate where a man scanned their tickets. Not saying a word, she took him to the skate rental counter.

"This should be fun," he said under his breath. "Kat, I've never had a pair of ice-skates on in my life. Are you sure you want to be seen with me?" He just watched as she took off her boots, handed them over, and had a tan pair of skates in her hands. Again, he followed suit, did the same, and had the same tan color skates. This was going to be one hell of a date. He had roller skated as a kid but never had any use for ice skates.

"Kat, what are you doing to me, I thought we were starting to like one another." She had her skates on and now stood over him, smiling down at him.

"Now, Mr. Fancy pants, Mr. Surfer dude, you can do this." She leaned down to help him lace up his skates. Kat pulled the laces tight over his foot, then put one lace through the hook eyelet, then moved her hand back and forth lacing them up the rest of the way. She managed to do this very fast, and Jeff found he was impressed, watching her lace his other skate just as fast.

"Where did you learn to do that, I've never seen someone lace up shoes so fast?"

"Not shoes," she corrected him. "Skates, and they're like boots, and I have plenty of experience lacing my boots."

He attempted to stand, it helped that he stood on a rubber mat. She took his hand, and he wasn't sure if that was a good idea, because if he went down he'd take her with him. Lucky for him, the mats went all the way to the ice. He watched her as she stepped out on the ice, gliding as if she had no worries. Jeff on the other hand, stepped on the ice very cautiously holding on to the side rail. The rink was crowded, and small children skated by him. Kat skated back to him, biting her lip with a half-smile.

"You have to let go of the rail, hold my hand, I'll help you." She took the one hand he was using to hold on for dear life. He should be able to do this. It was all about balance, and he knew balance. He let go and Kat pulled him away from the side, his lifeline. As long as he didn't pick up his feet, he was good. Kat skated backwards holding both hands, he couldn't even skate forwards, and she did it effortlessly. He felt like an ass because most dudes were the ones skating backwards with their girl. But he lived in California, and ice-skating didn't happen there.

He told himself he could do this, so he let go of one hand. Once he tried to move, it was a different story. Jeff's feet slipped right out from under him and down he went, pulling Kat with him. At least she fell on top of him, but damn that ice was hard.

Kat was laughing, "This is so, Kat two, and Jeff one."

"Oh, I see, we're back to that, are we?" He kissed her. His attempts to get up wasn't any better, he was on his knees looking up at her.

"You know they have walkers for the small kids to help them, do you want one? She asked as she didn't hide her smile.

"You know, pay back is going to be a bitch, right?" He managed to get to his feet again and when Kat held out her hands, he didn't take them. He didn't want to pull her down again. This time, he watched as the skater skated by, he bent his knees and tried to push off.

"It's easier when you're moving, let me help," Kat stood next to him.

He knew he was doing it wrong, but he tried as if he had roller skates on. With his arm flailing to try to keep his balance, he worried he might hurt someone, especially himself. Jeff knew Kat was enjoying herself at his expense, but seeing her smile and laughing, was well worth any discomfort. He'd get her back once they were home and she was learning how to surf. With his luck, she'd be good at it like Liz was.

Kat was having a great time, watching Jeff struggling was a bit underhanded. She skated round him, never leaving his side, but she stayed clear of his Frankenstein arms. He was trying, and she gave him a lot of credit for that, because most men would have already wanted to go, all because they weren't good at something, but Jeff just kept trying.

# ~ 12 ~

After almost an hour, Kat showed mercy and pulled him off the ice. His hands were so cold, he couldn't feel them anymore, and his ass hurt from falling so many times. Overall, he had a great time with her. He had gotten the hang of it toward the end. However, would he want to do it again, probably not? Still, it was about spending time with her, doing what she wanted to do.

Once they had their shoes back on and he was standing on solid ground, not that the ice wasn't solid because it was, he drew her into him and kissed her, he didn't dare try that when he had skates on, he might have bitten her tongue off. He was ready to be back at her place, but she leaned back and looked at him.

"I have one more thing I want to show you," taking his hand was getting easier each time she reached for it. "Are you getting hungry? After I show you this, let's get something and take it back to my place."

*Oh, hell yeah, that's exactly what he wanted to do.* He let her lead him through one of the buildings off the rink. Walking over to a bank of elevators, she showed her ticket again, and a young woman scanned it. They waited in line for a few minutes with many others. He didn't know where Kat was taking him, but he'd follow her. Standing there, it dawned on him, she kept showing her tickets, she must have had paid for them in advance. With the tickets, still in her hand, Jeff reached for them. She wasn't paying attention until he swiped them free from her grip.

"Hey, what are you doing, give those back," she tried to grab for them. He held tight and turned his back so he could try to look at them. She was fast though, so he stuffed them in his front pants pocket for later. He knew she wouldn't try to get them here in line, with all these people around.

"You are not paying for this date, I am the man, and you are the woman." He noticed they were attracting attention. He whispered in her ear, "I want to do this. You deserve to have someone treat you right, and part of that, is letting me pay. I'm going to have to insist," he felt her shiver, not certain if it was from the cold, or their proximity to each other.

"What the hell, you are man, I am woman. What's with the caveman routine? You told me we could do whatever I wanted, and what I wanted to do, you need reservations. We would have never gotten to skate otherwise, and to make reservations you must use a credit card. I might let you reimbursement me if you asked nicely." The doors opened and everyone crowded in, Jeff moved behind her and dragged her back.

In her ear, again he said, "I call bullshit. You know as well as I do, you would have never let me pay, no matter how nice I asked." He felt her shiver again, so he went a little further and kissed her neck, gliding his lips over her skin. Just then, the elevator dinged, and everyone moved to the front, but Jeff just held her tight. "Not so fast," he wanted to hold her to him for a little longer.

"We have to get out, we can't ride the elevator. Once we go down we have to pay again to come up." They stepped out, but Jeff still held on to her, he wasn't really regarding his surroundings, until he noticed the huge floor to ceiling windows, and she saw his face light up. The city lay out in front of them. The nighttime was the prettiest time to come up here with all the lights of the city. She watched as he moved closer to the windows. Never letting go of her, he moved around to each window.

"Wow, is all I can say. This is amazing, the way you can see all the cars moving in the streets. They look like little lighting bugs, moving through a maze." He put his hand to the glass and looked straight down. "Ok, maybe not," he stepped back. He heard Kat laugh and he looked down at her, she was watching him. He knew he totally looked like a tourist but couldn't help feeling overwhelmed by what he saw. He smiled back at her. leaning in he kissed her. He was at the top of the world, and he was sharing it with her.

They walked the entire observation deck, one window at a time. Jeff was as a small child, in awe of the city. She was getting hungry, but didn't want to stop Jeff from looking out over the city that never slept. Her stomach made a loud noise, and he noticed.

"You ready to go, I'm starving," he took her hand, and they made their way toward the elevator. While they waited, Jeff drew her in, her back to his front. Wrapping his arms around her waist, he held her pressed against him. "You know, you smell great," his face was in the crease of her neck. He tickled his nose along her jaw, letting the air escape over her skin.

Kat stood stock still, closing her eyes. The feeling of Jeff behind her set off so many warning bells in her head. He compelled the hairs on her neck to stand up, but this time, for different reasons. She wet her lips because her mouth was parched, and her body zinged with electricity. That damn elevator had better arrive soon because she just might jump him right here.

"Relax Kat, I can feel you getting tense," his hand progressed inside her coat and up her ribcage, and she sucked in as she held her breath. *Oh God, Oh God, what do I do.* She started to shake, and he stopped the movement of his hand. Did she want him to stop? Yes, she did. This was something that she needed to be behind closed doors.

"I can't do this here," she whispered. His hands eased a bit, and she could breathe again. She took a deep breath and another. Cleansing breaths, she told herself. The doors opened and she was never so happy to move and have some space. *This is just Jeff, not someone I don't know, I trust him, I think.*

Jeff didn't intend to make Kat uncomfortable, it was just his hands had a mind of their own. He wanted to be touching her. In the elevator, he didn't touch her, not even to hold her hand. He knew she needed the distance, he'd give her that until they reached outside the small, cramped space of the elevator. Once the doors opened she appeared to be ok, but he'd make sure.

He pulled her aside, away from everyone. "I'm sorry, I didn't mean..."

She cut him off, "I'm fine, let's forget it, and get something to eat." This time she took his hand, and he couldn't help giving it a little squeeze.

"What's your favorite restaurant to eat in the city," he asked. "I'm so hungry, I could eat a horse."

"Eww, that's disgusting. Don't make me lose my appetite, that doesn't sound very enticing." They walked out of the building and Kat pulled out her phone. Dialing the number by heart, she ordered from her favorite tofu restaurant and then gave her address to have it delivered. Walking to the curb, she hailed a cab, once in the back seat she said, "I know you're going to give me a hard time about dinner. I want you to try it, before you make up your mind. I did go with your selection for food the last time we were out," she reminded him.

"You mean our first date? Yes, I remember, and I recall you giving me a hard time about my choice. I will hold off any judgment until I see the food, but if I don't like the looks of it, I'm not eating it," he watched her as she laughed and shook her head at him.

"You sound like a little kid, I don't like it mommy, its green," she said in a childish voice. He couldn't help himself, he laughed, too. She added, "And that wasn't a date."

"I believe it was, because it ended with a goodnight kiss, so that makes it a date," Jeff said smugly.

"It most certainly did not, after the evening was finished, you chased me down on your motorcycle. Then you kissed me, so that doesn't count," Kat hammered back.

Jeff saw the cabby looking in her rearview mirror, with a smile on her face. "I think she has you there." So, Jeff rectified the situation and laid a kiss on Kat that knocked her back.

"Now, this is a date, and you're not going to get out of it." The look on Kat's face was worth being wrong about their first date.

The cabby now said, "I think he has you there."

"Well, of course, because I agreed to this date, and I didn't want a date previously..." she tailed off. She glanced over at Jeff and the son of a bitch had one of his hundred-watt smiles, so she punched him in the arm.

Once again, they were at her apartment building, Jeff could feel her hesitation. He put his arm around her shoulder and kissed her head. "It's going to be alright, I promise. I'll stop at any time, no pressure." She nodded and swiped her card to open the outer door. They walked in silence, and he pushed the button for the elevator. Turning toward her, he knew she was nervous, and he wasn't sure how to reassure her, because even if she freaked out, it would turn out fine. He was going to do his best not to do that, but when he was with Kat, it took everything he had not to go crazy on her. The way she made his body feel, he had to control himself and reel in his own needs.

The doors released and they walked in, it was empty. It gave Kat the chance to have that discussion she wanted to have with him earlier. She seized a deep breath and released it, closing her eyes she said,

"I'm concerned about freaking out on you. I could injure you, and I don't want to do that. I've never attempted this before because it's always been my way. The method that I'm most comfortable with, but it's the one obstacle, I haven't been able to hurdle. To be with someone without fear, to know I can release, be free. It's something I want, something I need. William took so much, and always thinking I couldn't trust a man again." Tears prickled her eyes, and she thought, *oh no, I don't want to cry*. She swallowed hard fighting back her emotions.

The elevator dinged and she felt Jeff take her hand. He hadn't said a word and when he was silent, she didn't know what he was thinking. They strolled to her door, and she stopped, she had to know where his head was. Was he on board or was he thinking of a way to walk away from her. Looking him in the eye she said, "Jeff, if you want to change your mind, I'll understand."

Before she could say any more, Jeff put his hands on her face. Framing her cheeks, he leaned in, and started with a soft kiss, gentle even. He kept his eyes open, and she could see the emotions in them. Kat put her hands on his forearm to hold him to her. She needed him, and that thought scared her to death. Pulling back Jeff said, "There is no way in hell I'm going to change my mind, about you, about us. I want you, I won't deny that. I need you to guide me, I don't want to push you into something you're not ready for. You have to talk to me and be honest for this to work." The elevator dinged behind them, Jeff stepped back, and two seconds later the doors open. A young man walked out and stopped short, he looked at the receipt in his hand and then back at them. Their dinner, Jeff paid the dude and Kat opened the door.

Kat walked to her kitchen, turning on lights as she went and stopped short, because there were a dozen red roses in a vase sitting on her counter. When she left this morning, they were not there. A small card sat propped against the vase. Opening it, her hands shook, who was in her apartment.

She read the note and laughed, Rose are red, Violet are blue,

I'm so glad to be with you.

I suck at this shit.

Love, J.

She turned on her heels to find Jeff watching her, "How did you get into my apartment? I have a security system, and yet, you still managed to get in here." She squinted her eyes, scrutinizing him once again. "I think I should be scared, not that I think you might hurt me, but has anyone ever told you, you have a little stalker in you. You're not planning a fatal attraction, are you?"

A devilish smile crossed Jeff's face, "I can't give away my secrets." He placed the bag on the counter next to the flowers and drew her in close. "I didn't mean to scare you. I wanted you to know how happy I am to be here with you."

She kissed him on his nose, "You may change your mind after…"

"Nope, not going to happen," he saw her resolve as she pulled away from him. He let her go, for now.

Kat went to get plates and napkins for dinner. She placed them on the bar and got out utensils. Opening the bag, she removed her meal first, and she noticed Jeff eyeballing her food. She then placed his tofu burger on the plate with tofu fries. He sat down, picked up one of the fries, and popped it into his mouth. As he chewed, she watched him closely, Kat knew he liked it.

"Ok, the fries are good, but this burger," picking it up, inspecting it. He took a bite, "So, I like it, not bad. You were right."

"Oh, how I do love a man that knows I'm right." She was playing around and Jeff stopped chewing and stared at her. "What?"

"Nothing," he shook his head, "It's just that you said you love a man…"

Realizing what she said and how he might interpret her meaning. "I was just playing with you, I didn't mean…"

"I know, but for someone who doesn't believe in love, it just threw me for a second. What are you eating, it looks pretty good too?" He took his fork and started to dive into her food. She didn't know how she felt about sharing food off her plate. Jeff didn't seem to mind, and she had kissed him, so sharing food should be no big deal, right?

He looked up and saw her face, "What you don't want to share with me, I thought you wanted me to try all the food."

"I didn't want you to eat yours, and mine," she eyed him.

"I'll give you half of my burger if you give me half of yours. What do you say?"

"I say no, if I wanted a burger, I would have ordered one and since I don't eat bread there is no reason to order a burger."

Jeff laughed, "I get it, you don't want to share. I'll just eat what's on my plate and anything you might not want."

Kat was enjoying the banter, and she realized she enjoyed his company, too. She went out on her first date tonight since high school. Knowing she had allowed this to go on too long, she never imagined that a guy like Jeff would be the one to get her over her fears. He was the kind of guy she thought was the scum of the earth, the ones who could get any girl, and knew it. Tonight, was going to be the night she'd work through that last hold, at least she hoped it would be.

Jeff tapped her on the head, "What are you thinking so hard about? You have your forehead all wrinkled," he moved his thumb over it to smooth it out.

"I never thought I'd be here with you, or that someone like you would be the one to help me get over my issues. You are the type of guy I'd either avoid, or lead on, and then dump. Is it wrong of me to judge men, when their good looking, overconfident, take what they want, and walk away?" She knew Jeff was one of those men and he dated many different women and walked away. Why was she letting him through her walls when he would do the same to her?

"Yes, it is wrong, but I understand why you think that way. Before Ben and I came to Boston, he made me realize I might be doing the same thing. I wasn't paying enough attention to my partners. I didn't see that they had deeper feelings for me, than I did for them. Once I understood what I was doing, I stopped. I thought everyone was having fun, going out, even sex. I took what they so freely gave, but after my talk with Ben, I could see that women see things differently. I never meant for it to be like that, I was having a good time, and I figured I would find someone that I felt something more with." Jeff didn't like that about himself once his eyes had opened. "Actually, it's one of the things I'm most ashamed of, although I never forced myself on any one and everything was consensual. Still, I'm not proud of my behavior." They were still sitting in her kitchen, with the food forgotten. He watched her surprised expression by his admission.

"Wow, I never expected you to admit it. We make a crazy pair, you the womanizer, and me the hard ass against womanizers." Kat laughed, Jeff liked the sound, and the little creases around her eyes. "What...why are you looking at me like that?"

"I like seeing you smile, hearing you laugh, you should do it more often." He got up from his chair and placed a hand on each side of her face. Framing it so she had to look at him, "Kat, I stopped dating, not only because I realized it was wrong, but because my mind was on someone else." He slowly leaned in kissing her and she returned the kiss. Pulling her from her seat, taking her hand, he moved them in the direction of Kat's bedroom.

"Jeff."

"I know, it's going to be ok, I'm going to tell you everything I'm going to do, so you can stop me if you don't feel comfortable." He stopped at the end of the bed, turning so her back was to the bottom of the bed. He turned on a small lamp across the room it illuminated the room to a dim glow. He wanted to see her, all of her. "You have a beautiful body, and I don't want you to worry about your scars, they don't bother me." He leaned down so he was looking directly into her eyes. "I will be looking at every part of this sexy physique you work so hard to keep in great shape."

Jeff went to his knees, opening the snap of her jeans, he looked up at her watching him. He kissed the skin that he uncovered. At the same time, he pulled down the zipper exposing her abdomen. Taking the waistband in his hands, he slowly slid her pants down her legs. Kissing the skin as he went, he helped her step out of them. He stood before her, taking the hem of her top, he slowly removed it, then sliding his hands into her hair pulling her in for a kiss. Once his tongue touched hers, his body wanted to drive into her. He had to remind himself slow, easy, and even soft. No sudden moves, he didn't want to freak her out.

Moving down her neck, he said into her ear, "I'm going to undo your bra, you ok with that?" When she nodded, and took a deep breath, his hands moved down her back and unhooked her bra. Sliding his fingers under the straps, he slid them down over her arms, letting it fall to the floor, "I'm going to move down your chest." His mouth sent open kisses as he moved she stood perfectly still. He wanted her to relax, "Breathe, Sunshine, I don't want you to faint on me. God, you don't know how many hours I've spent thinking about doing this very thing."

Kissing the top of her breast, he kept his eyes open this time. He wanted to see her breasts, her nipples. The site of her rose color nipples had him so hard, it hurt. Putting one into his mouth, he ran his tongue over it and slightly dragged his teeth over the little bud. Kat's unguarded sounds sent Jeff to the edge. He could feel her chest move as she breathed, and knew she was trying to hold on to her control. Moving to the other one, he knew she'd tense up, because this one had the long scar that ran from her collarbone down to her nipple. The fine white line didn't bother him, other than to know how it got there.

"You're beautiful, so fucking hot. I could stay right here. Do you have any idea what you do to me?" Sucking her, flicking his tongue over her, he kissed his way up the scar. "I want you lay on the bed," he slowly moved her back. She went willingly.

"Can I move over you? I won't put any body weight on you." She didn't answer right away, and he knew she might say no. "Remember, it's me ok, open your eyes Kat, and look at me." She did, opening her legs so he moved up her body, he placed his hands to each side of her head. Staying on his knees, he leaned in to kiss her, looking in her eyes. Looking for fear, but all he saw was her intense gaze back at him. "I love how you feel, your skin, the taut muscle." Leaning back on his knees, still looking at her, Jeff ran his hands over her chest and down her abs. He slid his fingers into her panties and slowly moved them down her thighs. "God, I want you so badly, I have to keep telling myself, slow." He positioned one finger to her core and deliberately teased his way down her pelvic bone. "What do you want Kat, tell me?"

"I want you naked. You're still fully dressed, and this isn't just about you touching me. I want to be able to feel and touch you. Until you, I've only had sex, just the act, and nothing more. I never wanted to touch or be touched." When he smiled, she said, "Don't go all macho."

"Too late, I can't help it if I love the sound of you wanting to touch me. However, now, if you touched me, I might explode. Why do you think I kept my clothes on? It's so I don't get too crazy and lose control."

"Well, I want them off," she was looking at him between her legs. She watched as Jeff slid off the bed and began removing his clothes. His body was all lean muscle with a board short tan. With his tan being so dark, it was as if someone sprayed the middle of his body in a white strip. Once he was completely naked he asked, "Now what, Sunshine?" She wasn't sure what would come next.

"Come and lay next to me," as he climbed back on the bed, she turned on her side, so they faced each other. His naked body revved up her need to touch him. Sliding her hand to his chest, feeling the contour of his pecks, she watched as Jeff closed his eyes. She let her hand roam further down over his abs. He had mentioned her abs, but his were hard, too. He might not be as obsessed with exercise, but his was all from surfing and being active.

"Telling you how hot you are, is hard for me. The way you have encouraging words for me, I can't." Jeff's eyes opened and when they met hers, she could see his raw desire.

"I don't need that," he skimmed her cheek with his hand, gliding his thumb over her lips. "I'm just glad we're here together, like this."

"This is just so foreign to me, to be lying naked next to a man, feeling your body next to mine, and the need to touch you. To think I would have gone on the way I was for years without knowing what I could feel. I still don't understand why I told you my secrets, because I was convinced you were like every other guy. I can't comprehend the reason, why I trusted you."

"I'm just glad you did, even if knowing your secrets makes me madder than hell that this dude would do what he did to you. How you might not ever trust a man again. I know you told me you didn't do relationships, but when you get back home, please tell me we can continue going out and spending time together."

"I don't know. I'll think about it." One hand still on his chest, she let the other one roam lower, over his hip. There was no more talking, she took charge and rolled him to his back. To the position, she was most comfortable in, but this time she leaned in to put her mouth on him. Starting with his lips, she initiated the kiss, and he let her take control. His hands rested on her ass, not groping, just relaxed. Kat could tell by Jeff's breathing he fought for his own control. To let her do what she wanted, that thought made her smile. She moved to his ear, never speaking dirty to anyone before, she was going to give it her best shot.

In a whisper, she said, "You fucking drive me crazzzy." The way she held out the last word, she felt him take a deep breath.

"Kat," the way he dragged out her name egged her on. Moving lower on his chest, she first kissed the bone of his clavicle. Swiping her tongue into the deep indention there, she heard her own shutter breath. Slowly moving her mouth south over his smooth chest, no hair to get in her way. Gliding her tongue over his nipple, made him tighten his grip on her butt cheeks and she chuckled, her breath blew across his skin, raising goose bumps.

"Kat, I'm not going to be able to take much more without flipping you." That got Kat's attention, how did she feel about that?

"I'm not done yet. I haven't even gotten to your bottom half. Come on, I know you can take it, with all the women you've been with, just a little." She didn't finish, because Jeff had her on her back with a shocked expression on her face.

"I can't let you go any further, and never compare yourself to anyone else, because you aren't the same." He was on top of her, but not really putting all his weight on her. "I need you to understand, I'm not sure why, why this is different, why you make me feel so much more. I know that must scare you because it does me. too, but whatever it is it's strong. I want you like I've never wanted anyone." He slammed his mouth over hers, kissing her hard. When she didn't try to pull away, he relaxed and pressed his cock against her core. He told himself to slow down, he wanted to make love to her, not maul her. Well, that wasn't true, but not this first time. He eased up, because wanting to make sure she was ok with what was going to happen next, he broke the kiss.

"Kat, I need to know what you want." He said a silent prayer and held his breath.

"I want… you inside of me," she said with no fear what-so-ever, because she felt that strong pull, and right now, she didn't want to try to understand it.

Jeff repeated in his head, *go slow, be easy*. He kissed her as he lined up their bodies, the only places they touched, were their lips, and where he entered her. Her legs were open, and he was in between hers. He watched her for any distress, but when she closed her eyes and rolled her head back on the pillow, somehow, he knew she wasn't suffering any affects from her attack.

"Fucking hell," he let slip from his lips. He hadn't even started to move yet and he knew he'd have to hold onto his control. When she pulled her legs up, so they wrapped around his back, with her heels pressing into his butt, he went deeper. Fuck, his cock jerked, he was pulled from his own hell when Kat started pushing her hips up to meet his.

Kat needed more, having Jeff on top of her with him buried deep inside of her was wonderful, but she wanted more. She entwined her hands around Jeff's neck and pulled him to her. He allowed her to pull him to her, kissing her, now moving his lower half slowly, it had Kat in heaven and hell at the same time. "Damnit, Jeff, I need more."

With having nothing between them, just skin to skin and the site of her pleasure, it was going be his undoing. He changed position, leaning back opening his knees to the outside of her legs, cradling her ass, he opened her legs and started to move. He wanted to close his eyes and savor the feeling of being with her but watching her to insure pleasure was what she was feeling, was more important. When she changed her own position, he almost lost it. Kat pulled her knee up to her chest, putting her feet to his chest. Now, he not only went deeper, but also his balls were slapping her ass every time he drove into her. With his hands on her knees, he could watch his dick slide in and out. Holy fuck he was going to come, that familiar tingling sensation that tightening in his balls, pulling them up like a vice grip. He reached down to where they connected to wet his finger. Swirling it around her clit, her eyes flow open, to link with his, and he said, "Come for me, Sunshine."

Her body shattered, stars, bright light shined in her eyes. Kat had no idea how long she laid there. She didn't know what happened after her mind shut down. It was as if she was dreaming, floating, or drifting. Freedom was the only sensation she could define, trapped for so long, she wasn't sure how to feel now.

Her entire life set on a course by one horrible night. Who she was, what she did, where she went, when she did things, all directed by him, and sheer survival. How was she to live her life now that he couldn't hold her back anymore? Who was she? That had always been easy to answer, who she was, because she played that roll and held her shield in place forever. It was the only character she knew how to play, the tough, hard ass, never give in to anyone. She felt him move in close and she didn't want to open her eyes to see the smug look on Jeff's face. How could she have let him in, to see her without her shield? She wished a black hole would open and swallow her, could she pretend to be asleep.

Jeff had a feeling Kat felt a little lost, he wasn't sure what he should do. Make her talk to him, knowing that would make him feel better. Would it be better for her though, there was the question? She couldn't keep quiet forever, and most likely it would be harder the longer she didn't talk about what just happened.

# ~ 13 ~

"Kat, talk to me, I know you're not out cold, and you're not sleeping." When she still refused to budge, he had to resort to drastic measures. She was facing away from him, so he slid his fingers over the curvature of her waist, he could see her attempts to resist. Her back began to quiver. He continued gliding just the tips ever so lightly, a little higher, then lower. He went over her hipbone, and that was it, she snatched his hand to stop his movement.

"You going to talk to me or am I going to have to do a full-fledged tickle," she made a noise and that drew a smile from him. He knew she was stubborn, and it might take some time to get her to open, but he was a patient man. "I've got all night, Sunshine." When she took a deep stubborn breath, he laughed, and that might not have been the best thing to do. She whipped around to face him, madder than he's ever seen her.

"What the hell do you want from me," she snapped and got up out of the bed, grabbing her robe as he watched her march out the door. Where was, she going? This was her house, now it was his turn to take that deep breath, but his was of frustration. Should he follow her or stay put until she came back. What if she didn't come back, that thought had Jeff moving grabbing his boxers as he went to find her. He found her putting workout clothes on in her guest bedroom.

"Kat, what are you doing?" She shoved her legs in a pair of yoga pants and pulled a t-shirt over her head. Not even looking at him she went on, putting socks on her feet, it wasn't until she jammed her feet into sneakers, he realized what she was about to do. Oh, hell no, was she leaving now to go exercise, because it was after one in the morning. He crossed his arms over his chest, blocking the doorway. He knew this was about to get ugly, but she wasn't going to run away from him.

"Get out of my way Jeff, I don't want to hurt you, but I will. So, step aside," she wouldn't look at him.

"No, you're going to have to hurt me Kat, I'm not letting you leave." He watched her as she mustered up the strength to fight with him. "You would rather run, than talk to me. What, you can't even face me, fuck that, Kat. I'm not someone you have sex with, and then just walk away. I told you, I'm not up for that anymore. I understand what tonight meant to you..."

Kat's head snapped up to look in his eye, "You have no fucking clue, what tonight means to me. You can't possibly understand how much I had to give up tonight to get back..." she stopped talking and pressed her lips together. "Get out of my way, I need to get out of here and kick the shit out of something, and if you don't move, then that something is going be you."

Jeff didn't move, he knew she was serious, but he couldn't let her leave. "Make me understand Kat, talk to me, you trusted me before why not now."

"I can't, I need to think," She started pacing the bedroom as if a caged animal, "and if I tell you anymore, I'll never be able to..." She didn't finish.

"You'll never be able to what Kat, pull back, you can walk anytime." Then he added, "Just not right now, it's after one, all the crazies are out there."

She murmured, "I am the crazies, listen Jeff, I need to work this out in my head. Working out is the only way I know how to survive." He could see she was losing stream, her movements slowed. She sat on the bed, and he moved to sit next to her.

"You did what you had to before, but now you have options. By talking to me, it helps me to understand, to know how to support you." He leaned over her legs to pull off her shoes, and she let him. He took that as a good sign. Then he went for the light, and once it was dark, he pulled her up onto the bed.

"Jeff, I can't share this with you, I've shared far too much of myself with you already." She rested her head on his chest as he rubbed her back, and she immediately felt the tension release. Although she knew, it would be back.

"How about you just listen, I'll do the talking. What I know, let's start there. I know you're working on not only the physical aspect, but also the emotional part of a relationship. For far too long you've only had yourself for everything, support, comfort, and now I want in. I want to help you, I want you to trust me, and I want to make love to you."

"Yes, and if I let you have those things, if I open myself up," Kat took a deep breath.

"You're afraid I'll hurt you, but did you ever stop to think that in the end, you might gain more than you lose. Kat, by confiding in me doesn't make you weak, it will empower you."

"I have to think about this, work it out in my head. Giving up so much power to anyone goes against every fiber in my body. What happened earlier was… I just need time and a hard workout."

"I can give you a hard workout," Jeff felt the hard shot she sent to his gut, "Owww."

"How about I give you the hard work out, because that would satisfy me." She rolled on top of him, "You going to give me what I want Jeff? Let me do what I want to you?"

"Kat, I'm not going to agree to what you might want to do to me." Then flipped her so now he was looking down at her, "I want to do whatever you need, but kicking the crap out of me is something I'll like to avoid, if possible." He heard her laugh and the sound made his tension calm. "What's so funny?"

"You are, you want to avoid a fight, and yet you stood in the doorway, knowing I could have pushed my way through." She moved fast to regain the control, and her movement sent them off the bed, onto the floor. They hit the floor with a thud, and both were laughing. Kat took advantage of her position, straddling and kissing him. All her anger gone, the need for him exploded inside her.

"I need you to stay put and not move, I'm going to touch you. I plan to explore everything with my fingers, mouth, and tongue can touch. Are you going to be a good boy for me Jeff?" He placed his hands over his head, and Kat knew he was going to comply with her request. "Good boy, now," She moved her hands up his biceps, lowering her face to his ear. "I find your body hot as hell, and since I've never felt that way about another man." She slid her lips over the stubble on his neck and he lifted his head slightly to give her better access. "I find it necessary," she bit him lightly then licked over the spot. "To discover every inch of you," moving her lips slowly down his shoulder. "You have no idea what you've started," still moving down his body.

Breathlessly, Jeff didn't move as he called on every ounce of control in his body. He wanted to allow her to do this, but he was just a man. Jeff felt his jaw clinch when she skimmed her tongue over his nipple, and he wanted to jump out of his skin when she sucked it into her mouth. She said something, but he couldn't listen and feel her movements, everything she did, or said, went straight to his cock, and it was already hard as nails. Her tits pressed in his crotch wasn't helping his control. He was going to have to stop her, or he would blow soon, like in the next second.

"Kat, you're going to make me cum if you don't stop. I can't take anymore," He could hear the agony in his own voice.

"I want to make you cum, Jeff, I want to watch you," the shaky sound he made gave her a surge of power. Lifting off his body to remove his boxers had her wanting the lights back on. "I want the lights back on, you okay with that?"

If he expected her to bare her sole, he would have to do the same. This was what she needed, and he would show her he could do whatever it took. He lay still, completely naked on the floor once she returned. She stood over him, looking her fill, and he felt his cock harden even more. He tried his best to look as if he was comfortable with her staring at him, but it made him feel unsettling.

"I like you like this, giving yourself up to me."

"Just remember Kat, turn around will be fair play, I will get my turn." He heard her take an unsure breath, but then he saw determination in her eyes. She came down on him again, kissing him on the lips and then a straight path down his chest over his abs. Jeff sucked in air through his nose and clinched his eyes closed. Everything in him screamed, flip her, and take control. He waited with anticipation to see what she was going to do next. Knowing what happened to her, he didn't want her to give him a blowjob, well he did, but not if it brought back terrible memories.

Kat skirted his dick, kissing his hip, and then down his thigh. He released the breath he held, but then she took him in her hand. Kat tight fisted him, moving her hand on him, and Jeff knew it wouldn't be long for her to get what she wanted. It was when she nuzzled her face into his groin and breathed him in, that made him lose it. He let a moan escape as he felt the warm spay of semen across his stomach, and when he could open his eyes, he saw her surprised expression.

"I didn't think that would make you cum, oh God, that was hot." He pulled her up to his side as he took his boxers to wipe his abdomen.

"I don't know why you'd be surprised, you sent my dick in overdrive. Anytime you're in the same room, my body knows. I've never felt anything like this before." He looked over to see her reaction to his words, and if the little mischievous smile didn't tell him, she knew exactly what she was doing to him.

"I guess, I thought you'd need more, you know a…" He stopped her by kissing her, he was going to have to straighten this out with her.

Rolling them again now with him on top, looking down at her he said, "I told you before, I don't need you to do that. I'll be honest here; I've fantasized about your gorgeous lips on my cock." Gliding his finger over her lips, "But, I couldn't ever enjoy anything that would bring you terrible memories, what goes on between us, will always be because you want it. What happens here with me, I don't want any of it to remind you of him, so, if or when, you want to give me a blowjob, then and only then, would I enjoy it. Kat, I don't want you to ever feel pressured into anything."

Kat started laughing, "That's funny, because if you didn't pressure me we wouldn't be here, so I guess a little coercing was needed. I'm here on my guest bedroom floor, with you on top of me. I don't feel the least bit frightened, or any flashbacks, and that would have never happened without you. I still have some thinking to do about what occurred earlier, but I would imagine it's going to take quite a few workouts to totally work that out in my head."

"Let's go back to your bed, I'm sure it's more comfortable than this floor. And there I can help you work off your mad." As he pulled her to her feet he said, "So, were you really going to hurt me? You understand why I couldn't let you leave. I would never want to hold you against your will."

"I don't know if I could have actually hurt you, I've never been in that situation before. I could hurt you, if you were attacking me, but just because I'm mad, I don't know. Jeff, I've lived in this city most of my life and gone where and when I wanted to, I would have been okay. I can take care of myself, I'd never leave this apartment if I didn't feel safe."

They walked to her room and Jeff couldn't help feeling proud of her for everything she had overcome. He turned to her, "Kat, you know you are an amazing woman, not just because you've survived something no one should have to go through, but because you are strong inside and out. I want you to know I admire how you live your life."

"I wouldn't go that far. I've lived my life protecting myself from everything, a predator, to emotional pain. Not trusting anyone, never giving too much away, and somehow you managed to do both, and I've let you in. I still don't understand why that is, but here we are, with you knowing more about me, than anyone in this world. You have no idea how much that scares me, to have you know everything there is to know about me."

"I would never intentionally hurt you or use anything I know against you. You should know, I realize what this means to you. I'd still like you to talk to me about what happened earlier, because I need to understand if it happens again."

"I'm fine," Kat started to pull away and Jeff let her go. "We need to get some sleep, you have a flight, and I have work in the morning." She went to her dresser and pulled out a silk nightgown and began to change. He still stood naked and once she removed her leggings and her top, Jeff couldn't help his body's reaction to the site of her.

"Kat," she turned as the cloth slid over her body. He could feel her withdrawing from him, not wanting to push her, yet he didn't want to allow her to retreat. Going to her, he wrapped his arms around her, "I want to see you when you get back, this is not over just because I'm heading home. I want to take you out on the town, maybe dancing where I can actually touch you. Take you to the movies, all the things people in a relationship do. What do you think about that?"

"Obviously, I have more to think about while you're gone, I'll consider it. I never wanted a relationship, and I'm not sure I'd be any good at it. Besides, if we go out in California, everyone in your family will have us married with kids."

Jeff chuckled because he knew she was right, but what was wrong with that? "Did you tell Liz that we had sex? Because you know as well as I do, if she knows than so does my mother, and everyone else. Not that they wouldn't be able to figure it out on their own, I'm not going to hide how I feel about you, Kat."

"And just how do you feel about me Jeff?"

"I think you know, but just in case you haven't figured it out." He put her hand on his chest over his heart, "I can't help how my heart pounds in my chest or how the blood rushes in my ears, when your close. I want to spend every minute I can with you, getting to know what makes your heart pound. You are not only the most challenging woman I've ever met, but also the most intriguing. You don't show all your cards, you hold them close, only showing one at a time. Then there's how my body responds to yours, how I can't help feeling aroused, no matter how many times we fool around or touch each other, it never seems to be enough. As much as I want to be the one to help you though the shit you went through. I'm not doing it just for you Kat, because I need you," then Kat kissed him. He walked her backwards to the edge of the bed. He had to have her one more time. Removing the silk gown in one full sweep, and discarding it, Jeff wanted to make love to Kat slow. Try to show her just how much he needed her.

After having her emotions strung like a rubber band, Kat didn't know what to think anymore. She needed to consider what she was doing and why, why now, with him. The only thing she did know, was how he made her body feel. Free from every inhibition she ever felt, the fear, the anxiety, and alarms that normally went off in her head, gone. Well yes, she heard alarms going off, but for totally different reasons. Feeling as though she could become addicted to him, to what he was offering concerned her. Could she trust herself to recognize when she should hold back, because now that the gate opened, she wasn't sure it could shut again. The key to her freedom tucked away for so long, almost lost forever. Never thinking someone like Jeff could be so significant in unlocking those emotions.

Jeff moved over her body, looking in his eyes, those beautiful golden brown eyes, warm, and caring looking back at her. The weight of his body didn't instill the need to escape, fight, or resist, in any way. Her want for him ran deeper than the need to control, she allowed him to have complete control. Jeff had their hands clasped over her head as he kissed her. Tongues mingled as he pressed his entire body to hers, forcing hers up to meet his, told her just how much she wanted him. Closing her eyes to revel in the amazing pleasure, a man's hard body, the weight of him swarmed her head. Before she knew it, she heard herself plead for more.

"Jeff, please," hearing the desperation in her voice, she felt his hand slide between them, and he slipped two fingers inside her. Slowly, he moved them, her hips encouraged him to move faster, but he kept his pace. His open mouth kisses nudged her head to the side.

"Open your eyes, Sunshine, I need to see your beautiful baby blues. I'm not going to be rushed here, this time we're going slow." When her eyes again connected with his, he asked, "Do you trust me?"

"Yes," strangely enough, it was true. She trusted him more than any male, except her father, in over fifteen years. He removed his fingers and began sliding the head of his penis over her clit. The sensation had her eyes wanting to close, soaking in the awareness that spread throughout her body. Feeling how intense the surge that shot through her body as he entered her, she needed to stay coherent. After losing consciousness the last time, she needed to breathe. Jeff caged her face with his hands, as he shifted in and out of her, her hands held onto his forearms, as she felt she could see his soul. He didn't seem to be holding anything back from her.

Slowly torturing them both, Jeff's body penetrated her and then withdrew. Each stroke, deliberate and precise, made her body melt, from the inside out. Soon, she would be a pile of mush.

"Do you feel it Kat, do you feel the connection we have to each other? I should have known after the first time we met and couldn't get you out of my head."

"Known what?"

"That you would be my downfall, the one I can't walk away from." She started to protest, and he kissed away her words. He started moving faster and she couldn't think of what she was going to say. Feeling her building orgasm coming on, her body tightened. Jeff tilted his hips and slammed into her, sending her insides into convulsion of spasms. The twinkling started again behind her eyes, immediately opening them, she caught Jeff's reaction. The cords in his neck strained as his teeth clinched, his own release was close. Clinching every muscle inside tight on him, he slammed into her one last time, and that sent Jeff over the edge. Watching his reaction, seeing, and hearing his pleasure, then his weight rested on her, as if he couldn't hold himself up. Feeling his body weight comforted her. Closing her eyes, feeling so tired, sleep would claim her soon. Sighing, her contentment, Jeff's head popped up. Opening her eyes once again, he stared down at her. She could see his hesitation, so she said, "I'm fine, just tried." Kat was surprised by his reaction when all he did was nod and got up. What no talking about what happened between them, no cuddling? Watching his bare ass as he walked to the bathroom, she thought isn't that what she wanted. Not to have to talk about them or what might be going on in her head.

Kat pulled a few tissues from the box on her nightstand to clean up with. When Jeff returned with a washcloth for her, she could feel the tension in the room, why did she sense walls were going up and they weren't hers. Taking the cloth from him, she noticed he wasn't looking directly at her.

"Something wrong Jeff?" She asked as she still watched him, not liking when he went silent.

"I'm going to shower off really quick, I'll be right back, and then we can talk." He disappeared and Kat couldn't help wondering what he was thinking.

Jeff fought the overwhelming feeling to tell Kat exactly how he was beginning to feel about her. Knowing she would never accept them at this point, so early in their relationship. Needing time to consider how he'd precede, Jeff didn't want to run her off before they even got started. Stepping under the water, he took a deep breath. Thinking about them making love, it was like nothing he'd ever experienced. Being with Kat excited him as much as his first sexual encounter, but he now knew what he was doing, and was at a point in his life he knew what this meant.

Rinsing his body as quickly as possible because he knew if he left Kat too long, she would talk herself right out of what they just shared. Of course, it didn't help that he pulled away from her first, right after they made love. As much as he needed time to think, he didn't want to give her time to change her mind about them. Stepping out of the shower, Jeff rapidly dried off. Moving back to the bedroom, Jeff noticed the lights off. That worked best to get Kat to talk to him. When she had to look at him, she didn't share her feelings.

Moving to join Kat in bed, she was facing away from him again. Pulling Kat into his body, she had put on in her silk gown. Liking the feel of it, Jeff stroked his hand over her breast and said, "Kat, I know we need to talk."

"No, we don't," she said quietly. "I have to get up in only a few hours, and I have a lot of work to do, before I need to return to Liz."

"Kat, listen to me, I'm working through my own feelings about us making love. How it's made me feel, how strong the pull is that I have for you."

"Stop, I need sleep. I can't think anymore, I've had my emotions stretched as far as they can go, and my head is spinning. Give me time, okay Jeff. We'll talk about this when I come back."

Knowing he shouldn't push her, but he couldn't help thinking if they didn't at least establish some ground rules, he'd be starting all over again once she returned to California. He kissed her cheek and said, "Good night, Kat, and this isn't over."

~ ~ ~ ~ ~ ~

The moment Jeff's mind became aware. He felt the weight, tugging and pulling on his chest, opening his eyes to find a gray face staring at him. His green eyes outlined in black didn't look so impressed with him. Jeff took in the hair coming out of his ears, his pink nose, and his grayish white chin. This cat in his face was a puff of gray hair. "Mr. Puss, I presume," Jeff turned to where Kat should have been in the bed. Not surprised when he found it was empty, he knew last night that she would withdraw from him. Trying not to take it personally, he'd move forward, because now he knew there was no going back. Jeff moved his hand over the cat's head and the cat rewarded him with rumbling purring. He was going home today, and he didn't even know when Kat would return, but he would use this time to plan, how he was going to woo Kat, so she wouldn't be able to withdraw from him again.

Removing Mr. Puss from his chest, Jeff got up. Starting with a shower, then he would call Robert to order Kat another music box. Grabbing his phone as he went, he noticed a few missed calls. Going through them, he deleted the ones from women he no longer had any interest in, but the ones from his mother he'd return, he knew he'd have to be careful, because she could be very compelling when it came to getting information. He even had a call from Liz, and he knew she wasn't that far from his mother when it came to wanting to know what was going on between him and Kat. Debating whether to stop by Kat's office one more time before he had to catch his flight, he decided to text her instead.

Pulling up the text screen on his phone, he started writing.

Jeff: Woke to Mr. Puss kneading my chest, looking me over and an empty bed.

Jeff thought about the last part of the text but hit send anyway. He didn't know if Kat would respond at all, much less anytime soon, so he went to getting his bags packed. When he heard his phone ping, he couldn't help the smile that crossed his face. Swiping his phone to life, he read her response.

Kat: Did he look unimpressed? Don't worry, he looks at all my house guests the same way.

What the hell did she mean about all her houseguest, he knew Shay had said only Liz and Paige had stayed with Kat. Hammering back, he wrote.

Jeff: All, your house guests, ah?

He waited, but she didn't text him back right away. So, he texted her again, asking what he really wanted to know.

Jeff: When will you be back?

Kat: When I can satisfy my boss, a day, or two, maybe more, I'm not sure.

After being with Kat for two nights, Jeff wanted her with him every night. Knowing he shouldn't, he did it any away and type, Jeff: When you get back will you stay with me?

"No," her response came immediately. Not that he was surprised, but he was still disappointed. Her next text cut off any further communication for now.

Kat: I have a meeting, text me when you arrive home.

Moving forward, it was going to take all the finesse Jeff had to convince Kat to stay with him.

Jeff was ready to go home. This trip had been a success all the way around, accomplishing everything he set out to do. Shafford Boards wanted Jacobs Surf Shop to carry their line. Even wanting to invest in enlarging the building itself, to accommodate their growing line of merchandise. Jeff took pride in knowing just how good this could be for the family business. He took one more look around Kat's apartment before he had to head out. He'd think about her here alone and what the last two days has meant for them. Closing the door and hearing the lock latch, he moved to the elevator. Trying not to think that by closing the door to her apartment, he was also closing the door on them. He wasn't going to let that happen.

Kat read Jeff's text again about staying with him when she went back to California. She was in a battle, between her mind, that thought she was crazy for getting involved with Jeff altogether, and her body, that wanted him and his touch more than her next breath. In her head, she went over every reason, every point why she needed to stay away from him. Once she'd made up her mind that staying away from him was in her best interest, her body would scream NO. Always in control of her body and mind, before he came along and set her world upside down. This conflict that raged in her, consumed her. Even going to the gym early this morning didn't do anything to settle her mind.

Giving herself up to him wasn't an option, and neither was walking away. How had she gotten herself into this predicament, and how in the world could she get herself out and survive. The floodgates were unlocked, wide open and there was no closing them again, not until all the water had passed through. Knowing what that meant for her, she had to hang on, ride the wave until she crashed, drowned, or came to the surface.

Closing her eyes, taking a cleansing breath, Kat attempted to calm her mind and body. As she relaxed, the image of Jeff on her floor with his hands over his head passed through her mind. Moving her hands over his body, feeling his tanned skin under her fingers, giving her what she needed from him. The raw power she felt by touching him, feeling free to do what she wanted. It wasn't only touching him, but him touching her that set her on fire. Having the need to be touched was new for her, making her feel more like a woman, a woman that was beautiful, desirable, and that was all because of Jeff.

Never wanting or caring about how a man saw her, was how she lived her life. Knowing she carried her scars on the outside, but they also ran deep on the inside, that didn't seem to effect how Jeff saw her, or how he didn't seem to care about the walls he'd have to climb over. The only man to see the real person, and apparently, he likes her for who she is.

# ~ 14 ~

Once on the plane, Jeff had time to sit back and replay every touch, every word they shared together. Closing his eyes, Kat's image in the shower came to mind. It was the first time he saw her naked body, the first time he ever had sex without a condom. Feeling her breasts in his hands, how they fit perfectly. The color of her nipples, how they tightened when he played with them. How her skin smelled and how soft it was when he touched her. He could feel his lower half stirring. God, he didn't want to stop thinking about their time together. The way Kat's ribcage stuck out, because of how lean she was, along with the flattest stomach he'd ever seen on a woman. Then, there was the beautiful butterfly tattoo that started just above her hipbone that continued into the crease of her leg and pelvis. The tattoo covered the scar that he knew she received from that douchebag. He didn't want to think about him, not when he was thinking about them.

He went back to the tattoo, the little stars at the top that went into delicate curved lines that attached to the wings of the butterfly. The inner part of the wings colored with pinks fading into purple, and the outer had blues fading into yellow. With several swirls positioned at the bottom and then going into tiny stars as it ended near her very smooth pussy. *Oh, hell yeah, when he got Kat alone again, he was going to show that tattoo homage.* He hadn't wanted to make a big deal about it before, because he didn't want to make Kat uncomfortable. If he kept thinking about her this way, he might join the mile-high club all by himself. Laughing at the thought of going to the restroom to jerk off, man, he had it bad for her, even her red toenails turned him on. He needed to think about something else.

The thought of how he called his mother just before the plane took off, so he couldn't talk about everything that happened. However, knowing she would be at the airport to pick him up, he needed to come up with something to tell her, without telling her anything. The thought of his mother did the trick, his dick relaxed. Maybe he could get his mother on board to help him convince Kat to stay with him. No, he X out that idea, although, he knew he couldn't keep her entirely in the dark either. Well, he had the next four hours to figure out what he would tell his mother.

~ ~ ~ ~ ~ ~

Today had been one of the longest days, and Kat didn't know what she needed more. To work out or go home and sleep because she needed both. Her mind needed the workout, and her body needed sleep. After getting no sleep last night and working out this morning, Kat felt spent. She kept looking at the clock, trying to figure when Jeff should be home. Calling Liz was out of the question because she had been avoiding her calls. Not wanting to talk about Jeff and what was going on with him, or anything pertaining to that man. Because Kat had not thought of anything else, no matter how hard she tried, he was there. His smile, his touch, and most of all, what she'd do about him. The decision made, she was going home to take a nice warm bath and then go to bed, even if she had to take something to help her sleep.

Kat gathered her things and headed for the door when her phone rang. Before she could control her reaction, hope filled her. Stopping in front of the elevator, she pulled her phone from her bag, looking at the caller. Liz, okay she'd tell her she was about to get into the elevator and would call her back.

"Hey Liz, I'm about to step into the elevator, I'll call you right back."

Kat heard Liz say, "Wait," as she almost hung up.

"Liz, I've had a very long day," Kat paused before saying, "Please let me call you back. I'm heading home to take a long bath, I'll call you then, and I promise to tell you whatever you want to know, okay."

"You promise to call me back?"

"Yes, give me an hour." At this point, Kat would spill her guts. After racking her brain all day, she might as well get Liz's take on her situation. Saying good-bye to Liz, Kat was on her way home. Sitting in the cab, Kat closed her eyes. She could feel her head bobbing as she drifted. It didn't take long before she was home, going into her apartment, she noticed a note stuck to her door. Not caring what it said, she pulled it free and stuffed it into her coat pocket. Moving to her bedroom, Kat kicked off her shoes and removed clothes as she went, turning on the water for her bath, as if she was on autopilot. She went to the sink, looking at her reflection. Not recognizing the person looking back at her, she never looked so exhausted. Her eyes appeared dull, lifeless. What was going on with her? She felt so out of control, always dominating and in charge of her life, this distraught feeling wasn't something she was familiar with, at least not in a long time. It was a feeling she didn't want to feel ever again.

Turning off the water, Kat stepped into the warm bath. Resting her head on the edge of the tub, her phone rang. "Shit, I forgot to grab my f-in phone," stepping back out she walked soaking wet to where she dropped her bag. She missed the call, but knew it was most likely Liz. Moving back into the tub, she swiped the screen, and sure enough, it was Liz. Kat dialed her number, and the phone barely rang before Liz answered.

"Liz."

"You said you'd call me back," Liz sounded concerned and quite frankly, Kat was, too.

"I just got into the tub and forget my phone. I had every intention of calling you back, but as I said, I've had a long day. So, give me a break, okay."

"What is going on with you?"

Kat took a deep breath and knew she was going to have to come clean with Liz. "I have so much going on with me, I almost don't know where to begin. I have something to tell you."

Liz interrupted, "Finally."

"This is not about Jeff. This is about something that happened to me. Jeff has just brought everything to the surface. Only one other person knows about this, well two people, I've kept this secret for a long time." Liz was quiet on the other end, so Kat went on. "When I was a teenager, I was raped," Kat heard Liz's gasp.

"I dealt with it in my own way, this is why, I am the control freak that I am. I've had issues with men, particularly men like Jeff. Because he reminds me of the guy…"

"Oh, Kat."

"In some ways, Jeff is just like him, and yet, he is so different. He managed to figure out so much about me, by watching me. No other man has ever taken the time to see past my aggressive behavior. To see the person under the huff and guff, I don't know what to do with that. He wants to help me work through my hang-ups, my head says run, but my body wants him. The way Jeff makes me feel, it's so unfamiliar, nothing I've ever felt before. The need for a man, his touch, it scares me, Liz. I don't know what to do with that." Now that she said the words aloud she knew what the problem is, she's afraid she will fall for him, and fall hard.

"Kat, you have to know Jeff would never hurt you. He may have a reputation, but he has changed. Ben and I have had many discussions on this subject. Ben told me Jeff stopped dating all together before they came to Boston. I don't know if that had anything to do with you, or the fact that he finally realized how much of a womanizer he was. Either way, he has changed. If you want my opinion, I think he has true feelings for you."

Kat drew a deep breath, and released it, "I'm not afraid of him hurting me physically, because I could kick his ass, but I'm not sure I have the emotional capacity to handle a real relationship. This is what Jeff is asking of me. I'm afraid I won't be good at it, and he will become tired of working so hard."

"There are no guarantees Kat, for anyone. Look at me, for instance, with Ben, I never thought in a million years I would be married again, much less, having a new family. All I'm saying is, you're going to have to try, and see where this goes. If things don't work out, you will be fine, because you're a strong woman. I didn't think I needed a man either, and now I don't know what I would do without Ben. The sex is a big bonus, too, well after the babies are born and the tubes are tied tight, it will be again." Liz laughed at her own joke and the sound loosened the tightness in Kat's chest. Kat's phone singled that she had a text message, hoping it was Jeff, she told Liz to hold on. The number was unknown, but it had a California area code so most likely it was from Jeff.

Opening it up, Kat read, made it home safely, but just by the skin of my teeth. My mom picked me up from the airport, so just imagine how that ride went. Miss, you already. J.

Kat laughed aloud, but she was still talking to Liz so she closed the text screen, she would text him back once she got off the phone with Liz.

"What's so funny?" Liz asked.

"I just received a text from Jeff, he's home and Linda picked him up so." She heard Liz chuckling, because everyone knows just how Linda can be when it comes to her children.

"She gave him the non-interrogation talk. I'm not interrogating you, just tell me what I want to know, talk."

"I'm sure, all I know is, I'm glad it was him and not me," and the thought that she would return to California, who would pick her up, hopefully it would be Jeff and not his mother.

They talked a little while longer and Kat did feel better, now she wanted to text Jeff back.

Kat: Glad you made it home safe although, I'm not sure if you are in one piece. I'm also pleased it was you and not me. (hee, hee) I've given your proposal of spending time together when I get back some thought. Maybe.

She hit send, wondering if he would text back. Getting out of the now cold water, she dried off and her phone pinged. Swiping her screen to life, she couldn't help the thrill that passed through her.

Jeff: Happy to know how you feel about my welfare. You will get your turn with my mother. She knows we're together. So, there is no maybe about it. When do you come back? I've thought of nothing else, except how we can work through your hang-ups. ;)

Kat didn't know what to say to his text, his mother knows we're together, just great. So much for not jumping into a relationship, Jeff was not going to take no for an answer. She had to ask herself did she want Jeff to give her no choice. If this went bad, she could always say he pushed for this, a relationship with her. She laughed at her earlier thoughts of having sex with him and kicking him to the curb, because now that she had, there was no kicking him anywhere. Somehow, he crept under her skin and now he had imbedded himself there.

Now knowing what she'd write, she started typing.

Kat: So, I have no choice in the matter, fine, but know if this goes bad, it will be your fault. What exactly do you have in mind for my hang-ups? I will be back the day after tomorrow and you had better not send your mother to pick me up. Not if you know what's good for you. What am I thinking, you want a relationship with me, so I know you don't know what's good for you.

She hit send and went to get ready for bed. Now, not so confused, but still tired, Kat needed sleep. The thought of spending time with Jeff, having sex with him, didn't scare her anymore. The forever part, she still didn't think she'd be any good at that. Boy, was she getting ahead of herself. *One-step at a time, Kat,* she told herself. Climbing into bed, looking over to the place Jeff slept the last two nights. Suddenly, the bed felt too big, and empty. Sleeping with Jeff was a first for her.

Kat got back out of the bed and went in search of her cat, he will sleep with her. She found him in her guest room, as she disturbed the sleeping gray puff of hair, giving her a dirty look, she picked him up. "Too bad, Mr. Puss, I need you, and you owe me, I feed you." She said to the very unimpressed cat. Placing him in Jeff's spot on the bed, the cat circled and laid down, closing his eyes. Now she wouldn't have to sleep alone, she found the thought unsettling, when had she ever wanted to sleep with anyone before.

On her nightstand, her phone was blinking, knowing Jeff had texted her back made her smile. Picking it up, she hoped he would tell her what he had in mind to work out her hang-ups. Looking over at Mr. Puss, she recognized he was a poor substitute for the real thing.

Jeff: If you only knew what I've been thinking about, I can't get that butterfly tattoo out of my mind. How I want to give it extra attention the next time we're together. Do you have any idea what you do to me? J. :-}~

Looking at the little face Jeff put after his initial, left no doubt about what he was thinking. The long drawn out day seemed to disappear, and arousal replaced tiredness. Although, Kat knew she needed sleep, sex-texting did have its appeal. She decided she wouldn't text him back and see what he did. Turning out the light she puffed up her pillow pulling her comforter to her chin, and she closed her eyes. Wondering if he texted her again, she dozed.

"Listen here bitch, you're a fucking tease." He pressed his face into hers as he shouted, "It's your own fault you're here." Kat shuddered awake, still seeing his callous eyes pinning her, she turned on the light. Trying to calm her breathing, she must have drifted off. As she sat up and noticed her phone blinking, not sure if she wanted to know what Jeff had to say. Her curiosity got the best of her, so looking at her phone, she had three messages unread and one missed call, all from Jeff. Now looking at the time, she had been asleep for hours, and it was late.

First message. Jeff: What no come back? Speechless, never thought I'd see the day. J.

Second message. Jeff: Kat, you there, hey, are you okay? J.

Third message. Jeff: Damn it, Kat say something, so I know you're alright!

Skipping the voice mail, she decided to call him. "I'll just explain that I fell asleep." The phone didn't even ring two times before he picked up.

"What the hell, Kat?" His voice was of anger.

"Hey, don't use that tone with me. I fell asleep, I'm tired, and it has been a long day, ok." She heard his intake of air, as if relieved.

"I'm sorry, it's just, I'm a million miles away and when you didn't answer your phone, it never was more evident just how far I am. If something happened to you…"

"Nothing happened to me, Jeff I'm a big girl and have taken care of myself for a long time. I don't need a man to protect me. Remember your three hours behind us on the East Coast, and you're not a million miles away."

"Sure, feels like it, damn I need to get my heart to stop pounding. I've paced this apartment a hundred times I've worn out the rug. When you didn't answer my text, I thought I might have said something... um... wrong."

"I'm fine," she said the words even though she didn't feel fine the dream shook her.

Jeff was quiet for a minute, "Kat, why do I get the feeling you're not fine?" She didn't respond and he said, "Kat, what aren't you telling me?"

"I had a dream, satisfied?" Why was she telling him this, it's not as if he could see her? Now that she had opened her mouth about the rape, it was as if she couldn't stop. Holding back her feelings, showing nothing was her claim to fame, the queen of the Poker face.

"FUCK...I'm so sorry Kat," she heard rustling in the background.

"Why are you sorry, Jeff, you didn't do anything."

"Because Kat, I wasn't there for you," he sounded frustrated and pissed.

"Jeff, I've handled these dreams for years, I don't have them very often. That's why I work out so hard, it helps keep them silent. When my body is exhausted, my mind knows I've muted the demons. All this talk about what happened has pulled everything front and center, that's all. Once I put it in the past where it belongs, things will settle down."

"So, what you're telling me, the dreams are my fault. I made them front and center by pressing you to tell me."

"No, I had one before I told you, and it has more to do with the change in my routine," she couldn't let him take the blame or feel guilty.

"Kat."

"No Jeff, I can't let you take any blame. If anything, you've helped me, yes, all the ugliness has resurfaced, but I'm facing it for the first time. I can't tell you how many times, I wished I could move completely past what happened to me. So, don't be sorry, because I'm not. If I can find some kind of normalcy for my life, it will be worth it." Knowing she wanted this change wasn't going to help her recognize who she is anymore. If she lets go of her anger, and always being on the defense, who will she be? *Can I totally take down my shields because I know I'll never be a victim again? I've made sure of that, but if I stopped fighting, will there be calm in my head, body, and soul. I've lived with this for far too long, I deserve peace, but this has made me who I am. Where do I go from here?*

"Kat, you still there?" Jeff asked, he must have said something, and she was quiet for too long.

"Sorry, I was just thinking."

"About?"

"Who I am, because of all this, and who will I be after..." Kat stopped talking, mostly because she was thinking aloud, and not wanting Jeff to see or know too much.

"You will be the same strong, stubborn, bullheaded woman I know and lo...um like. You will always stand up for yourself, being the toughest, kick ass, sexy as hell woman." Kat had to smile at his description of her because she was all those things. Well maybe the last part was Jeff's take on her because she never cared about being sexy. She couldn't help the tiny twinge of pleasure that coursed through her body knowing how he felt about her body. Knowing it wasn't just the physical aspect, he was attracted to, and this feeling was so foreign to her, a man wanting to be with her.

"I have to get some sleep, because I still have to get through tomorrow." The weariness was seeping back in and knowing she could dream again wasn't going to get her the sleep she needed.

"I wish I was there, next to you."

"Sorry, but your side of the bed is occupied at the moment." Kat snickered at Jeff's huff.

"Is it now, by whom may I ask? Male or female, oh, I know, who is with you. He's gray, very fluffy, and has green eyes."

"Why yes, you just described my most favorite male. He is very loyal to me, loving and he never wants to leave. He loves to cuddle, rubbing himself on me, wanting me to stroke him all over." Kat had to hold back the chuckles that wanted to escape.

"Holy shit, I'm jealous of your freaking cat. Damn, I want to cuddle, rub myself on you, and Sunshine, you can stroke me anywhere you want." Now Kat did burst out laughing.

"Mr. Puss knows he has it good with me." The cat lifted his head at the mention of his name, stretched and leaped off the bed, *well so much for him not wanting to leave me.*

"Can you catch a flight after work tomorrow?" Jeff's question surprised her.

"I wouldn't make it out there at a decent time, not to mention how tired I'd be. I wouldn't make someone come pick me up at that hour and your mother won't appreciate me coming in at that time, either." Why in the world would she ever want to leave so late, although, the time change was always better going than coming home?

"I was just thinking if you came a day early, you could come and stay with me, without anyone knowing you were here. I'd save you from my mother picking you up, and the third degree." The thought had its merits, what would she be like when she finally made it to him.

"I'll check into any flights leaving tomorrow night, but I'm not going to promise anything. Just so you know, there is a huge possibility you won't get the results you desire."

"Just so you know, I don't think I'm alone when it comes to desires and the possibilities. If you come and nothing happens, I still get to hold you and have you to myself before everyone starts asking questions."

"If that is what you really want, I will do my best, but in the meantime, I need to get some sleep. Especially if there are possibilities involved, then I need my rest." The sound on the other end of the phone was of Jeff's amusement.

"Is it terrible that I don't want to let you off the phone? I just left, and yet, now that we've gotten closer, I can't help wanting you." Kat had no idea what to say to that, because the changes in Jeff were as if someone flicked a switch. Before, his attentions were on many women, and now he seemed to be focusing solely on her. This kind of devotion, the music box, the flowers, and him just wanting to help her, gave her an amazing feeling. Wanting to trust those feelings was hard, this was all new to her, and even if Jeff had changed, he could always change back.

"Kat, did you fall asleep on me?" His question snapped her out of her thoughts.

"No, I'm here, but I need to go. I didn't get any sleep last night, and today I've felt of out sorts." Knowing how Jeff might take her admission, she quickly added, "I just need to wrap my head around all these new feelings. Dealing with a man's wants and desires is something I know nothing about, and of course, trusting in what I don't know, isn't easy for me."

"Okay Kat, sleep, I can't wait for you to be here."

"Good night," Kat hit end. She rolled over looking at the spot he had been last night. Grabbing the pillow, she pulled it in close to her chest and closed her eyes. She told herself no more thinking tonight, just sleep, no dreaming. If she were lucky, that would be all that happened in the next six hours.

Jeff sat in his bed, thinking that she might be there by tomorrow. Knowing he wasn't playing a very good hand of poker. He wanted her to know he wasn't just playing games with her. If that meant he had to show his hand, then that's exactly what he'd do. Kat had trust issues, and if he could help it, he wasn't going to give her any reason to not trust him. Having the experience with other women, he knew how some played games. Kat didn't understand the rules to the game of love. She never had someone care for her, to show her how it feels when her wants and needs come first.

Looking around his bedroom, he thought how she would see it. He had to clean his apartment before she came. Not that he was a complete slob, would it be up to her standards, because she had a housekeeper to keep her apartment spotless. That thought pulled him out of his bed, going into the kitchen to get his cleaning supplies. No time like the present, Jeff started in the bathroom. With thoughts of her coursing through him, he cleaned. His mother would be proud, not that she will know, because if he could, he'd keep Kat's presence unknown to everyone.

# ~ 15 ~

When Kat walked through the lobby of her building the next morning, the clerk at the desk stopped her. Telling her, she had a package that didn't fit into her mailbox, and it was stamped fragile, so he wanted to hand deliver it to her. Taking the box, she noticed the return address, she had a good idea what was inside and who had sent it. Instead of bringing it back upstairs, she just tucked it in her bag. She would open it once she was in her office, where she would have more time to admire the music box, she knew that was inside. Knowing what was inside, didn't stop the anticipation she felt about getting something Jeff sent her.

Kat arrived in the office before Vikki, which she knew she would, going on the theory of early in, early out. Now that Jeff put the idea in her head of spending the night with him, she wanted to make it happen, even if that meant coming in early, and missing her morning workout. Once at her desk, she pulled the box from her bag. Unwrapping it felt as if she was a child on Christmas. No one had sent her things just because. The box beyond the cardboard box was a smaller box wrapped in blue paper. Slowly gliding her finger under the seams, so she didn't rip the beautiful paper, taking a deep breath, she opened the inner white box. Pulling back the tissue paper, she revealed the blue glass Tiffany butterfly music box. Unfolding the sides of the white box to free the delicate treasure and carefully lifting the breathtaking piece, she wound the key, holding her breath until the music started to play. She knew the song well. It was one of her favorites, Butterfly by Jason Mraz. Swallowing hard, fighting back tears, she placed the box on her desk and listened. Then she noticed a white envelope amongst the white tissue paper. Jeff had sent a card, and on the last card, he stated the music box would be one of many. Sliding the card free he wrote. What was once ugliness, has changed into a beautiful butterfly.

Kat stared at the hand-written card that Jeff didn't sign. He must have bought the music box before he went home. Thinking about the note that was on her door, she went to her coat where she stuffed the message, and sure enough, it said she had a fragile package waiting for her. It was too early to call or text Jeff to thank him. She could always thank him in person. Unfortunately, she didn't have the time to dwell on the meaning behind his words. There was work to be done if she wanted to get to him sooner.

Kat's luck held, she worked through her day with efficiency and got out early. Knowing she could be in California in about seven hours, had her moving quickly. Getting her bags from home and heading straight to the airport was her plan. Vikki had booked a non-stop flight from LaGuardia Airport that left at 6:45. She would have to rush to make it in time to get through security. Texting Jeff her flight information and her response from him, was a smiley face. She realized she also felt a little giddy, sneaking around.

She made it to the airport, sitting and waiting for them to call her flight, when her phone beeped. Freeing her phone, that stupid giddy feeling came over her again. Feeling as if she was a teenager, she read his text.

Jeff: Can't wait until you get here, Sunshine. I even cleaned for you. I didn't want you to think I live like a pig. But, I don't have a Shay cleaning after me. J.

Kat laughed, the thought of Jeff cleaning was funny. Jeff was right, no one was as good as having Shay around, and she had worked a long time for Kat. The woman cleaned like no other and did whatever Kat asked her to, Kat valued loyal people. Even though, Shay had told Jeff how she didn't entertain men at her apartment. Responding to his text, she wrote.

Kat: I'm looking forward to being there, too. I'm waiting for them to call my flight. You never told me why you call me that. I think it was to make fun of my hair. By the way, I absolutely love the music box. Thank you. Oh, their calling my flight. See you on the other side. K.

Jeff had to wait until she got there, for now, he worked on getting the space Shafford Boards required. The surf shop had to devote a percentage of their square footage to the new product line. Moving the entire store around wasn't fun, but with the help of the new dude Ben hired, it wasn't so bad. This new dude was like a linebacker, he picked up displays as if they weighed nothing. He's Hawaiian, his name is Leo— something or another. Thank God, he goes by just Leo, although it is fun to watch his mother trying to pronounce his full name, as she does with all of us. Leo wasn't as tall as him or Ben, but he was still big, his chest was full, and his arm were like pythons. He had jet-black hair tied back, and looked as if you didn't want to make him mad. Jeff hadn't seen him surf yet, but Owen told him that Leo was great, and he knew his way around selling a surfboard. As much as it felt weird to have someone new working in the store, Jeff was relieved. It seemed everyone was going in different directions these days.

Ben with a new wife and twins on the way, him with Kat, and the new franchise and Dannie, well, he wasn't sure what she was up to these days, Owen coming and going when he had time to work around school, and then there was his mother, helping Liz while Kat was away and getting into her children's personal business. Thinking about the ride back from the airport came to mind, how relentless his mother was about finding out what was going on between him and

Kat. It didn't take long before he gave in and told her they were together and would be dating.

Leo pulled Jeff from his thoughts when he spoke, "Who's that?" Jeff turned to see who Leo was referring to and saw Dannie walking into the store. Jeff turned to Leo and watched him, watching his sister go down the hall and duck into his mother's office. "That would be my sister, and by the way you just watched her, she is off limits." Just then, Dannie came sweeping back out moving across the store to her own office. As she walked, her long hair tied into a ponytail swished back and forth. Leo's eyes were still tracking her movements. Jeff repeated his statement, "Off limits."

"Right, I'm not here for that anyway, but I can look." He heard Leo say, and Jeff had to laugh, because the irony not wasted on him. If a good-looking woman came into the shop, he would check her out, before Kat crawled under his skin. That was one of the benefits of owning a surf shop. He didn't want that anymore, going from one woman to another. Now just Kat filled his thoughts, she invaded his mind all the time. Even in the beginning, when he fought so hard to dispel her, she wouldn't go away. From that first night at the night club, on some level, there was an attraction, a lure, to her resistance to him. Of course, her body was what first caught his attention, but once he realized she would push him away, it was game on. Thinking about it now, it was that night she creeped under his skin. That's what he wanted to do, take Kat back to that club, where this time he could touch her, hold her.

Once on the plane, Kat sat back in first class and sipped her drink, knowing she should try to rest so she wouldn't be so tired once she made it to California. The threat of dreaming kept her from closing her eyes. She had to ask, why she was rushing to get to him, why she let down her guard? Her hard shell was melting away, the protective shield she depended on. Would she have to trade one for the other, to get past what happened to her, she'd have to give up always protecting herself. Let go of some control, allow Jeff to take care of her. She knew he was already doing that physically because her body craved him. Allowing him to show her what she'd been missing, has had a wonderful effect on her, although it freaked her out the first time when she lost consciousness.

He wasn't just taking care of her physical needs, sending her gifts, flowers, all new to her. The pull he instills in her, making her want and need him. Making her dependent on him, after only having herself to depend on, this was a strange feeling. Could she just let go, knowing she could, in the end, be devastated, a victim of a different kind. Anything worth having, takes hard work, chance, and knowing you could lose it all. Taking chances with her safety, she knew, her heart was an entirely different story. In the end, she wanted this.

Looking up at the inboard movie that she had no interest in watching, calmed her racing mind. Kat retrieved her briefcase from its position stowed beneath her seat. She could work for a few hours to keep her mind occupied. Placing her small reading glasses on, she started reading contracts. Next, she needed to read three chapters of a possible new client, and that should keep her busy until she lands.

Jeff waited for Kat's plane to land, and anticipation surged through his body. The strong need to have her in his arms almost overwhelmed him. Watching the people mull around the airport wasn't enough of a distraction for him. Fidgeting as her plane taxied to the gate, walking to the window to try to stop the squirming, he seemed to have no control over. People started to come down the corridor, and he knew she flew first class so she should be one of the first to get off. Then, he saw her blonde spiked hair, over a few people in front of her. Amazed by the relief he felt seeing her, she didn't appear to be looking for him. She just moved along with everyone else, he didn't want to rush her, but hell, he wanted her in his arms.

When she spotted him, he couldn't help the huge grin that crossed his face. When she smiled back, his heart started to pound, along with other body parts. He stepped up to her and opened his arms, as she moved into his embrace. Taking a deep breath, drawing a scent, that was all hers. Not truly understanding the effects it had on him, but knowing it intoxicated him.

"Hi," he whispered into her ear, not giving her time to respond he kissed her. Framing her face in his hands, she answered his demands. When his tongue touched hers, it sent blood rushing through his body. Wanting to get her back to his place, he ended the kiss, but not pulling back he asked, "You ready to go?"

Breathlessly, she answered, "Yes." Taking her hand, Jeff grabbed her bags and started walking. Noticing how tired she looked, knowing it had been a long day for her. Maybe he won't keep her up all night, although having her all to himself, without anyone knowing she was here, tempted him. He had already told Ben he would be late into work tomorrow, well actually today, because it was after mid-night, and no one was expecting Kat until much later today. So, they could stay in bed until mid-afternoon. The thought of having Kat all to himself had his body reacting, his pants getting a little tight.

Once they made it to his truck, he asked, "You hungry? We can stop by the diner and grab something if you are." He opened the door for her and noticed she slid to the middle seat, closing the door, he smiled as he walked around the front of the vehicle. Climbing in beside her, he put the key in the ignition, when she rested her head on his shoulder, he figured she didn't want anything to eat. Driving in silence, he glanced down at her and saw her eyes closed. He couldn't help resting his cheek on top of hers. Feeling her arm slide through his as she snuggled close had the same effect on him as being home, where you're supposed to be.

"I'm not really hungry, but sorry to say I'm exhausted. I worked on the plane, and now I'm feeling the effects of not getting enough sleep."

"That's ok, I understand you're tired. I'll just hold you so you can sleep." He felt her hand move to his groin as she stroked him. He heard her laugh under her breath.

"Somehow, I don't think that's what you had in mind for tonight." He liked how she was getting brave, openly wanting to touch him, but because she felt drained, he wasn't going to push her.

"Can't help how my body reacts to you being near, but I can control myself. Of course, if you keep that up, all bets are off and I'll be ripping your clothes off the minute I get you home."

He heard her chuckle as she said, "I might be in a comatose state by then." The fact that it didn't bother him because she was here with him, and that was all that mattered to him. She could sleep all night, just as long as he got hold her. Knowing she caught an earlier flight to be with him had him on a high. He could always let her sleep then wake her later.

"I can hear you thinking, don't worry, I'm sure I could muster up a bootie call before I pass out."

"Hey, you are no bootie call, I told you I'm not into that and that's not how I look at the time we spend together." He chastised her, he didn't want her to think that's how he felt or have her looking at herself as a bootie call.

"I know. I was just kidding. We're working through my issues…"

Jeff pulled his truck into the parking lot behind the shop, just in time because he wanted to be looking at her when he said his peace. Pulling the keys from the steering column, he was pissed, exited the truck and coming to her side. Not letting her get out, he said, "Kat, there is so many things I want to say to your comment, but first I'm here with you, not out of some pretense of just getting you past what happened to you. I want you to understand, I'm here with you because that's where I want to be. I don't just want sex, Kat. I want a relationship, someone to share my life with, the good times and bad.

I'm going to lay all my cards on the table, so there is no misunderstanding what I want. I want to see where we can go together. I'm willing to fight for what I believe that will be a very rewarding bond."

"Jeff," Kat slid her hand to the side of his face. "How could you be so sure about us, when I've never even considered being with anyone, much less any kind of lifetime bond. I know nothing, except what I know of other people's relationships. I don't know the protocol, much less how to do this. So, what I said before was, me not sure what to call what we're doing and making light of the situation."

Now getting her inside became important, before someone saw them. Jeff retrieved her bags as he took her hand walking them to the stairs that lead to his apartment. He sensed her apprehension, giving her hand a little squeeze before releasing her. He opened the door and ushered her into his home. Placing her bags by the door, he watched as she assessed her surroundings. Trying to see his place through her eyes, it was the exact duplicate of Ben's place.

"Do you want a shower or something, or do you just want to go to bed?" He was going to let her lead, whatever she needed he'd do. Kat moved through his apartment looking at his stuff, touching. He liked having her here, as he knew he would. Now if he could just talk her into staying with him permanently, or at least while she was staying in California. He followed her into his bedroom she went to his bed. She didn't look at him when she asked, "Have you had other women in here?" Jeff didn't want to lie to her, but he didn't want to tell her that he had.

"Not in a long time, but yes, I have. I stopped bringing women here because, one, my mother ended up finding out and, two, it was easier to leave someone else's place then to get them to leave." Again, his old lifestyle was up for discussion. It was something he'd have to live with because he couldn't change it. Not even for her.

"Why did you want me to come here? Not afraid I might want to stay," she said sarcastically.

Going to her, wrapping her in his arms, "Actually, I was hoping you would." He heard the hitch in her breath with his words, but they were true, he wanted her here. "I want you to stay with me every night, and I don't want you to go back to my mothers. I would like to wake up next to you each morning, and I intend to try to convince you to stay with me. If you choose to fight me on this, I'll just try harder to persuade you."

"Don't you think spending every minute with me might make you run the other way, rather than make you fonder of me." Standing next to the bed, he started to undress her. She was still in her work clothes, a pale blue skirt, and Jacket with a pink blouse underneath. Unbuttoning her jacket and gliding it off her shoulders, folding the jacket, he placed on his dresser. Next, he pulled her blouse from her skirt. Her eyes glued to his, he started at the top undoing her shirt, slowly removing it, and adding it to his dresser. Reaching behind her, he unzipped her skirt, sliding it down her long legs. She now stood stock still in her silk pink bra and panties.

Standing up, he caged her face with his hands, "I don't know where this will take us, but everything I learn about you, I find either fascinating, or I admire you for it. I want to learn what makes you happy, what makes you mad, at other people of course." He kissed her softly, "There's something in me that doesn't want to let you down, not stand up to your expectations. I hope to be the man you need Kat. Knowing how someone you trusted hurt you, I would never want to do that to you."

At his words, she melted, kissing him. He felt that deep need, to have her, to love her, and always care for her. Ripping his t-shirt over his head, he wanted to be inside her, with his body covering hers. The words repeated in his head, *slow down, slow the hell down.* Breaking the kiss that was running his blood to the boiling point wasn't easy.

Breathing hard he had to ask, "Kat, I need to know if this is what you want, because I need you."

"Yes," she whispered, and that's all he needed. Leaning her onto the bed, he stepped back to admire the view. Kat, in just her pink bra and very skimpy panties, was a sight of a major fantasy. Jeff quickly stripped off his pants taking his boxer briefs with them. Slowly moving up her lean body, he dipped his nose, so it presses against her panties, and inhaling her arousal. Biting the small scrap of fabric, wanting to tear them away, but fear of sending her into a flash back, he released them.

Tucking his fingers into the scrap of fabric he said, "I could rip this right off you," his eyes lock on hers. Gaging her reaction, he didn't see any fear but still slid the pink silk down to clear her ankles. Now he had the perfect clearance to her butterfly tattoo. "I haven't gotten this out of my head," gliding his fingertips over the permanent ink. "I know why you have it, but why did you pick this particular design? I love how it curls right here," he moved lower on the outline. As he moved over her mount, she lifted her hips. He knew she was tired, but he wasn't going to be rushed.

Slowly he kissed up her leg, and heard her say, "I wanted a design to cover the scar, but the butterfly symbolized freedom to me. To go anywhere, do anything I wanted without fear. I turned something I hated to look at into a beautiful image. I used to be very self-conscious when I had to wear a bathing suit, afraid my scar would show," slowing his movements even more, because he wanted her to continue talking. "The guy who did the tattoo understood what I wanted. He had done this kind of work on many who wanted something covered. He added the stars and the scrolls, to make it look more feminine and daintier. I just liked it because he covered the entire scar."

"Have you ever thought about getting any more tats?" Jeff asked as he continued touching her butterfly. Realizing he never liked tattoos on women before, this was different, because he absolutely loved Kat's ink. Not just because he knew why Kat had the tattoo, but also because where it was, it wasn't one of those huge tattoos he had seen on women. So why was he asking her if she was getting any more.

"I thought about covering the other scar but decided not to, because this one hurt like hell and..." she stopped talking when his lips pressed over her hip.

"I fucking love this," trailing his tongue over her, mapping the design. "On the plane home, all I could think about was this tat and how I wanted to pay it some attention. I didn't want to say anything about it before when you were so uncomfortable with me seeing your body." All the talking ended when he opened her folds. His movements over her sensitive bud made her hip bow off the bed.

Jeff smiled as his tongue twirled her tight nub, her sounds sent blood rushing south. He loved how responsive her body was to his touch. When her hands clutched in the sheets, he knew she was close. He watched her every move, the tightening of her jaw, her head pressed into the pillow. Reaching up, he pulled the cup to her bra down to expose her breast, pinching her nipple, just as he started sucking her clit into his mouth sent her over the edge. Her low, bewildering sounds of satisfaction, he could see she was trying to control her reaction to her orgasm. Transfixed by the satisfaction that he could see on Kat's face, it made him feel ten feet tall.

Once she gained her breath, Jeff climbed on top of her. Testing her reaction, to him being over her, he told her, "It's just me, ok. I want to make love to you on top, are you going to be alright with that?" When he saw, her shake her head, gesturing she would be fine. He kissed her as he slowly rested his weight on her. This would be the first time she had sex in the missionary position since the attack. "If you change your mind, just give me a hard shove."

"I won't change my mind, I want you on top, and I need to feel your body pressed to mine. I've never wanted this with anyone, but I want it with you."

That was all Jeff needed to hear, kissing her tenderly, he guided himself into her warmth. He waited a beat, then he started to move, slow strokes, in then out. Everything inside of him went crazy, his heartbeat, his need to possess her. His body demanded him to move faster, but he had to know if Kat could handle more. He asked, "You ready for more?"

"Yes," and her hips moved to meet his harder thrusts, his body started tightening, knowing this wasn't going to last much longer, he tilted his hips to penetrating her deeper. Relief spread when he felt her muscles clinch around him, he pumped into her one last time and let go.

When both of their breathing returned to normal, Kat couldn't move her body, she was so tired. "I can't stay awake a minute more," she turned to her side and within seconds her breathing slowed. She felt Jeff snuggle against her back, and she could only celebrate her triumph for the briefest moment before sleep took her under.

Having Kat in his bed, making love to her, this was the best night of his life. As crazy as it made him feel, he wanted to keep her here with him. Thoughts of tying her to his bed, and in the next second, how mad that would make her. Although he liked to ruffle her feathers, he didn't want to have a setback or freak her out. Wondering if he put on the charm, if he could get Kat stay with him, instead of going back to his mother's house. If he could convince her, he could have her every night. That was his last thought before he relaxed.

The next morning, Jeff woke with a start, the bed next to him was empty. Flipping back the covers, Jeff went looking for Kat. He didn't find her in his apartment, knowing she didn't have a car, so she couldn't have gone far. Most likely, she was out on the beach doing yoga or running. She worked out more than anyone he ever known. Going back to his bedroom, he threw on sweats and grabbed his acoustic guitar. Not even slipping on shoes, he walked down to the beach, and sure enough, she was there. Watching her for a minute, before he moved to where she did yoga. Remembering the last time when he watched her, and how she could flex her body into positions that induced so many sexual fantasies. Taking a calming breath, he sat to the side of her mat.

Feeling the presence of someone, Kat opened her eyes. Jeff sat about ten feet away from her, trying not to break her concentration. She noticed he had his guitar, and he didn't say anything, he just started to play. The music was soft when his fingers started to pick the strings. She found herself listening to each sound, the pings, pongs, and then a scrape across the strings. Then a strum, each sound peaceful and relaxing. She was very impressed, because he played quit well. Now, she found herself humming along with the tune. Finally, the last note before he started the next tune. With the sounds of his guitar along with the waves, she found an inner harmony.

Watching Kat move through her stance, her arms straight up, while one leg bent with the other extended behind her. Her head dropped back, with her body stretched out, he could see her ribcage and every muscle in her arms and legs. She was only wearing a sports bra and yoga pants that sat very low on her hips. It was a good thing he could keep playing, while he kept his eyes on her. He didn't need to think about playing the guitar. He could strum the damn thing all day if it meant he could watch her. Moving to the next move, she placed her forehead on her knee in front. His eyes roamed over her ass, and damn if his body didn't stir.

"Stop it, you're interfering with my Zen, I can feel your arousing thoughts."

"Can't help it, your half-dressed, and with those pants so low on your hips, I could just…"

"No, if you can't keep your thoughts to yourself, then you should go, no matter how much I was enjoying the music."

"I can try, but I have to tell you, no man alive, or maybe dead, could sit here and not have thoughts of unwrapping you, and I know what's under your clothes and yet I'm still imagining it."

"Okay, then maybe I should just do it naked then." Knowing it was an empty threat, but enjoying Jeff's surprised face, Kat had to laugh.

"That was just mean, you know. Offering something you never planned on delivering."

"Who said, I could always do this in your living room."

"Time to go," Jeff got up and started gathering all of Kat's stuff, even pulling her mat practically out from under her feet.

"You are so easy. All I have to do is mention being naked and you go all ape shit." The way Jeff reacted to her, now that they have had sex, was very empowering. Never having anyone act this way about being with her, made her feel wanted. "Hey, I never finished my yoga."

"Oh, don't worry about that, you can finish in my living room, like you promised." The way Jeff was nearly running to get her back to his place made her laugh.

"You're laughing now, but when I get you back to my place I'm going to strip you out of that outfit and then sink so deep inside you. I can guarantee you will not be laughing. You might be making other sounds, but differently not laughing."

The desperate tone in his voice, stopped Kat in her tracks. Knowing she shouldn't feel apprehensive, but her body was no longer humming with anticipation. Panic, that was the feeling she felt. Knowing how stupid it was didn't change anything.

When Jeff realized, she stopped walking, he turned to find Kat's complete demeanor had changed. No longer playing, she just stood there looking at her feet. He didn't know if he should touch her or give her a minute. "Kat," he said her name hoping to bring her back to the here and now. When she looked up, he knew. "I didn't mean I was going to attack you. I would never do anything you didn't want." Now he touched her arm, and he felt her stiffen under his touch. "I'm sorry if I sounded like a possessed man, I just got caught up. I didn't think how I sounded to you."

"I know you would never hurt me, and I got caught up, too. Until something in your voice, sent panic down my spine. I hate how suddenly something so small can freak me out." She needed to get past this shit, or William will always have a hold on her.

"Come on, let's get back to my place, I'll make you breakfast. You do eat eggs, right?"

Kat could tell he was trying to go back to the playful tone of their conversation. She just needed to move passed what just happened. Walking back, she felt she owed him an apology, "I'm sorry, I didn't mean to freak out on you, I do know you won't hurt me."

"Kat, you have nothing to apologize for, I need to watch what I say and how I say it." Walking up to his apartment, he hoped no one would see Kat, because he didn't want anyone to know she was here yet. He wanted a few more hours with her before she had to go upstairs to help Liz.

Jeff would do whatever she needed him to do, but he wasn't sure what that was. He knew hot sex was off the table for today. Maybe he could take her out on one of those dates he wanted to do.

# ~ 16 ~

After what happened on the beach, Kat needed to get away from Jeff's concerned looks. She knew he was mostly playing with her, but something in his tone and demeanor set her off. Needing some time, and space to herself, she asked Jeff to take her to his mother's right after breakfast. He wanted to spend the morning with her, but she couldn't take the pressure anymore. She hated this part, never knowing exactly what would set her off, most of the time, she could hide her anxiety. No one looked so intently at her every move. Jeff saw more than she ever wanted anyone to see, and now he was walking on eggshells. Treating her with caution, not to upset her and on some stupid level, it pissed her off, because she didn't need to be handled with kid gloves.

Moving through Linda's empty house, Kat got ready to go to help Liz for the day. She knew once she showed up, everyone would know she got back early. By avoiding Jeff's mother airport pick up service, Linda would find some other way to interrogate and grill her about her feelings toward Jeff. Not as if she didn't know it was coming, as Kat knew she couldn't dodge Linda for long. It might be best to just speak to Linda first and get it over with, because she could tell the woman things she didn't know herself. Kat was going to track down Linda once she made it back to the surf shop. She might need to talk to Ben, too, see where he was with buying the house. Not that if Ben and Liz moved to the house on the beach, there would be less eyes on her and Jeff's every move.

Walking into the shop for the first time since being back, Kat stopped short. Everything was different, it looked as if it was an entirely new place. She knew things would change with the deal with Shafford, but she didn't expect the store to be so unfamiliar. Moving toward the back of the store, where she knew Linda and Ben's office was, Linda's door was open, so Kat knocked on the door jam. Looking up, Linda smiled. Kat took a deep breath and walked in closing the door behind her.

"Linda, you got a minute?" Sitting across from the only person Kat might be a little afraid of, she waited for the questions to start.

"Kat, you're back. Did Jeff pick you up from the airport? Liz didn't tell me you'd be back this morning." Kat understood what Linda wasn't saying, she was there too early to have come in today, so she must have come yesterday, but didn't stay at Linda's.

"Yes, I got in late last night. I didn't want to disturb anyone so late. I know Jeff told you about us and I figure I'd come to you and save you the trouble of tracking me down." Kat watched Linda because she was calling the woman out.

"I appreciate the courtesy, but you know it's not necessary. I talked to Jeff and he's the one I was concerned with, you on the other hand, know your own mind."

"What's that supposed to mean, I know my own mind?"

"Kat, you are a strong, tough woman. Jeff has always been wish-washy when it came to women. I needed to know where his head is, and as I expected, he has feelings for you. Now is the feeling mutual?" Oh, Linda was good, she got right down to the main question she wanted to know.

"I'll be honest with you Linda, I don't know. I don't do relationships, and I don't believe in true love, except for maybe Ben and Liz. I didn't want to get involved with Jeff, but he just kept pushing until I gave in. Now he wants to date, and I've just stopped fighting him on that issue. This can't turn into anything Linda, I want you to understand right now, because I'm not moving, and Jeff isn't either. So, when the babies come, I will be returning home and that will end anything going on between myself and Jeff. No marriage, no grandkids, I want to make sure you understand this is where I stand, up front. As you stated, I know my own mind." Kat started to get up and could feel Linda watching her. She turned to look at the woman and regretted it when she saw the smile that shined bright as if she knew something. Closing the door behind her once more, she leaned on the wall trying to take in air. Standing there, she needed a minute to gather her thoughts. Then she saw Jeff walking toward her, along with a dark-haired man. The man with Jeff was big, and had coco colored skin, with his long hair tied back.

Jeff stopped in front of her, "Hey Sunshine, you looking for me?" He kissed her right in view of this stranger.

She pulled back, "Actually, I came looking for your mother, and then I need to speak to your brother before I tend to Liz," looking at the man standing behind Jeff.

Not paying any attention to the man behind him, Jeff said, "So, you're not looking for me then," and he smiled alone with the other guy. When Kat didn't take her eyes off the man, Jeff turned, "Oh, this is Leo, he just started working for us. Leo, this is my girlfriend, Kat." Kat couldn't believe how Jeff introduced her as his girlfriend.

"Nice to meet you, Leo," Kat put out her hand and Leo took it. Shaking her hand, she assessed him as he looked on, as he knew what she was doing.

"Same here," he let go first, but didn't take his eyes off her.

Jeff interrupted the odd moment, "What did you want with Mom?"

"I figured it was better if I came to her. Rather than have her track me down." Kat didn't know why Leo was still standing there, but it made her uncomfortable.

"Good game plan, and how'd that go?" Jeff noticed Kat still looking over his shoulder, he turns and told Leo he could go check if the truck delivering the new product line was here yet. When Leo walked away, Kat relaxed a bit.

"It went fine. I didn't have much to tell her because I have no idea what we're doing here." She didn't want to have this conversation outside his mother's office door. So, she said, "Can we talk about this later," she pointed her thumb to the door, and he nodded his understanding.

Leaning close to her ear he said, "I didn't think there was any confusion on what we're doing. Come talk to me when you're done talking to Ben," Jeff turned and walked away.

One down, one to go, Kat thought, now she needed to find Ben. She went up the back stairs, and knocked going in, to find Ben sitting at the table having a cup of coffee. He looked tired, but he smiled when he saw her, Kat knew how stretched he was in so many different directions. Kat got her own cup and sat down to have her exchange with him.

"How are Liz and the babies?"

She heard Ben exhale of breath, "She's hanging ten, but as you already know staying in bed is getting old. Doc says babies are growing and we're getting to the point where she can go into premature labor. He said, we need to keep that from happening if possible, the babies' lungs need more time. I don't want Liz to know how worried I am about the babies, because she doesn't need any more to be concerned with."

"Ben, you both need to talk, because you don't think she is doing the same thing. Worried about you and how your handling all this, isn't going to make things better for her. You're both in this together, and you're stronger if you rely on each other. How is buying the house going?"

"That's the only thing holding me together at this point, the closing is in a couple of days, and I can't wait to surprise her. I think she could really use something to take her mind off things she has no control over."

"Congratulations, that's great Ben. I think that will work to keep her occupied. I'll start getting her shopping online for the nursery. Getting ready for the babies' arrival will also help her feel prepared if they should come early." Kat found herself feeling anxious about an early arrival.

"Kat, I know we've had are moments, but I want you to know I couldn't have made it without your help. Liz and I appreciate what you've done for her and the friendship you have always given her." Ben went to get up, and Kat got the feeling he was going to hug her again, she put her hands up to stop his forward motion.

"Don't even think about hugging me, I'd hate to have to kill you before you get to see your babies." Ben laughed and went to put his coffee mug in the sink.

"So, now that you're caught up with Liz, what are you thinking getting involved with Jeff?" Kat let out a swift breath, not him, too. By the end of this day, she was going to have to explain about her and Jeff to every single person.

"I don't know what I'm thinking, but it's your fault."

"My fault, how'd you figure?" He leaned his back against the counter with his arms folded in front of him.

"I wouldn't be here to get involved with Jeff if you hadn't needed my help, so that's how it's your fault." She watched a huge grin cross his face, and he even had the nerve to chuckle under his breath.

"You could have said no, so don't go blaming me for this shit. I'm not taking any credit for what happens between you and Jeff," Ben opened the door and headed for the shop.

Kat sat there wondering if she could have said no to Jeff. Well, she had said no, but he didn't listen. As if she had agreed, Jeff moved forward giving her no choice in the matter. Now that Ben left, she couldn't go back down to talk with Jeff, it would have to wait until later. Putting her own mug in the sink, she went to see Liz.

The day passed quickly once Kat got Liz to take a break from writing and shopping. Liz picked out the theme for the nursery and from there, the items piled up. Not leaving much left for the baby shower Linda was planning to have for Liz. Kat couldn't help getting caught up in it too, because one thing was cuter than the next, and not knowing the sex of the babies made buying clothes a little harder. Liz wanted to paint the babies room, so Kat had plans of stopping by the paint store to pick up samples for Liz. Not remembering having so much fun shopping, Kat enjoyed being a part of the excitement. In what felt like no time, Ben was back, and Liz was showing him everything she bought for the babies. Kat slipped out to find Jeff.

As Kat walked through the store, all the new displays sat everywhere. Looking around she didn't notice the man watching her, but once she turned the corner, she bumped right into Leo. She immediately stepped back and took on a slight fighting stance. Leo put his hands up in front of his chest and stepped back, too.

"Man, you're jumpy." Kat narrowed her eyes.

"You shouldn't be lurking, and it would be in your best interest to remember that. I have no problem taking down a man your size." She didn't know what it was about this guy that incited this reaction from her.

When he laughed at her, she could feel her temper going hot. "I won't give you any reason to as you say, "take me down." I don't plan on getting in your way."

"I was looking for Jeff," she relaxed a bit as she scanned the store for him.

"He went into his office looking for the layout for some of these," Leo pointed to the displays she just walked by. Nodding, Kat turned and walked away, moving toward the new offices. Kat thought about Leo and how it must be his sheer size that unnerved her. Although he was a good-looking man, with his dark skin and beautiful eyes, she needed to get away from him. Kat found Jeff in his office rifling through a stack of paper.

He looked up when she walked in, "I didn't think you were going to come back. I thought I was going to have to chase you down." She just made a disturbed noise and shook her head. Watching her, he moved around his desk to take her into his arms then said, "But, I'm glad I didn't have too and you're here."

He felt her resist a little, "What's wrong, is it because we're back here?" Right away, he thought she was going to pull away from him now that they were back in California.

"No, I just ran literally into Leo, and I don't know why, but he makes me feel uneasy," Jeff was now looking concerned.

"He didn't do anything inappropriate, did he?" Jeff asked.

"He didn't do anything, that's just it. My reaction was to fight, and I felt I needed to tell him, I could take him down. He thought that was funny, which doesn't help how much I like him." She saw Jeff's tight smile threatening, "Have you forgotten what I can do to you?"

"Oh no, I know what you can do, but in Leo's defense he doesn't. Just so he doesn't do anything that makes you uncomfortable, and if he does, I want to know about it." He kissed the side of her head. "I like your hair like this," sliding his hand into her relaxed style.

"I didn't feel like doing it today, but obviously, I need my spikey hair to scare the bad guys away. This softer look doesn't have the same affect." Kat laughed at herself, and Jeff kissed her.

"I want to take you dancing tonight, but this time I plan on touching every inch of your body. Then I want you in my bed." Jeff kept his voice soft and nonthreatening. After what happened on the beach this morning, he didn't want to do anything that would upset her.

"I'll go dancing, but I don't think staying at your place is a good idea. With your mom watching us and then there's always a chance of running into other family members."

"My mom knows you stayed with me last night, so what's the difference, and Ben could care less what I do, unless you don't want to stay. If that's the case, then I guess, I'll just have to sneak into my mom's house." The look of shock Kat gave him was priceless.

"Oh, my God, I can't imagine how your mother would take finding us together in her house." Shaking her head because there was no way, she wanted any part of Linda finding out that Jeff snuck in to have sex with her.

"So, you see, it's much better if you come and stay with me. This way when I get you screaming, my mother won't come running, thinking you need help." Slapping him, Kat shook her head. "I'll pick you up at nine. I have more work to get done before I can leave tonight."

That meant she had a few hours to workout. Leaving out the back door, she didn't run into anybody this time. Once she got into the car and thought of going dancing, it brought back the memory of the first time she set her blue eyes on Jeff. Her thoughts going to how, she misjudged him, although he was a man-whore at the time. Even then, she wanted him on some level, even if it was just to tease him. In the end, he played her just as much as she played him. How could she go from not wanting him to touch her, to now she couldn't wait for him to be touching her? Tonight, it was going to be her turn to tease him, and she knew just the outfit to do the trick.

Jeff pulled up to his mother's house, the place where he grew up. The house was too big for just his mother, but she would never think about selling it. He didn't see his mother's car; most likely, she was out for the night, she was very active. Jeff didn't knock, but he didn't want to scare Kat, so he yelled, "Kat, I'm here." He almost swallowed his tongue when she came down the stairs. She was wearing a short red dress that had cutouts in all the right places to make a man's mind go into fantasy mode. Kat had on killer heels that made her legs go on forever, with her hair spiked and her kiss me red lips, along with her bluer than blue eyes, Jeff had to close his mouth, and damn if he didn't have to readjust his fly. She had a wicked smile, knowing what she was doing to him.

Jeff no longer wanted to take her dancing, he wanted to march her sexy ass back up those stairs, remove that dress, and fuck her. "Holy hell woman, you are mean, looking like that, you have to know what you're doing to me."

"I knew it would affect you, isn't that the point? Play to win or go home. Now you promised to take me dancing, you ready to show me off." Jeff placed his hand to her lower back and felt skin. Glancing to where his hand was, he could see one of the cutouts was almost to the top of her ass. The thought of her not wearing any underwear made his dick twitch.

"Tell me what you have on under this dress," he let his hand slide lower down her dress to her ass, he felt nothing, no signs of any under garment, and now he was looking at her back where her bra strap should be, nothing. Was she naked under this dress? Jeff's mind was reeling when he realized she was talking to him.

"You'll have to wait and see, it's all in the illusion." Jeff liked that Kat was being playful, but his body didn't want to wait.

"That must be some illusion, because I don't see how you can be wearing anything under there. I have to tell you, I don't want to take you dancing anymore, where I want to go is back to my place and strip you." They walked to his truck, and he opened the door for her, as she climbed in, Jeff tried to cop a feel, but all he felt was smooth skin. He was determined to find out what she had on underneath.

"Patience, the anticipation will be worth the wait, I promise." Jeff noticed how Kat was enjoying his enthusiasm with her dress. Driving was hard, he couldn't concentrate with her dress inching up her thighs. Resting his hand in that exact spot, he attempted to glide beneath the fabric. Kat stopped his progression with her own hand. It wasn't long before they were parking and walking into the club.

When they reached the bouncer, he looked Kat over with admiration. As Jeff walked by, he heard the dude say, "Damn, Jeff how do you end up so lucky?" As much as Jeff loved how Kat looked, he didn't want guys undressing her with their eyes. Even though he knew that was unrealistic because every dude would be fantasizing about Kat, but she was going home with him.

Once inside, Jeff took her hand leading her to the bar, turning to her he asked, "You want an apple martini?" Seeing her shake her head, he ordered her drink and a beer for himself. Noticing how the bartender gave Kat a once over, he gave Jeff a thumbs up. Jeff took their drinks and found a table. The table sat off to the side of the dancefloor, Jeff would have liked to get a table in the back. Sitting here, everyone could see them, and he needed to make it through the night without getting into a fight. The music was loud, and the lights flashed in every direction. Picking up her glass, he watched as she brought it to her lips, and again his cock jumped. She was playing him, when she pulled the apple slice off her glass and sucked on it, his mind went to her sucking on him. Making sure his chair was close to hers wanting everyone to know they were a couple, he pressed close to her ear and said, "If you want to stay, you need to stop doing that." She turned her blue eyes on him and gave him a wink. *Oh yeah, she knew exactly what she was doing to him.*

Once they finished their drinks, he pulled Kat to her feet, Jeff wanted to get her out on the floor. Right away, he took possession of her body, having his hands on her hips. They moved together through several songs. When she motioned to leave the floor, he followed. Jeff asked if she wanted another round and went to the bar. By the time, he came back, a dude sat down at their table. Jeff had to make it clear she was with him. He was starting to think it might be time to head back to his place when someone tapped him on the shoulder.

When Jeff looked up, he didn't like how this was going affect his night with Kat. Cindy, one of the women Jeff had dated, was standing there. She glanced in Kat's direction and sat in the chair on the other side of him. She tried to talk to him, leaning in close to his ear to speak because the music was so loud. Cindy has been texting him asking to go out, and Jeff was ignoring her, but with her sitting next to him, he couldn't be rude.

He turned to see Kat had slid her seat away from his, but she didn't look mad, more amused. Jeff had to draw the line when Cindy started pulling him to his feet to dance with her. He was just about to tell her no when Cindy turned to Kat and asked if she minded if she borrowed him for a dance or two. What he never expected, was when Kat waved her hand and told her she could have him. She said to have fun, next thing he knew, he was out on the dancefloor with Cindy and watching Kat get up from the table taking her drink and walking away. As Kat walked away, men stopped her, and she smiled at them and then moved on. Trying to keep Cindy at arm's length and keeping an eye on where Kat went, had Jeff pissed. He didn't want to be dancing with Cindy, and he didn't want Kat walking through the club without him. Not that he thought she couldn't take care of herself, because he knew she could.

Once he could get away from Cindy, Jeff went in search of Kat. He walked through the place twice and didn't see her. Knowing she wouldn't leave, he pulled out his phone to call her. When her phone went to voice mail, he hung up and started texting her. Moving his fingers over the keys he wrote.

Jeff: WHERE ARE YOU? Then he waited, looking over the people for her blonde spiked hair.

Kat sat on the counter in the ladies room, drinking her apple martini. Knowing Jeff was looking for her, she didn't respond right away. Figuring he could wait, not knowing why she was feeling jealous, because that was stupid. He was free to do as he pleased, he didn't have any ties to her. She didn't want any ties to him, that's what made how she felt irrational. The next text came about two minutes later.

Jeff: WHERE THE FUCK ARE YOU? I'M GETTING PISSED.

Smiling at his all capital letters, she decided to text back.

Kat: CHILL, I'M IN THE LADIES ROOM and you don't need to yell at me. I'm not the one dancing with someone else.

Two seconds and his next text came.

Jeff: You have two minutes, then I'm coming in after you.

Kat waited until her two minutes were up and then hopped down. Just as she pulled the door open, Jeff was starting to go in. He didn't look so happy to see her. Well, if he was mad, he could just get over it. He took her hand and pulled her down the hall and out an emergency exit. Once outside, he trapped her against the wall in the alley.

"What the hell Kat, this is not how I saw this evening going." He had his hands on either side of her body.

"I don't know why your angry with me," she spat back, "I was not the one dancing with someone who is not my date." Her own anger was showing, and she rained it in.

Jeff closed his eyes and took a deep breath before saying, "I didn't want to dance with her, I came here with you, but when she asked you, you waved your hand and gave her the go ahead. I must say Kat, that alone pissed me off. I guess, I expected you to at least put up some fight. Not just pass me off."

"That hurt your ego, well we have no ties, and you're free to dance, or fuck, anyone you want. I have no hold on you." She pushed him back, but he didn't budge. Leaning in she said, "You need to step back." The realization hit Jeff, and he did move, but not far.

Running his hand through his hair, his frustration was showing as he said, "Kat, you do have a hold on me, and yeah I guess it did hurt my ego. For the first time, I find myself wanting someone more than they want me, and I don't like how this makes me feel." He turned away from her, "I thought you at least had feelings for me, maybe I've been kidding myself."

"What do you want from me Jeff? I told you I don't do relationships and have no experience with this. But at any point tonight, did you introduce me as your girlfriend or tell her you were with me."

"No."

"Well, there you go."

A little calmer Jeff said, "I'm sorry, the first thing I should have done was make it clear to Cindy I was with you, by introducing you. No matter what you said, I should have never left your side, but Kat I have a past, one I'm not proud of, so women will come up to me. You should know, I do not want to be with any of them. We are together, so you are tied to me, and we are exclusive." He stepped closer, putting his hands on her hips, pulling her into him.

"Jeff, you are getting so far ahead of yourself. I don't plan to see anyone else, but as far as anything more, I can't give you that. We both know that after Liz has the babies, I'm going home. So, don't make the mistake of thinking there's more. I have a life, a job in New York, and you have a life and job here." Watching the emotions cross Jeff's face, had Kat feeling the sting of her own statement.

"I know you have a life across the county, but Kat I have never felt this strong pull before, and I have to go with my instincts. But, for now, we'll just take it day by day, ok, no pressure." Dragging her in close, he kissed those red lips that he'd been dying to kiss all night. Jeff slid his hand into the cutout, in the back of Kat's dress, and along the top of her ass. The only thing he felt was skin and once again, his body reacted.

"I want you to stay with me tonight, say you will," but he didn't give her a chance to answer before he deepened their kiss. Shifting them away from the wall, Jeff started moving down the alley toward the parking lot and his truck.

"I can't stay, it's too late to call your mother and tell her I'm not coming home. I don't want her to worry and come by your place looking for me, and we both know she will. We can go back to your place, but then you'll have to drop me off later."

Knowing she was going home with him, released some of his tension, but he wanted her to be there in the morning. They had argued, made up, and hopefully the makeup sex would be out of this world. Of course, with Kat in that dress, there was no doubt the sex was going to be hotter than ever before.

# ~ 17 ~

When they pulled up behind the surf shop, Jeff needed to make his intentions clear. Everything in his body wanted to rip that dress off Kat, but he wanted her to understand he didn't want to hurt her. Today at the beach, and then at the club, they had passion running high between them. He didn't want her to pull away. When he didn't move to get out he felt Kat looking at him.

Staring out the windshield he said, "Before we go up to my apartment, I need you to understand something. At any time, you can tell me to stop, but with you in that dress..." he paused. "I want to rip it off your body, and sink myself so deep inside you, and go all animal on you, but I don't want to scare you."

Kat's voice was soft when she said, "I want that too, all of those things. I want to be okay with you feeling so much passion, that you lose it a little bit. I want to be able to lose it, too, and not worry about anything else."

Getting out of the truck, Jeff walked to her side opening the door. Not moving to allow her to get out, but she turned to face the open door. Stepping between her legs, Jeff leaned in to kiss her. The kiss started soft and passionate, Jeff could taste the apple from her drink and the rest was all Kat. She slid her body against his, and right on cue, he was hard, with her hands in his hair, tugging him in close. Again, Jeff found the openings in the back of her dress with his hands, moving them over her ass. Her bare ass, he had to know if she was naked under her red-hot dress. Taking one hand now, moving it up her thigh and he encountered the end of tight shorts at the top of her leg. So, she did have something on, but how did it not show through the openings in the dress.

"You found me out. See it's all in the illusion. The entire night, you thought I didn't have anything on under my dress, and your mind went crazy. The bra and boy shorts are built into the lining of the dress."

"And now it's time for it to come off because it's done its job. I did enjoy the illusion, along with every guy in the club tonight. But, knowing you were coming home with me, made all the dudes fantasizing about you a little easier to handle. I do appreciate this little number, and you look hotter than hell in it, but knowing I have a tie to you, having a right to touch you." Pulling her out of the truck with him, he needed to get her upstairs. Before he stripped her right here, and she found herself fucked in his truck.

Kat went willingly, holding his hand as they moved up to his apartment. Once in the door, Jeff pressed his body against Kat, holding her in place as he kissed her. Still holding on to the smallest of his control, his hands roamed her body. In the next second, Kat had flipped them, so now he pressed against the wall. He liked when she took control, because then he knew she felt comfortable with what they were doing. She started kissing down his neck and he tilted his head to give her better access, gritting his teeth, when she moved down the opening of his shirt. She started opening buttons as she moved lower still. He let her remove his shirt, but when she went for his pants, he stopped her, not wanting to do this here.

"Why don't we move this into my bedroom," Jeff shifting so he could lead the way. He stopped her in the middle of the room and began kissing her. His hand run over her body, he couldn't wait any longer to remove her dress. Finding the zipper at the base of her neck, he slowly dragged it down. "I've waited all night to do that," whispering into her ear, his words filled with sexual desire. Pulling the back of her dress apart to slide it off her shoulders, he stopped just short of exposing her breasts. "You are so fucking sexy, holding back isn't easy. The things I want to do to you right now," he ran his nose along her collarbone, taking in her scent. "I love how you smell, how soft your skin is, and I can't get enough of you Kat. I don't know if I will ever get enough."

"I need you Jeff, do you have any idea how much I hate to admit that," she said breathlessly. "You make me feel things no one else..." he kissed away her words.

Sliding the dress past her chest, he kissed down her scar to her nipple. Rubbing his stubble over her sensitive skin, her nipples hardened for him, and Jeff sucked one into his mouth. Gliding his tongue over the nub, flicking it back and forth, along with the sounds she made, had Jeff close. With his hands in the back of her dress, he slid it over her hips, now she stood in only her heels. He wanted the shoes to stay on because she looked damn good in heels. His mouth roamed lower, over her tight stomach. Lower still until he was at her butterfly tattoo. God, how he loved her tattoo. He widened her stance as he stooped so he could glide his nose through her folds. Taking in the scent of her arousal, he heard her plead for more. Opening her up to him, he began pleasing her, loving how she clinched her fingers into his hair. To send her over the edge, he inserted two fingers and pressed the spot he knew that would send her into an amazing orgasm.

Jeff stood holding Kat as her body collapsed. Taking her to the bed, he laid her in the middle. He removed his pants. He admired her naked body in his bed, still only in her heels. He must have stood there to long because Kat opened her eyes, looking a little confused.

"I love seeing you in my bed," he whispered under his breath as explanation. Walking to the edge of the bed, he ran his hand down her leg. "I liked you in that dress, but I really like you in just those shoes."

"Don't tell me you have a woman's shoe fetish," as to make her point, she bent her legs, putting the heels on the bed. She watched him, then lifting one leg straight up, and slowly moving her leg over her head. Knowing he stared, she took ahold of her ankle, pushing her other leg up to join the other one. Looking at Jeff through her now straddled legs, Kat held her ankles wide.

"You want to fucking do me in," stepping closer, he trailed his fingers up her center. "You have no idea what you're doing to me, I want to fuck you just like this. With your feet over your head and you holding on to those red heels of yours," when she didn't move, Jeff climbed between her spread legs. Sinking deep, he had to hold his breath, so he didn't lose it.

Looking down at Kat, into her blue eyes and seeing her pleasure, had him feeling possessive of her pleasure. Jeff wanted to be the only one to make her feel like this, ever. His movements were harder, needing his own release, reaching between them, he touched her. Her orgasm set off his, he held tight to her legs until he could breathe again.

Breaking their connection, Jeff lowered her legs. It took her a minute to realize something was wrong because Jeff was very quiet. The sex had been great for her, and he had come, but he got up off the bed and walked away without a word. Wrapped up in her own pleasure, she didn't even notice Jeff. What kind of person does that, a selfish one? Was she becoming someone that didn't care about her partner's pleasure? Worrying about someone else was new to her, was she caught up in having someone who wanted to help her, that she paid no attention to him. She really needed to make this up to him because he had helped her so much. Deciding just how she could do that, Jeff walked back into the room.

Kat took off her shoes as she watched him move around the room. She couldn't help feeling as if she let him down somehow. When he pulled back the covers, she couldn't take it anymore. "Jeff, did I do something wrong? Your quiet, I hate it when you're quiet."

In the darkness of the room he, pulled her into him and said, "I have a problem Kat."

"I'm sorry if I didn't pay attention to your needs, please be patient with me. I'm a newbie."

"Kat, this problem has nothing to do with you not paying attention to my needs. Just you being here, has taken care of every one of my needs. When we started this, I told myself I would be honest with you. I wasn't going to play any games with you, because I knew from the beginning I felt more for you than any other woman. The more time we spend together, the more I want. Tonight, when you allowed me to make love to you, I understood the trust you must have in me. I've wanted you to trust me with you secrets, with your body, but I find myself wanting you all to myself."

Not knowing what to say to him, Kat turned to face him. Pulling his face to hers, she kissed him, "I want to show you how you make me feel, how safe." She started kissing down his body, but once Jeff understood what she was doing, he stopped her.

"No Kat, I don't need you to do that."

"Don't stop me Jeff, I want to give you something that I've never freely gave to any other man."

"Kat, that's not what I want from you, not the more I'm talking about." That stopped her short, protest forgotten. She sat up in the bed, and Jeff knew when it hit her, what he was talking about.

He pulled her back to him, and when she didn't resist he relaxed a little. "I'm not telling you this to put pressure on you, I just wanted you to know where my head is. I want more than just the time we have between now and when Liz has the babies."

"I can't give you that Jeff. I've given more of myself to you and I'm just not sure I can give away anymore."

"And I know that Kat, believe me, but tonight when you said I have no ties to you. You were wrong because I want nothing…"

Kat cut him off, "Don't you dare say you want to be tied to me. Not like, the forever kind of way, oh my God, you just convinced me to date you." The panic in her voice had Jeff holding her from running.

"Easy, relax, I didn't mean to upset you." He tried to calm her, knowing he shouldn't have brought it up, because she wasn't ready. "Listen, I shouldn't have said anything. Just forget what I said, we're just having fun."

"You can't just take back what you said, you can't back out… Wait I mean," she stopped talking because what did she mean?

Laughing, Jeff said, "I know what you're trying to say, I get it. Now about what you wanted to do to me, I understand what that would mean to you, and believe me, I'd love nothing more, but don't feel you need to do anything more than being who you are." Kissing her lips, his body stirred, wanting her again.

"Then I can do what I want to you, and you won't stop me." Hearing Jeff's sudden intake of air put a smile on Kat's face. Pushing him to his back, she climbed on top, kissing him hard. She may not want forever, but she wanted the here and now. If she could do this and enjoy giving Jeff pleasure, there was no telling where things would take her.

Breaking the kiss her words were explicit, "I want to give you pleasure." Her mouth moving south once again, "I want to take you into my mouth." She felt his body go rigid, she ignored that and continued her pursuit. "I want to suck you until you can't take it anymore," now her mouth rested just above his hairline. She could hear his accelerated breathing and felt his hand clinched in the bed sheets.

"Kat, if you can't do this, I understa—." That moment she licked the head of his penis. Jeff's mind went blank, except for the feeling of her on him.

"The first time, I pretty much blacked it all out," running her tongue down his length. "I'm going to experiment on you. So, if I'm not doing it right, tell me."

"No right or wrong here," was all he could say.

Chuckling as she held him, stroking him, "I'm going to put my__," that moment, she pressed him through her lips. Feeling him press his hips up to meet her mouth, she knew he wanted more. So, she took him in as deep as she could, then pulled back.

"Fuck, Kat," hearing the anguish in his voice, she stopped.

"Please don't stop," his plea made her start again. Taking him deep and withdrawing. He hardened in her hand as she squeezed the base of his cock. With her other hand, she explored his sack, moving between each testicle, testing how he liked that. Going by the sounds Jeff made, she was pleasing him. She was still taking as much of him into her mouth and sucking as hard as she could, then drew back. She felt his balls pull tight and that's when Jeff yanked her mouth off him. Unsure why, but two seconds later she felt a warm stream of semen coat her hand. Jeff placed his hand over hers, as he moved them up and down his shaft until he had nothing left.

Jeff couldn't believe how having Kat's mouth and hands on him, made him feel. Because if he felt he wanted more before, now he wanted forever. He'd had many blowjobs before, and nothing felt as the one that Kat had just given him. The electricity that charged through his body, physically overpowering all his senses, thank God, he had just enough to pull her mouth away before exploding. Now he needed her mouth on his, pulling her to him. He kissed her hard because he wanted her to know what she did to him. He rolled her under him, reaching between them he needed to know if she was ready for round two. When his fingers touched her center, he found her drenched.

He continued to kiss her as he entered her. A little concerned about having all his weight on her, he pulled back just enough to make sure. When she pulled him back to her, he knew she was fine. Jeff lost himself in her, she did things to him that he never felt before. Moving together, both making sounds of pleasure, he knew what he wanted to tell her, but held his tongue because if he told her he was falling in love with her, she'd run for sure.

Needing Jeff scared her, but the way he made her feel, having her body rule and not her mind, letting go to feel free, she knew she was becoming addicted to him. It wasn't about feeling safe anymore because it had gone way past that. Knowing she should get as far away from him was her brain thinking, but her body wasn't moving an inch. Once again, her body jumped off the cliff without a parachute, no safety net, flying, soaring alongside Jeff.

She heard him say, "Kat, I can't move," it was okay because she couldn't either. They stayed there, with Jeff on top of her for a long time. She could feel his body relaxing and he shifted to the side taking her with him. "I don't want to take you back to my mother's," he said and because she didn't want to move, she told him, "okay." He wrapped her in his arms and was asleep in no time, listening to him breathe, relaxed her enough to fall into a deep sleep.

Waking over heated, Kat tried to get out of the covers, when she noticed why she was so hot. Jeff's body was practically caging her in, as if in his sleep, he thought she might disappear. She did need to get up, so she slowly extracted herself out from under his body. Once she was free, she went to use the bathroom and get ready for a good long meditation on the beach. She'd truly miss not having the beach outside her door. There was just something about being outside in the fresh air to do yoga or her martial arts, or she could always run. She needed to get Jeff to teach her how to surf. Watching Liz surf looked like so much fun, and she could totally rock a surfboard. It was all in the balancing and moving with the water.

Walking out the door and down the stairs, Kat took in the sounds as she moved over the sand dunes. Today the tide had left a deep ledge along the beach it was never the same. Every day the water would pull sand out or push it in, some days, the sun peaked through clouds to make striking colors. Other times, the sun refused to shine, it just said, "not feeling it today." Those days felt gloomy. Thank goodness, there weren't many of those. Rolling out her mat, she sat looking out over the water. Crossing her legs, she moved into her meditation pose. Closing her eyes and steadying her breathing, she began to clear her mind of every negative thought.

Her mind began replaying last night, and again she tried to clear the thoughts away. After several attempts to clear Jeff out of her mind, she gave up on the meditation. Standing on her mat, she began to go through her martial art moves. Slowly, moving through one move into the next, controlling her breathing. Concentrating on the movement of the water, she went with the waves. Holding her pose as the water went out and moving to the next when the wave came in. This was working, keeping her mind off that certain person, along with what he could do to her body.

When Jeff's head cleared, he realized he was alone in the bed. He was almost sure where Kat was, out on the beach, because once again, she didn't have a car so where could she go. Getting out of bed, Jeff went to his kitchen window because that was where he had the best view of the beach. He didn't see her, but that didn't mean she wasn't down a little further. Sliding on a pair of sweats, he went to find her. Just as he cleared the dunes, he spotted her. Standing still, he watched her, he thought of how much he liked watching her, when she didn't know he was. He could scrutinize every inch of her, without looking as if he was a stalker. She came out here almost every day to do yoga or run. Today, she was going through some fighting moves. Watching her precise movement, seeing her deep in concentration, amazed him.

Pulled from his thoughts when someone stood next to him, at first, he thought it might be Owen, but when Leo spoke, Jeff turned.

"She's wound tight," he stopped talking when Jeff glared at him. Leo put up his hands, not wanting to get his new boss pissed.

"Look, you need to back off Kat, I know she warned you yesterday and you laughed at her. You think because she doesn't weigh more than a buck-fifty that she isn't someone to watch out for, well let me warn you again. She could take down a horse if she thought for one second she was in danger."

"I meant no harm, she's just skittish. When she ran into me yesterday, she went into a fight mode, putting up her fists. I didn't expect her to come around the corner when she did. I know you don't know me well enough, but I don't hurt women. I'm more the love'em type, but I'm not here for that. I'm here to work and stay off my father's radar." With that, he tilted his head in Kat's direction, "Something happened to her to make her that way," it wasn't a question more of a statement.

"Just don't get her pissed at you, is all I'm going to say," Jeff walked away.

Jeff went back to his apartment, not wanting to disturb Kat. He knew she needed this time, it was how she worked through things. Hopefully, she'd be back soon, and he could make her breakfast. Maybe he could even talk her into climbing back into bed with him. When he walked in the door, his phone was going off, and Jeff had a good idea who was calling this early. His mother, looking at the caller Id, he should be surprised.

"Good morning, Mother," he said in a sarcastic tone.

"Good morning, I was worried about Kat, she didn't come home last night, and I just wanted to make sure she's alright."

"You know damn well we went out last night, and that she stayed with me. So, if you were worried, then you must have thought I did something to her. We both know I didn't do anything to her," under his breath he said, "Nothing she didn't want anyway."

"Fine," his mother said and hung up on him.

Smiling, he went to start the coffee and making breakfast. Just as breakfast was ready, Kat walked in. He stopped what he was doing to kiss her. Taking her hand, he led her to his small table. He pulled out her chair and pushed her in. He loved confusing her and wanted to keep her guessing. Once he had her attention, he said, "I just got off the phone with my mother."

"Shit, I should have called her last night. Was she mad?" Kat looked concerned.

"Nope, I think she was just hunting for information. She tried to act all concerned about your wellbeing. I told her you were just fine, in more ways than one." Jeff's smile told her he was having fun with his mother, but she would have to deal with Linda, the next time she saw her.

"Thanks, so you told her I was here, safe and sound with you." It had been a long time since she had justified her movements to anyone. Even being a house guest and knowing she should give Linda the consideration, she hated the idea. Maybe it was time for her to start looking for her own place, one she could come and go, without anyone noticing. She would need a place of her own if she'd be coming to visit Liz anyway.

"I told her you were safe, as safe as you can be with me, and as far as sound well last night I think we both were loud," he chuckled. "You hungry, I made you breakfast," Jeff pulled plates from the oven and sat one down in front of her.

He watched her as she looked over what he made for her. "I didn't know what you liked, but I figured you would eat only the egg whites. I made them scrambled and added cheese, bacon on the side, although I wanted to add it to the eggs, but didn't know if you ate bacon."

"Thank you, it smells great. I usually eat before I work out, but I'm not on my regular schedule." She picked up her fork and started eating, looking over at Jeff he just watched her. "What, aren't you going to eat?"

"Yeah, I just like taking care of you, Kat." Picking up his own fork, he couldn't help the feeling of contentment. She didn't need anyone, but he still felt she could use someone to care about her. In a way, no one had ever done before. Keeping his mouth shut this time he ate quietly, watching her pull the meat away from the fat on the bacon. Smiling he asked, "You're not going to eat the best part of the bacon," and reach over and took it from her plate, shoving it into his mouth.

"Oh gross, do you know what that's going to do to your arteries? You probably have high cholesterol and will end up with heart disease."

"You have to go somehow, might as well be happy, and thanks for worrying about my health, but doc says I'm healthy."

"Not if you keep eating like that you won't be. I can show you some healthy options."

"I'll do some of your options…" He paused, "If you do some of mine." Locking eyes with hers, he watched her expression.

"Trying to pull me to the dark side?" When she saw his wicked smile, she had to wonder, "Are we still talking about food?"

"Do you want it to be about food, or maybe something different all together? Either way, I'm in, just tell me what you want Kat."

"I want to learn how to surf, as you promised. I want to learn more about what makes both are bodies happy and I guess we can explore the food options."

Something about how she put all her wants, surfing, sex and then food, it made him think if she was doing it on purpose, putting sex in the middle. Not most important and not least important, and somehow it stood front and center. Jeff sat back in his chair, "What time do you get off tonight? The surfing lessons can start then, as for the second thing on your list, you have to stay here for us to truly explore that option, and for the third, we can work on that as we go." He said hoping he could convince her to stay with him.

"I know what you're doing here, so don't think for one second I'm going to fall for that. If you want me, and I know you do, I don't have to stay here." It was her turn to sit back and watch him.

"That is true, I want you anyway I can get you but think about all the time we could have if you didn't have to go back to my mothers. Also, she won't know things, like what time you come home, and you won't have to check in with her when you stay here." He was going to fight for what he wanted and having her in his bed every night was what he wanted.

"That is true, I don't like the idea of checking in with anyone, but I'm sure I could speak to your mother, and we can come to an agreement about my sleeping arrangements. I think you might have forgotten that I negotiate contracts every day."

Jeff got up from his seat, "Yes, I'm sure you do, and most of the time, the incentive is to get a great deal for your client." Taking her hand and pulling her to her feet, he said, "This time, the incentive is for you, a great deal for you Kat."

"Are you telling me, you're the good deal?" Her blue eyes boarded into his.

"I think it's a great deal, because I'm a sure bet, Kat." He leaned in to kiss her, but she stopped him.

Kat had to think about what Jeff was offering. If he started kissing her, her mind would turn to mush. As she suspected, that was what he had in mind, she had to pull away. She needed to get upstairs, maybe then she could think. "I have to go," grabbing her clothes she had left at his place, she went to change.

Jeff watched her go, knowing he was close to convincing her, and that's why she was running. It was a give and take, he'd give her this time, and then later he'd take what he wanted. She was no push over, but he already knew that. Kat was going to make him work for it, and that was fine with him. After watching his brother fight for Liz, he knew Kat would make him feel many different things. Knowing she has already made him feel different, because his feelings about being with one person had changed. Give all that you are to that one special person, concentrating on the other ones needs. In the end, Ben and Liz are happy and in love, so it must have some merit. Just then, Kat came out of the bathroom.

"Do you need anything from my mother's house because you don't have a car here? I can take you over there before you go upstairs."

"That would be great. I can't get any work done without my laptop."

Jeff stepped close and said, "I'll just be a minute," and kissed her. Walking into his room, he quickly changed and made a mental note to speak to his brother about wooing Kat. Knowing Ben would have a field day with him asking for help, but right now, he'd take all the help he could get. Ben managed to win Liz over, so he had to have some advice that could help him. He spent every night with Liz, and that was what Jeff was after. The time with Kat, to show her there was more than just sex. Even if the sex was out of this world, he didn't want Kat getting the wrong idea about his intentions.

Dropping Kat off at his mother's, he headed back to the shop, knowing he most likely wouldn't see her until after the store closed, because he had so much work to do. He kissed her hard, sending a message he needed to get his fill of her. When he finally released her, she was breathless, and he was rigid. The thought of running her upstairs to take the edge off his need, passed through his mind. Deciding it wasn't a good idea, he left.

Kat watched as Jeff pulled away. On one hand, the man made her body sing, and on the other, he just down right pissed her off. Now she was left with wanting him, a feeling she wasn't accustomed to feeling. He kissed her as if he wanted her, then turn on his heels and left her standing there looking after him. Not understanding her body's reaction to him, well she knew what she was feeling, but why him. He was a very good-looking man. She'd give him that, and he had a way about him that turned her insides to mush. The strong pull her body felt, she wanted to spend as much time as she could with him.

However, she had fear of becoming obsessed with the man, and how he made her feel. She could very easily become accustomed to his touch and the warmth of his body. A mighty fine body, Kat felt her teeth biting down on her bottom lip. Yes, the thought was pleasing to her. Having Jeff around has been a pleasurable experience. Now that she had a taste of him, she knew it would be hard to give him up, but she was not staying. No matter what her body wanted, she had worked too hard to establish herself in the business to throw it all away. Gathering her stuff, she needed to work, she drove to Liz's apartment, where she would help her until she didn't need her anymore. Then go home, back to the life she worked so hard to have, alone.

# ~ 18 ~

When Jeff got to the shop and he had to unlock the door, he knew Ben wasn't in yet. The days of just walking in whatever time he wanted, were over. Having Ben in the shop was something Jeff could always count on. He was the first one in, and most of the time was the last to leave, but now with Liz on bed rest, Ben had other priorities. It brought Jeff a lot of pride to know that Ben now depended on him to open the shop on time. Turning on the lights as he went, the shop came to life. The place that his father opened so many years ago, didn't look anything like it did today.

Making him laugh to think as a kid, he hated and loved that his family owned a surf shop. Working the summers sucked, but the influx of girls was great. Here he was now, an adult, and up until recently, he still loved and hated it. Now that he had taken on ordering and the new line of surfboards, the place brought him satisfaction to be a part of it all. To know he was truly adding to the legacy that his father started. Going into his new office, he started looking over the floor plans, what he wanted to accomplish today. With the help of the new guy, they could almost get finished with the new displays. Then, they had to figure out what they would do with the old product with the space they had left. After this was over, the shop was going to look as if it was stuffed, bursting at its seams. Maybe he needed to talk to Ben about having a big sale to reduce the stock. Also, he needed to go over what products they no longer had room to sell.

Jeff must have been deep in thought, because he didn't hear his brother come in, startled by Ben's voice, "How's the move going?"

"I was just thinking we need to go over some things, like what we don't have room for anymore. Maybe we can figure out what we don't sell well, or don't make any money on, because we're going to run out of room soon. I still need to find places for the old stuff we have in the stock room. I thought we could have a huge sale."

"That's a good idea, but can we wait until I tell Liz we bought a house. I don't think I can prepare for a big sale, with advertising and getting everything ready."

"Wow, you got the house, congratulations. That was a great place. I was impressed when Liz invited everyone for dinner that time. Having the ocean outside your door, the hot tub, and of course along with all the good memories," Jeff shifted his brows up and down.

"Yeah, I think Liz is going to love it. It was a great suggestion that Kat had. I should give her credit. She really has been a great help. Not just with taking care of Liz's everyday needs but helping me to keep my sanity."

"Speaking of Kat, I know you're going to have a ball with this, but I need your advice. I'm attempting to get Kat to stay with me. I want to prove to her we have something, and if she runs back to mom's, then I can't work my magic." Jeff watched as Ben stepped into the room and sat in the chair across from his desk.

"I should give you shit about this, but I'm not, because I've been where you are. As far as Kat goes, you have your hands full, and I knew that the first night at the club. How to convince Kat to do anything she doesn't want is an undertaking. The best thing I can tell you, is make her want to stay, and stop pushing her to stay. The more you insist she stays, the more she is going to fight against you. I don't know if that helps, good luck, you're going to need it." Ben got up, started out the door, and stopped, "Hey, do you think you and Kat could do me a big favor, I'd like to have the babies room painted before I take Liz to the house. I don't want her breathing any paint fumes, and I think she'd really like that the room will be ready."

"Sure, I'll talk to Kat tonight. I'm giving her first surfing lesson. If she's not into painting I'll ask Owen, we'll get it done for you. When are, you going to tell Liz?"

"The closing is tomorrow, and I thought if you paint the room within the next couple of days, I'd like to bring her over on the weekend."

"Doesn't she have to be at the closing, how are you going to hide that from her until the weekend?"

"Under the circumstance, with her on bed rest, they said I can sign the papers and have her sign with a notary present. Mom can do that for us, and I can turn the paperwork back to them, but in the meantime, they will give us the keys."

"When do you plan on moving in? I have a feeling we are volunteering to help you move too."

"All we have to move is our personal belongings because the house is furnished. I bought everything that was in the house lock, stock, and barrel. Hey, on a different subject, how is the new guy working out?"

"Leo's working out fine, I don't know why but he freaks Kat out. She ran into him in the store, I mean physically and went into fight mode. He thought she was funny, and you could only imagine how that went over. I told him to back off, but he truly didn't seem to be into upsetting her. I think it was just a misunderstanding. As a matter of fact, I think he is more into Dannie. I've caught him watching her, even though he says he's not here for that. I told him she's off limits just in case he gets any ideas."

Ben nodded, "I don't think Dannie is ready to get involved with anybody right now. So even if he's interested, he won't get far. She will shut him down, besides, he's an employee, and I happen to know she won't go there."

Jeff had known something happened at Dannie's last job that sent her home, but he didn't know any details, as he was sure Ben did. He wasn't sure he wanted to know, because if someone took advantage of his sister, he might have to kill someone. It wasn't unusual for Ben to know what was going on in Dannie's life more than him. Ben was always the one they turned to for advice. Jeff didn't bother to ask Ben what he knew, because if Dannie wanted him to know, she would have come and talked to him.

Ben left to open the doors to the public, and Leo strolled in. Getting the day started, Jeff laid out where he wanted the new product for Leo. Moving between the shop and the stock room, Jeff thought about the kiss this morning with Kat. Wishing he could have stayed. He pulled out his phone to send her a quick text telling her just that.

Jeff: Hey, Sunshine, thinking about you and that kiss. I'm missing you!

He waited, but after a few minutes, he didn't think she was going to text back, so he went back to work. Maybe she was busy with Liz, or on a conference call. As Jeff worked, the thought that she hadn't returned his text plagued his mind. Everything in him wanted to text her again or he could just march upstairs and find out what she was doing. But, he had to play it cool, if he pressured her, he would push her away that he knew for sure. He would see her tonight when he'd teach her to surf. The thought made him smile, Kat on a surfboard. He figured she'd do great, the way he had seen her go through her fighting moves, and of course those yoga poses.

~ ~ ~ ~ ~ ~

Kat moved through the apartment, bringing boxes into Liz's bedroom, ever since Liz started ordering things for the babies the apartment had become a UPS hub. Every day, more boxes arrived, and as Liz opened them, she became excited. Which Kat knew was benefiting Liz greatly, because her demeanor had changed. Kat couldn't help the feeling of dread. Liz would have the babies, and she would go home, to the empty apartment. She was happy for Liz, but if she looked deeper, beyond the happiness she wanted for Liz, jealousy, over what Liz, and Ben had together, that's what she was feeling. Not that she was proud of that, but before Ben and Liz, she didn't believe in true love. Now seeing it with her own eyes, how Ben has moved heaven and earth for Liz's happiness. The question was, could she ever completely trust someone to give her happiness. She couldn't help wanting that for herself.

As she brought yet another box for Liz to open, seeing all the cute baby clothes, made Kat yearn for something else, she never thought she wanted. It wasn't until she noticed, Liz looking at her, how transparent she felt.

"Kat, what's going on with you? You've been quiet, and that's never good." Liz pushed the contents of the box aside.

Kat didn't want Liz to look too closely, because she didn't want to have to explain what was going through her mind. "I'm not being quiet. I'm just moving the boxes and the stuff you bought. Soon, this apartment will look like a Babies R Us store and it is totally strange that I even know what that is."

"Kat, look at me." When she glanced over at Liz, Kat could see she was not going to let this go. "Come sit with me," Liz patted the bed. Kat felt overly exposed, she tried to avoid looking directly at Liz. Moving toward the bed, Kat pulled up the covers as she sat down.

"You do know this friendship goes both ways. You've put your life on hold to help me out, and I don't think I could have gotten this far without you. I sense you don't think I can be the same kind of friend. You haven't said very much about what is happening between you and Jeff. I've tried to give you space to figure out how you feel, but now I'm thinking I'm going to have to pull some teeth. Either you start talking, or I'm going to have to call Jeff and get his take on what's going on."

Kat took a deep breath and released it, closing her eyes. "You know what's going on. Jeff and I are having a physical relationship. He is helping me work through the issues I have from the rape, that's all."

"Kat, this is me you're talking to, I know you. This is so more than you workin' through things, and you know it. Why can't you trust me? Talk to me, Kat."

"Liz, for the first time in my life, I want more. More than just my job and the life I have now. You and Ben have shown me that love does happen, and Jeff has shown me how good my body can feel. I'm just not sure what to do about how I feel, or if I trust someone like Jeff with forever after. He knows how to make my body rock, I'll give him that."

Kat heard Liz chuckle, "I bet he does. Kat, there is no guarantee in life. Jeff has a bad track record, for sure, but I also think he is changing. I know what Ben has said about how much he is doing for the shop, and I've talked to him myself about you. He looked me in the eye, Kat and told me he has feelings for you. Not that I think he understands what he's feeling, as I'm sure you don't either. I do think he is being sincere, and for the first time, he wants more."

"I can't stay here, and he's stuck here. The same as it was for you, but I'm not willing to move like you did."

"I didn't think I'd move so far away from Paige, but in the end, I had to do what was best for me. You showed me it was time for me. I did love Ben, there was never any doubt about that. He added so much to my life, things I didn't even know I needed."

"Yeah, but you can write anywhere, I have to be in New York. I'm pushing my luck with my boss now, so as soon as the babies are born, I must go home. I can't just relocate. As you can see, my situation sounds the same but will have a different conclusion."

"Why can't you start your own business here?"

"I don't want to start all over, and if I chose to do that, I couldn't be your agent anymore, because you have a contract with the company not me."

"So, when is my contract up? Because I won't renew it with them, I want you."

"It's not that easy Liz, I have a stipulation in my contract. If I leave the company, I can't take any clients with me. You would have to self-publish your books and I couldn't legally represent you."

"So, I could do that, and I don't need it to be legal. I can have you look over anything before I sign it, as my lawyer not my agent."

"I don't want to do that Liz. I like my job. I just don't want it to be my entire life anymore."

"Kat, what are you looking to get out of this relationship with Jeff? Are you just using him for sex to get past what happened to you? Or do you have real feelings for him?"

"I don't know, Liz. I really don't know what I'm doing. I never wanted to get involved with Jeff in the first place, and yet here I am. He didn't give me much of a choice. I tried to push him away, but all the things that normally worked on men, didn't work on him. I even went home to get away from him, and he showed up at my job. Thanks to you, by the way. So, if you want to imply I'm using him then it's his own fault, because up until New York, there was nothing going on between us."

"Just enough sexual tension to choke a horse. I hate to tell you Kat, but everyone in the same room could feel it. This was going to happen, it wasn't if, it was when."

"Yeah, well now what, because he wants me to stay with him and not go back to Linda's? If I do that, I'm not sure how I will ever keep this just about sex, and I can't fall for him. I just can't. So, any suggestions would help." When Liz didn't say anything, Kat knew this wasn't going to end well. She needed to go home as soon as

~ Love's Dangers Undercurrents ~ Part 1

possible, do not pass go, do not collect two hundred dollars. Knowing it and making it happen, were two different things.

After working all day, and not hearing from Kat, Jeff's mood wasn't the best. He was hoping at some point, she would text him back. He thought about what Ben had said about making Kat want to stay and not pushing her. Making it her idea, she would feel more in control that way. How could he make her want to stay, and the thought came to mind? A wicked smile spread, and he knew just what he was going to do. The shop was closing in a half hour, so Jeff got everything he would need for Kat's surfing lesson. Tonight, he would show Kat why it was best if she stayed with him.

Once he had everything set, he headed up to his brother's apartment to collect Kat, for what he hoped to be a great night. Going up the back stairs, he knocked and went in. Not waiting for someone to open the door, Jeff was surprised to see boxes everywhere. Moving through the small pathway, he made his way to the bedroom. He knocked on the doorjamb before entering the room. Not wanting to catch his sister-in-law exposed, because that was something he truly didn't want to see. When Liz looked up from her computer on her lap, she smiled.

"Jeff, come in. Kat's changing for her surfing lesson. I wish I could go down to the beach and watch." Jeff could see how bed rest was wearing on Liz.

"Maybe one day we can get you down to the beach, you know, like we did when we worked on the new offices." In fact, she could watch them surf on the deck of her new house. Not that he was going to say anything, but he knew she would like that. "So, what's going on in here, you look like your buying out the baby stores?"

"Well, once I got started, I just couldn't stop. Kat thought if I felt more prepared for the babies, I would relax. Just because I'm on bed rest, doesn't have to mean I can't have things ready. I've bought cribs, and more clothes than the babies could possibly wear. Not knowing

~ 283 ~

what I'm having doesn't make it any easier, but I want to be surprised. As long as they are heathy, that's all I care about, and of course, getting through giving birth to twins." Jeff hadn't realized just how much his brother's life was about to change. Having babies in the house, he knew nothing about kids. Looking at all this stuff, made him feel overwhelmed, he couldn't imagine how his brother was feeling.

He could tell in Liz's face, that she was happier, and Jeff had a good idea that it had a lot to with Kat. She might try to come off as a hard ass, but deep down, she cared. If he could get her to feel that way about him, he found himself wanting that more than anything. It was that moment, when Kat walked into the room, with just her bikini and a small lace dress coving her body. Jeff stepped in close, pulled her into him, pouring all his frustrations into a kiss. Tilting Kat's head so he could get better access to her mouth, feeling his body react to her closeness. He felt her pull back before he was ready to release her, but he ended the kiss.

"Hi, you ready for your lesson?" There was so much more in that question than just wanting to know if she wanted to go surfing. Watching Kat glance over his shoulder at Liz, he knew Kat felt uncomfortable with Liz in the room, so he pulled back just a bit.

"Yes, I'm ready. I've been looking forward to riding a surfboard, waiting for my lesson to start." Jeff knew what she was doing. Her meaning wasn't lost on him. Yet, he couldn't help how her saying she was ready to ride the surfboard, made him think about her riding him. They said their good-byes to Liz, and Jeff pulled Kat from the room, and down the stairs to his apartment. He knew they didn't have long to surf before it would get dark. He needed to have her alone, even if only a few minutes, he had to have her close, pulling Kat into his apartment. Before he knew it, he had Kat pinned against the door and he slammed his lips on hers. Holding her arms over her head with one hand, he couldn't get enough of her. Gliding his other hand along her jaw, he lifted her face. Wanting nothing more than to take her right here, he knew he had to pull back. Slowly, as if it killed him, he ended the kiss. Pressing his forehead to hers, he whispered, "Do you have any fucking idea what you do to me?"

"If it's anything close to what you do to me, then I have some idea," she said in the same hush tone, both needing a moment to catch their breath. As Jeff glided his thumb over Kat's porcelain skin, he looked into the bluest eyes he'd ever seen, it seemed like she could see right through him.

"I need to change if we are going to surf, and you need a wetsuit," he said to break the spell she had over him. Stepping back, he said, "I'll be just a minute." Turning his back on her, he heard her release the breath she had been holding. He totally understood how she was feeling because he found himself in the same boat. He had to tell himself, he would have her later, and knowing what he had in mind for her, only made him want the lesson to be a short one.

Once they were out on the beach, Jeff started Kat off on the sand. He had her on her stomach and taught her to pop up into a stance that she would do once she was on a surfboard. She did well with all that, and was anxious to get out on the water, so Jeff figured he would just let her try, and see how well she did. Before he let her go completely, he made her lay on the board to feel the lift of the wave and told her when to pop up. He sat on his board next to her, watching her, and it didn't hurt that her ass was right there. This was the first time he ever taught a woman to surf or even had a woman out here with him. Except Liz, but she didn't count, because she wasn't really with him, she was with his brother.

Knowing he didn't care enough to share this part of his life with anyone else, and the fact that Kat wanted to share this with him, made what he was feeling about her, more real. Kat was trying so hard, but each time she popped up on the board, it flew out for underneath her. Jeff tried to correct what she was doing wrong, but she wasn't really doing anything wrong, as much as she attempted to control the board, instead of going with the board. After many attempts, Jeff wanted to give her a rest and show her how it feels to ride a wave. He had her climb onto his board, and he lay on top of her. Once the wave came in, he popped up in between her legs, riding the wave with her on his board. Next time, he had her on her knees, so when he rode the wave, she could see. Then he made her stand with him, and they rode the wave together. He knew she had to be exhausted, and twilight was setting in. The sun setting was a beautiful site, and having Kat to share it with was prefect.

Sitting with Kat between his legs he asked, "So, how did you like your first taste of surfing. Not as easy as it looks, is it?"

She chuckled, "You make it look easy, and I can't believe you can do it with me on the board. When I tried, the board wanted to go somewhere else. I don't think my board likes me."

"You know the board is just that, a board. You want control and the board goes where it wants, until you get better at it, you need to go with the board. Learn to ride the wave in, before you try to do anything else," Jeff's hands wrapped around her waist.

"I watched Liz surf, and I thought, I got this. I'm in better shape than her, so of course I thought I wouldn't have any trouble. I've worked my ass off tonight, and I still don't think I've got it," Kat leaned against Jeff's chest.

"Liz did great for a first timer, not many do that. I know dudes that had surfed for years, and still not master it."

"You know, it could be that her teacher is better than mine."

"Is that so, well he just might be? Ben teaches underprivileged kids all the time, and to tell you the truth, you are the first girl I've ever taught. You know, there is a bit of a distraction teaching you."

"Is that so, I might need to get Owen to teach me, you know so he doesn't get distracted?" Kat said in a playful tone.

"He'd be distracted, too," Jeff went silent for a while, then asked, "Kat, can I ask you something?" He felt her body tighten up, but she nodded.

"Where do you see, this going, I know where I want it to go?"

Before she could answer, the water moved next to her leg and a head popped out of the water. Kat screamed, and Jeff laughed. Two dolphins splashed them when they got scared with her scream.

"Easy, they won't hurt you. Stay still and they will come back." Sure enough, after a minute one put his nose on the tip of the board. "Relax, he will move closer, he wants you to pet him."

"Oh, my God, you have to be kidding, you want me to touch it." The other dolphin surfaced on the other side of the board. Kat didn't know where to look, there was one on each side of the board. Jeff put his hand out and the dolphin next to them moved in closer, placing his nose on Jeff's leg. Jeff rubbed his hand over the dolphin and the other one then moved in, too, wanting his attention. Taking Kat's hand, he moved it down the dolphin's head. It made a sound in the back of its throat of pleasure. Kat relaxed, but the more attention she gave one, the other tried to get her attention. They pushed her hand with their noses. Before she knew it, she was petting both. One even attempted to get on the board with them. Then just as they showed up, they were gone.

"Wow that was crazy. Wait until I tell Liz, I pet two dolphins. As New Yorker, I never would have thought I'd come close to anything like that."

"They like the attention, but it's getting dark, and we need to head in, dolphins aren't the only thing in the water." At that, Jeff started paddling in.

Jeff and Kat made their way back to Jeff's place. Leaving the boards on his back deck, they went in to clean up and get to the part of the evening Jeff was looking forward to. He took her hand and led her into his small bathroom. Sliding down the zipper to her wetsuit, he watched her reaction to his hands on her. Slowly, he removed it off her shoulders, taking it to the floor. Looking up at her, he helped her free her feet. Seeing she was holding her breath, he said, "It's just me Kat," moving his hands up the back of her legs.

"I know, that's what I'm afraid of." With her statement, he stopped moving his hands.

Not looking at her anymore, he asked, "What are you afraid of, Kat? You know I won't hurt you," placing small kisses on her legs.

"I'm afraid of how you make me feel," she whispered.

"Tell me how I make you feel," he moved higher up her legs, rubbing his stubble as he went.

"Great, fantastic, scared, out of control, confused." Her voice drifted off and her eyes closed.

"You have no idea how scared and out of control you make me feel. You make everything inside of me go crazy," wanting to say more, but he knew this wasn't the right time for more.

"I'm scared, because I'm becoming addicted to your touch, I crave it."

With her words, Jeff removed her bikini bottoms, kissing the butterfly tattoo. He'd make sure she craved just his touch, not only for her pleasure, but his own, too. He craved her, needed her, body, mind, and soul. Pulling the string to her top, he let it hit the floor before coving her breast with his mouth, drawn to the one with the scar, as if it needed special attention.

Kat stood stock still, absorbing the feel of Jeff touching her. His every caress, sent shock waves throughout her body, and it was something she didn't understand. How could, after all these years, she come to have this amazing sensation with the completely wrong man, as if there was a right man for her. He was touching her body, and she no longer cringed, no longer afraid, well she was, but not for the same reasons. Afraid he would stop, or this would end before she could get her fill, before she went back to her old life. Feeling the pull as he sucked her nipple, made her almost stop breathing. Would she ever get enough of him? Could she stop after what he made her feel?

She had no idea when he had turned on the shower, or when he removed his wetsuit. However, when the warm spay of the water cascaded down her body, it brought her back. Watching him move in the small space, as he started washing her hair. With no shoes on she was shorter then him, looking up, seeing the concentration in his face, as his fingers moved through her hair, he massaged her head. The feeling was exquisite, and she found herself wanting to return the favor. She wanted not only to wash his hair, but she wanted to make him feel the way he made her feel. Raising her hands to his chest, her hands roamed over his flat nipples. Leaning in she took one nipple into her mouth, running her tongue over it.

Jeff's response was a moan, closing his eyes as she continued her quest over his chest. Moving her hands lower, exploring his abs, he leaned against the wall for support. She bit him, and sucked, Jeff pulled her in closer with his hands on her ass. Lifting one leg, she wrapped it around Jeff's waist. The water running down the back of her body washed the shampoo away. Jeff picked up her other leg and turned them, so she was now pressed against the wall. He kissed his way down her chest, as he held onto her ass. Lost in the feeling, he slipped deep inside of her. Her body ached, for him, the feel of him moving inside her. She began her own movement as her legs clinched around his waist. They moved together, one moved up and down, while the other moved in and out. It didn't take long before both had found release and were now sitting in the bottom of the tub. This was not getting old, nor was she getting her fill. Never having this sensation before, of wanting more, was very confusing to her. This wrong man was the right guy to make her body sing.

Having this out of body experience, she didn't know if this happens with everyone having great sex or was it just with him. Not having anything to compare it to, she didn't know, and asking Jeff was out of the question. He would think she, was what? More, why did she care? Somehow, she knew the answer to both her questions, she did care, and that was the problem.

Jeff pulled her to her feet, looking in his eyes she said, "Jeff, I have to know," she paused before asking, "Is this how it is with everyone, I have nothing to compare my reaction to."

Looking down at her, he took her face in his hands. "No, this isn't how it is with everyone, just you, Kat." Slowly he leaned in to kiss her, his tender kisses were almost her undoing. "I've never felt this way before you."

Now that she had her answer, she didn't know what to do with it. Realizing she had begun to like Jeff, not just for what he did for her body, but him. The question, that continued to plague her, was can she trust him? Of course, the why now, why him questions remained. Right from the beginning, her instincts said to stay far away from this man and yet she couldn't seem to do that. His pull, she felt drawn to him. His question from earlier came to mind, he asked her where she saw this relationship going. She didn't have an answer, on one hand she knew she was going home, but on the other, she wanted to stay and see where this took her. She still didn't understand why she let her guard down to begin with, but here she was.

As all these thoughts went through her mind, Jeff continued to wash her body. She found she wanted to return the favor, taking the body wash, she spread the soap over his shoulders and down his chest.

"Why do you look so deep in thought? What's going on in that pretty little head of yours?" He made her look at him.

"The truth, I'm confused. For the first time in my life, I don't understand my own feelings. After what happened to me, I always had my feelings in check. Controlling them and knowing myself, I prided myself on that fact. Now as an adult, I should know what I'm feeling, sort through them, but I find I'm more lost now, than I ever was."

"You think you're alone? You're not. Just because you're an adult, doesn't mean you have all the answers. At some point, you need to stop trying to understand and just go with the flow. If it is meant to be it will be." Rinsing them both off, Jeff pulled her from the shower.

"We don't have to have all the answers tonight," he said.

# ~ 19 ~

After drying her off, Jeff took her to his bedroom. He made love to her, making every inch of her body a bundle of nerves, sending impulses through her spine and out every muscle. How did he do this to her body repeatedly? Her body felt so sated, she didn't have an ounce of strength. When Jeff announced, it was time to take her back to his mother's house, she couldn't move. Knowing she should get up, and making her body move, were two entirely different things.

"No," was the only word Kat could form.

"What do you mean, No? I thought you didn't want to say with me," he leaned over her shoulder to speak in her ear.

"I can't, now go away," she heard the jerk laugh, but she didn't care.

"Ok, but don't tell me I didn't try to take you home." He slid down under the covers and drew her in close. His plan was working, surfing, then fantastic sex, and now she didn't want to move. He closed his eyes and listened to her breathing slow.

The next morning, Kat opened her eyes and knew right away, where she was. The light wasn't even shining in through the window yet. She glanced over at the alarm clock on Jeff's nightstand, it read five am. She could get up and go for a run? Or she could stay in bed, waking Jeff to her roaming hands. That idea sounded better than a run to her. Slowly she turned to face him, knowing she couldn't see him. Kat moved her hand to his waist, and he slightly shifted. Moving her hand lower, over his hip, he mumbled something. That made Kat smirk, wishing she could see his face. When her hand slid over his lower abs, his hand landed on top of hers, gliding hers down over his very hard penis. She didn't know if he was awake, or if he was just reacting to her touch.

She took him in her hand, sliding up and down him. In the dark, she heard a sound of his pleasure, and she gripped him tighter. Within a few minutes, she knew he was awake, but not saying anything, she continued her pursuit. Kat started to kiss down his chest, loving how his body felt. When she reached his abs with her mouth, she felt him shift. Knowing he was going to stop her, she went for what she wanted. Taking him, she slid her tongue over the head of his penis. She heard him say her name, with a tight tone, as if he was holding on by a thread. After what he did to her last night, he deserved to feel out of control, the way he made her feel, every minute they spent together.

This was payback in the best kind of way. Moving down his shaft, she sucked him in hard. Going as deep as she could, then, backing off, only to do it again. Taking her free hand, she moved it down between his legs, taking hold of his sac, and shifting it amongst his testicles. She could tell he was close and wanted to take him over the edge. Never in a million years, did she ever see herself doing this of her own free will, much less wanting it more than her next breath.

"Kat, you need to stop, I can't hold back any longer." Jeff said in a stranded voice.

She ignored his words, and in the next second, she felt his release. His hips jerked to meet her mouth, and she rode out the wave. His hands threaded through her short hair, as he pulled her up to meet his lips. Rolling her to her back, Jeff kissed her tenderly. His hands moved from her face to over her body, lighting the fire within her once again. She couldn't help wanting to touch every inch of him, too.

His words in her ear were soft and unrushed, "I love waking up next to you." She liked it, too. Having Jeff next to her to have anytime she wanted was a big plus. Maybe she'd pack a small bag to leave at his place, so when she stayed, she'd have clean clothes to wear. That thought went right out the window when Jeff slid into her. All she could think, was just how great he felt. They moved together, kissing, touching each other as they both found freedom to free fall. She lay in his arms, feeling as if there was no other place she ever wanted to be.

Once they caught their breath, Jeff broke the silence, "I forgot to ask you last night, but Ben asked me if we could paint the babies room for them. He doesn't want Liz breathing any paint fumes. I told him I'd ask, and if you don't want to do it, I could always get Owen to help. The closing is today, and he'll get the keys, so we could do it anytime. Ben wants to take Liz over the weekend. I think Liz is going to be so surprised."

"I don't mind helping out, but just so you know, I'm not a painter. I've never painted a room before. I don't know the first thing painting a room." She felt his chest move, and she knew he was laughing at her.

"Something else I can teach you, surfing, and now painting. This is going to be fun, make sure you wear old clothes."

"I don't have any old clothes, and surfing wasn't the first thing you taught me," rolling on top of him so she could look at him. "You taught me how good my body can feel, and you showed me, I can trust you with my body. You helped me with my hang-ups, and showed me I can be normal," he kissed her forehead, and she leaned into him.

"I'd like to say I did it all for you, but we both know that would be a lie, and I told you, I'd always tell you the truth. Speaking of the truth, you never answered my question last night, about where you see this going."

"I don't know, Jeff, I told you I'm confused. I want more in my life then just work, but I'm not willing to give it all up either and move. I like my job. So right now, I'm just taking it day by day." She laid her cheek on his chest, because as much as she didn't want to give up her life in New York, she didn't want to end what they had either. She felt his hand run over her hair, as if he was comforting her.

He tilted her head up to his, "I get it, I do, but what we have is special. Not many people find this. I told you last night, when we're together, it's like nothing I've ever felt before. You may not have the experience in relationships that I do, and I'm not proud of that fact, but I can tell you that you're different, I feel different with you. I want more with you, and I've known it for a long time now. Not that I wanted it at first, because I knew I was going to have to work for it. You had me all over the place one minute, I was pissed off and in the next, I was so hard."

"From the first time, I met you, you've had this way about you. You are the kind of guy I would avoid, or I'd belittle. Everything I did, you just kept coming back for more. Most men don't stick around for more abuse. You provoked a part of me that I thought was dead, and that scared and aroused me. I still don't know what to do with that."

Jeff knew that at this point Kat wasn't capable of a commitment, and he wasn't going to push her. So, he changed the subject, "You hungry? I could make you breakfast in bed." He started to get up, and when he looked back at her, he realized how much he liked seeing her in his bed. She had shocked the shit out of him with her morning wake-up call. That was something a man could really get used to, and if he had his way, he would.

"Do you have anything healthy," she asked as she stretched. Watching her move around unashamed of her body, being naked in front of him didn't seem to bother her anymore.

"I have eggs, and I bought turkey bacon for you." He slipped on his boxers and went to her. "I want you to stay in bed, because after we eat, I have plans for you." He lightly run his fingers down the center of her body, watching her pale skin break out into goose bumps.

"You can't possibly want more," she watched the smile cross his face as he turned and walked out. She yelled after him, "Just the egg whites, and make sure you drain the bacon."

Jeff sat at his desk, thinking about the night before and this morning. It couldn't have gone any better, because Kat had stayed with him of her own free will. Although, he had made sure she was completely satisfied. He knew how much surfing would take out of her, and she did work it. He smiled at the thought, Kat had tried repeatedly, and each time she wiped out. He would have thought she'd be a natural, but it seemed she was going to have to work at it. It just meant that they would be spending more time out on the water, and that was fine with him.

He closed his eyes as he sat back in his chair, thinking about their discussion on the future. He didn't want her to have to give up her job and her life in New York, but for them to be together, someone had to give up something. Thinking back to when his brother faced the same dilemma, his brother was willing to walk away from the shop, the place he worked so hard to keep afloat after their father's death. At one time, Jeff would have loved to move away, and do something else, but now that he felt invested in the shop, he didn't want to leave. For the first time, he liked where he was, and what he was doing. He was happy to have Kat by his side, and the fact that the shop was doing well, the only thing he could think that would make his life perfect would be if Kat decided to stay in California. If that were possible, he'd have to allow Kat to make up her own mind. The only thing he could do, is make her want to stay. Jeff pulled out the card for the music box store and dialed the number.

~ ~ ~ ~ ~ ~ ~

Kat went upstairs to Liz's apartment, standing there feeling more confused than ever. Jeff had her head spinning. He had her wanting to pack a bag to stay with him, when she knew that would only lead to trouble, if she became more dependent on him. This was turning into something she couldn't pass off as just sex. She was entering territory she was very unfamiliar with, not knowing how to proceed. When it was just her, doing what she wanted when she wanted, her life was easier. Now, he was there in her head, what he wanted, when he wanted it. Kat shook her head to clear it, as she knocked.

Ben opened the door as he did every morning, but today he had a huge smile on his face. "Hello, Kat," Ben leaned in and asked quietly, "Did Jeff talk to you about helping me out?" His question threw her, then she realized what he was talking about, and she nodded.

She whispered, "Painting, yes. When will you have the keys?"

"Later this afternoon, I figured I'd pick up the paint on my way home, and you can do it anytime. If it has a few days to dry, I think Liz will be alright with the smell." Knowing the smell wouldn't hurt Liz, Kat didn't say anything to Ben, because she found it to be sweet that he worried about her and the babies so much. Also, the way he wanted to surprise her was very endearing. "This is all happening because of you, Kat. I don't think I would have come up with the prefect plan without you. You have to help me surprise her, I plan on bringing her over there on Saturday."

"Ben, you don't want to do it with just the two of you?" Kat was stunned that Ben wanted her there.

"No, I want everyone there. Well, once we get her down the stairs, I want everyone to go to the house and wait inside. I'm going to blindfold her, and you are going to make sure she doesn't peek as we drive over to the house." Kat couldn't help getting caught up in Ben's excitement.

Smiling Kat said, "Okay, I'd love to be a part of your surprise." That's when she saw Ben move toward her and once again, he pulled her into a hug. This time she returned his embrace, he said in her ear, "Thank you, Kat."

When she made her way into Liz's bedroom, she found herself smiling. This was going to be good for Liz and her family. Liz was finally getting everything she deserved, and Kat was happy for her. She found herself feeling as if she wanted that same happiness. Kat found Liz sitting up with her arms folded over her huge chest. Liz was big on top before she became pregnant, and now she was just huge, chest, belly, everywhere.

"Kat, do you know what my husband is keeping from me? And don't give me any bullshit because I know something is going on. He is walking around with a smile on his face until he sees me looking at him, then he tries to hide it. He's jumpy, anxious, and I know it's not just about the babies. At first, I was worried I was spending too much money, but he didn't care about that. So, spill it."

"Okay, yes I know what he's hiding, no, I won't tell you anything, so forget it." Kat said and walked away from Liz's intense stare.

"Kat, you come back here," Liz commanded in her sternest mother voice.

"Don't try and use that tone with me, it's not going to work."

"Kat, how fair is it that everyone knows what's going on, while I'm stuck in this bed, hidden away from everything." This time Liz pouted, and Kat still didn't fall for her act.

Kat went to Liz and sat on the bed next to her, then said, "I will tell you this much, you'll like it. Now, until Ben is ready to tell you, I can't say anymore, so don't even try." Liz made a humph sound and attempted to cross her arms tighter across her chest, as her nose went in the air. It made Kat laugh to see Liz so upset over a surprise her husband had for her.

The rest of the day flew by, with more packages coming, and Liz moving past the secret she didn't know. Kat didn't realize what time it was until Ben and Jeff walked in. Jeff asked if she was ready, not knowing exactly what she was agreeing to, she nodded her head. He took her hand and as she walked out of the room, she heard Liz tell Ben that Kat had told her everything. Kat yelled back, "I said nothing, don't believe her Ben."

Jeff led her down to his apartment, and once inside, Jeff went straight into his bedroom. Kat wasn't sure if he wanted her to follow, but in a few minutes, Jeff was back, handing her a t-shirt and a pair of his boxers. Looking down at her hand with a puzzled look, he said, "We're going to paint, remember? You don't have anything that can get paint on them, so I'm lending you some of mine."

"Oh," she said, still looking down at the clothes in her hand.

"You going to change, or you just going to look at them," he asked.

"Right," she started stripping right there in his living room. Sliding his boxers on, she rolled down the waistband and pulled the t-shirt over her head. Both were too big on her small frame, but somehow, she liked them.

"I like the way you wear my boxers, they look good on you," and before he got any ideas he, moved to the door.


Jeff unlocked the door to the house that Ben was going to surprise Liz with the house Kat had stayed in when she came to check on Liz. It felt weird to be inside, without Liz being here, even more so, because Ben hadn't given it to her yet. Walking through the kitchen, Kat looked out the French doors to the beach. Remembering the few times they had sat on the deck, that first talk when she had told Ben that Liz had left. Kat smiled, she thought how far she and Ben had come. Hell, he was hugging her just this morning, but of course, he didn't like her much that day. Turning away from the memories, she asked Jeff if he knew what room they were painting.

"I didn't ask, maybe I should give Ben a call and find out." Jeff pulled out his phone.

"I would think Liz would want the room closest to the master bedroom as the nursery," she said, because that's the room she would want for her child. If she were preparing a room for a child, that's what she'd do.

"Right," he said as they walked down the hall. Knowing what room Liz stayed in, Kat showed Jeff the room she thought Liz would want. They moved the small amount of furniture out of the room. Then, Jeff went back to his truck to get the paint and the supplies. Kat looked out the window as she waited for Jeff to return. She could imagine a rocking chair sitting here, and Liz, with a baby in each arm, rocking them. A melancholy feeling passed over her and she felt her eyes tear up.

Jeff's arms wrapped around her, "Hey, you ok?" How did he know she was in a funk?

"I was just thinking of Liz sitting here in a rocking chair with both babies in her arms. She really hit the jack-pot when she fell for your brother," she turned in his arms.

"Yes, we Jacobs men are a great catch, just in case you need reminding how good." He held her chin and kissed her. He chased away any sadness she felt and replaced it with need.

Pulling back, Kat said, "I'd like to get Liz a rocking chair, and have it sitting here when she comes into this room."

"We can do that, but first we need to paint." He moved the supplies to the doorway. "We need to spread out these tarps, to keep any paint off the floor." They worked together, once they finished, Kat waited for what came next. When she said, she had no experience in painting a room, she wasn't kidding.

"Now, do you want to trim out the walls or use the roller?" Seeing her expression, he started to laugh. She had no idea what he was talking about, so he showed her. Kat choose the trim work, so Jeff put some of the paint in a container and gave her the brush. She worked along the floor, and he poured paint into the roller tray. Knowing it was going to take her awhile to get enough done so he could start rolling, he also took a brush and started working around the windows and the doorway. He took out his phone and played some music for them to paint to. After a while, he could hear her humming to the music, and when a song came on that she knew the words to she sang softly. Pretending to paint, he watched her, she concentrated on keeping the paint on the wall and not to get any on the molding.

Once she finished one wall, Jeff started rolling on the paint. With the ceiling, so high, Jeff's reach wasn't even close to touching. He moved faster around the room than she did, and when he was right over her, a drop of paint hit the top of her head. Looking down, Jeff could see the pale-yellow drop, and he thought, oh shit, but Kat kept painting. Maybe she didn't know it was there, so he kept rolling, until he felt a wet spot on his ankle. Looking down he had a dash of yellow paint streaked there. So, this is how it was going to go. Up until now, the paint was going on the wall, but now it was game on.

Kat felt the drop hit her, but she didn't react. When Jeff stepped closer, she swiped the brush across his ankle. She saw him looking down and knew what was coming next. The roller made a pass over her head, now she no longer had just a drop in her hair.

"Really, just remember you started it," that's when her brush shot up and hit him in the crotch. With a yellow stain on his shorts, he started rolling it wherever he could touch her. She jumped to her feet and smacked paint on his cheek. He held out the roller, and she held her brush, as if they were dueling, walking around each other. He didn't have nearly as much paint on him as she did, but she planned on rectifying that. She jabbed the brush at him, hitting him in the ear. He tried to hit her with the roller, but she jumped out of the way. He tried again and she anticipated his move, hitting him in the chest. His weapon held more paint, so when he did hit her, she ended up with a lot more on her. Her brush didn't have any more paint, but that didn't stop her from trying.

Jeff was laughing so hard, he couldn't even protect himself anymore, so he wrapped his arms around her. Once she stopped moving, he kissed her. They had more paint on them then the walls.

"Truce, we still have a lot to paint," kissing her again, he released her.

Pointing her brush at him she said, "You started it."

"I didn't mean to start it, but damn, if that wasn't fun." He turned to look at the room that now had paint flung everywhere. Thank God, they covered the floor before they started. They would have to take off their shoes before leaving the room, so not to track paint through the rest of the house. Kat went back to her job, and Jeff grabbed the ladder to trim out around the ceiling. They moved in a comfortable silence. Moving around the room in no time, when they finished, both stood back to admire their work. The pale-yellow color brightened the room, and Kat liked it.

Jeff stooped down to take Kat's shoes off. She rested her hands on his shoulders to steady herself. He then picked her up and brought her to the doorway, placing her back on her feet outside the room. Then he removed his own shoes and stepped out with her. Taking her hand, he moved them into the master bedroom.

"I happen to know there is a really big shower in here, and I think you might want to get that paint out of your hair."

Kat reached up to feel her dry, stiff hair and that's when she caught site of her reflection in the mirror. She had paint on her face, on her chest, down her body. Laughing, because she never would have done anything like this before meeting Jeff. She had fun painting and fighting with Jeff. Because of this man, she realized how much she was missing. Fun, the word wasn't one she would use to describe herself. Uptight, formal, or disciplined, that's how she saw herself, but with Jeff, she wasn't any of those things. Looking past her reflection, she saw Jeff watching her.

"What?" She asked.

"Nothing, I just like seeing you smile and hearing your laughter. When I first met you, you didn't do either, but now you seem happier. I'd like to think I have something to do with that, but truly, I don't think I can take all the credit." He moved in behind her, "I know, I'm feeling happier. I've never thought painting a nursery could be so much fun. As a matter of fact, I don't think I've ever had a better date."

"I was just thinking how I never saw myself painting a room, much less, having so much fun doing it. I don't know if it's being away from my normal routine. Get up, go to work, workout, then go home, work some more, then bed. Now with taking care of Liz, I still manage to get work done, but it's not everything. I don't feel the pressure, or that everything is an ASAP thing. Things can wait until tomorrow. I guess because something has become more important. Like having fun, I don't remember the last time I did anything just for the fun of it. I sound like such a loser, a very uninteresting person."

Jeff laughed, "Now, that is not how I see you at all, and there is nothing wrong with being a hard worker. Having pride in your job and what you do, wanting to do it to the best of your abilities. I just think you needed to meet someone who knows more about having fun, then hard work."

"You work hard, look what you're doing for the shop. This new line is going to bring in big bucks for the surf shop. Without you pushing Ben into something new, it wouldn't be happening."

"The funny thing about that is, I started changing just around the time I met you, when Ben wanted to spend more time with Liz and wasn't in the store every day. He gave me more responsibilities, making me see that I had more to give to the store then I had been. He gave me the freedom to look at new items the store could sell. All these years I hated my job, it was just what paid my bills. Now that I've become more invested, I look forward to going to work."

Kat smiled, a mound of pride swelled within her for Jeff. He deserved to find success, working hard and putting the best interests of the shop first. Of course, none of that helped the situation that was building between them. Not wanting to think about that now, not after a great night, Kat put that thought out of her mind.

"You know, if we shower now, we don't have any clean clothes to change into." She turned to face him.

"We could always stay the night and worry about clothes tomorrow." Jeff's eyebrows moved up and down.

"No, I'm not doing that. This is Liz's house, not ours, I will just put these clothes back on until we get back to your place." Kat stepped away from his embrace.

"You're no fun," he said playful.

"I've tried to tell you that," Kat moved to the shower to turn on the water. Turning back to him she said, "Give me your clothes, I'll throw them into the wash. They shouldn't take long and I'm sure you can figure out something to do in the meantime."

Now standing in just his birthday suit, with the biggest grin he said, "Now you're talking."

Kat took their clothes and went in search of the laundry room. Moving through the house, she couldn't help thinking of Ben and Liz raising a family here. Ben will be surprising Liz in just a few days. This was going to be one of the best things for Liz, besides finding Ben to begin with. With them, falling in love had set off a chain reaction, she wouldn't be here if they hadn't met. She wouldn't be exploring her own sexuality, and she would have never divulged any of her secrets.

Finding the washer and dryer, Kat looked for detergent. She really didn't know what she was doing, because Shay, her housekeeper, always did any laundry that didn't go to the drycleaners. However, how hard could it be, she could read the directions to know how much to put in. Starting the small load, she went back to the master bath. Jeff had already stepped into the shower, and Kat found herself watching him through the glass enclosure. This man was a site to see, his male form in the steam coming in and out of focus. She stepped closer, seeing his hands moving over his body, had heat spreading throughout her own body.

"You going to just stand there gawking at me, or you going to join me and wash my back?" That pulled Kat out of her stupor, he was so cocky.

"Gawking, huh," she opened the door and stepped in with him. Immediately he took her into his arms and smashed his lips to hers. She could feel his need because her body was feeling the same way. Returning his kiss, she tangled her fingers into his hair at the nape of his neck, loving that his hair was longer, and her fingers could hold him to her. His hands caressed her face, as he shifted her so he could deepen the kiss.

Pulling back just a whisper, "What are you doing to me," his voice deep and raspy.

Kat repeated his words in her head because it wasn't what she was doing to him, it was what he was doing to her. He was changing her, showing her his tender touch, his caring ways. He was making her want him, in ways that would end badly for her. Even knowing that, she couldn't pull back. He had put a spell on her, and she was falling for the man that bewitched women. The warning bells went off in her head, and yet, her body didn't want to listen.

Her body must have stiffened, because when she opened her eyes, Jeff's concerned look stared back at her. Needing to move past this, because she certainly didn't want to explain what was going through her head. Going for distraction, she reached down taking hold of his manhood, kissing him.

Jeff knew something was up with Kat, but he also knew she didn't want to tell him what it was. For now, he wouldn't press her. He was beginning to be able to read her, and his words right before her entire body tightened must have had something to do with it. She will talk to him when she was ready. Knowing something was bothering her, had turned arousal into concern. Pulling back, he grabbed for the shampoo to wash out the paint that he put in her hair.

Feeling the change in the mood Jeff asked her, "Have you always had short hair?"

"Yes, ever since high school," she was gazing into his eyes, and he didn't look away.

"Ever think about letting it grow out?" He asked as he massaged her head.

"No, I've always felt it gave me an edge."

"Do you think you still need that edge because I like when your hair is soft. Like that first time I saw you at the gym, when your hair was flat from your sweat. I think it gives you a relaxed look and I like running my fingers through it." He rinsed out the soap, running his hands over her head.

Looking up at him she said, "Before I cut it, I had very long hair. It was something I changed after... Well, you know," she didn't finish.

"I know, but don't you think he has taken enough from you. You must have liked the way your hair was before, and since you're regaining some of the other things he took from you, I just thought you might want to take back everything."

"You think I should let it grow out for me, or you'd like it if my hair was longer?" Now he had soap in his hands lathering them up.

"I can't say that I wouldn't like to truly run my fingers through your hair. Or, feel it on my skin." He moved his hands over her shoulders and down her arm, where he hit her with the paint roller.

"Okay, you would like me to grow my hair out. If I do this for you what will you do for me?"

The words were out immediately, "Anything."

# ~ 20 ~

The next few days went by so fast with Liz being busy with the new boxes. As Kat brought the boxes to Liz to open, she found one addressed to her. Jeff had sent her a snow globe, but this one didn't have any snow, there were stars that floated around. It was of two dolphins that moved around in a circle, and it lit up. Kat couldn't help holding it to her chest and remembered being on Jeff's surfboard when the face of a dolphin appeared. How calm and gentle Jeff was with them. Kat realized, Jeff was cataloging their time together with music boxes. Turning it over, she saw the name of the song, it played Breakfast in Bed, by Train. Again, she was reminded how he had made her breakfast that morning. It was a two for one, the dolphins, and breakfast in bed.

Today was the day Ben would bring Liz over to the house, and Kat felt caught up in the excitement of the surprise. That morning, Ben wanted to set up the cribs, so Kat kept Liz busy. Once Ben returned, it was time to bring Liz downstairs. Everyone walked into the bedroom as Liz sat in the wheelchair. She was talking non-stop about wanting to know what was going on. No one said a word, just moved methodical to get her down three flights of stairs. Ben and Jeff took the front, Linda and Kat took the back, Owen helped guide them around the landings. When they hit the last step, everyone took a deep breath, getting a very pregnant Liz down three flights, wasn't easy.

"Okay, now what," Liz asked.

"Now we get you in the car, and then I put this on you." He held up a blindfold in his hand.

"You've got to be kidding me, why would I need a blindfold? I think I can handle just closing my eyes."

Ben and Kat said at the same time, "I don't think so."

"I hate when you two gang up on me, I almost miss the days when you two couldn't stand each other."

"Just get in the car Liz," Kat helped her up, turned her so she could slide into the seat.

Once Ben put her seatbelt on, he slid the fabric blindfold over her eyes, and he said in her ear, "Kat is going to make sure you don't peek."

"I'm not a child, I think I can manage this," but Ben and Kat knew differently.

The short ride over to the house, had Kat's anticipation flying higher. She could feel her heart beating so fast. They pulled into the driveway, and Ben parked the car as close to the door as he could. Getting Liz out of the car with the blindfold on, wasn't easy, but they managed. In the yard, there was a real estate sign with the word SOLD sprayed across it. Ben pushed Liz to the front walkway. He stood behind her and Kat stood next to her. Ben pulled the fabric away from Liz's eyes and said, "Welcome home."

It took Liz's eyes a few seconds to readjust to the light. When her only reaction was, to look at the house in wonder, Kat was a little worried, however, when it dawned on her, Ben's words, "welcome home," she looked at him then the house.

"Welcome home," Liz, whispered with tears in her eyes. "You bought our house, my house, for me."

"For us Liz, room for the kids to grow up, and always room for Paige to come home."

Tears now streamed down Liz's face, and Kat felt her throat tighten up. Hating she couldn't control her emotions, Kat walked away from Ben and Liz. Both followed her up the walkway, when she heard Liz say, "You knew about this Kat, and didn't even give me a clue." Then Ben spoke, "It was her idea, about buying this house to surprise you. I wanted to buy a house for us, but you couldn't go looking, so she suggested I buy this one, because we both knew you loved it here."

"This is where it all started, oh my God, Ben, what have I ever done to deserve you." That's when the door opened, and Linda was standing there in welcome.

"You loved me Liz, and I feel the same way, how'd I get so lucky." He knelt and kissed Liz.

Kat walked past Linda, she needed to find a quiet corner to get herself together. She walked beyond Jeff and Owen, and she found herself in the babies' room. The only thing that was in here was the rocking chair that she and Jeff had picked out for Liz, and the two cribs. Walking to the window, she took a deep breath. This was all too overwhelming for her, but when she heard voices, she snapped every ounce of control front and center. Turning in time to see Ben wheel Liz into the room, once again, she had to hold tight to her emotions.

"Oh… my…God," she said each word as if she couldn't believe what she was seeing. "When did you have time to paint the babies room?" Kat could see she wasn't the only one emotional, because Liz looked as if she might explode and Linda appeared stunned, too.

That's when Jeff stepped into the small room and said, "We painted it for you, Liz. Kat and I did it the other night, so you wouldn't smell any fumes from the paint."

"Come here you two," Liz waved her hands for them to come to her. They move toward her, she made Jeff come down to her, and she took both of his checks in her hands as she said, "Thank you." Then kissed him right on the lips, just a quick peck, but Kat could see how that surprised Jeff. His face immediately turned red, and he glanced up at his brother, but Ben didn't seem to be concerned. Then Liz waved him off, so she could do the same to her and Kat had to say she felt a little taken back. She didn't even kiss her father or mother on the lips, in fact her mother only air kissed her, and her father kissed her on the forehead.

Ben's voice pulled her from her thoughts, "Mom cleaned, and washed all the linens, so if you want to stay here tonight Liz, we can."

"Linda where you are," Liz yelled. The small room became crowded, so Kat moved to exit as Linda came into the room. As she walked away, she knew Liz was kissing Linda as she did with Jeff and herself.

Walking into the living room where Owen was standing, she realized she hadn't spoken to him in a long time. He looked as if he was uncomfortable, Kat didn't understand why. Then she heard Liz calling Owen's name, and she knew his discomfort. She noticed Ben's sister wasn't here and wondered why, but no sooner than the thought passed through her mind, she heard the front door open.

"Hello, I have boxes. Let's go, ya big lugs," Dannie walked into the room. "Hey, where is everyone?"

"Everyone is in the nursery, and just to prepare you, Liz is very emotional and handing out kisses, on the lips." Kat made a face, and Dannie started laughing.

"Thanks for the warning. Leo loaded some of the boxes that were in Ben and Liz's apartment into my van. He's waiting for me to come back to load up again."

"I'll help you," but Dannie was shaking her head.

"I'm not going to do it, when I have three very capable dweebs to do it." This time it was Kat's turn to laugh at Dannie's description of her brothers and Owen. Dannie walked down the hall, and Kat started out the door to get the boxes. The same boxes she had moved at least ten times already. When Kat returned with a stack of boxes, she passed all three dweebs heading out. Ben told her Liz wanted her in the nursery. Kat walked down the hall and found Liz alone sitting in the rocking chair.

"If you're going to kiss me again, I think I'll just stand here."

Liz turned from the window, "I need you to come over here, I promise not to kiss you." When Kat moved in next to Liz, she said. "There are no words that I can say, to thank you enough. Kat, I've never had anyone in my corner, until I met you. You have become my very best friend, but even that doesn't sound good enough. You might do this for all your clients, going above and beyond the call of duty, but I want you to know, I love you, and you mean the world to me. You even have Ben loving you, and I'm pretty sure you have Jeff, too."

"Liz," for the first time in her life she didn't know what to say.

Jeff almost walked into the room to ask where Liz wanted this stuff. When he heard, Liz speaking to Kat, listening in, he knew it was wrong, and if his mother caught him, she wouldn't be happy.

"You come off as such a hard ass, but you have a huge heart and I'm so glad I get to have a part of it. You are the strongest woman I know, I have found strength, and courage to face things I never thought was possible, with your help."

Kat was shaking her head, "I am not strong, and I haven't had the courage to face things that happened to me, until recently. Therefore, I don't think you should hold me on some high pedestal. I've been a fraud almost all my life. Playing the role of someone who has her shit together, I've almost convinced myself with the attitude I walk around with."

"No Kat, maybe it is because of what happened to you that made you tough. But it has also made you stand up for the underdog, the person that needs someone in their corner, like me."

"No, I'm a fraud, and I'll tell you why. I see what has happened to you, falling in love with Ben, having a family, and all the wonderful things. I don't believe in that, although I've watched it, but it's not for me. I don't see myself giving everything to someone, that same someone that can rip my world apart. I'm afraid, afraid to give love, to be loved. Even here with you, telling me you love me, I have a hard time listening to your praise. I find myself wanting what you have, but most of all, I want to be open to love, and I don't know if I can do that."

"I think you can, maybe you don't know it yet. Maybe you just need to forgive yourself for trusting the wrong person so long ago. You were just a kid, and didn't know better. Kat, I guess what I'm trying to say is, now that you're an adult, you should allow yourself to trust again, because with love, comes happiness."

Jeff could hear voices coming, so he backed down the hallway and yelled as if he just got there, "Hey Liz, where do you want all this baby stuff?" When he walked into the room, he noticed that Kat didn't look at him. Everything he had overheard wasn't news to him. He knew most of what she said. She told him she didn't believe in love, at least not for her. He had hoped he was changing her mind, but apparently, he still had work to do.

The excitement exhausted Liz, so Kat took her into her new/old bedroom to rest. Settling her down, Kat seized this moment to tell Liz that she loved her, too. Closing the door behind her, she met Jeff waiting for her. Moving away from Liz's door, she turned to him.

"I want to take you somewhere special tonight, wear pants, and bring your bathing suit and a jacket. I'll pick you up at my mother's house around seven." He kissed her and was gone.

Well, she guessed she'd get a ride with Linda back to her house. Kat had no idea what Jeff was planning, but whatever it was, she knew if she had to dress in a bathing suit, most likely sex would be involved. The sex part she could totally handle, but the love part got a little wish-washy.

Kat was ready and waiting for Jeff to show up. She had packed a few things in a bag just in case she stayed at his place again. Boy, how things had changed, from her refusing to stay with him, to hoping she would stay. She tried to tell herself it was just for the great sex, even if, deep inside, she was starting to have feelings for Jeff that went way beyond the sex. She pushed those thoughts away when she saw him pulling up on his Harley. Smiling like a fool, she walked down the front steps to meet him. The one time he gave her a ride on his motorcycle, she had loved it.

The engine died and he slid the kickstand down. Not getting off he asked, "You ready?"

"I packed a bag just in case I stayed over, but now there's nowhere to put it." She laughed at herself.

"Just slide it in the side bag and we can go. Here's your helmet." She shoved the bag in and took the helmet. Noticing it looked new, she wondered if he had bought it just for her or was it the helmet he gave all the women he took on his bike. Not wanting to think about just how many that might be, she stuck it on her head and buckled it up, then hopped on the back.

He glanced over his shoulder to make sure she settled and asked, "You okay?"

"Yes, I was just wondering how many heads this helmet has been on. I'm not much for sharing things that go on my head." There, that should sound normal, without coming right out and asking how many people have had it on their head before her. He laughed at her because he so knew what she was saying.

"No one has had that helmet on their head, so no cooties." Shaking his head, he started the bike, and it roared to life.

Taking a deep breath, she snuggled in close and wrapped her arms around his waist. Taking hold of her upper thighs, he ran his hand down over them, stretching her legs out next to his, then he slid back just the slightest bit, so her entire body shaped his. He was wearing a t-shirt and jeans, just as she was. With just two thin layers of cotton between her chest and his back, Kat felt him inhale deeply, tapping the pedal with his foot. Giving the bike gas, they were off, she had no idea where he was taking her, but she didn't care.

Jeff had to concentrate on shifting through the gears and staying on the road. With Kat's lethal body pressed against him, his mind wasn't completely on what he was doing. Moving through the streets, he couldn't wait to get away from the main roads. Once they were out and away from the central traffic, he could open the bike up. Where he was taking Kat, wouldn't take long, but Jeff wanted to give her more of a ride. It didn't hurt that he liked having her pressed tight to his body. As the buildings, cars disappeared and the road opened to houses and trees, they just road. That's when he accelerated, moving smoothly through the empty streets. Before he fully opened her up, he wanted to make sure Kat was okay, so he shifted to speak to her over his shoulder.

"You okay back there? I haven't heard a peep out of you." He liked how she pressed even closer to hear what he was saying.

"I'm more than okay, just enjoying the ride, scenery, and of course, my chauffeur." She could feel him laughing.

"I'm going to open the bike up, you gonna be alright with that?" He didn't want to scare her, just give a little thrill.

"Do it," was all she said, and he nodded. The bike took off like a rocket and she released his body, holding her arms in the air, as if she was on a rollercoaster. "Oh, my God, YES," she yelled, and Jeff found himself feeling ten feet tall. She was acting as a small child, but it was her carefree reaction, that incited Jeff's own excitement. He had to slow down, because they were going off road, and this bike wasn't made for this kind of terrain. He felt her arms wrap around him again, just that small touch comforted him.

They came to a gate with a big sign saying, Keep Out, Private Property. Jeff just turned to her and asked, "Can you hop off and open the gate, and I'll drive through, then close it again."

She had a question of her own, "Are we allowed in here?"

"Its fine, I know the owner." He put both feet on the ground to stabilize the bike for her to get off. She did, and he couldn't help enjoying her image walking in the headlight from the bike. Kat moved to open the gate, and he drove through, and then waited for her to close it and hop back on. Driving a little longer on the dirt path, he stopped the bike and turned the engine off. Immediately the quiet took over the harsh sounds of the bike. It was getting dark, but not quite there. Jeff let her get off the bike before he put the kickstand down and got off. They both removed their helmets, hanging them off the handlebars. Going to the saddlebags on the bike, he pulled out a blanket and a few other things.

Reaching for her hand, he smiled when she didn't even hesitate and put her hand in his. Walking down a path, she didn't say anything, so Jeff left the comfortable silence between them, but he wanted to know what she was thinking.

When they came over the hill and reached the point where Jeff wanted to show Kat, he heard her gasp. The view from the top of the hillside was beautiful. Down below, was a small lake, with the last of the day's sun shining on it. Turning to her, he pulled her into him, his hands wrapping her waist. With her eyes opened wide, looking out over the water, Jeff couldn't help kissing the side of her head. He knew the site was overwhelming, one of the reasons he wanted to show her one of his favorite places, where he would come to think things through, his spot. When she turned toward him, her clear blue eyes sparked. She kissed him, broke his embrace, and started running down the path to the water. Jeff had to catch up, the carefree feeling was back, and Jeff loved how she seemed so relaxed. As if, her self-protection had evaporated right before his eyes. The unguarded Kat was sexy and playful. Jeff couldn't help wanting to make her feel this way every day. He just had to make sure he never did anything for her to mistrust him.

When he caught up she was already stripping out of her jeans, Jeff had to swallow hard. Just standing there watching her was an amazing site. She had her suit under her clothes, but that didn't help the boner in Jeff's pants. Slowly, walking toward her, he needed a minute to get control over his body. In fear, he might strip her and do what his body wanted.

She looked up at him confused, why was he just standing there, "Jeff, you goin' to come swimming with me, or you just going to watch? That's why we came here, why you said to bring my suit?" Kat stopped taking her clothes off and just stood there.

"That is why we came here, but now that you put it that way. It makes it a hard decision, get in the water with you half-naked, or watch you swim half-naked. Both are making taking my jeans off, difficult."

She smiled, "Now come on, seeing me naked can't possibly have that much of an effect on you. You've seen me naked like a hundred times."

"Oh, I hate to differ with you, but every time you come even close to me, my body reacts. You don't even have to remove any clothes, and when you do, I appreciate the hard work you do to keep your body in shape," if the grin and his hands in his pockets wasn't a dead giveaway. He didn't have his board shorts on under his jeans. It would have been too uncomfortable to ride the bike. He just thought he'd change once they got here, but now, if he took off his clothes, this would undoubtedly, get them off track. If they were going to swim, it needed to done before it got too dark. He loved the smile she gave him, so open and easy.

"So, what you're telling me, is you have a problem and if I keep taking my clothes off…" She pulled the hem of her t-shirt over her head. She stood before him in just her bikini, and she watched his eyes rack over her body. Seeing him like this made everything in her feel invincible. Tugging on her top just in the slightest, so a little more of her breast showed.

His voice was raw as if he had been yelling when he said, "Get in the fucking water, and believe me I will be right behind you. Just know Kat, all this teasing me is going to come back on you. I'm feeling that tiny bit of control slipping," with that, she turned tail and run into the water yelling, "I'll be waiting."

Jeff started to remove his boots, slowly, he unbuttons his jeans. Taking deep breaths wasn't helping his need to rip his clothes off and chase her down. Sitting down, he pulled off his jeans and slipped his shorts on over his massive erection. Willing it too ease just a bit, he tried to think about anything except the beautiful woman splashing around in the lake, calling his name.

Kat never swam in a lake before, so she wasn't sure about touching the bottom. She ran into the water and picked up her feet as soon as she was deep enough. Yelling for Jeff to join her, knowing he wasn't kidding when he made his threat of coming after her. It excited and turned her on, to know how she still affected him. Within what felt like seconds, he was running down the embankment and into the water, and Kat felt the need to swim, fast and hard to get away from him. He caught her in no time, what was she thinking, he swam almost every day of his life. She was strong though and could fight him off in the water. She slipped out of his hold and kicked him as her attempt to get away from him again failed. He snagged her ankle and pulled her back, which forced water up her nose. Coming up choking, Jeff stopped playing for her to catch her breath.

Once Kat regained air in her lungs and felt his grip on her ease, she immediately pulled away from him again. He was fast, she would give him that, but what he might not know is, she didn't give up easily. This was something she never had with anyone before him. To play fight, she didn't want to hurt him, but her will to be uncaught was stronger. He stopped chasing her, just stood still in the water. An eerie feeling came next, why was he not going after her.

"Kat, come here," he said in a stern voice. She looked at him, was he crazy, no way.

"Why?" She looked at him from about twenty feet away.

"I said come here, and I won't say it again." He just stood so still, the fight left her, she found herself moving in his direction. She bit her lower lip as she stepped up next to him, "That's better," his voice softer now. "I don't want to hurt you, playing around."

"I was enjoying the fight, but I didn't want to hurt you either." He made a sound in the back of his throat, as if he didn't believe she could hurt him, if he only knew what she could do to him if he was attacking her.

"I know you could hurt me, so don't even go there. I don't want to chase you. I want to catch you. I know you're new to this game, but you are actually supposed to let me catch you."

"Why should I do that?" She asked and it made him smile because she was so new to all of this.

"So, I can do this," he drew her in, cradling her head in his hands. He slowly lowered his lips over hers. Feeling her legs wrap around his waist and her hand in his hair, had him deepening the kiss.

"Hey, you kids, this is private property, and I don't call the law. I shoot first and ask questions later." A man yelled from the top of the hill, and Kat found herself shifting behind Jeff. He just laughed.

"Jeb, it's me, Jeff Jacobs."

"Oh, you alone down there, I could have sworn I heard kids down here." Just a shadow of a huge man stood looking down at them.

"No, I'm not alone. I brought my girlfriend to show her your beautiful lake." The man walked closer, so he was standing on the edge of the water. Now that Kat could really see him, he was huge. "Jeb, I'd like you to meet Kat Jackson," Kat didn't feel like coming out from behind Jeff, so she just leaned around him to wave.

"Hi, you have a nice place here," as an afterthought she added, "It's stunning as the sun goes down." The man didn't move a muscle. The only thing that moved was his face. His eyes looked her over and a smile crossed his face.

"Nice Jeff, so you going to come out of the water to shake my hand, and bring your pretty lady friend," his smile got a little sleazy looking.

"Not a fucking chance, no way am I going to let you even have a peek at her, so you can forget it." Kat had a feeling they were kidding, but she didn't like the way they were talking about her, and she found her voice.

"Hey, I'm standing right here. I don't know who you are, but you don't want a piece of me, you might be a big man, but I've taken down bigger than the likes of you." Her body started moving around Jeff when he held her back.

"You have a live one there Jeff, good luck." He turned laughing as he walked away and yelled over his shoulder, "Make sure you close the gate when you leave. I'll be thinking about all the fun you're going to have in my lake."

Jeff's only response was to say, "Fuck you."

"Oh, I was hoping you'd be fucking her," Jeb said as he cleared the hill. "The fantasy isn't as good to thinking about you fucking me." The man was gone, and the lake got quiet again.

"Holy shit," she said slowly.

Jeff turned to face her, "Were you going to fight him, because it might have been worth him seeing you. Even if after Jeb got a good look at you, he would be at a major disadvantage." It didn't escape him, how she moved behind him. Even knowing she could handle herself, her instinct was to trust him to protect her.

"He's a friend of yours, but he didn't seem to be very friendly and a little creepy, too," Kat shook off the creepy feeling she got for him.

"His father owned this property when I'd come here as a kid, but I always came alone, so he never chased me away, like the other kids who tried to have parties back here. I didn't cause any trouble, not that I should have been swimming alone. Jeb, inherited it after his father passed away, he comes off as a jerk, but has a few social skill problems. He's a bit older than I am, but he'd come down and hang out with me. Jeb was always a big boy, and he kinda scared girls with his size. So, I tried to help him out in that department, but every time he tried to talk to a girl, he got frustrated and scared them off."

"No one got to know him, you know, get past his size. How sad, and here I was, going to take him on, well you know." There was just something in Kat that always felt for the underdog.

Jeff laughed, "He did find a girl who wasn't afraid of him, eventually. She is as big as he is, so his size didn't bother her. But he would have loved it if you got out of the water, just sayin'." Jeff took her in his arms again, getting back to what they were doing before being rudely interrupted. When her legs rewrapped him, they stood in the water embracing each other.

"I hate to say it, but we need to get out and dry off before we head back. If we are still wet when we get back on the motorcycle, it's going to be a cold ride home."

"I know what we can do to dry off," she bit his bottom lip. "Of course, first thing, is to get out of these wet bathing suits." She still had her arms and legs enclosed Jeff's body. He walked out of the water holding her as close as two people could be.

"I know, I said Jeb is an okay dude, but I wouldn't put it past him to hang around, to find out what could happen," he said into her ear.

Immediately she looked around, seeing if she could spot someone watching them. Jeff told her she wouldn't see him if he didn't want her too. Even with his size, he knew the woods around the lake like the back of his hand. Once they were out of the water Kat felt very exposed and she covered up as soon as Jeff handed her a towel. He had her sit on an old tree trunk that had fallen years before. He straddled the trunk, pulling her in close and she rested her head on his chest. They wouldn't be having sex, but she had a great time with Jeff tonight. Spending time with Jeff was becoming her most favorite thing to do, realizing it had been day's since she'd worked out, at that thought, she had not one ounce of guilt, or regret.

"Penny for your thoughts," he said.

"I was just thinking how long it's been since I've worked out, and somehow, I don't care. You could almost set your watch by my routine. I've had more fun in the last few days, than I can ever remember having. Swimming here with you, even painting the nursery was fun, going to pick out the rocking chair for Liz." The night after they painted, she dragged Jeff out to the baby super store to help pick out a chair. He didn't act as if he was happy about it, but she saw him smiling at some of the cute crap they sell for babies. Jeff moved over to where all the cribs lined up and he wound every mobile once he found out they played music, so they all were playing as he walked away.

"You mean to tell me, going into that baby store was fun," he sounded as if he didn't believe her.

"Yes, even that was fun," she said to herself, *because you were with him, he made it fun.* If it was just her, she would have just ordered something out of a catalog, or off the internet, and have the item sent to the person. Even at times, she would have her assistant Vikki pick out gifts and send it with a card she didn't even sign, the realization that she wasn't a very personable person, never taking the time to personally shop for anyone. Seeing Liz sitting in the chair they picked out, somehow gave Kat a satisfying feeling.

# ~ 21 ~

"What's going on in that beautiful mind of yours?" the brush of his lips on her forehead pulled her from her thoughts.

"Why do you like me? I don't understand what you see in me. I'm a very selfish, self-centered person, that hardly takes the time for my own family. Buying the rocking chair for Liz is the first time I've ever took the time to actually go to a store for someone." His laughter had her turning to face him.

"Have you ever had fresh coconut or the milk from inside?" His question didn't have anything to do with her question for him.

"Yes," she said with inquiry in her voice.

"Did you like it?" Again, she had no idea why they were talking about coconuts.

"Why are you talking about coconuts?" He didn't answer her, just asked another question.

"Do you know how hard it is to climb a coconut tree."

"No, why would I have any idea," getting a little short with him.

"Well, if you want the coconut bad enough, you will climb the almost impossible tree. Then, once you get up far enough to reach the fruit, you need to chop it down without falling out of the tree, because it's a long way down."

"Uh-huh," she said not sounding as if she cared.

"When you chop it down, you try to get as many as you can, not to have to climb the tree again. Once you have the coconut on the ground, you now have to climb down."

"I think a chainsaw would work better," she said with no humor.

He laughed at her off handed comment, "Yeah, well that would mean no more fruit from that tree. Anyway, now that you have the coconut in your hand, you have to get inside of it to get to the good stuff."

"Okay, good lesson on how to get a coconut out of a tree, although you never actually said how to get up the damn tree." She started to get up, but he held her in place.

"I'm getting to the point, hang ten. If the fruit were so easy to harvest, it wouldn't be such a commodity. The fruit must be worth all that work because they do it every day. I see you for the good stuff inside, I know getting through the tough shell is going to mean a lot of hard work, but you're worth it. You are sweet and juicy on the inside."

"Oh, my God, did you just compare me to a coconut?" Now she was pulling away from him.

"What, I love coconuts, and I'm willing to climb your tree, do a little chopping and enjoy the fruit for myself." He went after her, when he caught her, he could tell she wanted to act insulted.

"Jerk," was all she said, but when he kissed her, she melted.

"I didn't mean it as an insult. I just see past your hard shell." Kat pressed her face into his chest. "The part you don't want anyone to get through. I happen to know because I've seen it and felt it. You do have a sweet inside, Kat, I think you and Jeb have something in common though. No one has taken the time to get to know you, Kat. That might be some of your own doing, but I already know you." His finger under her chin tipped her face up to his, "More than you might think."

Thank God, it was already dark, and he couldn't see her face, because he would have seen the panic that flooded her body. Okay, this is the part that scared her to death, him knowing her. She has left the gates open, let down her guard, and he is now inside her compound. Dispel the enemy, in her anxiety she pulled away from him. Turning to where she put her clothes, she quickly started to change, making sure her back was toward him.

Right away, Jeff felt the shift in Kat, watching her rigid movements in the dark told him she was closing herself off to him. He might have pushed her a little too far, telling her how much he knew her. He didn't move, he'd let her do her thing and once she was dressed, she had to talk to him. He'd wait her out, but what he knew for sure, she was going to pull away from him. What he didn't know, should he let her. Once she was finished, she turned on him and he stood his ground and said nothing.

"Why are you just standing there?"

"Because, I'm not moving until we talk," he crossed his arms over his chest.

"I don't want to talk. I think we've talked too much, tonight, and not enough sex." He was not going to let her gloat him into a fight.

"You know, this isn't just about sex for me."

"Yeah, well it is for me, I don't want anything more than steaming hot sex from you, Jeff. You know just like you gave every woman you've had. I'm ready to go back to your mothers, because I'm done talking, I'm all talked out."

"Okay, you be quiet, because I have a lot to say." Now he did move and stepped right in her space. "We both know what we're doing, both adults, so anytime you want out, just let me know. I have feelings for you Kat, and no matter how hard I fought them, I still feel them in here." He took her hand putting it over his heart. "I know this scares you, it does me too, but I'm not going to stand here and allow you to make what we're doing, just about sex. It might be easier for you to tell yourself that's all it is, but at some point, you're going have to face the truth."

"And, I've already told you, I have a past, and I'm done apologizing for it. I also told you how different you are to me. I will lay my heart on the line here, Kat. As crazy as it may be, I'm falling for you, no, I've already fell, hard, so don't you stand there and belittle me and what we're doing. I realize why your lashing out, but remember I have feelings, too." Jeff felt the anger but tried to control it by stepping back. He grabbed his jeans, yanking them up over his wet shorts. Finding his shirt, he tugged it over his head, jamming his feet into his boots. Rolling up the towels and blanket, he started walking toward his bike. The path was pitch-black now, so he pulled out his phone to light the way for them. She was a few steps behind him. Once they made it back to the bike, Jeff stuffed the balled-up fabric back into the saddlebag. Taking her helmet from where it hung on the handlebar, he handed it to her and, when he turned to get his, he heard her speak. Turning back to face her, he acted as if he didn't understand what she said. He knew it was childish, but he wanted her to apologize to his face.

"What?"

"I said," she stumbled on her words. "I shouldn't have brought up those things, about you with other women."

"Is that the only thing you think you shouldn't have said, because I can think of a few more?"

"I don't want to fight with you, Jeff, but we both know this started out with you wanting to help me through my issues. That night in my apartment, when you pushed for this, I told you then, it would be about sex. I don't want this. I...I don't want to get hurt again, and I don't want to give anybody the power over me to do it. Don't you see, I can't give you what you want from me? I can't give you all of me because I will never fully surrender to someone again." The hurt of her submission was clear, out there for him to see, even in the dark, it was right there. There was never going to be more for her. She couldn't trust him, nor herself anymore. This had to end, as she felt her body screaming inside she tamped down the pain and did what she should have done in the beginning.

"I don't think we should see each other anymore. I want out."

Those three little words stopped Jeff in his tracks. He knew he had to play it slow with Kat, and he still pushed too hard. But, he never thought she would break things off completely. His mind was spinning, thoughts racing, did he try to convince her to change her mind? Did he let things stand and give her time to think, he didn't know the right thing to do? If he gave her time to think, she could convince herself right out of any feelings she might have for him and if he continued to push, she possibly would shut down entirely. He felt powerless, it was a feeling he didn't like, not where a woman was concerned. He stood there frozen to the spot.

"Kat," her name was all he could manage, and even he could hear the desperation in his voice.

"No, Jeff, don't, it needs to stop. I need to go back to your mother's." Putting the helmet on her head was as if she sealed herself off.

Jeff nodded and climbed on the bike, buckling the helmet that he wanted to throw. He waited until she mounted the bike to start the engine. Feeling how she kept her body as far away from his killed him. He even slid back a bit, but her body wasn't there, pushing the bike forward so the kickstand retracted, clicking the clutch into gear. The bike slowly moved down the path they came. All Jeff could think, was he didn't want to take her to his mothers. He didn't want to break things off. He didn't want to stop being with her, and how easily she could just not want to be with him. It hit him hard. She could because it was just sex to her. With the revelation brought pain, and anger. He was mad at her, but he was angrier with himself. Then calm resonated throughout him, along with his mother's voice.

*"Jeffery, you remember when we had those stray cats at the shop? How you worked so hard to gain the trust of the mamma cat, so you could feed her. How patient and determined you had to be, before the mamma found out you weren't going to hurt them, and let you hold her kittens. Kat has to know you're not going to hurt her, and that's going to take the same amount of patience and determination."*

Then her father's voice, *"If you don't get discouraged, she will come around."*

The message was loud and clear, don't give up. Give her what she needed to allow herself to open to him. Even if it took more effort, more determination, and more time, he'd win her over in the end. He refused to look at it any other way. Now, pulling up the drive, he felt better about this time he'd have to give her.

Once the bike stopped, and his feet stabilized the motorcycle, he knew she would attempt to run. He wasn't going to let her go without leaving her with something to think about.

Kat had unbuckled her helmet as they turned off the road. She knew this was going to be awkward between them and wanted to get it over as soon as possible. Before he was even off the bike, she grabbed the bag she had stowed in the side bag. Kat was hoping he would stay on the bike and just let her go inside without saying a word. Somehow, her mind and body didn't agree, and until she could figure out what she was doing, she needed to stay as far away from him as she could.

Jeff didn't rush, just moved behind her up the stairs to his mother's porch. Kat spoke over her shoulder, about not needing to walk her in. Ignoring her protest, he stepped in close, as she tried to get the door open. Positioning his hand over hers, stopping her from slipping away, she turned to face him.

"I'm going to respect your decision to end the relationship, even if I don't agree. But, I'm not going to end our friendship, just because we won't be having sex, doesn't mean I'll stop caring about you, Kat." Jeff slid his hands in along her jaw, caressing her face as his thumbs softly brushed her smooth skin. Studying her amazing blue eyes, he said, "I do want more from you, Kat, so much more, but, I also know how hard this is for you. I understand you need time to process what's happened tonight, and us." Kat started to object, but Jeff silenced her protest with the slightest touch of his lips on hers. Jeff pulled back just an inch, not giving her the space to rebuff him. "I'm not going anywhere, Kat. You'll always know where to find me if you change your mind. I know what I want, and when you figure out you can't live without me." With his arrogance, she shoved at him, laughing he said, "In the meantime, I'll be waiting for you to catch up." Before she could get two words in, he was sliding his helmet into place. All he heard was her yelling that he was a "jerk," and he was in so many ways. But when it came to her, he didn't want to be jerking her around.

Pissed off, Kat moved inside the safety of Linda's house. Standing against the closed door, it gave her first chance to take a deep cleansing breath. Somehow, Jeff could push and pull her in every direction in the matter of two seconds. With her thoughts flying in and out of focus, her only hope was to move up stairs before Linda realized she was there.

"Kat, is that you?" Linda's voice came from the kitchen.

*Shit, shit, shit*, she said repeatedly in her head, "Yes, it's me Linda."

"I didn't expect you back tonight."

Thank God, she didn't come into the room, "I needed a break." Crap, that didn't sound good. How was Linda going to take her needing a break, a break from Jeff, a break from the sex, or maybe she just needed sleep. Kat groaned and looked to the stairs thinking she could make a run for it.

"Everything alright?" It was a loaded question and Linda knew it.

"I'm fine, just tired," as much as Kat knew that wasn't true, she didn't want to talk about Jeff. "I'm going to head up stairs, good night."

"Good night, Kat, see you in the morning." Kat thought by the time she saw Linda again, she would know exactly what was going on between them anyway. Moving to her private hell, where she knew she wouldn't escape her own thoughts. Tonight, would not be a good night. Feeling the strong need to work out, but she couldn't go back out, without Linda knowing she was leaving, and she just told her she was tired. For someone who always had control over her life, she has made a huge mess of it. What happened to the person that made precise decisions, knowing exactly what to do, never wavering? Wish-washy, soft, that is what has become of her. Can't even decide without flip-flopping a hundred times.

It was all Jeff's fault, because he's the one that made her this way. Made her feel things, things she didn't want to feel, like need and passion. Wait, Kat thought, that was what she liked feeling, not the feeling of losing control, or fighting the urge to rip Jeff's clothes off. No, she liked that, too. All those feelings tied into sex, and the sex with Jeff, she loved. It was the emotions that she didn't know what to do with. Wanting him, the deep pull he had over her, that's what she didn't like. The powers he possessed, it was no wonder women fell at his feet.

Right then, she realized why she was so angry with herself, because she was no better than any other woman that Jeff encountered. Thinking she was stronger to resist his charm, to rebuff his advances, falling for his wicked appeal, his great smile, and those eyes. She wasn't the tough, badass she always felt she was, now she had become soft, a pushover, that's what he turned her into, falling for his words. The way Jeff used his sense of humor, to make her laugh and relax around him. Making her believe he felt something for her with his kisses.

Kat laughed at the thought of him wanting more with her, because the thought of Jeff settling down, with a wife and kids, no way. Wondering if she agreed to a real relationship, how fast it would take him to move on. He wanted her because she was a challenge to him and to conquer her was a huge notch on his bedpost. Well, she had fallen for it, but now she was the one with all the power. She left him wanting more, and what did he say, when she figured out she couldn't live without him, she knew where to find him. When hell froze over, she thought.

~ ~ ~ ~ ~ ~

Jeff didn't want to go home, not to the cold empty bed that awaited him. Riding his bike with his wet board shorts still under his jeans, wasn't an option either. Pulling into the parking lot of the shop and his apartment, Jeff parked the bike under the stairs. Taking both helmets with him, he walked up the two flights of stairs. Once inside, he went to change his clothes, but he didn't want to stay in his apartment. It was too dark out to surf, besides it was unsafe to go alone, the things that always helped him clear his mind, he couldn't do right now. Grabbing his guitar, he went out on the landing of the steps. Now that Ben and Liz weren't upstairs anymore, he didn't have to worry about disturbing anyone. Leaning his back against the post, Jeff started playing, just moving his fingers over the strings. Mindlessly, he sat back thinking about Kat, and how she ended things tonight.

He knew she'd do it eventually. It was a part of who she was, the scared teenager who had every right not to trust a man again. Even if she knew he wouldn't physically hurt her, the fear of being hurt emotionally, was just as strong. He knew she would go back to working out and most likely would be out on the beach in the morning. Thinking if he should be out there, too, maybe he could go surfing. On the other hand, he may need to give her some space, because it wasn't as if they wouldn't see each other at all.

Taking a deep breath, Jeff started playing the song I'm Yours, by Jason Mraz. Singing the words, he realized what the next music box song would be. Tomorrow, he'd call Robert to set it up. Just because she ended things between them, didn't mean he was going to pull back. Just move a little slower, slip back in, and show her, he wasn't going to give up on her or them. Three days, he would give her without seeing him. He was going to have to become more creative, with the fact that Kat won't be right upstairs helping Liz anymore.

"Hey, do you mind I'm trying to sleep here," the voice came from upstairs. The voice belonged to his sister, what was Dannie doing in Ben's apartment? Jeff leaned out over the edge of the steps, to in fact, see his sister leaning over the rail looking down at him.

"What are you doing up there? I didn't think anyone was up there when I started playing."

"Ben said I could move in, since they didn't need his furniture, I moved right in." He heard her move and then he saw her coming down wearing a pair of men's boxers and a tank top to where he sat.

"Why didn't I know you were moving in, not that it don't make total sense for you to live here."

"I didn't think I had to check in with you, Ben's place, and all," Dannie sat down next to him.

Jeff pulled on her long ponytail, "You don't need my permission. I just would have liked to know you were up there, that's all. I know you don't usually talk to me, but you do know I'm here for you, right?" When Dannie didn't say anything, Jeff knew something was going on with her. "Dannie, you okay?"

"Yeah, I've just had a lot of stuff going on. Working through issues," he could see her turmoil and just waited for her to continue. "I left my job in Dallas, because of my old boss. He was such an asshole. Besides the fact that mom almost made it impossible for me to stay and still get my check at the end of the year. I still don't understand how she can do that, we own the shop, so how does mom still rule the roost."

Jeff laughed, because he knew just how Dannie felt about how their mother worked. If Linda wanted something bad enough, she would end up getting it. Recalling the exact conversation Dannie was referring to, because he also got a lashing from his mother, for not doing enough for the shop. That was part of why he started working harder, but it had more to do with Ben giving him more responsibility. Linda wanted him to do more, she also wanted Dannie to come home, and she got both.

"Don't laugh," she said as she smiled herself. "Mom is out of control, Jeff. Why do you think I stayed with a friend instead of moving back home? I refuse to be under her thumb. My God, you would think I was still a teenager."

"Sorry Squirt, in mom's defense, she loves you, and as much as it can be a pain in the ass, she's not going to change, so get used to it. Just think, you've been gone, and we still live here, you think you had it bad. Now, why don't you tell me about your asshole boss?"

"We worked close together, late at night sometimes, one thing, leads to another. We became involved, and then I found out the hard way, I wasn't the only one. It went all downhill from there."

"He didn't hurt you, did he?" Jeff could feel everything inside go taught.

"Not physically, he hurt my self-esteem, mostly. After I caught him, my work wasn't good enough, I wasn't dressing appropriate, and he found reasons to make me feel as if it was my fault he cheated. I worked on some of the major accounts most of the biggest companies, but still, just not good enough and he took all the credit with his boss. He called me into his office, and I knew, because he didn't shut the door, he wanted the new girl he was doing to overhear him. Before he could fire me, I resigned my position, effective immediately. I knew it would be hard to get another job with a major firm, but I went off on him. At the time, it was worth it, but then I had nowhere to go. Mom doesn't know any of this, so I'd really appreciate it if you didn't say anything to her about it."

"Man Dannie, I'm so sorry. I know you loved your job, but you're right, he was a huge fucking asshole."

Dannie started laughing, "You crack me up Jeff, a fucking asshole, and you pegged him."

"Your secrets are safe with me. I have enough trouble keeping mom out of what's going on in my own life."

"Speaking of your life, what the hell is going on between you and Kat? Last I knew you, said you liked her, like you like all women."

"Since you shared with me, I'll tell you exactly what's going on. I plan to marry Kat. Now the question, is will she marry me?"

Dannie's eyes got huge, "Holy shit, does she know? Hell, does mom know, damn."

"Just you, so I trust you to keep your mouth shut. I've already said some things that scared Kat, so I'm giving her some time."

"You know what this means for me, right? Once mom gets you married off, she will put all her concentration on getting me married. Shit, Jeff, I thought I could count on you to keep mom busy. I figured she would eventually start to overlook you and move onto me, but you and Kat, you guys do make such a power couple. I knew something was up when she was listening to everything I said about you in the car when we went to look at office furniture."

"Thanks, the crazy thing is, I knew almost immediately. I didn't want to have feelings for her. When we first met, she rubbed me the wrong way. Her attitude, the bold, I don't give a shit about you, way about her did something to me."

"She was a challenge," Dannie said quietly.

"At first, I might have agreed with you, but it wasn't long before I found myself thinking about kissing her. Then, I'd get mad for even thinking it, and then, I was thinking about her all the time. Out on a date and here she was taking up my every thought."

"Is that why you stopped dating, you knew she was the one?"

"Oh no, I put up a good fight at first, because I didn't want to like her. I was glad she went home after the weekend she was here, and then I found myself wanting to go with Ben to Boston. I said it was for support, but I knew I had to see her again. I needed to know if I'd get that feeling when I saw her, and I did."

"The feeling?" Dannie asked.

"Yeah, seeing her made my stomach leap, and my heart pound. I could feel the reaction, but it was her reaction when I stepped into her space that told me I affected her as much as she did me. I noticed for the first time just how much I liked how someone smelled. Somehow, her bold attitude became so appealing to me, and I saw how she treated Liz, I knew there was something there."

"And the fact she didn't just fall under your spell." Dannie got up, and started up the stairs, turning she said, "I don't want to fall under a spell again."

"Dannie," when he said her name she stopped and looked at him. "Be careful, the new guy has a thing for you. I know it's not really my place, but I told him your off limits."

"Thanks, I'm not in the market for a man right now," she said and then she was gone.

Thinking about his conversation with his sister, Jeff couldn't remember the last time, or any time, they both shared with each other. What she said about her, boss pissed him off. Good thing the dude didn't live anywhere around here, otherwise he'd know what it felt like to get his ass handed to him.

The thought of going inside sucked, Jeff pulled out his phone, knowing he shouldn't, but did anyway. He typed out a quick text to Kat.

Jeff: Miss you already, good night, Sunshine.

He didn't expect her to text him back, so he went to bed.

Kat was sitting up in bed looking over contracts, attempting to divert her attention off tonight. When her phone chimed, knowing it could be important, she pulled up the message. Reading Jeff's text, made Kat take a shallow breath. She wished she could just turn her phone off or just ignore it, but she knew she couldn't. Not when Liz was in her last trimester and could go into labor at any time. That was a good thought if the babies were healthy. Then, she could go home, get away from the thought of him, along with what he could do to her body. She knew, going across the country was not far enough away to forget about Jeff.

This was a perfect example of not knowing the right thing to do. Should she text him back, or just ignore him? What would she say to him anyway? She said to no one, "Good night, sweetheart, I hate how you've managed to suck me in. How you've made me want you." Throwing her phone back on the bed, *ignore.* Going back to the contracts on her bed, she read the same line three times. "God, what am I going to do?" Grabbing her phone again, she typed back.

Kat: Why are you doing this to me?

Looking at the screen, she wanted to hit delete but hit send instead. "Shit," she tried hitting the button again to stop the text from going through, but it sent.

Right away, her phone chimed, almost not wanting to read his text, she still looked.

Jeff: What am I doing to you?

Now what Kat thought, again with the decisions?

Kat: Why are you texting me? She hit send this time on purpose. She didn't even have time to put the phone down, before his next text came in.

On the screen, she read, Jeff: I think it was clear enough, I miss you.

Kat: Jeff, we broke up, I know I don't have any experience with this, but I think once things end, you're not supposed to contact the other person.

She looked down to see his next message.

Jeff: Just because you stopped things, doesn't mean things changed for me.

Would she ever get away from him, how would she get over him? Did she really want to get over him, she knew her body certainly didn't want to get away from him? Clearing her bed off, she turned out the lights. Sliding into the covers, she looked over to where she placed the dolphin globe on the dresser. The glow from the small light inside, showed the dolphins going around. That was a fun day, attempting to learn to surf. Of course, the one thing she wasn't going to be any good at, no, that wasn't going to be the only thing, also erasing Jeff from her mind, she knew she wasn't going to be any good at that either.

# ~ 22 ~

Kat no longer had to go to the surf shop now that Liz was in her new house. She figured that would make her situation with Jeff easier, because she wouldn't have to see him. She kept busy helping Liz set up the nursery, putting up curtains, putting diapers in the diaper-caddy, and hanging the little baby clothes in the huge walk-in closet. Kat unpacked box after box, putting things away, as Liz sat in the rocker instructing her where to put them. Doing the mindless work felt good, no pressure, she could just move around completing each task at her own pace. Liz could only sit for short periods of time, when she needed to rest, Kat helped her to her room to lie down. When Liz slept, that was when she did her work. Talking to Vikki on the phone, and doing video calls, kept Kat busy the rest of the time.

In the next few days, the house would become very busy. Linda would normally have Thanksgiving dinner at her house, but with it being easier for Liz, everyone was coming to her home. Paige was flying in, Liz was just ecstatic about seeing her daughter. Liz hadn't seen Paige in months, at least not in person. They would Skype every week, because that was the only way Liz could relax about her daughter being so far away at college. Owen was picking her up from the airport tomorrow. Linda was in and out of the house bringing in groceries and preparing food. Liz wanted to help but couldn't stay up long enough.

Jeff had kept his distance. It had been days since she broke things off. Although when she went to the gym, she felt him, she didn't see him but somehow, she knew he was there. She knew she was going to see him when everyone got together. Telling herself often how she could handle seeing him again, and not reacting to him being near, then the thought came to her, *oh crap what if he brought a date to Thanksgiving dinner*. But then she knew he wouldn't do that to her. At least Kat hoped he wouldn't do that to her.

~ ~ ~ ~ ~ ~

Doing his best to keep busy, Jeff tried everything to take his mind off Kat. He told himself it would only be a few days. He said he could manage, but after one day, he found his truck driving to the gym. Under false pretense, he drove through the parking lot, looking for a parking spot. If he happened to pass several, only after seeing his mother's car, the one Kat was using, did he find the right spot to park. Knowing damn well what he was doing, he went inside. Thinking if he could just see her, it would relieve the ache. It was the craziest thing, how she made him feel. Never in his life had he ever stalked anyone, but Kat made him do things he never had before.

When he was inside, he didn't start his workout. Jeff moved through the gym, staying out of sight. He wanted to get a glimpse of her, without her seeing him. Once he spotted her, he moved to a place where he could see her better. Kat was out on the main floor, so Jeff went up to the upper floor. She was working with a trainer, and the site of him touching her, sent a sharp jolt of jealousy throughout his body. If he weren't hiding, he would march down there and claim her as his. At that moment, she looked around the gym, as if she felt him watching her. He quickly ducked behind the ellipticals, which earned him a strange glare from the woman on the machine next to him. Jeff sent the woman one of his sexy smiles and her face immediately turned shy. Knowing he couldn't stay there much longer without Kat spotting him, or someone might even turn him in for being a creepy dude. Taking one last look at Kat, Jeff headed for the door.

Then the next morning, he found himself out on the beach, doing the same thing, watching her. Kat moved through numerous martial art stances, her arms, and legs flowing effortlessly. It was a site to watch her turn her sexy body into a lethal one. Her strength was one of the things that attracted him to her. Strong, fierce, and aggressive, never called to Jeff before. Not the way Kat did, it was a powerful draw. His feelings for her, the intensity was like no other. He wondered if she was missing him, the way he missed her. Kat's deep need to control, and years of fighting to overcome what happened to her, wouldn't allow her to chase after any man. So, he knew she wasn't stalking him or working hard to get a glimpse of him. He realized early on that he was going to have to be the aggressor in this relationship. Convincing Kat that he was worth a long-term commitment was going to be the hard part. After telling his sister the other night how he planned to marry Kat, had set the wheels in motion.

Today she should receive the music box with the song, I'm Yours, and hopefully, she will contact him. Either she would be like, "Why are you still sending me music boxes?" Or, she just might not contact him at all. Whichever way, he would see her in two days, when they all got together for Thanksgiving. The music boxes were going to play a big part of telling Kat, just what he wanted.

~ ~ ~ ~ ~ ~

Owen was standing waiting for Paige's plane to disembark. He watched as people started to walk by him. He felt a little anxious about seeing Paige again. When she was here for Liz and Ben's wedding, they got along great. Talking to Paige was so easy because they had a lot in common. Both starting college, although it wasn't just that, they liked the same music, and many other things. It didn't hurt that she was beautiful, not that anything could happen, because they were family now. He promised to teach her to surf when she came back, so they would be spending time together. Paige had a sweet, innocent, a pureness to her. Owen didn't quite understand his reaction to Paige, he would think about her from time to time, she even texted him once or twice.

He spotted her as she slung her backpack over her shoulder. Paige had her long strawberry-blonde hair tied back, her ponytail swished as she walked. When she smiled at him, he felt it in a place he shouldn't.

"Hey Owen, how's things going?" She gave him a quick hug.

Sliding the bag off her shoulder and slinging it over his, he said, "Good, how about you. Glad classes are out?" He looked down at her as they walked through the airport.

"I don't mind the classes, but I miss my mother. I know that kinda sounds babyish, but it feels like I haven't seen her in forever."

"Na, I don't think it sounds bad, you love your mom. Liz is a great person, but wait until you see her," Owen chuckled.

"Big, huh, mom and I Skype every week, but it's hard to get the big picture." They both laughed as they made it to Owen's car. Unlocking Paige's door for her, he then placed her backpack on the back set and climbed in. "So…" She was biting her lip, looking very unsure about something.

Owen looked over at her, "What?" Not sure he wanted to know what was making Paige nervous.

"Are you going to have time to teach me to surf? I know this is your break also, so if you have other things planned I understand."

"Yeah, I have things planned," before he could finish the look of disappointment crossed her face. "Hey," he touched her cheek to make her look at him. "Teaching you to surf is at the top of my list.

You do know it's going to take more than four days, right. Unless you take after your mom, because she took to it pretty easily."

"Oh good, because I thought you just might have been being nice, you know to the new girl. I didn't know if Ben told you to... you know, to make me feel welcomed."

Owen started the car, "Paige, Ben never said a word about being nice to you. I imagine that finding out your mother was getting married to someone you've only met once before the wedding, was a little bit of a shock. I did want to make you feel comfortable, but I wouldn't promise anything that I wouldn't follow through on. I'm glad to be spending time with you, I like you, Paige."

"Oh...I...um like you, too."

Paige got all flustered, he didn't want Paige to misunderstand, "We're friends, well, family." This time he didn't look at her, because he didn't want to see her reaction to his, "we're just friends" speech.

The day Paige was supposed to arrive, Liz was beside herself. She must have asked Kat a hundred questions, "Owen knows what time to pick her up, right," to "What time is it," and then, "Do you think Paige is going to like it here." Liz couldn't rest, which meant, Kat got no work done, and by the time Paige was due to appear, Kat felt exhausted.

"Liz, you need to calm down, your blood pressure is going to be through the roof." Kat knew her words would fall on deaf ears, because she was still bouncing up and down in the bed. There was a very good reason why Kat made Liz stay in bed today, if she was reacting this way in bed, Kat could only imagine what her excitement level would be out of bed.

"Paige is coming, Kat! I can't calm down."

"This isn't good for the babies Liz, and you don't want to spend the four days you have with Paige in the hospital." That got Liz's attention, because she stopped bouncing. Almost as if she forgot about the babies for a second, and what all this excitement could do to push her into premature labor.

"I just want to see my first baby," Liz said, as she heard Paige yelling as she came into the house.

"MOM, I'M HERE, WHERE ARE YOU," Paige yelled at the top of her lungs. In the next minute, she was standing in the doorway. Running to her mother's side, Paige wrapped her arms around her very large mother. Liz was crying, hugging her daughter so tight. Paige climbed in the bed with her mother.

"I missed you, mom," Paige put her head on her mother's chest, as her mother ran her hand over the back of her head.

"I'm sorry we couldn't come for parent's weekend. I wanted to go, but the damn doctor said no flying."

"Mom, I know," Paige put her hand over Liz's belly, leaning down she said, "Hi babies, I'm Paige, your big sister."

Kat slipped out of the room, to give Liz and her daughter some privacy, closing the door behind her. Owen was still standing in the living room, looking a little lost. Kat understood, because she was feeling the same way.

"Hey, Owen," when he heard her he looked up from where he had been staring at his feet.

"Kat, can I talk to you about something, and can this be just between you and me?"

"Sure, what's up," Kat sat on the couch and waited for Owen to get up his nerve to say what was on his mind.

He sat on the other couch looking at his clasped hands, "I think I might be in trouble."

"Trouble, what kind of trouble," when Owen wouldn't look at her, her heart started beating fast.

"I might like Paige."

Kat started laughing, she couldn't help it, with all the things Owen could have said, Kat never thought it would be that. If this is what he thought trouble was, then the kid didn't know what real trouble was. Owen looked up from his hands.

"Kat, don't laugh, it's not funny, I can't like her. She's practically my sister, and Ben will kill me."

"First, you both are too young for anything serious. Besides the fact that Paige is going to school, on the other side of the country, you won't see her, but a few days a year. Be friends, have fun, nothing more. You both have four years left of school, and I don't see why Ben would kill you. If and this is a huge IF, I think Ben and Liz couldn't ask for any one better for Paige. But understand a lot can change in four years, you find someone, she finds someone. College is not just about good grades. It's about learning about yourself. You find out who you are Owen, away from your parents, how to make good decisions for yourself."

"When she was coming off the plane, she smiled at me. I'm not proud of my body's reaction, and no matter how many times, I tell myself how stupid it is, I can't seem to get it to go away. I'm thinking what it would be like to kiss her and stuff I shouldn't be thinking."

"Well, part of that is you're a red-blooded male. It's a natural reaction to seeing a beautiful girl. Paige is pretty, in a way she doesn't even know that she is. I'm going to tell you something, but if you repeat this, I will hunt you down and hurt you bad, do you understand me, Owen?" When he just nodded, Kat said, "Paige is very innocent when it comes to boys, and she would be horrified if she knew I was telling you this. So, when you're thinking all those thoughts that you shouldn't, remember how inexperienced she is."

"Thanks, Kat," Owen went to get up, but Kat had one more thing to say to him.

"Owen, don't start anything you can't finish, because Paige isn't the love'em and leave'em kind of girl, she's more the forever kind of girl."

"I get it," just then, Ben walked into the room.

"I guess the fact that Owen is sitting here with you, means Paige is in with her mother," Ben said to Kat.

"Yeah, I gave them some privacy. When I left, Paige was introducing herself to the babies. You planning to stay, because I have to get some work done, with the excitement, Liz didn't rest today."

"We closed the shop early for the holiday, so you can take off if you need to." Ben turned to Owen and asked, "Did you need something Owen?"

"Na, I was just talking to Kat, then I figured I'd wait around to see if Paige might want to hang out, you know go down to the shop and get her set up for the surfing lesson, I promised her." Ben nodded and went down the hall, knocking on the door, before slipping inside.

"Hello," Linda's voice boomed as she came walking in and going straight into the kitchen. "Owen, dear could you help bring in the rest of the bags in my car for me?"

Kat thought, and so it begins, Owen went to help Linda. Ben was with Liz and Paige. It was time to make a run for it before Linda put her to work. Walking to the kitchen, Kat knew she couldn't just leave without talking to Linda first. Kat, found it made things easier if she somewhat kept Linda in the loop. At least it made Linda feel as if she was in the loop. Linda was emptying bags when Kat walked in.

"Linda, I'm heading out. I need to get some work done before tomorrow. Ben is with Liz and Paige, but Liz is going to need a nap soon, and I can tell you she's going to give you a hard time about it." Linda just gave Kat a face, as if, not likely, that made Kat smile, because that's what her and Linda had in common. Neither one took any crap from anyone. Kat liked that about Linda. Of course, not so much when Linda was calling her out.

"Kat, the ladies are getting together in the morning, I'd like for you to come. We will be gathering here, around seven-thirty. I start a little earlier because I put in the turkey. We sit around drinking coffee and start preparing the dinner."

"Linda, I don't cook. I have no idea how to make a Thanksgiving dinner. I don't think I'll be of any help, more like getting in the way."

"You don't need to know how to do anything. I'll tell you what I need from you, I promise you can handle cutting up veggies. My Mother-in-law started this tradition, and I found we had a lot of fun. We all pitch in, and no one has to make the entire dinner."

"So, who all is going to be here, because I can think of only like three people?"

"There will be six of us, you, Liz, Paige, Dannie, Helen, and me," as she said each name, she counted them out on her fingers.

"Who's Helen?" Kat asked, because she never heard anyone speak of Helen before.

"That's my mom," Owen said as he brought in the last of the bags. "Linda has done this for years. Ever since I started hanging out at the surf shop, and Linda found out it was just my mom and me. We've had Thanksgiving dinner here, well at Linda's house. Linda adopted us. My mom loved how Linda asked for her help. You know, it made her feel like we weren't freeloaders."

"Owen, you, and your mother were never freeloaders. Your mother and I were both single parents, trying to raise our children the best we could. I had a little more to share, that's all, and I did what I did because I fell in love with a scrawny teenager that kept hanging around the shop. I could see you were special, and you gave Ben and Jeff someone to be responsible for."

When Kat left the house, she realized Linda wasn't kidding when she said she took in strays. Not just Owen but his mother, too, whom else has Linda taken into her family? After Ben and Liz married, it gave Kat comfort to know Liz would have Linda. Kat knew Linda was pulling her in, and she wasn't sure if she could, or even wanted, to stop it. Besides, getting into everyone's business, Linda was a very loving person. It was just the fact that Kat wasn't used to anyone caring enough to look deeper into what people needed. Linda didn't miss a thing, she could see through what you were saying, or what you weren't. Unlike her own mother, who didn't want to see anything more then what was on the surface. If Linda was her mother, Kat had no doubt that William McDonnell would be in jail right now. That would be after Linda got ahold of him and ripped him to shreds.

The thought made Kat smile, as she drove back to Linda's house, knowing the house was empty, gave Kat a well-needed breather. When Kat stepped up to the door, she noticed a package, thinking Linda ordered something, she picked it up and saw her name on it. Knowing what was most likely inside, Kat wasn't going to open it. Moving into the quiet house, Kat went upstairs to change her clothes.

The sun was shining, and she was going to sit out on the back patio while she got her work done. After getting herself some iced tea, she went out to set up her outside office. Thinking how nice this was, and no way could she be doing this back home. Everyone was freezing their butts off. She had heard from Vikki that it was snowing the other day. Not feeling the least bit guilty, she shared the weather they had in California. Vikki had asked if she could come, and Kat laughed and told her sure, there's plenty of room.

~ ~ ~ ~ ~ ~

Jeff left the shop and headed over to his brother's house, with every intention of talking to his mother. With the holiday, he didn't see her today at the shop. Knowing full well that Kat would be there, too, he could kill two birds with one stone. When he pulled into his brother's driveway, he noticed Kat's car wasn't parked among all the other vehicles. Ben's Jeep, Owen's, and his mother's car, all lined the driveway. Thinking Kat could have run an errand for his mother or Liz, pulling up he parked his truck and walked to the door. Knocking and then walking in was how he went into Ben's apartment, so this was no different. He found his mother in the kitchen as he expected, she was moving from one end to the other talking to Owen and Paige.

His mother was giving Owen the safety talk, the one Jeff had heard a hundred times before. Apparently, Owen was going to be taking Paige surfing, and Linda wanted to make sure Owen understood she wanted Paige to come back in the same condition as she was leaving. All in one piece, and poor Owen was trying to reassure Linda that he wouldn't let anything happen to Paige.

Linda noticed him standing there and said, "She's not here, Kat went to get some work done." With break in the conversation, Owen and Paige slipped out the French doors.

"I know she isn't here, I came to find out if you needed any help, and what time dinner is tomorrow," Jeff leaned against the counter.

"You know I don't need your help, but thanks for asking. Tomorrow's dinner is the same time it has been your entire life, you know the drill." Leave it to his mother to call him out, because she knew exactly why he was there. "This time, be here before dinner is ready and just in case you are not bright, no date."

Jeff had to laugh, "Mom, give me some credit here. I want Kat and only Kat, so what would I gain by bringing a date, besides the fact how wrong that would be for me to use someone that way. I want more with Kat, and right now, I've scared, her because I see her for who she is. Anyway, I need to talk to her, as you already know."

His mom gave him a knowing look, "I think she went back to my house." Jeff kissed his mom's cheek and whispered his thanks in her ear.

Kat was working for hours, when suddenly, the hairs on the back of her neck stood up. She knew why and attempted to control her breathing. After a few minutes, Kat yelled, "Are you just going to stare at me, or you going to come out here? We both know what you want." Just then, the back-screen door opened, and Jeff came strolling out. She watched as he walked to the lounge chair next to hers. He sat on the seat sideways, facing her, with his knees apart and his elbows resting on them. The jolt that went through her body, was unnerving, how he still managed to make her want him against her better judgment. Knowing what Jeff could do to her body, how he could make her feel made her breathing accelerate. She let her eyes rake over his body.

"Stop looking at me like that Kat, it's been days, and I've missed the hell out of you. You're in that fucking bikini, that I could have off your body in two seconds. I only have so much control, and when I'm around you, I have none." He was watching for her reaction, when he saw her shiver, her nipples harden, and his body reacted by becoming hard as nails. Trying to control himself, because this wasn't what he came here for, he had to show Kat there was more than just sex between them.

"You looking for sex, Jeff, is that why you're here?"

Damn, even her voice sounded sexy, but he had to pull all the strength he could to answer her. "No, Kat I'm not here for sex." Again, watching her, he saw disappointment cross her face.

"Why are you here, or better yet, why did you send me another music box? You know I can't keep it." Clicking a few buttons on her computer, she closed it and placed it on the table next to her. Giving Jeff her undivided attention, she wanted to look in his eyes when he talked to her.

"I'm here because I want to talk to you. Did you even like the music box?"

"I didn't open it, there was no sense to it, because I wasn't keeping it."

Jeff didn't count on her not opening the damn thing, he needed her to open it. "Where is the box, Kat," he asked as he stood.

"In my room," she watched as Jeff headed back inside, she added, "It's on my bed," but he was gone. Kat knew he would find it, and he could take it with him. Jeff looked a little perturbed when she said she didn't open the box. *Oh well, he could just get over it,* she thought.

Jeff retrieved the box and marched back out the door, she was going to open the damn box. Kat had reclined her chair and now had her arms over her head and her long legs spread open. Jeff had to take a deep breath and not look at anything but her face. He put the box on her amazing stomach and looked down at only her face.

"I want you to open it. I sent it to you because I wanted you to have it. I can't send it back, so fucking open the damn thing." He released a harsh breath, taking in another breath, and swallowing hard to calm the tension rushing through him. Kat sat up, glaring at him with her beautiful blue eyes and he could see she was gearing up for a fight. "Don't fight me on this Kat, please."

Taking her eyes off him, she started to open the box. Very slowly, she removed the tape and pulling back each flap, she removed the wrapped box. Unwrapping the bubble covering, the box began to come into view. A very delicate glass box sat in her hand with pink roses etched into its sides. Kat didn't want to look on the bottom to find out the song he chose, she gently opened the lid. When the music started to play, she closed her eyes to listen to the tune. Knowing the song well, Kat opened her eyes to see him staring at her.

"I picked that song Kat because I am yours. You have done what many had tried to do and failed. You captured my heart, and I don't want anyone but you. Nothing else matters to me, where we live, or what we're doing. I'm yours, and I want you to be mine Kat, forever."

"Hold up," she shot up ramrod in her seat. "Did you just propose to me, because I can't even think straight right now?" Kat was blinking fast and was shaking her head as to clear it.

"If your answer is yes, then I did propose. If it's no, then I didn't just propose."

She opened the music box again looking inside, "I don't see a ring anywhere, so this isn't a real proposal. You were just testing me. I get it. The joke is on me, ha, ha," she started to get up.

Jeff had to stop her, he sprang into action, he didn't want her to think this was joke. Caging her in, he placed a hand on each armrest. Jeff couldn't have stopped his next move because his lips were on hers before he even knew he was going to kiss her. Somehow, his knee ended up in between hers, and then he was on top of her. Kat wasn't fighting him as their tongues tangled with each other. She had her hands up the back of his shirt, yanking it over his head. Breaking the kiss just enough to get it free, he went back to her mouth. His mind wasn't thinking, it was all his body and the need for her that took over. He didn't even take the time to remove her top as he slid it aside to free her breasts. Moving down her body, his hands caressing her round firm mounds and his lips finding her taunt nipple, Jeff sucked, drawing her deep into his mouth.

Kat's moans were driving him insane. He could feel her raw need, as her nails scraped down his back holding him to her. Fighting the need to be inside her, he slowed down, taking his time. Moving to lavish her other nipple, pulling back just the slightest he said, "Kat, tell me you want me."

"Oh, God, of course I want you. Please don't stop," Kat's words came out in piqued, breaths as she begged him not to stop.

"Tell me you want more, with me. Tell me your mine." His kisses moved slowly down her body, over her tight abs. He knew he wasn't playing fair, but he didn't care.

"I want more," her voice was barely there.

"With me," he untied her bottoms, and scraped his jaw along her tattoo. Opening her up to him, he couldn't help running his nose over her mount and taking in her scent. She said yes, but through clinched teeth, Jeff looked up her body, to see her head pressed into the chair. He wasn't sure if she knew what she was agreeing to or not, but he would have to work that out later. Reaching under her bottom, he lifted her to his mouth, and that's when Kat's legs went wider than he'd ever seen. Her legs touch each side of the chair, and Jeff thought *oh yeah, here's to her flexibility.*

Jeff's mind was only on making Kat feel good, but he also wanted to make this last. He wasn't sure if she was going to agree to get back together. If this was going to be the last time, then he would go out with a bang. His tongue swirled around her clit, like he knew she liked. When she stretched down to grab his hair, he knew she was close. Pulling back, he changed tactics and inserted two fingers. With his other hand, he took one of her nipples and pinched it between his thumb and index finger. Switching between pinching and tugging it taunt, he felt she was close again, he went back to sucking her clit. This time, he hooked his fingers to hit the spot, and that was it, Kat exploded. Her insides clinched his fingers as her cream coated his face. Lapping up her juices as Jeff brought her down from her hard orgasm. Moving up her body, he kissed her, the way her tongue came out to lick his lips clean of her come, freaking turned him on big time, he hadn't planned on having sex, but she drove him crazy.

"Kat, I don't want us to be just about sex." Jeff caressed her face, as her beautiful eyes open to stare up at him.

"Jeff, if I could be with anybody, I'd be with you, but I don't think you will end up happy with me. Not when I can't give you everything you need."

"Kat, all I need is you, the person I've spent time with. If you're honest with me, I will work hard to earn your trust. I'm not going to make the same mistake and tell you how I know you, but admit it, you've shared more with me, than anyone else. So, on some level, you must think I'm worth the risk."

"I need time, Jeff. I need to think things through. I don't just jump in with both feet, ever." He rolled back so his body no longer pressed against hers. Replacing her top and then tying her bottoms.

"Take all the time you need. I'm not going anywhere. You know what I'm looking for, so when you figure out what you want, let me know. For now, I don't want to stop seeing you." He kissed her, got up, and left.

Kat laid there long after Jeff was gone, still wondering what just happened.

**Watch for Love Dangerous Undercurrents Part 2**

# Find me on the Web.

Facebook ♥ Trish Collins – Author

Instagram ♥ trish_collins_author

Twitter ♥ Trish Collins – Author @collins_author

Website ♥ https://TrishCollinsAuthor.net

Email ♥ TrishCollins.Author@gmail.com

Facebook Store ♥ https://www.facebook.com/TrishCollinsAuthor/shop

♥ Amazon.com/TrishCollins

Made in the USA
Columbia, SC
21 March 2025

55454766R00202